"This is a chilling, compulsive portrait of a psychopath, and proves that Carter is now in the Jeffery Deaver class."

—*Daily Mail*

"There's a touch of the Patricia Cornwell about Chris Carter's plotting."

—*Mail on Sunday*

"Part comment on our reality TV–obsessed society, it's punchy and fast-paced."

—*Sunday Mirror*

"A chilling, dark thriller, *An Evil Mind* will have readers running to lock their doors, book in hand. Carter's knowledge of the intricate details of the criminal mind and his portrayal of a sadistic, psychotic serial killer had me sleeping with the light on and the soothing sounds of HGTV humming in the background. For thriller readers who think they can't be shocked, try this one!"

—Susan Crawford, author of *The Pocket Wife*

"A thrilling and unsettling look at a killer from a new perspective. *An Evil Mind* is absorbing and a must-read."

—James O. Born, author of *Scent of Murder*

"An especially sadistic serial killer taunts the feds in this . . . compelling read. A true battle of good versus evil."

—*Kirkus Reviews*

CHRIS CARTER

AN EVIL MIND

A ROBERT HUNTER THRILLER

POCKET BOOKS

NEW YORK   LONDON   TORONTO   SYDNEY   NEW DELHI

Pocket Books
An Imprint of Simon & Schuster, Inc.
1230 Avenue of the Americas
New York, NY 10020

This book is a work of fiction. Any references to historical events, real people, or real places are used fictitiously. Other names, characters, places, and events are products of the author's imagination, and any resemblance to actual events or places or persons, living or dead, is entirely coincidental.

Copyright © 2014 by Chris Carter

Originally published in 2014 in Great Britain by Simon & Schuster UK Ltd.

First Pocket Books paperback edition October 2016

POCKET and colophon are trademarks of Simon & Schuster, Inc.

For information about special discounts for bulk purchases, please contact Simon & Schuster Special Sales at 1-866-506-1949 or business@simonandschuster.com.

The Simon & Schuster Speakers Bureau can bring authors to your live event. For more information or to book an event, contact the Simon & Schuster Speakers Bureau at 1-866-248-3049 or visit our website at www.simonspeakers.com.

Manufactured in the United States of America

10 9 8 7 6 5 4 3 2 1

ISBN 978-1-5011-4190-4
ISBN 978-1-4767-6570-9 (ebook)

AN EVIL MIND

Part One

THE WRONG MAN

Morning, Sheriff. Morning, Bobby," the plump, brunette waitress with a small heart tattoo on her left wrist called from behind the counter. She didn't have to check the clock hanging on the wall to her right. She knew it would be just past 6:00 a.m.

Every Wednesday, without fail, Sheriff Walton and his deputy Bobby Dale came into the unassuming truck stop, just outside Wheatland in southeastern Wyoming, to get their pie fix. Rumor had it that Nora's Diner baked the best pies in the state, a different original recipe for every day of the week. Wednesday was apple and cinnamon, Sheriff Walton's favorite. He was well aware that the first batch always came out of the oven at 6:00 sharp, and you just couldn't beat the taste of a freshly baked slice.

"Morning, Beth," Bobby replied, brushing rainwater off his coat and trousers. "I'll tell you, the floodgates of hell have opened out there," he added.

Summer downpours in southeastern Wyoming were common occurrences, but this morning's storm was the heaviest they'd seen all season.

"Morning, Beth," Sheriff Walton followed, taking

off his hat, drying his face and forehead with a hand-kerchief, and quickly looking around the diner. At that time in the morning, and with such torrential rain outside, the place was a lot less busy than usual. Only three out of its fifteen tables were taken.

It was easy to match each table's occupants to their vehicles parked outside. The couple in their mid-twenties having a pancake breakfast probably drove the beat-up silver VW Golf; the obese, shaved-headed man and the tall, gray-haired guy by the window pensively toying with his cigarettes would've driven in the eighteen-wheelers, while the dark-blue Taurus to the diner's side had to belong to the stylish, well-groomed forty-something flipping through the morning's newspaper.

"Just in time," Beth said, winking at the sheriff. "They are just out of the oven. As if you didn't know."

The sweet smell of freshly baked apple pie had already engulfed the place.

Sheriff Walton smiled. "We'll have our usual, Beth," he said, taking a seat at the counter.

"Coming right up," Beth replied before disappearing into the kitchen. Seconds later she returned with two steaming, extra-large slices of pie, drizzled with honey cream. They looked like perfection on a plate.

"Umm . . ." the well-dressed man sitting at the far end of the counter said, tentatively raising a finger like a kid asking his teacher's permission to speak. "Is there any more of that left?"

"There sure is," Beth replied, smiling back at him.

"In that case, can I also have a slice, please?"

"Yeah, me too," the large truck driver called out

from his table, lifting his hand. He was already licking his lips.

"And me," the horseshoe mustache man said, returning the cigarette pack to his jacket pocket. "That pie smells darn good."

"Tastes good too," Beth added.

"*Good* doesn't even come close," Sheriff Walton said, turning to face the tables. "Y'all are just about to be taken to pie heaven." Suddenly his eyes widened in surprise. "Holy shit," he breathed, jumping out of his seat.

Bobby Dale swung his body around fast to track the sheriff's stare. The large window just behind where the young couple was sitting framed the headlights of a pickup truck coming straight at them—and fast. The car seemed completely out of control.

"What the hell?" Bobby rose to his feet as everyone in the diner turned to face the window. The shocked look on their faces was uniform. The truck was headed toward them like a guided missile, and it was showing no signs of diverting or slowing down. They had two, maybe three seconds before impact.

"EVERYBODY TAKE COVER!" Sheriff Walton yelled. At that speed, that pickup truck would crash through the front of Nora's Diner and not stop until it reached the kitchen at the back, destroying everything in its path.

Desperate screams and scrambling took over the restaurant floor. They all knew they didn't have enough time to get out of the way.

CRUUUUNCH-BOOM.

The deafening noise sounded like an explosion, making the ground shake under everyone's feet.

Sheriff Walton was the first to look up. It took him a few seconds to realize that somehow the car hadn't crashed through the building at all.

Confusion replaced the frown on his face.

"Is everyone all right?" the sheriff called out, frantically looking around.

"Yeah" was returned from all corners of the room.

The sheriff and his deputy rushed outside, checking their weapons as they ran. Everyone else followed just a heartbeat later. The rain had definitely gotten heavier in the past few minutes, now pouring in thick sheets that severely reduced visibility.

Out of sheer luck, the pickup truck had hit a deep pothole on the ground just a few yards from the front of the diner and had drastically veered left, missing the restaurant by just a couple of feet. As it detoured, it clipped the back of the dark-blue Ford Taurus before smashing headfirst into a side building that housed two bathrooms and a storage room, completely destroying it. Thankfully, there had been no one inside, as Walton gathered from Beth's relieved exclamations.

"Holy shit!" Sheriff Walton coughed the words out, feeling his heart race inside his chest. The collision had turned the pickup truck into a mangled wreck, and the outside building into a demolition site.

Skipping over the debris, the sheriff was the first to get to the truck. The driver was its only occupant—a gray-haired man who looked to be somewhere in his late fifties, but it was hard to be sure. Sheriff Walton didn't recognize him, and he was certain he'd never seen that pickup truck around Wheatland before. It was an old and rusty early 1990s Chevy 1500, and though the driver had been wearing his seat belt, the impact had been way too violent for a truck like this with no air bags. The front of the truck, together with its engine, had caved backward and into the driver's cabin. The dashboard and steering wheel had crushed the driver's chest against his seat. His face was covered in blood, torn apart by shards of glass from the windshield. One had sliced through the man's throat.

"Goddammit!" Sheriff Walton said through clenched teeth, standing by the driver's door. He didn't have to feel for a pulse to know that the man hadn't survived.

"Oh my God!" he heard Beth say in a trembling voice from just a few feet behind him. He immediately turned to face her, lifting his hands in a *stop* motion.

"Beth, do not come over here," he commanded her. "Go back inside and stay there." His stare moved to the rest of the diner patrons, who were coming toward the truck fast. "All of you, go back into the diner. That's an order. This whole area is now out-of-bounds, y'all hear?"

Everybody stopped, but no one turned back.

The sheriff's eyes searched for his deputy, and found Bobby standing behind the small crowd, back in the parking lot. The look on his face was a mixture of shock and fear.

"Bobby," Sheriff Walton called. "Call for an ambulance and the fire department NOW."

Bobby didn't move.

"Bobby, snap out of it, goddammit. Did you hear what I said? I need you to get the radio and call for an ambulance and the fire department right now."

Bobby stood still. He looked like he was about to be

sick. Only then did the sheriff realize that Bobby wasn't even looking at him or at the mangled pickup truck. His eyes were locked on the Taurus. Before crashing into the bathroom building, the truck had clipped the left side of the Taurus's rear end hard enough to release its trunk door.

All of a sudden, Bobby broke out of his trance and reached for his gun.

"No one move," he yelled out. His shaky aim jumped from person to person. "Sheriff," he called in an unsteady voice. "You better come have a look at this."

2

In lunchtime traffic, the seven-and-a-half-mile drive from Huntington Park to the LAPD headquarters in downtown Los Angeles took Detective Robert Hunter a little over forty-five minutes. He wasn't supposed to be in for the next two weeks. Officially, he was supposed to be on vacation, but just under an hour ago he'd received a call from his captain, Barbara Blake, asking him to come in for an urgent meeting.

The Robbery-Homicide Division, located on the fifth floor of the famous Police Administration Building on West First Street, was a simple, large, open-plan office crammed with detectives' desks—no flimsy partitions to separate them. The place sounded and looked like a street market on a Sunday morning, alive with movement and chatter that came from every corner.

Captain Blake's office was at the far end of the main detectives' floor. The door was shut—not that unusual because of the noise—but so were the blinds on the oversized internal window that faced the floor. That was undoubtedly a bad sign.

Hunter slowly started zigzagging his way around people and desks.

"Hey, what the hell are you doing here, Robert?" Detective Perez asked, looking up from his computer screen as Hunter squeezed past Perez's and Henderson's desks. "I thought you were out for a couple of weeks."

Hunter nodded. "I am. I'm flying out tonight. Just having a quick chat with the captain first."

"Something up?" Perez asked.

Hunter shrugged. "I guess I'll find out," he said before moving on. He paused before the captain's door. Instinct and curiosity made him tilt his head to one side and check the window, but he couldn't see past the blinds. He knocked twice.

"Come in," Captain Blake called from the other side in her usual firm voice.

Hunter pushed the door open and stepped inside.

Barbara Blake's office was spacious, brightly lit, and impeccably tidy. The south wall was taken by bookshelves packed with perfectly arranged, color-coordinated hardcovers. The north one was covered by framed photographs, commendations, and achievement awards, all symmetrically positioned in relation to each other. The east wall was a floor-to-ceiling panoramic window, framing the captain's twin pedestal desk and two leather armchairs.

Captain Blake was standing by the window, looking out over South Main Street. Her long jet-black hair was gracefully styled into a bun, pinned in place by a pair of wooden chopsticks. She wore a silky white blouse, tucked into an elegant navy-blue pencil skirt. Standing next to her, holding a cup of steaming coffee and wearing a conservative black suit, was a slim and very attractive woman Hunter had never seen before.

She looked to be somewhere in her early thirties, with long, straight blond hair and deep-blue eyes. Despite her polished appearance, there was something a little apprehensive about her expression.

As Hunter entered the office and closed the door behind him, the tall, slender man who was sitting in one of the armchairs, also clad in a soberly dark suit, turned to face him. The heavy bags under his eyes and his fleshy cheeks gave him a somewhat hound-like look, and aged him at least ten years, despite his fit figure. The thin locks of gray hair he still had left on his head were neatly combed back behind his ears.

Taken aback by these unexpected attendees, Hunter paused, narrowing his eyes.

"Hello, Robert," the man said, standing up. His naturally hoarse voice, made worse by years of smoking, sounded surprisingly robust for a man who looked like he hadn't slept in days.

Hunter held his gaze before moving to the blond woman and finally to Captain Blake.

"Sorry about this, Robert," she said with a slight tilt of the head before allowing her stare to go rock hard as it homed in on the man facing Hunter. "They turned up unannounced about an hour ago. Not even a goddamn courtesy call."

"I apologize again," the man said in a calm but authoritative tone. That slight edge revealed that he was someone who was used to giving orders, and having them followed. He addressed Hunter. "You look well. But then again, you always do, Robert."

"So do you, Adrian," Hunter replied, stepping toward him and shaking the hand he proffered.

Adrian Kennedy was the head of the FBI's National Center for the Analysis of Violent Crime and its Behavioral Analysis Unit 4—a specialist FBI department that provided support to national and international law enforcement agencies involved in the investigation of unusual or serial violent crimes.

Hunter was well aware that unless it was absolutely mandatory, Adrian Kennedy never traveled anywhere. He coordinated most of NCAVC operations from his large office in Washington, DC, but he was no career bureaucrat. Kennedy began his life with the FBI at a young age and quickly demonstrated a tremendous aptitude for leadership and motivation that didn't go unnoticed. Very early in his career, he was assigned to the prestigious Secret Service. Two years later, after foiling an attempt on the president's life by throwing himself in front of the bullet that was supposed to kill the most powerful man on earth, he received a high commendation award, and a personal thank-you letter from the president himself. The National Center for the Analysis of Violent Crime was officially established in June 1984. When it came time to change directors, Adrian Kennedy's name was at the top of the list.

"This is Special Agent Courtney Taylor," Kennedy said, nodding at the blond woman.

She moved closer and shook Hunter's hand. "Very nice to meet you, Detective Hunter. I've heard a lot about you."

Despite her delicate hands, her handshake was firm and confident, like that of a businesswoman who had just closed a major deal.

"It's a pleasure to meet you too," Hunter replied

politely. "And I hope that some of what you've heard wasn't so bad."

She gave him a small but genuine smile. "None of it was bad."

Hunter turned and faced Kennedy again.

"I'm glad we managed to catch you before you left for your break, Robert," Kennedy said.

Nothing from Hunter.

"Going anywhere nice?"

Hunter held Kennedy's stare.

"This has got to be bad," he finally said. "Because I know you couldn't care less about where I am going on my vacation. So how about we drop the bullshit? What's this about, Adrian?"

Kennedy paused, as if to savor the drama of the moment.

"You, Robert. This is about you."

3

Hunter's gaze flashed to Captain Blake for a brief moment, and as their eyes met, she shrugged apologetically.

"They didn't tell me much, Robert, but the little I know sounds like something you would want to hear." She went back to her desk. "It's better if they explain."

Hunter waited.

"Why don't you have a seat, Robert?" Kennedy said, offering one of the armchairs.

Hunter didn't move.

"I'm fine standing, thank you."

"Coffee?" Kennedy asked, indicating Captain Blake's espresso machine in the corner.

Hunter's gaze hardened.

"All right, fine." Kennedy lifted both hands in surrender, while at the same time giving Special Agent Taylor an almost imperceptible nod. "We'll get on with it." He returned to his seat.

Taylor put down her cup of coffee and stepped forward, pausing just beside Kennedy's chair.

"Okay," she began. "Five days ago, at around six in the morning, while driving south down US Route 87, a Mr. John Garner suffered a heart attack just outside a small town called Wheatland, in southeastern Wyoming. Needless to say he lost control of his pickup truck.

"Maybe you already know this, but Route 87 runs all the way from Montana to southern Texas, and like most US highways, unless the stretch in question is going through what's considered a heavily populated area, it has no guardrails, high curbs . . . *nothing* that would keep a vehicle from leaving the highway and venturing off in a multitude of directions."

"The stretch that we're talking about here doesn't fall into the category of a heavily populated area," Kennedy commented.

"By pure luck." Taylor moved on. "Or lack of it, depending on what point of view you take. Mr. Garner suffered the heart attack just as he was driving past a small truck-stop restaurant called Nora's Diner. With him unconscious at the wheel, his truck veered off the road and drove across a patch of low grass, heading straight for the diner. According to witnesses, Mr. Garner's truck was in a direct line of collision with the front of the restaurant.

"At that time in the morning, and because of the torrential rain that was falling, there were only ten people inside the diner—three employees plus seven customers. The local sheriff and one of his deputies were two of those." She paused to clear her throat. "At the last second, Mr. Garner's truck drastically changed course and missed the restaurant by just a few feet. Road accident forensics figured that the truck hit a large pothole just a few yards before getting to the diner, and that caused the steering wheel to swing a hard left. The truck crashed into the adjacent building. Even if his heart attack hadn't killed Mr. Garner, the collision would have."

Taylor picked up on a hint of doubt dancing across Hunter's expression. She could tell that he was still trying to figure out why he was being told all of this.

"Now," she said, lifting her right index finger and nodding at Hunter, as if signaling that she'd understood his silent question. "Here comes the first twist. As Mr. Garner's truck missed the diner and headed toward the outside building, it clipped the back of a blue Ford Taurus that was parked just outside. The car belonged to one of the diner's customers."

Taylor reached for the briefcase resting by Captain Blake's desk.

"Mr. Garner's truck hit the Taurus's rear hard enough to cause the trunk door to pop open," Taylor said. "The sheriff missed it, because as he ran outside, his main concern was to attend to the truck driver and passengers, had there been any."

She reached into her briefcase and retrieved an eight-by-eleven-inch color photograph.

"But his deputy didn't," she announced. "As he ran out, something inside the Taurus's trunk caught his eye."

Hunter waited.

Taylor stepped forward and handed him the photograph.

"This is what he saw."

4

Special Agent Edwin Newman had been standing inside the holding cells' control room in the basement of one of the several buildings that made up the nerve center of the FBI Academy for ten minutes. Despite the many CCTV monitors mounted onto the east wall, all of his attention was set on a single and very specific one.

Newman wasn't one of the academy's trainees. In fact, he was a very experienced and accomplished agent with Behavioral Analysis Unit 4, who had completed his training over twenty years ago. He was based in Washington, DC, and had specially made the trip to Virginia four days prior just to interview the new prisoner.

"Has he moved at all in the past hour?" Newman asked the room operator, who was sitting at the large controls console that faced the wall of screens.

The operator shook his head.

"Nope, and he won't until lights off. Like I told you before, this guy is a goddamn machine. I've never seen anything like it. Since they brought him in four nights ago, he hasn't broken his routine. He sleeps on his back, facing the ceiling. His hands are always locked together and resting on his stomach—like a fucking body in a coffin, you know what I'm saying?" He linked his fingers together and placed his hands over his own torso to emphasize his point. "Once he closes his eyes, he doesn't move—no twitching, no turning, no restlessness, no scratching, no snoring, no waking up in the middle of the night to go pee, no nothing. Sure, at times he looks scared, as if he has no fucking idea why he's here, but most of the time he sleeps like a man with absolutely no worries in life, crashed out in the most comfortable bed money can buy. And I can tell you this." He pointed at the screen. "That bed ain't it. That is one goddamn uncomfortable piece of wood with a paper-thin mattress on top."

Newman scratched his crooked nose, but said nothing.

The operator continued. "That guy's internal clock is tuned to Swiss precision. I shit you not. You can set your watch by it."

"What do you mean?" Newman asked.

The operator let out a nasal chuckle. "Every morning, at exactly five forty-five, he opens his eyes. No alarm, no noise, no lights on, no call from us, no agent bursting into his cell to wake him up. He just does it by himself. Five forty-five, on the dot—*bing*—he's awake."

Newman knew that the prisoner had been stripped of all personal possessions. He had no watch or any other kind of timepiece with him.

"As he opens his eyes," the operator moved on, "he stares at the ceiling for exactly ninety-five seconds. Not a second more, not a second less. You can watch the recording from the past three days and time it if you like."

No reaction from Newman.

"After ninety-five seconds," the operator said, "he gets out of bed, does his business at the latrine, and then hits the floor and starts doing push-ups, followed by sit-ups—ten reps of each in each set. If he isn't interrupted, he'll do fifty sets with the minimum of rest in between sets—no grunting, no puffing, and no making faces either, just pure determination. Breakfast is brought to him sometime between six thirty and seven. If he hasn't yet finished his sets, he'll carry on until he's done. Then he'll sit down and calmly eat his food. And he eats all of it without complaining. No matter what tasteless shit we put on that tray. After that, he's taken in for interrogation." He turned to look at Newman. "I'm assuming *you* are in charge of that?"

Newman didn't acknowledge the question. He simply continued staring at the monitor.

The operator shrugged and carried on with his account.

"When he's brought back to his cell, whatever time that might be, he goes back to a second serving of his exercise routine—another fifty sets of push-ups and sit-ups." He chuckled. "If you lost count, that's one thousand of each, every day. When he's done, if he isn't taken away for further interrogation, he does exactly what you can see on the screen right now—he sits on his bed, crosses his legs, stares at the blank wall in front of him, and I guess he meditates, or prays, or whatever. But he never closes his eyes. And let me tell you, it's fucking freaky the way he just stares at that wall."

"For how long?" Newman asked.

"Depends," the operator replied. "He's allowed one visit to the shower every day, but prisoners' shower times change from day to day. You know the drill. If we come get him while he's wall staring, he'll simply snap out of his trance, step off the bed, get shackled, and go to the shower—no moaning, no resisting, no fighting. When he comes back, he goes straight back to the bed-sitting, wall-staring thing again. If he isn't interrupted at all, he'll keep staring at that wall until lights off at nine thirty."

Newman nodded.

"But yesterday," the operator added, "just out of curiosity, we kept the lights on for an extra five minutes."

"Let me guess," Newman said. "It made no difference. At *exactly* nine thirty he lay down, went back to his body-in-a-coffin position, and went to sleep."

"You got it," the operator agreed. "Like I said, he's a machine." He paused and turned to face Newman. "I'm no expert here, but from what I've seen in the past four nights and days, mentally, this guy is a fucking fortress."

Newman said nothing.

"I don't want to overstep my bounds here, but . . . has he talked at all during any of the interrogation sessions?"

Newman considered the question for a long moment, but the operator leaped in once more.

"The reason I ask is because I know the drill. If a special prisoner like this one hasn't talked after three days of interrogation, then the VIP treatment starts, and we all know how tough that gets." Instinctively the operator checked his watch. "Well, it's been four days, and if the VIP treatment was about to start, I would've gotten word of it by now. So I'm guessing he talked."

Newman observed the screen for a few more seconds before nodding once. "He spoke for the first time last night." He finally looked away from the wall monitor and stared back at the room operator. "He said seven words."

5

As Hunter studied the photograph Special Agent Courtney Taylor had handed him, he felt his heartbeat pick up speed, a rush of adrenaline surging through his body. Several seconds went by before he allowed his stare to finally leave the picture and wander over to Captain Blake.

"Have you seen this?" he asked.

She nodded.

Hunter's eyes returned to the photograph.

"Clearly," Kennedy said, standing up again, "Mr. Garner's pickup truck clipped the back of the Ford Taurus hard enough not only to release the trunk door, but also to knock that ice container over."

The photograph showed a family-sized picnic-style ice container that had been tipped on its side inside the Taurus's trunk. Large cubes of ice had spilled out of it, rolling off in all directions. Most of the ice cubes were stained crimson with what could only have been blood. But that was only a secondary shock. Hunter's full attention was on something else—the two severed heads that had been stored inside the container. Both heads were female—one blond with longish hair, one brunette with a short, pixie-styled cut. Both heads had been severed from their bodies at the base of the neck. From what Hunter could tell, the cuts looked clean— experienced.

The blond woman's head lay on its left cheek, her long hair covering most of her face. The brunette woman's head had rolled away from the container and wedged itself in such a way that the back of her head was flat against the trunk's floor, her features clearly exposed. And that was what made Hunter pause for breath. Her facial wounds were more shocking than the decapitation itself.

Three small locked metal padlocks crudely and sav- agely pierced the flesh of her lips at uneven intervals, keeping her mouth shut but not completely sealed. Her delicate mouth, crusty with blood, was still swollen, in- dicating that the padlocks had ripped through her flesh while she was still alive. Her eyes had been removed, the sockets just two black holes caked with dried blood, which had also run down her cheeks, creating a crazy dark-red lightning-bolt effect.

She didn't have the skin of an old woman, but it was practically impossible to guess her age from the picture alone.

"That photograph was taken by Sheriff Walton just minutes after the accident," Kennedy offered, walking over and pausing next to Hunter. "As Agent Taylor mentioned earlier, he was having breakfast in the diner that morning. Nothing was touched. He acted fast be- cause he knew the rain would start destroying evidence pretty quickly."

Taylor reached inside her briefcase and retrieved a new photograph, handing it to Hunter.

"The forensics team took this one," she explained. "They had to travel all the way from Cheyenne, which is only about an hour away, but when you add the delay of assembling the team and getting them on the road, they got there four hours after the accident."

In this new photograph, both heads were placed side by side, facing up, still inside the Taurus's trunk. The blond woman's face showed exactly the same wounds as the brunette's. Again, guessing the second woman's age was nearly impossible.

"Were their eyes inside the container?" Hunter asked, his attention riveted on the picture.

"No," Taylor replied. "There was nothing else." She looked at Kennedy, and then back at Hunter. "And we have no idea where their bodies might be."

"That's not all," Kennedy said. "Once those padlocks were removed from their lips, we could see that they'd both had all of their teeth extracted." He paused. "And their tongues cut out."

"Since we have no bodies," Taylor said, taking over again, "and consequently no fingerprints, one could argue that the perpetrator removed their teeth and eyes to avoid identification, but that is still unclear."

For a fraction of a moment Taylor almost sounded doubtful, and this time it was Hunter who picked up on a ghost of a concern in her and Kennedy's expressions. He breathed in slowly.

"And you're thinking that given the sheer brutality of the wounds inflicted on both victims, there's a chance that this could've been an act driven by simple sadistic pleasure, and not a maneuver to avoid identification."

Kennedy wasn't surprised that Hunter had so quickly

read their thoughts. Despite not being part of the FBI National Center for the Analysis of Violent Crime, or Behavioral Analysis Unit 4, Robert Hunter was the best criminal profiler Kennedy had ever met. He had tried to recruit Hunter into the FBI for the first time many years ago, after he first read Hunter's PhD dissertation, *An Advanced Psychological Study in Criminal Conduct.* Hunter had been only twenty-three years old at the time.

The paper had impressed Kennedy and the then FBI director so much that it became mandatory reading at the NCAVC, and it remained so. Over the years, Kennedy had made several further attempts to recruit Hunter. In his mind, it made no sense that Hunter would rather be a detective with the LAPD's Robbery-Homicide Division than join the most advanced serial killer–tracking task force in the US—arguably in the world. True, he knew Hunter was the lead detective for the Ultra Violent Crimes Unit, a special unit created by the LAPD to investigate homicides and serial homicides where overwhelming brutality and/or sadism had been used by the perpetrators, and Hunter was the best at what he did. His arrest record proved that, but the FBI could still offer him a lot more than the LAPD could.

Even so, Hunter had never shown even an ounce of interest in becoming a federal agent, and had declined every offer made to him by Kennedy and his superiors.

"Interesting case," Hunter said, handing the pictures back to Taylor. "But the FBI and the NCAVC have investigated a ton of similar cases . . . some even more disturbing. This isn't exactly something new."

Neither Kennedy nor Taylor disputed that.

"I take it that you don't have an identity on either of the two victims," Hunter said.

"That's correct," Kennedy replied.

"And you said that their heads were found in Wyoming?"

"That's also correct."

"You can probably guess what my next question is going to be, right?" Hunter asked.

A second of hesitation.

"If we don't know who the victims are," Taylor said, nodding at him, "and their heads were found in Wyoming, what are we doing in Los Angeles?"

"And why am I here?" Hunter added, quickly checking his watch. "I have a plane to catch in a few hours, and I still need to pack."

"We're here, and you're here, because the federal government of the United States needs your help," Taylor replied.

"Oh, please," Captain Blake said with a smirk on her lips. "Are you going to give us the patriotic bullshit speech now? Are you for real?" She stood up. "My detectives put their lives on the line for the city of Los Angeles, and consequently for this country, day in and day out. So do yourself a favor and don't even go there." She pinned Taylor with a stare that could melt metal. "Does that bullshit actually work on people?"

Taylor looked like she was about to reply, but Hunter cut in just a second before she could speak.

"Need me? Why?" He addressed Kennedy. "I'm not an FBI agent, and you guys have more investigators than you can keep track of, not to mention a squad of criminal profilers."

"None of them are as good as you," Kennedy said.

"I'm not a profiler, Adrian," Hunter said. "You know that."

"That's not really why we need you, Robert," Kennedy replied. He nodded at Taylor. "Tell him."

6

The tone Kennedy used caused Hunter's right eyebrow to twitch up just a fraction. He turned, faced Agent Taylor, and waited.

Taylor used the tips of her fingers to tuck a strand of loose hair behind her ear before beginning.

"As I mentioned, the Ford Taurus belonged to one of the customers who was having breakfast in the diner that morning. According to his driver's license, his name is Liam Shaw, born February thirteenth, 1968, in Madison, Tennessee." Taylor paused and observed Hunter for a second, searching for signs that he'd recognized the name. There were none.

"According to his driver's license?" Hunter questioned, his gaze ping-ponging between Taylor and Kennedy. "So you have doubts." It wasn't a question.

"The name checks out," Kennedy said. "Everything looks aboveboard."

"But you still have doubts," Hunter pushed.

"The problem is . . ." Taylor spoke this time. "Everything looks aboveboard if we go back a maximum of fourteen years, but beyond that . . ." She shook her head faintly. "We could find absolutely nothing on a Liam

Shaw, born February thirteenth, 1968, in Madison, Tennessee. It's as if he never existed before then."

"And judging by the way you were observing me when you mentioned his name," Hunter said, "you were looking for signs of recognition. Why?"

Taylor had always been very proud of her poker face, but Hunter had read her like a book.

Kennedy smiled smugly. "I told you he's good."

"Mr. Shaw was arrested on the spot by Sheriff Walton and his deputy," Taylor said. "But Sheriff Walton also quickly realized that he had stumbled upon something that he and his small department simply wouldn't be able to handle. The Taurus's license plates were from Montana, which created a cross-state reference. With that, the Wyoming sheriff's department had no option but to bring us in."

She paused and shuffled through the contents of her briefcase for a new document.

"Now, here is the second twist to this story," she said, moving on. "The Taurus isn't registered under Mr. Shaw's name. It's registered under a Mr. John Williams of New York City."

She handed the document to Hunter.

He barely glanced at the sheet of paper he'd been given.

"Surprise, surprise," Kennedy said. "There was no John Williams at the address the car was registered to."

"John Williams is a common name," Hunter said.

"Too common," Taylor agreed. "About fifteen hundred of them in New York City alone."

"But you have Mr. Shaw in custody, right?" Hunter asked.

"That's correct," Taylor confirmed.

Hunter looked at Captain Blake, still a little confused. "So, you've got Mr. Shaw, who is apparently from Tennessee, two unidentified female heads, and a vehicle with Montana license plates, which is registered to a Mr. Williams from New York City." He shrugged at the room. "My original question still stands—why are you in LA? And why am I here and not at home packing?" He checked his watch one more time.

"Because Mr. Shaw isn't talking," Taylor replied, her voice still calm.

Hunter stared hard at her for a couple of seconds.

"And how does that answer my question?"

"Agent Taylor's statement isn't one-hundred-percent accurate," Kennedy cut in. "We've had Mr. Shaw in our custody for four days. He was transferred to us a day after he was arrested. He's being held in Quantico. I assigned Agent Taylor and Agent Newman to the case."

Hunter's eyes moved to Taylor for just a second.

"But as Agent Taylor said," Kennedy continued, "Mr. Shaw has been refusing to speak."

"So?" Captain Blake interrupted, a little amused. "Since when has that stopped the FBI from extracting information from anyone, regardless?"

Kennedy was unfazed by the spiked remark.

"However," he continued, "during last night's interrogation session, Mr. Shaw finally spoke for the first time." He paused and walked over to the large window on the east wall. "He said just seven words."

Hunter waited.

"I will only speak to Robert Hunter."

7

Hunter didn't move. He didn't even flinch. If Kennedy's words had affected him in any way, he showed no signs of it.

Taylor had to admit that she was a little surprised by how calculated Hunter seemed after everything he was told.

"You can watch the recording of our last interview if you like," she offered. "I've got a copy right here." She gestured toward her briefcase.

Hunter's gaze scanned the room.

"That's why we thought that maybe you might recognize the name," Kennedy said. "But then again, after what we found out, we were expecting *Liam Shaw* to be a bogus alias anyway."

Hunter shifted his weight from foot to foot.

"Do you have a photograph of this Liam Shaw?" he asked Taylor.

"Of course." Taylor retrieved one last picture from her briefcase and handed it to Hunter.

He stared at it for a long moment, then took a deep breath. His eyes moved up to meet Kennedy's.

"You have got to be shitting me."

8

Hunter eventually made it back to his apartment to pack his bags, but the flight he took just a couple of hours later wasn't the one he had booked to Hawaii.

After taxiing its way up the runway, the private Hawker jet finally received the takeoff go-ahead from the Van Nuys airport control tower.

Hunter was seated toward the back of the plane, nursing a large cup of black coffee. His job didn't really allow him to travel much, and when he did, he usually drove, if at all possible. This was his first time inside a private jet, and he had to admit that he was impressed.

Luxurious and practical in equal measures, the cabin was twenty-two feet long by seven feet wide. Eight very comfortable cream leather seats were set out in a double-club configuration—four individual seats on each side of the aisle, each with its own power outlet and media system. All eight seats could swivel 360 degrees. Low-heat LED overhead lights gave the cabin a warm, atmospheric feel.

Agent Taylor sat directly in front of Hunter, typing away on her laptop on the foldout table in front of her. Adrian Kennedy was to Hunter's right, across the aisle.

He'd been on his cell phone since they'd left Captain Blake's office.

The plane took off smoothly and quickly climbed up to a cruising altitude of thirty thousand feet. Hunter kept his eyes on the blue, cloudless sky outside his window, wrestling with a multitude of thoughts.

"So," Kennedy said, finally getting off his phone and placing it back inside his jacket pocket. He had swiveled his seat around to face Hunter. "Tell me about this guy again, Robert. Who is he?"

Taylor stopped typing on her laptop and slowly rotated her seat around to face both men.

Hunter kept his eyes on the sky for a moment longer before meeting Kennedy's gaze.

"He's one of the most intelligent people I've ever met," he said at last. "Someone with tremendous self-discipline and control."

Kennedy and Taylor waited.

"His name is Lucien; Lucien Folter," Hunter carried on. "Or at least that's the name that I knew him by. I met him on my first day at Stanford University. I was sixteen."

"You said he was your roommate?" Taylor asked.

Hunter nodded. "From day one."

"How many sharing the room?"

"The two of us, that's all. It was a tiny room."

"Was he also a psychology major?"

"That's right." Hunter's gaze returned to the sky outside his window as his memory started to take him back. "He was a nice guy. I never expected him to be so friendly to me."

Taylor frowned. "What do you mean?"

Hunter shrugged. "I was a lot younger than anyone around. I was very skinny and awkward, long hair, and I didn't dress like most people did at the time. In truth, I was a bully magnet. Lucien was almost twenty then, loved sports, and worked out regularly. The kind of guy who'd usually have a field day with someone who looked like me."

Hunter grew up an only child of working-class parents in Compton, an underprivileged neighborhood of South Los Angeles. His mother lost her battle with cancer when he was only seven. His father never remarried and had to take on two jobs to cope with the demands of raising a child on his own.

Hunter had always been different. Even as a child his brain seemed to work through problems faster than anyone else's. School bored and frustrated him. He finished all of his sixth-grade work in less than two months, and just for something to do, he read through all the curriculum modules for the rest of his middle-school years. He then asked his school principal if he was allowed to take the final exams for grades seven and eight. Out of sheer curiosity, the principal allowed him to. Hunter aced them all.

It was then that his principal decided to contact the Los Angeles Board of Education, and after a new battery of exams and tests he was accepted into the Mirman School for gifted children, at the age of twelve.

But even a special school's curriculum wasn't enough to slow his progress.

By the age of fourteen he'd glided through Mirman's high school English, history, math, biology, and chemistry offerings. Four years of high school were condensed into two, and at fourteen he'd graduated with honors. With recommendations from all of his teachers, Hunter was accepted as a special-circumstances student at Stanford.

By the age of nineteen, Hunter had already graduated summa cum laude in psychology, and at twenty-three he received his PhD in criminal behavior analysis and biopsychology.

Surprise danced across Taylor's face once again. From Hunter's look and physique, she'd imagined him to have been a typical high school jock, the exact type she had no sympathy for. All throughout elementary and high school she too was bullied to tears almost every day for being overweight.

"But he didn't," Hunter continued. "In fact, it was because of him that I didn't get picked on as much as I would have. We became best friends. When I started going to the gym, he helped me with workouts and diet."

"And how was he on a day-to-day basis?"

"He wasn't the violent type, if that's what you're asking. He was always calm. Always in control. Which was a good thing, because he sure knew how to fight."

"But you just said that he wasn't the violent type," Taylor said.

"That's right."

"But you've also just implied that you've seen him in a fight."

Half a nod. "I have. There are certain situations that, no matter how calm or easygoing you are, you just can't get out of without a fight," Hunter replied.

Taylor could easily relate to that, but she had to insist. "I understand, but in this particular case, can you be a little more specific?"

"I only remember seeing Lucien in a fight once," Hunter explained. "And he really tried to get out of it without using his fists, but it didn't work out that way."

"How so?"

Hunter shrugged. "Lucien had met this girl in a bar one weekend and spent the night chatting with her. As far as I am aware of, that was it, just a few drinks and a little flirting. On the Monday after that weekend, we were coming back from a late study session at the library when we got cornered by four guys, all of them pretty big. One of them was the girl's very pissed off ex-boyfriend. Lucien had always been a great talker. The guy could sell ice to an Eskimo. He tried to reason his way out of the confrontation. He said that if he'd known, he would've never approached her and so on. But the guys didn't want to hear it. They said that they weren't there for an apology. They were there to fuck him up, period."

"So what happened then?" Taylor asked.

"They just went for him. Me? Even skinny as I was, I wasn't about to sit and watch my best friend get beat up by four Neanderthals, but I barely got a chance to move. The whole thing was over in ten . . . fifteen seconds, tops. I couldn't really tell you what happened in detail, but Lucien moved fast. All four ended up on the ground. After we got out of there, I asked him where he learned to do that."

"And what did he say?"

"He gave me a bullshit answer. He said he watched a lot of martial-arts movies. One thing I knew about

Lucien was that there was no point in trying to push him for an answer when he didn't want to give you one. So I just left it at that."

"When did you last see him?" Kennedy asked.

"The day I got my PhD," Hunter explained. "After getting my BS in psychology, I stayed at Stanford. I was offered a second scholarship to earn a doctorate. So I took it. Lucien and I continued to share the dorm for one more year, until he graduated. After that, he left California."

"Did you keep in touch?"

"Not for very long," Hunter said. "He took a few months off after he graduated. Went traveling for a little while, and then decided that he wanted to go back to get a PhD."

"At Stanford?"

"No. He went to Yale."

"Was his family from the East Coast?" Taylor asked.

Hunter paused for a second, trying to remember.

"I don't know," he said. "He never talked about them, and I never talked about mine."

Most people would've probably found it a little odd that two best friends could've spent years sharing a dorm room together in college and never talked to each other about their families, but not Taylor. The last time she talked to anyone about hers, she had been seventeen years old.

"So you last saw him when you got your PhD," Kennedy said.

Hunter nodded. "He flew over for the graduation ceremony, stayed for a day, and flew back the next morning. I never heard from him again."

"He just flew back to Connecticut and disappeared?" Taylor asked. "I thought you were best friends."

"Maybe I was the one who disappeared," Hunter said.

Taylor hesitated for an instant.

"Why? Did he try to get in contact with you?"

"Not that I am aware of," Hunter replied. "But I didn't try to keep in touch with him either." He paused and looked away. "After my graduation I didn't keep in touch with anyone."

9

The Hawker jet touched down on Turner Field landing strip in Quantico, Virginia, almost exactly five hours after taking off from Van Nuys airport in Los Angeles.

After Hunter's conversation with Kennedy and Taylor about what he could remember of his former best friend, they sat in near silence for the rest of the long flight. Kennedy fell asleep for a couple of hours, but Hunter and Taylor stayed awake, both lost in their own thoughts.

Taylor had left Los Angeles, the city where she was born, when she was twenty years old. Her visit to the LAPD was the first time she had been back, and as she'd dreaded, the bad memories flooded in.

Her father had died of an unexpected heart attack, triggered by a coronary aneurysm, when she was fourteen years old. Taylor took his death very badly, and so did her young mother. The next couple of years were a tremendous battle, emotionally and financially, as her mother—who had been a housewife for the previous fifteen years—struggled with a series of odd jobs and the pressures of being a recent widow and a single parent.

Taylor's mother was a tender woman with a kind

soul, but she was also one of those people who just couldn't handle being by themselves. What followed was a string of deadbeat boyfriends, some of them abusive. Taylor was just about to graduate from high school when her mother became pregnant again. Her mother's boyfriend at the time told her that he just didn't want that kind of responsibility, that he wasn't ready to become a father and have a family, and that he had no intention of becoming a father to someone else's daughter—a girl that he couldn't care less for. When Taylor's mother refused to follow through with the abortion-clinic appointment he'd set up for her, he simply dumped her and left town the next day. They never heard from him again.

With her mother heavily pregnant and unable to work, Taylor gave up on the idea of going to college and started working at the local mall full-time. A month later her mother gave birth to a baby boy, Adam—born with an abnormality on chromosome eighteen, resulting in moderate mental retardation, muscle atrophy, craniofacial malformation, and huge difficulty in coordinating movement. Adam's birth threw Taylor's mother into an out-of-control depression. She didn't know how to cope with her new baby's needs and found solace in sleeping tablets, antidepressants, and alcohol. At the age of seventeen, Taylor had become not only big daughter and big sister but also man of the house.

Their government subsidy wasn't nearly enough, so for the next three years Taylor worked whatever jobs she could get and took care of her little brother and mother. Despite all the medical support, Adam's health deteriorated rapidly, and he died two months after his third birthday. Her mother's depression worsened considerably, but without medical insurance, adequate professional help was nearly impossible to find.

One rainy night, when Taylor came back from working a late shift in a restaurant downtown, she found a note from her mother on the kitchen table:

> *Sorry for not being a good mother to you or*
> *Adam, honey. Sorry for all the mistakes. You're the*
> *best daughter a mother could ever hope for. I love*
> *you with all my heart. I just hope that you can*
> *one day forgive me for being so weak, so stupid,*
> *and for all the trouble I've put you through. Please*
> *be happy, honey. You deserve it.*

Reading the note filled Taylor with a heart-stopping dread, and she rushed to her mother's room, but it was too late. Her mother had overdosed on sleeping pills and a whole bottle of vodka.

Taylor still had nightmares about that night.

• • •

A black GMC SUV with tinted windows, FBI style, was already waiting for them on the runway when they landed.

Hunter stepped off the plane and stretched his six-foot frame against the early-morning breeze. It felt good to be breathing fresh air again. No matter how luxurious the jet's passenger cabin was, after five hours inside, it felt like a prison.

Hunter checked his watch. The sun wouldn't be up for another two hours, but surprisingly, the early-morning air in Virginia felt just as warm as in Los Angeles.

"We all need to try to get some sleep," Kennedy said, shifting his attention from his cell phone once again, as all three of them boarded the SUV. "And a decent breakfast later on. Your quarters are ready," he addressed Hunter. "I hope you don't mind staying at one of the academy's recruit dorms."

Hunter shook his head.

"Agent Taylor will come get you at ten a.m." Kennedy consulted his timepiece. "That'll give everyone around six hours' break. Get some sleep."

"Can't we make it any earlier than that?" Hunter asked. "Like now? I'm here already. I don't see the point of delaying this any longer."

Kennedy looked straight into Hunter's eyes. "We all need some rest, Robert. It's been a long day and a long flight. I know that you can work on very little sleep, but that doesn't mean your brain doesn't get tired like everyone else's. I need you sharp when you walk in there to talk to your old friend."

10

S pecial Agent Courtney Taylor knocked on Hunter's dorm door at exactly 10:00 a.m.

Hunter opened the door, checked his watch, and smiled.

"Wow, you timed your arrival to absolute perfection."

Hunter's hair was still wet from his shower. He was wearing black jeans, a dark-blue T-shirt under his usual thin black leather jacket, and black boots, in contrast to her black pin-striped suit and professional, slick ponytail.

Dozing on and off, he had only managed to sleep a total of two and a half hours.

"Are you ready, Detective Hunter?" Taylor asked.

"Indeed," Hunter replied, closing the door behind him.

"I trust that you got breakfast okay?" she said, as they started walking down the corridor toward the staircase.

At nine o'clock, an FBI cadet carrying a healthy breakfast tray of fruit, cereal, yogurt, scrambled eggs, coffee, milk, and toast had knocked on Hunter's door.

"I did," Hunter said with a questioning smile. "But I didn't know the FBI did room service."

"We don't. This was a one-off. You can thank Director Kennedy for that."

Downstairs, another black SUV was waiting to drive them across the compound. Hunter sat in silence in the backseat, while Taylor sat in front with the driver.

The FBI Academy was located on 547 acres of a marine corps base forty miles south of Washington, DC. Its nerve center was an interconnected conglomerate of buildings that looked a lot more like an overgrown corporation than a government training facility. Recruits in dark-blue sweat suits, with the bureau's insignia emblazoned on their chests, and *FBI* in large golden letters across their backs, were just about everywhere. Marines with high-powered rifles stood at every intersection and at the entrance to every building. The sound of helicopter blades cutting the air provided a constant hum. A palpable sense of mission and secrecy cloaked the entire place.

The SUV stopped at the heavily guarded gates of what could only be described as a compound within a compound, completely detached from the main network of buildings. After clearing security, the SUV moved inside and parked in front of a three-story brick building fronted by tinted, bulletproof-glass windows.

Hunter and Taylor exited the car, and she escorted him past the armed marines at the entrance. Inside they went through two sets of security doors, down a long hallway, through two more sets of security doors and into an elevator, which descended three floors down to the Behavioral Research and Instruction Unit. The elevator opened onto a long, well-lit hardwood corridor, with several portraits in gilded frames lining the walls.

A big man with a round face and a crooked nose stepped in front of the open elevator doors.

"Detective Hunter," he greeted them, his voice harsh. "I'm Agent Edwin Newman. Welcome to the FBI BRIU."

Hunter stepped out of the elevator and shook Newman's hand.

Newman was in his early fifties, with combed-back peppery hair and bright-green eyes. He wore a black suit with a pristine white shirt and a silky red tie. Despite his brusque tone, he smiled suddenly, flashing gleaming white teeth.

"I thought that we could have a quick chat in the conference room before we take you to see . . ." Newman paused and looked at Taylor. "Your old friend, as I understand."

Hunter agreed and followed Newman and Taylor to the opposite end of the hallway.

The conference room was large, with the majority of its space taken up by a long, polished mahogany table. A digital screen showing a detailed map of the United States glowed at the far wall.

Newman sat at the head of the table and nodded for Hunter to take the chair next to him.

"I know you've been made aware of the delicate situation we have here," Newman began once Hunter had settled himself.

"I have."

Newman flipped open the folder on the table in front of him. "According to what you told Director Kennedy and Agent Taylor, the real name of the man we have in our custody is Lucien Folter, and not Liam Shaw, as his driver's license stated."

"That's the name I knew him by," Hunter confirmed.

"Do you think that Lucien Folter could also be an alias?"

"I see no reason why he would have used a false name back in college," Hunter theorized. "You also have to remember that we're talking about Stanford University here, and someone who was just nineteen at the time. That means this nineteen-year-old kid would've had to have expertly falsified his records to an impeccable extent, in an era where personal computers did not exist. Not an easy task."

"Not easy," Newman agreed. "But it was doable."

"I suppose," Hunter replied.

"The only reason I ask is because of the meaning of his name," Newman said.

"Meaning?" Hunter looked at the agent curiously.

Newman nodded. "Did you know that the word *folter* means *torture* in German?"

"Yes. Lucien told me."

Newman stared at him.

Hunter didn't look too impressed. "The name *Lucien* comes from the French language, and it means *light, illumination*. It's also a village in Poland, and the name of a Christian saint. Most names have histories behind them, Special Agent Newman. My family name means *he who hunts*; nevertheless, my father was never a hunter in any shape or form. A great number of American family names will, by coincidence, mean something in a different language. That doesn't actually constitute a hidden meaning."

Newman's jaw tensed.

Hunter took a moment, and then allowed his gaze to move to the folder on the table.

Newman got the hint and began reading. "Okay. Lucien Folter, born October 25, 1966, in Monte Vista, Colorado. His parents, Charles Folter and Mary-Ann Folter, are both deceased. He graduated from Monte Vista High School in 1984, with very good grades. No youth misdemeanor record whatsoever. Never got into any trouble with the police. After graduating from high school, he went to Stanford University." Newman paused and looked up at Hunter. "I guess you know everything that happened during the next few years.

"After obtaining his psychology degree from Stanford, Lucien Folter applied to Yale for a PhD in criminal psychology. He was accepted, did three years of coursework, and then simply disappeared. He never completed his doctorate."

Hunter kept his eyes on Newman. He *hadn't* known.

"And when I say *disappeared*," Newman said, "I mean *disappeared*. There's nothing else out there on a Lucien Folter after his third year at Yale. No job records, no passport, no credit cards, no listed address, no bills . . . no anything. It's like Lucien Folter ceased to exist." Newman closed the folder. "That's all we have on him."

"Maybe that was when he decided to take up a new identity," Taylor offered. She was sitting across the table from Hunter. "Maybe that was when he got tired of being Lucien Folter and became someone else. Maybe Liam Shaw, or maybe even someone completely different that we don't yet know about."

"The truth is that whoever this guy really is, he's a living, breathing, walking mystery," Newman said. "Somebody who might've lied to everyone throughout his whole life."

Hunter had entertained that same thought over-night, but not for very long. He had passed most of the night recalling the time he'd spent at Stanford with his old friend. True, Lucien had always been enigmatic, but that was no reason to think that he might've lied to everyone for his whole life. What reason would he have had?

"I wanted you to understand this before you go talk to him," Newman added. "Because I know that things can get a little emotional when we're dealing with people from our past. I'm not trying to tell you what to do. I've read your file, and I've read your dissertation— *An Advanced Psychological Study in Criminal Conduct*, right? I know that you know what you're doing better than most. But you're still human, and as such you have emotions. No matter how prepared we are, emotions can and will cloud our best judgments. Keep that in mind when you walk in there."

Hunter knew exactly what he meant.

Newman then proceeded to detail Lucien's uncon-ventional behavior since he had arrived in Quantico— the extreme silence, the mysterious up-to-the-second internal timekeeping, the long exercise sessions, the wall staring, the extraordinary mental strength.

None of that surprised Hunter very much. In col-lege, Lucien had been the most focused and determined student Hunter had known. Every time he had set his mind on doing something, he had achieved it, whether it had been academic or physical.

"He's waiting," Newman said at last. "I guess we better get going."

11

Newman and Taylor guided Hunter out of the conference room, back down the hallway, and into the elevator, which descended another two floors to sublevel five. This level was nothing like the Behavioral Research and Instruction Unit's floor. There was no shiny hallway, no fancy fixtures on the walls, no pleasant feel to the place whatsoever.

The elevator opened onto a small concrete-floored anteroom. On the right, behind a large safety-glass window, Hunter could see what had to be a control center, with wall-mounted monitors and a guard sitting at a large console desk.

"Welcome to the BRIU holding-cells floor," Taylor said.

"Why is he being held here?" Hunter asked.

"Your friend's potential psychopathy has triggered several bells within the behavioral unit," Newman replied. "No one in the unit has ever come across anyone quite like him. If he really is a killer, judging by the level of brutality that was used on the two victims' heads, there might be a whole lot of other dead girls in his past."

Taylor signaled the guard inside the control room and he buzzed open the door directly across the room from them. The marine standing by the door took a step to the side to allow them through.

The door led them into a long cinder-block corridor. There was a distinct sanitized smell in the air, something that tickled Hunter's nose, reminding him of a hospital. The hallway ended at a second heavy metal door—breach and assault proof. As they approached, Taylor and Newman looked up at the security camera high on the ceiling above the door. A second later, the door buzzed open. They zigzagged through another two smaller hallways and two more heavy doors, before arriving at the interrogation room, halfway down another nondescript hallway.

This new room was nothing more than a square box, sixteen feet by sixteen feet, with light-gray cinder-block walls, and a white linoleum floor. A square metal table with two metal chairs at opposite ends was securely bolted to the floor. Also bolted to the floor, just beside the chairs, were two sets of thick metal loops. Fluorescent tube lights encased in metal cages bathed the room in crisp brightness. Hunter also noticed the four CCTV cameras, one at each corner of the ceiling. A water cooler was pushed up against one of the walls, and the north wall was covered by a two-way mirror that spanned the room's width.

"Have a seat," Taylor said to Hunter. "Get comfortable. Your friend is being brought here." She gestured with her head. "We'll be next door, but we'll have eyes and ears in this room." It was a reassurance tinged with a hint of warning.

Without saying anything else, Taylor and Newman exited the interrogation room, allowing the heavy metal door to slam behind them, leaving Hunter alone inside the claustrophobic square box. There was no handle on his side of the door.

Hunter took a deep breath and leaned against the metal table. He'd been inside interrogation rooms countless times, often face-to-face with people who turned out to be violent, brutal, and sadistic killers. But not since his first few interrogations had he felt this tingle of anticipation.

Then the door buzzed open again.

12

To Hunter's surprise, he found himself holding his breath.

The first person to walk through the entryway was a tall, well-built marine carrying a close-quarters combat shotgun. He took two steps into the room, paused, and then moved to his left, clearing a pathway from the door into the room.

Hunter tensed and stood up straight.

The man who then entered was about an inch taller than Hunter, his hair brown and cropped short. His beard was just starting to become bushy. He wore a standard orange prison jumpsuit, and his hands were cuffed and linked together by a metal bar no longer than a foot. The chain that was attached to the metal bar looped around his waist and then moved down to his feet, hooking onto thick, heavy ankle cuffs, restricting his movements, and forcing him to shuffle his way along as he walked.

His head hung low, with his chin almost touching his chest. His eyes were focused on the floor. Hunter couldn't clearly see his face, but he could still recognize his old friend.

Directly behind Lucien followed a second marine.

Hunter took a step to his right, but remained silent.

Both guards guided the prisoner to one of the chairs. As they sat him down, the second marine quickly shackled the prisoner's ankle chain to the metal loop on the floor. Once all was done, they left without uttering a word, or even looking at Hunter. The door closed behind them with a heavy clang.

The tense silent seconds that followed seemed to stretch for an eternity, until Lucien finally lifted his head.

Hunter stood across the metal table from him, immobile. Their eyes met, and for a moment they both simply stared at each other. Then, the prisoner's lips stretched into a thin, nervous smile.

"Hello, Robert," he finally said, his voice full of emotion.

Lucien had gained a little more weight since Hunter had last seen him, but it looked to be all muscle. His face looked older but leaner, and the expression in his dark-brown eyes had changed. They now possessed a penetrating quality often associated with greatness, and an intensity that spoke of tremendous focus and purpose. With high cheekbones; full, strong lips; and a squared jaw, Lucien was still an attractive man. There was something else that was new: a one-inch-long diagonal scar on his left cheek, just under his eye.

"Lucien," Hunter greeted him.

The staring continued for several seconds.

"It's been a very long time, my friend," Lucien said, looking down at his shackled hands. "If I could, I'd hug you. I've missed you, Robert."

Hunter stayed quiet simply because he didn't really know what to say. He'd always hoped that one day he would see his college friend again, but he'd never imagined that it would be in this type of situation.

"You look well," Lucien said with a renewed smile, his eyes analyzing Hunter. "I can tell you've never stopped training. You look like . . ." He paused, searching for the right words. "A lean boxer ready for his championship fight. And you haven't aged. Looks like life has been good to you."

It took a moment for Hunter to shake the fog of confusion that enveloped him, for his ears to recognize the sound of his old friend's voice.

"Lucien, what the hell is going on?" Hunter's voice was calm and composed, but his eyes couldn't hide his surprise.

Lucien took a deep breath, and Hunter saw his body tense. Hunter had never seen Lucien scared of anything before, but he sure looked scared just then.

"I'm not sure, Robert," he said, his voice a little weaker.

"You're not sure?"

Lucien's eyes returned to his cuffed hands and he shifted in his seat, looking for a more comfortable position. For someone as versed in body language and criminal behavior as Hunter, it was a clear sign that he was struggling with his thoughts.

"Tell me," he said, avoiding eye contact, "have you ever heard from Susan?" For an instant he looked surprised by his own question.

Hunter frowned. "What?"

"Susan. You remember her, don't you? Susan Richards?"

Hunter remembered Susan well. How could he not? The three of them had been together most of the time during their years at college. Susan was also a psychology major. She had moved from Nevada to California after being accepted into Stanford. Susan Richards was one of those incredibly bright, happy-go-lucky girls, always smiling, always positive about everything. Very little ever fazed her. She was also very attractive, having inherited most of her Native American mother's delicate features—tall and slim, with chestnut hair, beautiful almond-shaped hazel eyes, a petite nose, and plump lips. She looked more like a Hollywood star than a college student.

"Yes, of course I remember Susan," Hunter said.

"Have you ever heard from her in all these years?" Lucien asked.

Hunter's psychological training overcame his initial confusion, and he finally realized what was happening. Lucien's defense and fear mechanisms were kicking in. Subjects too afraid or nervous to talk about a delicate topic might, almost unconsciously, try to steer the conversation away from it and avoid talking about it, at least for a little while, until their nerves settled. That was exactly what Lucien was doing.

Hunter knew that the best way to deal with that reaction was to just play along.

"No," he replied. "After her graduation, I never heard from her again. Did you?"

Lucien shook his head. "Same here. Not even a postcard."

"I remember she'd said that she wanted to go traveling. Europe or something. Maybe she did and decided to stay over there for some reason. Maybe she met somebody and got married, or found a career opportunity."

"Yes, I remember her talking about traveling. Maybe she did," Lucien agreed. "But even so, Robert. We were together pretty much all the time. We were friends . . . good friends."

"Things like that do happen, Lucien," Hunter said. "You and I were best friends too, after all, and we didn't keep in touch after college."

Lucien looked up at Hunter. "That's not entirely true, Robert. We did keep in touch for a while. A few years, actually. Until you finished your PhD. I went to the ceremony, remember?"

Hunter nodded.

"I just thought that maybe she had kept in touch with you." Lucien shrugged. "Everyone knew that Susan was into you." He gave Hunter a tentative smile. "I know that you never got together with her because I really liked her."

Hunter remained silent.

"That was nice of you. Very . . . considerate, but I don't think I would've minded. The two of you would've made a nice couple."

Lucien's eyes darted away from Hunter's for a second.

"Do you remember when we went with her to that tattoo parlor because she wanted to get that horrible thing on her arm?" he asked.

Hunter did remember it. Susan had wanted to get inked with a red rose, with its thorny stem wrapped around a bleeding heart.

"I do remember," Hunter said with a melancholy smile.

"What the hell was that? A rose strangling a heart?"

"I liked that tattoo," Hunter said. "It was different, and I'm sure it meant something to her. I thought it looked good on her arm. The artist did a great job."

Lucien made a face. "I don't really like tattoos. Never did." He paused and his eyes moved to a random spot on the cinder-block wall. "I miss her. She could always make us laugh, even in the worst of situations."

"Yes, I miss her too," Hunter said.

Silence took over the room for several seconds. Hunter filled a paper cup with water from the cooler and placed it on the table in front of Lucien.

"Thank you," he said, taking a quick sip.

Hunter poured himself one as well.

"They've got the wrong man, Robert," Lucien finally said.

Hunter paused and looked back at his old friend.

"I didn't do it," Lucien said, his voice full of emotion. "I didn't do what they're saying I did. You have to believe me, Robert. I'm not a monster. I didn't do those things."

Hunter stayed quiet.

"But I know who did."

13

Behind the two-way mirror, inside the observation room next door, Special Agents Taylor and Newman were watching attentively.

On a table by the east wall, two CCTV monitors showed highly detailed images of Lucien taken from different angles. Dr. Patrick Lambert, a forensic psychiatrist with the FBI Behavioral Research and Instruction Unit, was patiently examining every facial movement, and scrutinizing every voice inflection the prisoner produced, but that wasn't all. Both monitors were also hooked up to a computer equipped with the latest state-of-the-art facial-analysis software, capable of reading and evaluating the most involuntary movements—movements triggered subconsciously as the interviewee's state of mind altered from calm to nervous, to anxious, to irritated, or to angry. Everyone inside that observation room was confident that if Lucien Folter lied about anything at all, they would know.

But neither Dr. Lambert nor Special Agents Taylor and Newman needed that technology to pick up the anxiety in Lucien's demeanor. They'd expected it. After all, he was talking for the first time since he'd been arrested for a brutal double homicide. Add to that the fact that he was now face-to-face with an old friend he hadn't seen since his college days, and Lucien was bound to be nervous. It was a common human reaction, as was his initial avoidance of the subject. But his last few words had caught everyone by surprise.

They've got the wrong man, Robert.

The tension inside the observation room went up a notch, and everyone looked in the direction of the monitors.

"I didn't do it. I didn't do what they're saying I did. You have to believe me, Robert. I'm not a monster. I didn't do those things."

"Of course he didn't," Newman said with a half chuckle, looking over at Taylor. "They never do. Our prison system is full of innocent people, isn't that right?"

Taylor said nothing. She was still carefully watching the screens, and so was Dr. Lambert.

"But I know who did."

Those last five words were something no one was expecting, because in truth, those words were an admission of complicity. Even if Lucien Folter hadn't been the one who'd murdered and decapitated both of those women, admitting that he knew who'd done it, not alerting the police, and being picked up transporting the women's heads across state lines, made him an accessory to murder with at least a couple of aggravating circumstances. And in Wyoming, where he was arrested and the death penalty was still enforced, the district attorney's office would no doubt push for it. Lucien Folter was a dead man.

14

Despite his surprise, Hunter did his best to appear relaxed. Now that Lucien's nerves had seemed to settle enough for him to start talking, Hunter knew he had to keep the conversation going as smoothly as possible. He'd simply steer it in the right direction.

Hunter pulled over a chair and sat across the table from Lucien. "You know who did it?" he asked, his tone as tranquil as someone asking for the time.

Interrogators usually hold a standing, more authoritative position, while the person being interrogated is kept in an inferior, seated one. It works as an intimidation technique—the person asking the questions is at a higher level, talking down at the person who is answering them. It echoes common childhood memories of a parent's reprimand. But the last thing Hunter wanted was for Lucien to feel any more intimidated than he already was. He hoped the move would produce an unthreatening effect, keeping the tension in the room to a minimum.

"Well," Lucien said, leaning forward and placing his elbows on the table, "I don't really know *exactly* who did it. But it has to be either the person who I was supposed to be delivering the car to, or the one who delivered the car to me. If they didn't do it directly, they'll know who did. They are the ones you have to go after. You have to help me, Robert. I'm not the one the FBI wants. I didn't do this. I'm just a delivery boy."

For the first time, Hunter noticed real trepidation in Lucien's voice. He knew the car wasn't registered in Lucien's name, the FBI had told him that, but this was the first he'd heard of Lucien delivering the car to someone else.

"You were taking that blue Taurus to someone?" Hunter asked.

Lucien averted his eyes once again. When he finally spoke, his tone was as calm and controlled as ever, but it carried a hint of anger this time.

"The reality is, life doesn't treat everyone equally, my friend. I'm sure you know that."

Hunter did, but he was unsure of where Lucien was going.

Lucien's gaze quickly moved to the cameras on the ceiling, and then to the two-way mirror just behind Hunter. He knew he was being recorded. He knew that nothing he said could remain private, and for the briefest of moments he looked embarrassed.

Hunter picked up on his friend's sudden discomfort, following his stare, but there was nothing he could do about others listening in. This was the FBI's show, not his. He gave Lucien a moment.

"After I left Stanford, I made a few mistakes," Lucien said. Paused. Rethought. "Actually I made *quite* a few mistakes. Some of them very bad." He finally looked back at Hunter. "I guess I should start from the beginning."

15

For some reason, Lucien's words chilled Hunter, as if someone had switched on an air-conditioning unit inside the interrogation room.

Lucien took another sip of his water, and as he did so, the look in his eyes grew sad.

"I met a woman during my second year at Yale," he began. "Her name was Karen. She was British, from a place called Gravesend, in southeast England. Have you heard of it?"

Hunter nodded.

"I hadn't," Lucien said. "I had to look it up. Anyway, Karen was . . ." He seemed to consider what to really say. "Different from what most people would expect a Yale PhD student to be like . . . or look like."

"Different?" Hunter prodded.

"In every aspect. She was a free spirit. You remember the kind of girls I used to go for, right?"

Hunter nodded again, but said nothing, allowing his old friend to carry on uninterrupted.

"Karen was nothing like any of them." A timid smile parted his lips. "When we met, she was forty-two. I was twenty-five. She was five foot one. A whole twelve inches shorter than me . . . and curvy."

In college, Lucien had been attracted only to tall and slim women.

"She also had quite a few tattoos," Lucien continued. "A lip piercing, a nose piercing, her left earlobe was stretched to a full half inch, and she had these Bettie Page–style bangs."

This time it was hard for Hunter not to show surprise.

"I thought you didn't like tattoos."

"I don't. And I don't much care for facial piercings either. But there was just something about Karen. Something I can't really explain. Something that grabbed hold of me and didn't let go." Another sip of his water. "We started dating just a few months after we met. It's funny how life is always full of surprises, isn't it? Karen looked nothing like any of the girls I used to go for, she didn't act like them either, but nevertheless, she was the one I fell head over heels for." Lucien paused and looked away. "I guess I can say that I was truly in love."

Hunter saw a muscle flex on his friend's jaw.

"She was a very sweet woman," Lucien said. "And we got along fantastically well. We did everything together. Went everywhere together. Spent every second together. She became my haven, my heaven, my heart. I was living a dream, but there was one problem."

Hunter waited.

"Karen had gotten involved with some very bad people."

"What kind of bad?" Hunter asked.

"Drugs bad," Lucien said. "The kind of bad you don't mess with, unless you've grown tired of this life and feel like exiting it in a very violent way." He finished the rest of his water in three large gulps before crushing the paper cup in his right hand.

Hunter took note of his friend's silent angry outburst, stood up, poured him a new cup of water, and placed it on the table.

"Thank you." He stared at the cup. "I'm sorry to say that I wasn't strong enough, Robert," Lucien continued. "I'm not sure if it was because I was too much in love, or if I was just swallowed up by the moment, but instead of talking her out of it, I ended up joining her, and trying some of the stuff she was using."

There was a pain-stricken, embarrassed pause.

"The problem is," Lucien went on, "and I'm sure you know this—some of that shit is hard to only *try.*" He looked down at his hands. "So I got hooked."

"What kind of drugs are we talking about here?"

Lucien shrugged. "The heavy kind. Instant-hook stuff—crystal, heroin, crack, GHB, coke, K . . . whatever was going, really . . . and alcohol. I started drinking a lot too."

Hunter had seen so many strong people fall victim to drugs, he'd lost count.

"From then on everything went downhill, and in a hurry. All the money I had went into supplying Karen's habit and mine. It ate away at my finances faster than you could imagine. My entire life suffered. I dropped out of Yale in my third year, and would do anything to get my daily fix. I ran up debts everywhere, and with the wrong kind of people. The people Karen had introduced me to. The really bad kind."

"You didn't have anyone you could turn to for help?" Hunter asked. "I'm not talking about financial help. Someone who could help you kick the habit, bring you back."

Lucien's gaze met Hunter's and he chuckled derisively. "You know me, Robert. I never had that many close friends. The few I had, I had broken contact with."

Hunter took the hint. "You could've still looked me up, Lucien. You knew where I was. We were best friends. I would've helped you." Hunter paused, and his stare went hard as he realized his mistake. "Shit, you were already hooked when you flew down for my PhD graduation, weren't you? That's why you stayed in LA less than twenty-four hours. But I was so consumed by the moment that I didn't even notice. That was you asking for my help."

Lucien looked away.

Hunter felt a stab of guilt cut through his flesh. "You should've said something. I would've helped you. You know I would've. I'm sorry I didn't notice it."

"Maybe I should have. Maybe that's just another one of my bad mistakes. But I'm not going to cry about things long gone, Robert. Things that can't be changed. Everything that happened to me was my own doing, my own fault, nobody else's. I know it, and I accept that. And yes, I know that everyone needs a little help every once in a while. I just didn't know how to ask for it."

It was Hunter's turn to take a sip of water. "Were you still with Karen when you went to LA?" he asked.

Lucien nodded. "She also quit Yale, and did some very . . . very stupid things to get hold of cash." He hesitated, took a deep breath, and his eyes saddened again. "We stayed together for three years. All the way until she overdosed." A long pause. "She died in my arms."

Lucien looked away as his toughness began to crack. Tears came into his eyes, but he held steady.

"I'm so sorry," Hunter finally said.

Lucien rubbed his face with his shackled hands and rested his forehead on his palms.

"What happened then?" Hunter asked.

"Then I really went to hell, and I did it a step at a time. I lost my way, big time. I hit depression hard and at full speed. Instead of learning from what happened to Karen and kicking the habit, I got deeper into it." Lucien stole a peek at the two-way mirror once again. "I should be dead by now, and in many ways, I really wish I were. The fight back was very long, very slow, and very painful. It took me many years to manage to get my addiction under control, a few more to finally kick it. But along the way I just got myself into more and more debt, and involved with the worst kinds of characters society has to offer."

The FBI's blood tests had shown that Lucien Folter was clean. Hunter knew that.

"So when did you finally kick your habit?" he asked.

"Several years ago," Lucien said. Hunter wondered if he was being deliberately vague. "By then, I had lost all hope of a career in psychology or in anything decent, really. I went through a series of odd jobs, most of them awful, some of them not quite legit.

In the end, I hated what I had become. Even though I was clean, I just wasn't the person I once was anymore. I wasn't Lucien Folter. I had become someone completely different. A lost soul. Someone I didn't recognize. Someone *no one* recognized. Someone I really didn't like."

Hunter could guess what was coming next.

"So you decided to change identities," he said.

Lucien looked straight at Hunter and nodded.

"That's right," he agreed. "You know, being a junkie, living life as 'scum' for as long as I did, puts you in contact with some very colorful folks. People who are able to get you anything you want . . . for a price, obviously. Getting hold of a new identity was as easy as buying a newspaper."

Hunter understood the reality of the world they lived in. All one needed to obtain whatever documents they like in a different name was to know the right people . . . or the wrong people, depending on which way you looked at it.

"Once I became Liam Shaw," Lucien said, "I concentrated on getting healthy again. It took me quite a while to manage to put weight back on . . . to regain focus. With all the drugs, I had the body of an anorexic. My stomach had shrunk. My mouth was full of ulcers. My health had deteriorated to a hair away from death. I had to keep on forcing myself to eat." He paused and looked at his arms and torso. "I look okay on the outside now, but my insides are royally fucked up, Robert. I've caused a lot of damage to my body. Most of it irreversible."

Despite his blunt words, Hunter picked up no self-pity in Lucien's tone of voice or in the look in his eyes. He simply accepted what he had done to himself. He had acknowledged his mistakes, and he seemed okay with paying the price.

"Tell me about this car delivery thing," Hunter said.

16

The problem with getting involved with the kinds of people I got involved with," Lucien began, "is that they get their claws deep into you right at the beginning. And once they do that, they never really let go. They own you for life. I'm sure you understand that these people can be very persuasive when they want to be."

Lucien read the question in Hunter's eyes. "Yes, I did change my name. And yes, I moved as far away as I could at the time, but who do you think put me in touch with the people who organized the name change and all the false documents, Robert?" He let go of an angry sigh. "I was stupid enough to believe that I had finally managed to get away, but no one ever does. Not from these people. If they want to find you, they will. And they did."

Lucien didn't need to tell Hunter how powerful organized crime was in the United States.

"So help me understand this 'car delivery' thing, Lucien," Hunter said.

"It started about a year and a half ago. The way it works is, I get a call on my cell phone telling me where to pick up a car. They give me a delivery address and a time frame. No names. When I get there, there's always someone waiting to collect the car. I hand the car over, he gives me enough money for a bus ticket back . . . maybe a little extra, and that's all. Until the next phone call."

"I'm guessing you don't always deliver the cars to the same place," Hunter said.

"Not so far," Lucien agreed. "A different pickup and delivery address every time." He paused and looked at Hunter. "But I've always delivered to the same person."

That came as a surprise.

"Can you describe him?" Hunter asked.

Lucien made a face. "About six foot tall, well built, but deliveries were always made at night, in a dark field. The person receiving the car was always wearing a long coat with its collar up, a baseball cap, and dark glasses." He shrugged. "That's as good a description as I can give."

"So how do you know it was the same person?"

"Same voice, same posture, same mannerisms." Lucien sat back in his chair. "I'm telling you, Robert, it was the same person every time."

Hunter saw no reason to doubt Lucien. "What about the person who delivered the car to you?" he asked.

"As I've said, the instructions came over the phone. They'd leave it in a parking lot. Keys, a parking stub, and the delivery address were left inside an envelope in a safe place for me to collect. No human contact."

"And you had no idea what you were delivering?" Hunter asked. "I mean—you didn't know what was in the trunk?"

Lucien shook his head. "It was always part of my instructions: *Don't ever look in the trunk.*"

Hunter pondered that for a second or two, but Lucien anticipated his next question, and offered an answer before Hunter could even ask it.

"Yes, I was curious about it. Yes, I thought about taking a quick peek many times, but like I said, these are the kinds of people you simply don't fuck with. If I'd opened that trunk, I'm sure they would've had a way of knowing. Curious or not, that was one stupid mistake that I wasn't prepared to make."

Hunter had a quick sip of his water.

"You said that this all started about a year and a half ago?"

"That's right."

"How many deliveries were there?"

"This was supposed to have been my fifth one."

Hunter held steady, but alarm bells started ringing everywhere inside his head. *Five* deliveries. If Lucien was telling the truth, and if he was delivering the same or very similar cargo every time, then this whole thing had just escalated into a serial-murderer investigation.

Lucien paused, a smug look overtaking his features, like a rookie poker player who'd just gotten a great hand and was unable to disguise it. "My trump is—I know who the person on the phone was."

Hunter's eyebrows arched.

Lucien took a moment before speaking again. "For now, I'll keep that information to myself, together with all the previous pickup and delivery locations."

That answer caught Hunter completely by surprise and he frowned.

"I know you're not running this show, Robert," Lucien explained. "The FBI is pulling all the strings here. The only reason you're here is because I asked for you. I know they've probably told you that you're only here as a guest . . . a listener. You have no authority over anything. You can't guarantee me anything because here you have no bargaining powers. *My* only bargaining chip, meanwhile, is this information."

"I understand that," Hunter agreed. "But I don't see how withholding it can help you, Lucien. If you are innocent, you have to help the FBI prove that, not play games with them."

"And I will do that, Robert, but I'm scared. Even a child can see that the evidence against me is overwhelming. I know that I'm facing death row here, and I'm petrified. I didn't tell them anything so far because I know there's no way they'd believe me."

It was easy to see how fear could've distorted Lucien's vision of reality. They both knew how seriously the FBI was committed to punishing criminals. Hunter had to reassure him.

"It doesn't quite work like that, Lucien. Why wouldn't the FBI believe you? They're not in the business of sending innocent people to prison. They want to find the person who's responsible for those murders, and if you can help them do so, of course they'll listen to you, of course they'll follow up on what you tell them."

"Okay, maybe they would, but I panicked, all right? I didn't know where to start." He took a deep breath. "Then I thought of you. I have no family left, Robert— everyone's gone. There's no one on this earth who even cares if I live or die. I've met a lot of people in my life, but you're the only real friend I've ever had. The only one who knew the real me, and you were also a cop. So I just thought that maybe . . ." Lucien's voice croaked, filled with emotion once again. His face crumpled. "I didn't do this, Robert. You have to believe me."

Back in college, Hunter could usually tell when Lucien was lying because he had a subtle tell. Hunter had identified it in his second semester at Stanford. As he was telling a lie, Lucien's stare would intensify, becoming more determined, as if somehow the hard look in his eyes could hypnotize you into believing him. Consequently, for just a fraction of a second, his lower left eyelid would tighten, producing not exactly a twitch, but a delicate, definite flutter. He couldn't help it because he didn't even know he was doing it. It'd been over twenty years, but Hunter remembered. There had been no hardening of the stare. No movement of the lower left eyelid whatsoever, no matter how subtle.

"Remember when I told you that I didn't know how to ask for help, your help?" Lucien paused for breath. "Well, I'm doing it now. Please help me, Robert."

Hunter felt the stab of guilt slash through him for the second time.

"How *can* I help you, Lucien?" he asked. "You said yourself just a moment ago, I'm here as a listener. I have no authority over anything. I'm not even an FBI agent. I'm a detective with the LAPD."

Lucien locked eyes with Hunter for a long moment, and then, all of a sudden, his gaze softened.

"If I'm brutally honest, Robert, I don't think I really care if I live or die anymore. I messed up a long time ago. I made way too many mistakes, and since then, I've done nothing but live a substitute life. I lost everything, including my dignity and the only person I truly loved. I guess I can say that I'm ashamed of most of my life . . . but I'm not a murderer. I know that this might sound silly, but I don't care what anyone thinks of me—except you, Robert. Regardless of what happens to me, I want *you* to know that I'm not a monster."

Hunter was about to say something, but Lucien interrupted him.

"Please don't say that you already know that, or that you don't believe I am one, because I don't want your pity, Robert. I want you to *know. Really know.* That's why I'm going to tell you what I'm going to tell you, because I know that you will check on everything I say, with or without the FBI."

Hunter knew Lucien was right. There was no way he would walk away from that interrogation room and forget anything Lucien was about to tell him, no matter what sort of pressure the FBI tried to put him under.

"So what is it?" he asked. "What would you like me to do?"

Lucien looked down at his hands before meeting Hunter's stare . . . and then he spoke.

17

S pecial Agents Taylor and Newman, together with Dr. Lambert, stepped into the interrogation room thirty seconds after Lucien was taken back to his cell. Hunter was leaning against the metal table, facing a blank wall, a pensive look on his face.

"Detective Hunter," Taylor said, grabbing his attention. "This is Dr. Patrick Lambert. He's a forensic psychiatrist with the BRIU. He also watched the entire interview from the observation room."

"It's a pleasure to meet you, Detective Hunter," Dr. Lambert said, shaking Hunter's hand. "Impressive work you've produced. And to think that you wrote that dissertation when you were so young."

"For someone who had said only seven words in five days, he sure had a lot to say just now," Taylor said.

"We didn't pick up anything relevant," Newman announced, pouring himself a cup of water from the cooler.

"What do you mean?" Hunter asked.

Newman told Hunter about the facial-analysis software they were using inside the observation room.

"There were a few nervy eye, head, and hand movements," Dr. Lambert said. "A few emotional qualities here and there in his towne of voice, but nothing that would flag as too unreliably anxious or nervous. Bottom line is—we have no clear indication that he was lying about anything." He paused for effect. "But we also have no clear indication that he was telling the truth about anything."

So much for your expensive facial-analysis software, Hunter thought.

"And that includes everything he told you in the last few minutes of your interview," Dr. Lambert added.

Lucien had tried keeping his voice quiet, quieter than throughout the rest of the session, but the powerful multidirectional microphone on the ceiling directly above the metal table had picked up every word he said to Hunter.

"*I know that only you will know the answers to the questions I'm about to throw at you, Robert.*" Lucien had placed both elbows on the table, leaned forward, and looked over Hunter's shoulder at the two-way mirror behind him. "*Paranoia or not, I still don't trust those fuckers.*"

His voice had become almost a whisper.

"*For the past several years, I've been living . . . or hiding, if you prefer, in North Carolina. The house is rented, and I pay cash in advance directly to this old couple, so the place can't be traced back to me.*" A pause, followed by a sip of water. "*In our dorm room back in Stanford, I used to have several posters on the wall by my bed. But there was a particular one. The largest of them all. The one that you also liked . . . with the sunset. If you think about it, you will remember it. My county in North Carolina carries the same name as the figure in that poster.*"

Hunter's expression had turned thoughtful.

"*I'm sure you'll also remember Professor Hot Sauce.*" The right edge of Lucien's mouth had lifted in a devious smile. "*Susan's dare? Halloween night?*" He waited just a second before seeing recognition dawn across Hunter's face. "*By sheer coincidence, the city I've been living in shares his name.*

"*After I got the phone call asking me to make the first car delivery, something inside my head told me that this would end badly. So, out of precaution, I started keeping a diary, so to speak. I noted everything I could—dates, times, and duration of calls, conversation details, pickup times and locations, car types and license-plate numbers, stops I did on the way, the name of the person at the other end of the line . . . everything. I keep the notebook in the house, down in the basement.*"

Hunter caught a new glint in his old friend's eyes. Something that wasn't there before.

"*The house is right at the end of the wood's edge. The keys are in my jacket pocket, which I believe was seized by the FBI. You have my authorization to use them and get into the house, Robert. You'll find a lot in there. Things that can help you clear this mess up.*"

That was all Lucien had said.

"So," Newman said to Hunter, "do you know the answers to all that crap he threw at you at the end?"

Hunter said nothing, but Newman seemed to read his demeanor as an affirmation.

"Great. So if you give us the name of the county and the town in North Carolina where his house is, your job here is all done." He finished drinking his water. "I understand that you were on your way to Hawaii for a long overdue vacation." Newman checked his watch theatrically. "You've only missed a day. You could be there by tomorrow morning."

Hunter's gaze lingered on Newman for a few seconds, before moving to Taylor, and then back to Newman.

"There's a reason Lucien hid the location of his house inside questions that only I would know the answers to," he said, standing up straight and adjusting the collar on his leather jacket. "Because the only way any of you are getting there is if I take you."

18

I thought that you couldn't wait to go on vacation, Robert," Adrian Kennedy said, staring straight into the webcam.

Hunter, Taylor, and Newman had gone back up to the BRIU main floor and were now sitting inside an ample office, facing a flat-screen monitor mounted onto the west wall. The dot-sized green light at the top of the monitor indicated that their images were being transmitted to Kennedy's office in Washington, DC.

Despite his being less than an hour away, Kennedy's overbooked schedule had prevented him from making the trip back to Quantico.

"Well, that plan got screwed up yesterday when you showed up in LA, Adrian," Hunter said matter-of-factly.

"I'm sure we can fix it, Robert," Kennedy replied. "If you just give Agents Taylor and Newman the information they need to proceed, I can arrange to have a jet fly you to Hawaii tonight."

Hunter looked incredulous. "Wow. Is the FBI budget that loose that you can actually justify getting a jet just to take me all the way to Hawaii, from Virginia? Damn, and at the LAPD we don't even get a big enough budget to cover new bulletproof vests."

"Robert, I'm serious. We need this information."

"So am I, Adrian." Hunter's voice went grave all of a sudden and his stare hardened. "I didn't ask for this. You came to *me*, remember? You threw me into this mix and now I'm part of it, whether you like it or not. If you think I'm just going to hand over my information and walk away like an obedient little boy, then you don't know me at all."

"Nobody really knows you, Robert," Kennedy hit back, his voice still calm. "But now you're playing a very risky game, my friend. You do understand that what you're doing is withholding information that's pertinent to a *federal* homicide investigation? I can have your ass for that."

Hunter looked unfazed.

"If that's how you want to play it," he replied evenly. "I've never explicitly told anyone that I knew the answers to Lucien's questions. I can't be withholding information if I have none, Adrian, because I don't think I remember seeing any posters in my old dorm room, and Professor Hot Sauce is no one I can recall." Frustration began to color Agent Newman's face. "You're not the only one who knows how to play hardball, Adrian, and I'm not one of your puppets."

"Sorry to interrupt, Director Kennedy," Newman said, leaning forward in his seat. "But we still have the subject in our custody. If Detective Hunter is refusing to cooperate, sorry, but *fuck* him. Let him go back to LA." He looked at Hunter. "No offense, pal."

He got absolutely zero reaction.

"We can still extract the information from the subject," Newman continued. "Just give me a few more sessions with him."

"Of course we can," Kennedy said. "Because that has worked brilliantly so far, hasn't it, Special Agent Newman?"

Newman was about to say something else, but Kennedy lifted a finger, silencing the agent. The intent look in his eyes was clear indication that he was mentally revising his options.

"Okay, Robert," Kennedy said finally. "I'll play nice if you play nice. You and Agent Taylor go check out this property in North Carolina. Agent Newman, I need you back in Washington . . . today. I've got something else I want you on."

Newman looked like he'd been slapped across the face. His mouth half opened to say something, but Kennedy cut him short again.

"*Today*, Agent Newman. Is that understood?"

Newman took a deep breath. "Yes, sir."

Kennedy addressed Hunter again. "Robert, no more games. You do know what this Lucien character was talking about in his riddles, right? You know the answers to those questions?"

Hunter nodded once, confirming.

"Okay." Kennedy consulted his watch. "We're lucky. North Carolina is close enough that we can move fast. Agent Taylor, get everything organized. I want you and Robert there by tonight, at the latest. Let's go seize the notebook, or whatever it is, and start figuring this whole mess out. Call me directly with any news as soon as you get it."

"Yes, sir," Taylor replied.

Kennedy cut the connection.

kay," Agent Taylor said, using a wireless keyboard to type a new command into a desktop computer.

Taylor and Hunter had gone back to the same conference room they were in earlier, the one with the large monitor showing a detailed map of the United States on the far wall. As she hit the Enter key, the map changed to a county-detailed version of the entire state of North Carolina.

"So what was this poster that Lucien Folter had on his wall?" Taylor asked. "The one you liked. The one with the sunset."

Hunter stepped closer to the map, studying it closely.

"It was a poster of the mountains," he said. "The sun was just about to set over them. The sky was this striking reddish-purple color. That was what I really liked about that poster—the sky's colors. But there was also a campfire, with a lone figure sitting by it, looking off into the distance."

"What figure?"

Hunter's eyes had stopped searching the map.

"An old man."

Taylor frowned. "An old man?" she said, joining

Hunter by the map. "So what are we looking for here? Oldman County? Granddad County? Or did this old man have a name? Lucien Folter said that the county carried the same name as the figure in that poster."

"No name," Hunter clarified. "But that old man was a Native American. More precisely, a . . ." He pointed to a county on the far left-hand side of the map. The county of Cherokee, the westernmost county in the state.

Taylor's attention returned to the map as she considered the county's location in relation to Quantico. It was as far away from Virginia as it could be, as it bordered both Georgia and Tennessee. "Damn," she said, returning to the computer. "That will be a hell of a long drive."

"At least eight hours each way," Hunter agreed.

Taylor typed in a new command, and on the map, a route was immediately traced between the FBI Academy in Quantico and the eastern border of Cherokee County. On the left-hand side, a detailed, step-by-step breakdown of the entire itinerary was displayed. According to it, the 535-mile journey would take them approximately eight hours and twenty-five minutes, and only if they made zero stops.

Hunter checked his watch—12:52 p.m. He sure as hell wasn't in the mood for a seventeen-hour drive there and back.

"Can we fly there?" he asked.

Taylor made a face. "I don't have the kind of clearance necessary to authorize a plane," she said.

"But Adrian does," Hunter suggested.

Taylor nodded. "Director Kennedy can authorize anything he likes."

"So let's get him to authorize one," Hunter said. "Just minutes ago he was ready to authorize a jet to take me on vacation to Hawaii, and I'm not even with the FBI."

Taylor had no argument against that.

"Okay, I'll call him. So where are we going?"

Hunter looked at her.

"The second question," she clarified. "The name of the city? Who was this Professor Hot Sauce? Your friend Susan's dare? Halloween night?"

Hunter wasn't ready to show all his cards yet, at least not while they were still at the FBI Academy. He checked his watch. "One step at a time, Agent Taylor. Let's get going first. I'll tell you when we're airborne."

Taylor studied him for an instant. "What difference does it make?"

"My point exactly. If it makes no difference, then I can either tell you now or later. I'll do it later. We need to get going."

Taylor lifted both hands, giving up. "Fine, we'll play it your way. I'll call Director Kennedy."

20

Taylor's telephone conversation with Director Adrian Kennedy lasted less than three minutes. He didn't need much persuading.

Lucien Folter had been arrested six days ago. The FBI had two decapitated and mutilated female heads on their hands—no bodies, no identification. The questions were piling up like dirty dishes, and so far they had no other leads. Kennedy wanted answers, and he wanted them pronto, whatever it took.

Within ninety minutes, everything was arranged and a Phenom 100 light jet was waiting for Hunter and Taylor at the Turner Field landing strip. This plane was about half the size of the one they took from Los Angeles to Quantico, but just as luxurious.

The cabin lights dimmed momentarily, and the plane took off swiftly. Hunter sat nursing a cup of strong black coffee, while carefully revisiting every word he and Lucien had spoken inside the interrogation room that morning.

Taylor was sitting in the black leather swivel chair directly in front of Hunter. Her laptop rested on her legs; its screen displayed a detailed map of Cherokee

County with all its cities and towns. "Okay, Robert, we're airborne, so where exactly are we heading? Who's Professor Hot Sauce?"

Hunter smiled as he remembered the anecdote.

"Lucien, Susan, and I went to a Halloween party in an Irish bar in Los Altos; there we bumped into our neuropsychology professor. Nice guy, great professor, and he loved to drink. That night we all had had a few, but then, out of the blue, he decided to challenge us to a shot-drinking competition. Lucien and I declined, but to our surprise, Susan took him up on the offer."

"Why were you surprised?"

"Susan wasn't that good a drinker," Hunter said, with a slight shake of the head. "Four, five shots, and she was gone. What we didn't know was that she had a trick up her sleeve."

Interest lit Taylor's face. "What trick?"

"Susan's grandparents were Latvian, and because of that, she knew a few Latvian words, including the word for water, *ūdens*. The deal was, each one took turns downing a shot of their favorite drink. Susan knew the bartender, who was Latvian too. The professor was drinking tequila, and Susan kept on ordering shots of *ūdens* from the bartender. Fourteen shots later, the professor threw in the towel. His forfeit penalty was to drink an entire two-ounce bottle of hot sauce, which he did. He didn't turn up for class for the next three days. From that day on, the three of us only referred to him as Professor Hot Sauce."

Hunter quickly studied the map on Taylor's screen. It took him just a second to find what he was looking for.

"So who was your neuropsychology professor?" Taylor asked.

Hunter pointed at the screen. "His name was Steward *Murphy*."

The city of Murphy was the largest city in Cherokee County, situated at the confluence of the Hiwassee and Valley Rivers.

"It doesn't look like there's an airport in Murphy," Taylor said, analyzing the map, before typing in a new command. A second later she had an answer. "Okay, the closest airport to Murphy is Western Carolina Regional Airport. Thirteen and a half miles away."

"That will do," Hunter said. "You can tell the pilot that that's where we're heading."

Taylor used the intercom phone on the wall to her right to give the pilot his instructions.

"We should be there in an hour and ten minutes, give or take a few," she told Hunter.

"Much better than eight and a half of driving," he said.

"Do you mind if I ask you something, Detective Hunter?" Taylor said, breaking the silence after they'd been airborne for a few minutes.

Hunter peeled his eyes from the blue sky outside his window and looked at her.

"I do if you're going to continue calling me Detective Hunter. Please call me Robert."

Taylor seemed to hesitate for a moment. "Okay, Robert, as long as you call me Courtney."

"Deal. So what would you like to ask me, Courtney?"

"You felt responsible, didn't you?" She waited a couple of seconds and decided to clarify. "When Lucien told you about his drug problem and how he got involved with it all."

Hunter kept his gaze on Taylor.

"While everyone in the observation room had their attention focused on Lucien, I was observing you. You felt guilty. You think it was your fault."

"Not like it'd been my fault," Hunter said slowly. "But I know I could've helped him. I should've noticed he was hooked when he came to see me in Stanford for the last time. I don't know how I missed that."

Taylor bit her bottom lip and looked away, clearly debating if she should say what she was thinking. She decided that there was no point in being coy. "I know he was your friend, and I'm sorry to say this, but junkies don't get a lot of sympathy from me. I've worked on too many cases where someone, high on some cheap fix, or trying to get some cash to buy some cheap fix, committed the most atrocious murders." She paused for breath, anger underlying her tone. "He could be lying, you know? He could still be hooked on something, and he could've killed those two women while under the influence."

"Your lab tests showed that he was clean," he said.

"Certain drugs exit your system in a matter of hours, you know that," Taylor retorted. "Plus, those heads had been preserved in an ice container for who knows how long. Those two women could've been murdered months ago."

"That's true," Hunter admitted. "And certain drugs do exit your system in a matter of hours, but you've seen junkies before, right? They just can't stay away from drugs for too long, and they all show typical psychological and physical signs of dependency—you can see it in their skin, eyes, hair, lips. And then there's the paranoia, the anxiety . . . you know what to look for. Lucien showed none of it, even though he's been in custody for days." Hunter shook his head. "He isn't hooked anymore."

This time it was Taylor who couldn't debate Hunter's argument. Lucien showed no signs of dependency, but she wasn't ready to let it rest quite yet.

"Okay, I agree, he does appear to be clean, but he still gets none of my sympathy. According to what he told you, nobody forced him to take any drugs. He decided to do so of his own free will. He could've just as easily walked away from it. You know this better than most, Robert, with your work in LA. It's a *choice*. In his case, it was *his* choice, no one else's. No one but Lucien should feel guilty about him becoming a junkie."

The plane hit a spot of turbulence and Hunter waited until it was all clear before speaking again.

"I'm not trying to defend junkies, Courtney," Hunter said. "I just believe that a very large number of addicts out there know that they've made a mistake, and all they want is to find the strength to kick the habit. Most of them can't seem to find that strength on their own, they need help . . . help, which most of the time isn't very forthcoming. Probably because so many out there share the same thoughts as you do."

Taylor's blue eyes honed in on Hunter intensely before darting away.

"So how do you think you could've helped him?" she asked. "What would you have done?"

"Everything I could," Hunter replied without missing a beat. "I would've done *everything* I could. He was my friend."

21

Precisely an hour and eight minutes after taking off, the Phenom 100 touched down at Western Carolina Regional Airport. The weather had started to change. Several large clouds were now lurking in the sky, keeping the sun from properly shining through, and bringing the temperature down a few degrees. In spite of the lack of sunshine, Taylor put on her sunglasses as soon as they stepped out of the plane. It was basic FBI training—once in public, always hide your eyes.

Outside the airport, Hunter and Taylor met a representative from a local rental car company she had spoken to on the phone. He delivered them to a top-of-the-line black Lincoln MKZ sedan.

"Okay," Taylor said, flipping open her laptop as she and Hunter got into the car. She took the driver's seat. The car looked and smelled brand-new, as if it had been purchased that morning for them. "Let's figure out where we need to go from here."

Taylor used the laptop's touch pad and quickly called up a satellite-viewing application. In a fraction of a second, she had a photographic bird's-eye map of the city of Murphy on her screen.

"Lucien said that the house was at the end of a wood's edge," she continued, angling the laptop Hunter's way.

They both studied the screen for a long moment, and as Taylor used the touch pad to drag the map from left to right and top to bottom, her demeanor changed.

"Was he kidding?" she finally said. Her voice was still calm, but it was now tinged with annoyance. She lifted her sunglasses and placed them on her head before pinning Hunter with a concerned stare. "This place is surrounded by woodland. Just look at this."

Her gaze returned to her screen as she used the touch pad to zoom out on the map. She wasn't joking. The city of Murphy looked like it had been built slap bang in the middle of a large, hilly forest. There seemed to be more woodland than buildings.

Hunter said nothing. He was still staring at the screen, trying to figure it all out.

"He was fucking with us, wasn't he? Even if this house does exist, which I now doubt, it could take us a couple of days to find it, maybe more. He sent us on a wild-goose chase, Robert. He's playing games." She took a moment to think about it. "I'm sure he's been here before. Maybe even lived here for a while. He knows Murphy is mostly forest. That's why he sent us here with that crazy riddle. We could spend days here, and never come across this . . . fantasy house."

Hunter spent a few more seconds analyzing the map before shaking his head. "No, this is wrong. This isn't what he meant."

Taylor's eyebrows arched. "What do you mean?

That's exactly what he said. *The house is right at the end of a wood's edge.* Unless you've got this riddle wrong, and we came to the wrong place."

"I didn't," Hunter assured her. "We came to the right place."

"Okay then, so Lucien *is* playing games. Just look at that map, Robert." She nodded at her laptop. "*The house is right at the end of a wood's edge,*" she repeated. "Those were his words. I've got the recording here with me if you want to listen to it again."

"I don't have to," Hunter replied, turning the laptop to face him. "Because that's not exactly what he said."

"I'm sorry?"

"He said that the house was at the end of *the* wood's edge, not *a* wood's edge. And there's a big difference. Can you get us a searchable map of Murphy? Locations, streets, things like that?"

"Yeah, sure."

A few keystrokes later, the bird's-eye-view map on the screen was substituted with an up-to-date satellite street map of the city of Murphy.

"Here we go," she said, passing the laptop over to Hunter, who quickly typed something into the search feature. The map panned out, rotated left, and then zoomed in on a narrow dirt road located between two woodland hills on the south side of the city. The road's name was Woods Edge.

Even Hunter was a little surprised at the obviousness of it all. He was expecting that perhaps one of the woodlands, or maybe even a park, carried the name *Woods Edge*, but not a road.

"Oh, ye of little faith," he said.

"I'll be damned," Taylor breathed.

The road looked like it was about a half a mile long. There was nothing on either side of it, except forest, until the very end, where a single home stood—the house at the end of the Woods Edge.

22

Once Taylor took the wheel, the thirteen-and-a-half-mile drive from the Western Carolina Regional Airport to the south side of Murphy took just under twenty-five minutes. The trip was punctuated by hills, fields, and forest. As they approached the city of Murphy, a few small farms sprang up by the side of the road, with horses and cattle moving lazily around the fields. The expected smell of farm manure coated the air, but neither Hunter nor Taylor complained. Hunter, for one, couldn't remember ever having been in a place where everywhere he looked was painted by trees and green fields. It was striking scenery, he had to admit.

As Taylor exited Creek Road and veered right onto Woods Edge, the road got bumpier by the yard, forcing Taylor to slow down to a snail's crawl.

"Jesus, there's absolutely nothing here," she said, looking around. "Did you notice that we haven't seen a lamppost for over a mile?"

Hunter nodded.

"I'm glad we still have daylight to guide us. There's no doubt Lucien was hiding from something, or someone. Who in their right mind would want to live down here?"

She tried her best to avoid the larger potholes and bumps, but no matter how carefully she swerved, or how slowly she negotiated, it still felt as if they were driving through a war zone.

A couple of slow and bouncy minutes later, they finally reached the house.

The place was a small single-story ranch. A low wooden fence in desperate need of repair and a new paint job surrounded the front of the property. The grass beyond the fence looked like it hadn't been cut in months. Most of the cement slabs that made up the crooked pathway that led from the front gates to the house were cracked, with weeds growing through the slabs. An old and ragged Stars and Stripes fluttered from a rusty flagpole on the right, and while the house had once been white, with pale-blue windows and doors, the colors had faded drastically. The paint was peeling from just about everywhere. The roof also looked like it could do with a few new shingles.

Hunter and Taylor stepped out of the car. A cool breeze blew from the west, bringing with it the smell of damp soil. Hunter looked up and saw a couple of darker clouds starting to close in.

"He certainly didn't take very good care of this place," Taylor said, closing the car door behind her. "Not really the best of tenants."

Hunter checked the dirt road. Except for their own, there were no tire tracks. The house had no garage, so Hunter looked for a place where a car could park by the house. He knew that people tend to park in the same spots. That would've undoubtedly left some sort of lasting impression on the ground, maybe even some oil marks or residues. He saw none. If Lucien Folter really lived here, it didn't look like he owned a car.

Hunter and Taylor gloved up before Hunter checked the mailbox by the fence. Empty.

As they both moved toward the house, Hunter paused a second, allowing Taylor to take the lead. As it'd been pointed out to him more than once, this wasn't his investigation.

The single wooden step that led up to the porch creaked like a warning signal under Taylor's weight. Hunter, who was right behind her, decided to skip it, stepping straight onto the porch instead.

They checked the windows on both sides of the front door. They were all locked, with their curtains drawn shut. The heavy door to the right of the house that led to its backyard was also locked. The wall surrounding it was high enough to dissuade anyone who might've been thinking about climbing over.

"Okay, let's try these," Taylor said.

Lucien's utilitarian key chain could've belonged to a building's supervisor—a single thick metal loop, packed with similar-looking keys. There were seventeen in total.

Taylor pulled open the mesh screen door and tried the first key. It didn't fit into the lock. The second, third, fourth, and fifth keys all slid in easily, but none of them turned.

The smell of damp soil became stronger and the air cooler as the first drops of rain came down. Taylor paused a second and looked up, wondering how many holes would reveal themselves once the rain got stronger.

Keys number six and seven were repeats of the first five. Key number eight, on the other hand, slid into the lock with tremendous ease, and as Taylor turned it, the lock came undone with a muffled clunk.

"Bingo," she said. "I wonder what all these other keys are for."

Taylor turned the handle and pushed the door open. Surprisingly there was no creaking or squeaking. The hinges had been well oiled, and recently.

Even before stepping into the house, they were hit by the smell of disinfectant and mothballs. Instinctively, Taylor brought a hand to her nose, but the smell didn't bother Hunter.

Taylor found a light switch on the inside wall to the right of the door and flicked it on.

They found themselves in a small, completely bare, white-walled anteroom. They quickly moved past it and along to the next room—the living room.

Once again Taylor found the light switch by the door and flicked it on, activating a single lightbulb that hung from the center of the ceiling. The thick red-and-black shade around it dimmed its already weak strength considerably, throwing the room into semidarkness.

It wasn't the most spacious of living rooms, but with no furniture save a small table and a couple of chairs, it didn't feel cramped. The overly sanitized smell was much stronger in this room, making Taylor cringe.

"You okay?" Hunter asked.

Taylor nodded unconvincingly. "I hate the smell of mothballs. It messes my stomach up."

Hunter gave her a few seconds, and allowed his eyes to slowly scan the room. There was nothing that indicated that the house was home to anyone: no pictures, no paintings, no decorative items, nothing.

It was like Lucien had been hiding even from himself.

The open door on the west wall led into a dark kitchen. Across from where they entered the living room, a corridor led deeper into the house.

"Do you want to check the kitchen?" Hunter asked with a head gesture.

"Not particularly," Taylor said. "I just want to find this diary of his, and go get some fresh air."

Hunter nodded his agreement.

They crossed the living room and entered the corridor on the other side. The light here was just as weak as the one in the living room.

There were four doors down the hallway—two on the left, one on the right, and one down the far end. The two on the left and the one at the end of the corridor were wide open. Even with the lights off, Hunter and Taylor could tell that they led into two bedrooms and a bathroom. The thick, heavy door on the right side of the corridor, on the other hand, was secured with a large padlock.

"This has got to be the door to the basement," Taylor said.

Hunter agreed, checking the padlock. He was surprised to find it to be military grade, made by Sargent and Greenleaf—supposedly resistant to every form of attack, including liquid nitrogen. Lucien certainly didn't want anyone going down into that basement uninvited.

"And we're back to playing key roulette," Taylor said, retrieving Lucien's key chain once again.

As she started going through the keys, Hunter quickly checked the first room on the left—the bathroom. It was small, tiled all in white, with a heavy musty and wet smell. There was nothing interesting in there.

Click.

Hunter heard the metal noise coming from the corridor and stepped out of the bathroom.

"Got it," Taylor said, letting the padlock drop to the floor. "Took me just twelve tries this time." She twisted the door handle and pushed the door open.

A light cord hung from the ceiling on the inside of the door. Taylor clicked it on. A yellowish fluorescent-tube lightbulb flickered on and off a couple of times before finally engaging, revealing a narrow cement staircase that bent right at the bottom.

"Do you want to go first?" Taylor asked, taking a step back.

Hunter shrugged. "Sure."

They took the steps slowly and carefully. At the bottom, another two fluorescent bulbs lit a space about the same size as the living room upstairs, with a crude cement floor and faded white walls. Furniturewise, it was as bare as the sparsely decorated living room. A tall wooden bookcase overflowing with books hugged the north wall. A large rug, together with a flowery sofa, centered the room. Directly in front of it stood a beech-wood module with an old tube TV on it. To the left of the module was a chest of drawers and a small beer fridge. A few framed drawings adorned the walls. Everything was covered in a thin layer of dust.

"The diary must be there," Taylor said, nodding at the bookcase.

Hunter was still looking around the room, taking everything in.

Taylor stepped toward the bookcase, paused before it, and ran her eyes over all the titles. Unsurprisingly, several of them were on psychology, a few on engineering, a few on cooking, a few on mechanics, several paperback thrillers, and a few on self-motivation and how to overcome adversity.

In one corner, though, a small collection of books looked different from all the others. They had no titles. They were hardcover notebooks, the kind easily found in any stationery store.

"It looks like we've got more than one diary here," Taylor announced, reaching for the first book.

She got no reply from Hunter.

She flipped the book open. As she started flicking through it, her triumphant gaze turned to a frown. There was nothing written on any of the pages. They were all covered with drawings and sketches—a few male and female faces, still lifes, and what looked to Taylor to be schematics for building tools, possibly carpentry ones.

"Robert, come have a look at this."

Still no word from Hunter.

"Robert, can you hear me?" Taylor finally turned to face him.

Hunter was standing in the middle of the room, immobile, staring at the wall straight in front of him. Taylor couldn't quite identify the look on his face.

"Robert, what's going on?"

Silence.

She followed his stare toward one of the framed drawings.

"Wait a second," she said, squinting at it and moving

a little closer. It took her several seconds to understand what she was looking at, but as realization dawned, her whole body was suddenly covered in gooseflesh.

"Oh my God," she whispered. "Is that . . . human skin?"

Hunter nodded slowly.

Taylor breathed out, took a step back, and looked around the room again.

"Jesus Christ . . ." Her throat went completely dry, as if she were being choked by a pair of invisible hands.

There were five different frames.

Hunter still hadn't moved. His stare was still locked on the frame directly in front of him. But the fact that what seemed to be framed prints were actually framed human skin wasn't what had shocked him the most. What had frozen Hunter to the spot was what was drawn onto the human skin in the frame he was staring at. It was a very unique tattoo, one that Hunter remembered well, because he had been there when it was done. A tattoo of a red rose with its thorny stem wrapped around a bleeding heart, giving the impression that the rose was strangling it.

Susan's tattoo.

Part Two

THE RIGHT MAN

23

This time, Lucien Folter was waiting at the metal table inside the interrogation room when the door buzzed open and Hunter and Taylor walked in. Just like before, his hands and feet were shackled, linked by a metal chain.

Lucien was leaning forward on his chair. His hands rested on the table with his fingers interlaced. He was calmly tapping his thumbs against each other in a steady rhythm, as if to the beat of some song that only he could hear. His head and his eyes were low, his stare fixed on his hands.

Taylor deliberately allowed the door to slam shut behind her, but the loud bang didn't seem to reach Lucien's ears. He didn't flinch, didn't look up, didn't stop with the tapping. Once more, he'd returned to a world of his own.

Hunter stepped forward and stopped across the table from him, his arms loose and relaxed by the sides of his body. He didn't take a seat. He didn't say a thing. He simply waited.

Taylor stood by the door, anger burning behind her eyes. On their trip back to Quantico, she had promised herself that she wouldn't let that anger show, that she would be pragmatic . . . professional . . . detached. But seeing Lucien again, sitting in that room seemingly unperturbed, made her blood boil inside her veins.

"You sick son of a bitch," she finally blurted. "How many did you actually kill?"

Lucien just kept staring at his thumbs, following the beat that no one else could hear.

"Did you skin them all?" Taylor demanded.

No reply.

"Did you make one of those sick trophies out of every victim?"

Slowly Lucien stopped tapping, lifted his head, and locked eyes with Hunter. The two men studied each other like strangers about to go into battle. Lucien's demeanor had totally changed from their previous interview. The emotional Lucien, the one who seemed scared that a huge injustice was being done, the one who needed help, was gone. The new Lucien looked stronger . . . more confident . . . fearless, tougher, like a fighter who wouldn't walk away from any sort of confrontation—someone who was ready, come what may. His dark-brown eyes were cold and disconnected, void of any emotion. It was an empty look that Hunter had seen several times before, but never in Lucien's eyes. It was a look he recognized all too well.

It was the look of a psychopath.

Lucien breathed out.

"By the expression on your face, Robert, I'm sure you recognized the tattoo in one of the frames on my wall."

Hunter now knew the real reason Lucien had mentioned Susan in their first conversation. Lucien hadn't been trying to steer the conversation away from a fragile topic until his nerves settled after all. He had wanted to make absolutely sure Hunter would remember the tattoo before sending him to the house.

"That piece is by far my favorite," Lucien continued. "Do you know why, Robert?"

Lucien smiled, as if the memories filled his heart with joy.

"Susan was my first."

"You sick son of a bitch," Taylor said again, stepping forward as if she was about to attack Lucien. Hunter moved to stop her, but the agent's sense seemed to take over at the last second and she paused by the metal table.

Lucien's icy gaze slowly moved to her. "Please stop repeating yourself, Agent Taylor." His voice was flat. "Maybe I *am* one, but swearing doesn't really suit you." He ran his tongue over his lips to wet them. "Name-calling is for the weak. For people who lack the intellect to argue intelligently. Do you think you lack the intellect, Agent Taylor? Because if you do, you have no business being part of the FBI."

Taylor took a deep breath to steady herself.

"I understand that right now you're still in shock from your discovery back at the house," Lucien continued. "So your emotions are running a bit high." He shrugged, unconcerned, pushing her. "Understandable. But that little outburst of yours isn't really what's expected from a senior FBI agent, is it? I bet it surprised even you, because I bet you promised yourself that you wouldn't lose it. You promised yourself that you would remain calm and professional, didn't you, Agent Taylor?" Lucien gave her no time to reply. "But even with the best of intentions, your emotions can still easily boil up. It takes a lot of training to be able to properly control them." Another shrug. "I'm sure you'll get there someday."

Taylor held her tongue with effort.

"How many were there, Lucien?" Hunter asked in a steady voice, finally breaking his silence. "You said Susan was your first. How many victims were there?"

Lucien sat back and offered a smile that looked rehearsed.

"That's a very good question, Robert." He looked deep in thought for a long instant. "I'm not really sure. I lost count after a while."

Taylor felt her skin starting to get goose bumps again.

"But I have it all written down," Lucien said, as he began nodding. "Yes. There really is a diary, Robert. Actually, more than one, where I documented everything—places I've been, people I've taken, methods I've used—"

"And where are they?" Taylor asked.

Lucien chuckled and moved his hands to an outstretched position, making the chain rattle against the metal table. "Patience, Agent Taylor, patience. Haven't you ever heard the saying *Good things come to those who wait*?"

Though Lucien's condescending words were intended for Taylor, all his attention was on Hunter.

"I know that right now you have a thousand questions tumbling over each other inside that big brain of yours, Robert. I know that all you want is to understand the *why*s and *how*s . . . and obviously, since you're a cop, to identify all the victims and deliver some justice." Lucien rotated his neck from side to side, releasing tension. "That could take a while. But believe me, Robert, I really do want you to understand everything."

Lucien looked past Hunter at the two-way mirror behind him. He wasn't speaking to Hunter or Taylor anymore. He knew that after what they had uncovered in North Carolina, a more senior FBI figure would be on the other side of that glass. Someone with the authority to call all the shots.

"I know that you also want to know why I am how I am," he said in a chilling tone, staring at his own reflection. "After all, this is the famous FBI Behavioral Science Unit 4. You live to study the minds of people like me. But I can guarantee you this—you have *never* encountered anyone quite like me."

Hunter could practically feel the tension swelling behind the glass.

"More than that," he continued, "you need to identify the victims. It's your duty. But I'm telling you now, you'll never be able to do that without my cooperation."

Hunter saw Taylor shift her weight from foot to foot, uneasily.

"The good news is that I'm willing to do that," Lucien said. "But I'll do it on my terms, so listen up." His voice took on an even more serious tone. "I will only speak to Robert. No one else. I know he isn't with the FBI, but I also know that can easily be remedied." He paused and looked around the room. "The interviews will not be conducted in this room anymore. I don't feel comfortable here, and . . ." He lifted his hands and moved them about, allowing the chain between his wrists to rattle against the metal table. "I really don't like being shackled. It puts me in a very bad state of mind, and that's not good—for me, or for you. I also like to move around when I talk. It helps me think. So from now on, Robert can come down to my cell. We can talk there." He stole a quick peek at Taylor. "Agent Taylor can sit in on the interviews if she wants. I like her. But she'll have to learn how to control that temper of hers."

"You don't get to negotiate," Taylor said, keeping her voice as calm as she could muster.

"Oh, I think I do, Agent Taylor. Because I take it that by now you have a team of agents going over every inch of my house in Murphy. And if they're competent in the least, they should find out that what you and Robert saw in that house earlier . . ." Lucien paused and he and Hunter locked eyes once again. "Well . . . that's only the beginning."

24

Lucien was right in his assumption—a specialized FBI team had already been deployed to scrutinize every inch of his house back in Murphy.

Special Agent Stefano Lopez was the agent in charge of the experienced, eight-strong search team who'd been deployed to Murphy. Director Adrian Kennedy, who had little trust in forensic specialists, had assembled them himself, nearly eight years prior. A few years back, most forensic work around the country had started being outsourced to private companies. Their agents (if one could call them that) were severely overpaid. Their numbers, no doubt fueled by the increasing number of forensic-investigation TV shows that had hit the airwaves in the past decade, had swelled. But worst of all was that most of them truly believed they were stars, and acted accordingly.

On the other hand, Kennedy's team had been highly trained in the collection and analysis of forensic evidence, and all eight of them had degrees in chemistry or biology or both. Three of the agents (including Lopez) had been premed students before joining the FBI. They had brought enough lab equipment and gadgets with them to Murphy to perform a variety of on-the-spot basic tests.

To expedite the search, Agent Lopez had compart-mentalized the house and split the crew into four teams of two. Team A—Agents Suarez and Farley—was in charge of going through everything in the living room and kitchen. Team B—Agents Reyna and Goldstein—was searching both bedrooms down the corridor and the small bathroom. Team C—Agents Lopez and Fuller—was downstairs in the basement. Team D—Agents Villegas and Carver—was outside searching the property grounds.

Team C had already photographed the entire base-ment in its original state and was now in the process of sieving through everything as it was collected, tagged, and placed inside plastic evidence bags for further anal-yses. The first items to be taken down were the framed pieces of human skin.

As Agents Lopez and Fuller carefully unhooked the first frame from the east wall, they realized that the frames had been simply but cleverly homemade. First, skin had been either soaked or sprayed with a preserving substance. Their lab technician back at Quantico would be able to tell whether it was treated with formaldehyde or formalin, a solution of gas formaldehyde in water. Then the pieces had been stretched out and placed flat against a sheet of Plexiglas that was about one-tenth of an inch thick. A second sheet of Plexiglas, of identical thickness, was then placed over the skin, sandwiching it between both Plexiglas sheets. To keep skin deteri-oration to a minimum, the sandwich of Plexiglas and human skin was finally made airtight with a sealant.

"This is one hundred percent fucked up," Lopez said, after dusting the last of the frames for fingerprints. There were none.

Lopez was tall and slim, with short curly hair, piercing dark-brown eyes, and a hooked nose that had earned him the nickname Hawk.

"No shit, Hawk," Agent Fuller said as he started tagging and bagging the frames. "You know we've seen enough killers' trophies over the years. Quite a few body parts among them, but this is pushing the boundaries." He gestured toward the frames. "This guy didn't just cut a finger or an ear off his victims. He *skinned* them, at least partially, maybe even while they were still alive. That's a whole new category of fucked-up I haven't seen before."

"And what category is that?"

"Psychopath freak show—level: grand master. One with a lot of skill and patience too."

Hawk agreed with a nod. "But what really gets me is this room." He looked around.

Fuller's gaze circled the room, following Hawk's. "What do you mean?"

"How many serial killers' trophy rooms would you say that we've seen over the years?"

Fuller made a face and shrugged. "I don't know, Hawk. More than enough, for sure."

"Since this unit was put together, thirty-nine," Hawk confirmed. "But we've all seen hundreds of photographs of others, and you know they all look similar—small, smelly, grimy, dark, you know what I'm talking about. Most of them filled with human parts. It's usually just a cupboard-sized space or a shed somewhere where the perpetrators keep whatever they've chopped off their victims. Somewhere they can go to jerk off, or fantasize, or whatever it is they do. You've seen them. They all look like some sort of sick shrine out of a Hollywood horror movie." Hawk paused, turned both of his gloved hands upward, and looked around the room again. "But look at this place. It looks like an average family's sitting room. It's just a little dusty." He ran two fingers over the top of the chest of drawers just to emphasize his argument.

"Okay, and your point is?"

"My point is that I don't think this guy came down here to be reminded of his murders, or of the time he spent with his victims. I think this guy came down here to watch TV, drink beer, and read, just like regular folks. The difference is that he did all that surrounded by the framed skin of his victims."

Hawk had walked the entire house before assigning the agents to their teams. He knew that the only TV set in the entire house was the old tube one down in the basement. He also knew that the small fridge in the corner had nothing but a few bottles of beer inside. He knew he was right.

Something in Hawk's voice concerned Fuller.

"So what are you really saying, Hawk?"

Hawk paused by the bookcase and scanned some of the titles.

"What I'm saying is that I don't think those were trophies." He pointed to the evidence bags on the floor now holding the five frames. "Those were just simple

decoration. If this guy really has a trophy room somewhere, this isn't it." He paused and breathed in a worried breath. "I'm saying brace yourself, Fuller, because if
this guy has a trophy room, we haven't found it yet. And
it will be worse than you can even imagine."

25

Upstairs, team B—Agents Miguel Reyna and Eric Goldstein—had just finished their swipe of the small bathroom and the first bedroom. They'd managed to collect several fingerprints from both rooms, but even without a more in-depth analysis, Goldstein, who was the team's expert when it came to fingerprints, could tell that their patterns seemed identical. They'd likely all come from the same person. The size of all the thumbprints found also indicated that the prints had probably come from a male subject.

The shower's drain had given them several hair strands, all of them short and dark brown in color. The high-intensity UV light test they'd conducted in the first bedroom and in the bathroom had revealed no traces of semen or blood. Several spots, some small, some large, did light up on the floor all around the toilet seat, and on the seat itself, but that was to be expected. Urine is extremely fluorescent when illuminated with ultraviolet light.

Just to be sure, they also ran a UV light test on the corridor walls. It's not uncommon for perpetrators to try to cover bloodstained walls by giving them new coats of paint. The problem is that paint-covered blood-stains will still quite clearly reveal themselves under high-intensity UV light scrutiny.

A few scattered speckles did light up on the corridor walls. Reyna and Goldstein collected samples of them all, but none of them were hidden behind the topcoat. Both agents had their doubts that the samples they collected in the hallway would turn out to be blood.

They approached the last room at the end of the corridor, the master bedroom, and paused by the door, allowing their eyes to take everything in before proceeding.

The decor inside was sparse, cheap, and messy, like a college dorm room furnished on a budget. The double bed pushed up against one of the walls looked like it had come from the Salvation Army, and so did the mattress and the black-and-gray comforter and pillowcases. A wooden bedside table supporting a reading lamp was also pushed up against the same wall, on the right side of the bed. A shabby double-door wardrobe was centered against the west wall. The only other piece of furniture was a small bookcase, crammed full.

"At least this shouldn't take very long," Reyna said, slipping on a new pair of latex gloves.

"Good," Goldstein agreed. Even with his face mask the smell of mothballs had started to burn the inside of his nostrils.

They started as they had in the two previous rooms, with a high-intensity UV light test, and as soon as they switched the UV light on, the bedcovers lit up like a Christmas tree.

"Well, no surprise there," Goldstein said. "These sheets look like they've never been washed."

While a variety of bodily fluids are fluorescent under high-intensity UV light—semen, blood, vaginal secretions, urine, saliva, and sweat—several other nonbodily fluid substances, like citric fruit juices or toothpaste, will also light up bright under a UV light test. It could be anything they were seeing: a bloody murder, or a breakfast in bed gone wrong.

"Let's bag everything," Goldstein said. "The lab will have to deal with this."

Reyna quickly pulled the comforter and sheets off the bed and placed each item into an individual evidence bag. The white mattress under the sheets showed no visible signs of any blood spatter, but they ran a UV test on it anyway. Once again, several speckles lit up here and there, but nothing that set any alarm bells ringing. Nevertheless, Reyna and Goldstein marked and collected samples of them all.

When they were all done, Goldstein crossed over to where the small bookcase was, and carefully began retrieving each and every book. Reyna stayed by the bed, dusting its frame for fingerprints. As he moved over to the other side, he noticed something on the side of the mattress—a long horizontal flap, made from a thick white fabric that blended easily with the mattress. He frowned and set about slowly ripping the careful stitches. He found a long slit in the mattress concealed underneath.

"Eric, come have a look at this," he called, beckoning his partner to his side.

Goldstein put down the book he was looking through, and walked over to where Reyna crouched.

"What do you think this is?" Reyna asked, pointing to the slit.

Goldstein's eyes widened a touch. "A hiding place."

"You bet," Reyna replied, slipping his fingers into the slot, and pulling both sides apart, horizontally, as wide as he could.

Goldstein bent down and shined his flashlight into the aperture. Neither of them could see anything past Reyna's hands.

"I'll check," Goldstein said, putting his flashlight down, and slowly slipping his right hand into the gap. Very carefully he started feeling his way around the inside of the mattress. First left, then right—nothing. He slid his arm in a little deeper, all the way up to his elbow. Left, right. Still nothing.

"Maybe whatever was hidden here is already gone," Reyna offered.

Goldstein wasn't about to give up just yet. He bent forward and shoved his whole arm into the mattress—all the way up to his shoulder. This time he didn't have to feel around. His fingers immediately collided with something solid.

Goldstein paused and looked at Reyna.

"You've got something?" Reyna asked, instinctively bending his head to one side to look into the gap again. He saw nothing.

"Give me a sec," Goldstein said, spreading his fingers to grab whatever object was hidden inside. Whatever it was, it was about five inches thick.

"Hold on," he said. "I've got it." He tried to pull it out, but the object slipped from his grip. "Hold on, hold on," he said again, now sliding his other arm into the mattress. With his arms shoulder length apart, he grabbed hold of the object with both hands. "It feels like some sort of box," he announced, and slowly started dragging it out.

"Okay, here we go," Goldstein said as he got the object to the opening.

Reyna felt a familiar excitement run up and down his spine.

Goldstein dragged the whole object out of the mattress and placed it on the floor between them. It was indeed a wooden box of about two feet long by a foot and a half.

"Gun box?" Reyna asked.

Goldstein's thick eyebrows arched. The box was certainly large enough to hold a submachine gun like an MP5 or an Uzi, or even two or three handguns.

"Only one way to find out," Goldstein said.

Surprisingly, the box had no locks, just two old-style flip latches. Goldstein undid them both, and opened the lid.

There were no guns inside, but still, its contents made both agents pause, their eyes opening wide.

The box had a division down the center, splitting it into two separate compartments.

After several seconds of absolute stillness, Goldstein finally used a pen to cautiously rifle through the contents.

"Holy shit," he whispered before looking over at Reyna. "You better go get Hawk."

26

At 1:30 a.m., Hunter and Agent Taylor were called into a special NCAVC meeting inside a soundproof conference room on the third floor of the BRIU building. Four men and three women sat around a long, polished red oak table. A projection screen had been lowered from the ceiling against the far wall. As soon as Hunter was ushered into the room, he could sense the worried atmosphere, which was further emphasized by the tense looks on everyone's faces. Director Adrian Kennedy sat at the head of the table.

"Please come in and have a seat," he said, indicating the two empty seats by his side—one to his right, one to his left.

Hunter sat at Kennedy's right.

"Okay, let's start with introductions," Kennedy continued. "I know everyone here is familiar with Detective Robert Hunter's paper," he said to the group. "But I believe this is the first time most of you have met the man behind that work." He glanced at Hunter then in turn nodded at each person around the table. "Jennifer Holden oversees our PROFILER computer system; Deon Douglas and Leo Hurst are with our Criminal Investigative Analysis Program, CIAP; Victoria Davenport is with the FBI's Violent Crime Apprehension Program, ViCAP; Dr. Patrick Lambert, whom you met earlier, is our chief of forensic psychiatry; and Dr. Adriana Montoya is one of our chief pathologists."

They all nodded a silent *hello* at Hunter, who gave them a nod of his own.

"To my left is FBI Special Agent Courtney Taylor," Kennedy said. "She'll be heading this investigation.

"I already took the liberty of contacting your captain with the LAPD once again, Robert," he said to Hunter. "We now certainly need you on this case, and I know you want in, but we've got to do this by the book. A request has already been expedited and sanctioned by both sides. You're now officially 'on loan' to the FBI." He placed an FBI ID card with Hunter's name and photograph on the table in front of him. "So until we've got this all figured out, you are Special Agent Robert Hunter."

Hunter internally cringed at the title. He left the ID card where it was.

"Okay," Kennedy said, now addressing the whole room. "Sorry to have dragged you all out here for such a late, unscheduled meeting, but there's no doubt that today's turn of events constitutes a major game change." He sat back on his seat, locked his fingers together, and rested his hands on his lap before addressing Hunter and Taylor directly.

"Dr. Lambert and I were in the observation room earlier today during your second interview with Lucien Folter."

Hunter wasn't surprised. He knew that Taylor had called Kennedy from the house in Murphy right after their discovery, and used her smartphone to email him pictures of the framed human skin, as well as a short video of Lucien's basement. Hunter had expected that Kennedy would've postponed whatever he had going on for the rest of the day and made the trip back from Washington, DC, to Quantico ASAP.

"Everyone in this room has also watched the recorded footage of both interviews at length," Kennedy added before nodding at Dr. Lambert, who took over.

"The transformation Mr. Folter went through in the space of just a few hours, from interview one to interview two, was nothing less than astounding." He looked a little embarrassed. "I must admit that after the first interview, after the drug-addiction story he told you, some part of me had started to believe him. I felt sorry for him."

Victoria Davenport with ViCAP nodded her agreement before Dr. Lambert carried on.

"I had really started to entertain the possibility that Mr. Folter had in fact been just another victim of an elaborate plan by a very sadistic killer, or killers. That he'd been just a pawn, a delivery boy in something much bigger." The doctor ran a hand through the little hair he had left on his head, just a handful of white strands that didn't seem to want to stay in place. "In all my years as a forensic psychiatrist, I've seen very few people who were able to lie so convincingly, and most of those suffered from dissociative identity disorder."

He looked straight at Hunter. "And you know that's not the case we have here."

Hunter said nothing, but he knew Dr. Lambert was right. Lucien had never claimed to be, or hinted at being, two or more different people.

In the case of someone suffering from dissociative identity disorder, once an identity takes over, an entirely different set of feelings, emotions, history, and memories comes with it. These individual attributes aren't shared between identities. So if Lucien suffered from DID, causing him to display a different identity in the second interview from the identity he'd displayed during the first one, the second identity wouldn't have remembered the first interview, or anything that had been said. The crimes committed by that identity would have also been forgotten. But that hadn't been the case. Lucien knew exactly how he'd acted, and what he'd said.

"After what I saw," Dr. Lambert said, "I have very little doubt that during the first interview Mr. Folter had simply acted a well-thought-out part to perfection. The real Lucien Folter is the one we all saw and heard in the second interview—cold, emotionless, psychopathic, and in absolute control of his actions."

He paused, allowing his words to hang in the air for a moment before proceeding.

"He might have been caught by chance after that freak accident in Wyoming, but he willingly guided Detective Hunter and Agent Taylor to his house in North Carolina, knowing very well that they would find the victims' remains, and knowing that Detective Hunter would personally recognize one of them. That shows a very high level of sadism, arrogance, and pride, together with a tremendous sense of achievement and pleasure in what he's done." The doctor paused for breath. "This guy really likes hurting people . . . both physically and emotionally."

D r. Lambert's last few words caused almost everyone sitting inside the conference room to shift uneasily in their seats.

Kennedy took the opportunity to glance over at the pathologist in the room, Dr. Adriana Montoya. She was young, with short black hair, striking hazel eyes, full lips, and a tiny tattoo of a broken heart on her neck, just behind her left ear.

"DNA analysis might still take a couple of days," she said, leaning forward and placing her elbows on the table. "We might have the results of the skin-pigmentation test and epidermis analysis sometime later today. There's a chance that they will show that the pieces came from five different people." A short pause. "If that's the case, that'll give us seven victims so far, which already makes Lucien Folter a prolific serial killer, and one the FBI had no knowledge of until about a week ago. And I have to agree with Dr. Lambert. His level of brutality and cruelty is astonishing. The two victims in his trunk were decapitated. The five in his basement were skinned." She softly shook her head as she considered the possibilities. "And according to him—*this is only the beginning.*"

Hunter noticed that Dr. Montoya's last words made Kennedy tense a fraction further.

Leo Hurst from CIAP—early forties, heavily built, and somber—flipped a page of the document sitting on the table in front of him. It was a transcript of Lucien's interviews.

"This guy knows his game," he said. "He knows that the FBI doesn't give in to psychopaths' demands. Whatever the situation is, we dictate the rules . . . always. The problem is that in this case he has managed to tip the scales in his favor, and there isn't much we can do about it. He knows that we'll have to play ball because the investigation's priority has just shifted from arresting a subject to identifying the victims."

Everyone's attention moved to him.

"Okay, let's suppose for a moment that he's lying about this being only the beginning," he continued. "Let's suppose that all we get are these possible seven victims. Yes, there's a likelihood that we could positively identify all seven of them without his help, depending on DNA analysis, and if they had all been added to the national missing-persons database." He scratched the skin between his two thin eyebrows. "But even if we manage to identify them all without his help, we're faced with problem number two."

"Finding the bodies," Kennedy said. For a brief moment he locked eyes with Hunter.

"Precisely," Deon Douglas, Hurst's partner at CIAP agreed. He also looked to be in his early forties, with a shaved head and a stylish goatee that no doubt took some maintenance. "Their families will want closure. They'll want to give the bodies, or whatever remains are found, a proper burial, and this Folter character knows that without his cooperation, we probably won't have a prayer of finding the location or locations where he disposed of them."

Again, Hunter noticed that Kennedy seemed to tense up more than anyone else in the room. That was odd. Adrian Kennedy had been with the FBI NCAVC and Behavioral Science Unit 4 for as long as Hunter could remember. He wasn't easily rattled by any sort of crime or perpetrator, no matter how brutal or unusual. Hunter sensed that there was something else bothering the director. Something that Kennedy wasn't telling them, at least not yet.

"He could be lying about this being only the beginning," Jennifer Holden said. "As you've said." She nodded at Leo Hurst. "He seems to know his game. He knows that by saying that, the scale would tip in his favor. Maybe we should put him through a polygraph test."

Hunter shook his head. "Even if he's lying, he could easily beat it."

"He would beat a lie-detector test?" Jennifer Holden asked, a little surprised.

"Yes," Hunter replied with absolute conviction. "I've seen him do it before just for fun, twenty-five years ago, and my guess is that he's only gotten better at it."

A few odd looks circled the room.

"You all saw the recording of the first interview," Hunter offered. "Even the facial-analysis software you used failed to pick up any significant changes in his expressions. It looks to me that Lucien has almost no physiological response to lying. His pupil dilation and breathing remained exactly the same throughout. I'm sure that he's trained himself, and we'll find that even his pore size and skin flush will remain unchanged. He's probably *counting* on a polygraph test, in fact. Whether we put him through one or not, it will make no difference to him."

Dr. Lambert nodded his agreement. "Long, elaborate lies take a certain type of individual and a great amount of talent to tell convincingly. They require creativity, intelligence, control, great memory, and—most of the time—very high improvisational skills. And I'm only talking about regular circumstances here. When a person has to do all that before an authority figure, knowing that his freedom is on the line, those qualities will multiply themselves by a factor of X. Judging by how convincing he was in that first interview, I really wouldn't be surprised if Lucien Folter waltzed his way through a polygraph test."

"Do you think he's lying about this being only the beginning?" Taylor asked Hunter.

"No, I don't, but what I or any of us think is irrelevant. Like Agent Hurst said, Lucien knows his game. He knows that after what we've seen, we don't have the luxury of doubt. Right now, he's calling the shots."

Hunter took the room's silence as an opportunity and turned to face the man sitting at the head of the table.

"How's the house search going, Adrian?" he asked. "Any news?"

Kennedy looked at him as if Hunter had read his thoughts.

There was a stretched, worried pause.

"Well," Kennedy said at last. "That's the real reason we're here tonight. The search team found something inside Lucien Folter's bedroom. It was hidden inside his mattress."

The tension in the room climbed up a few degrees.

Everyone waited.

"And this is what they found."

Kennedy clicked a button on the small remote-control unit on the table in front of him, and the image of the closed wooden box Goldstein and Reyna had found was immediately projected onto the white screen on the far wall.

"Looks like a gun case," Deon Douglas commented. "Big enough for a machine gun, or a disassembled long-range rifle. Has it been opened yet?"

Kennedy nodded. "Unfortunately, a weapon wasn't what was found inside," he replied.

"So what did we get?" Taylor asked.

Kennedy's eyes circled the table and paused on Hunter before he pressed the remote-control button one more time.

"We got this."

28

Despite the total darkness that surrounded him down in sublevel five of the BRIU building, Lucien Folter lay awake in his cell. His eyes were open, and he stared at the ceiling as if fascinated by something that only he could see. This time he wasn't lost in one of his meditative trances. The time for meditation was well and truly over.

A step at a time, he thought. *Take it a step at a time, Lucien.*

Step one seemed to have gone perfectly so far.

Lucien would've given anything to have seen Hunter's face when he entered the basement in the house in Murphy and finally realized that the wall frames weren't drawings. He would've given anything to have seen Hunter's face when he recognized Susan's tattoo.

Yes, that would've been worth a small fortune.

He felt his blood warming as memories of his last night with Susan came rushing back to him. He could still remember the sweet smell of her perfume, how soft her hair felt, how smooth her skin was.

Lucien wondered how long it would take the FBI search team to find the box he had hidden inside the mattress in the master bedroom.

Probably not that long, if they're any good.

Going over the contents of the box in his head filled him with excitement, bringing a proud but curbed smile to his lips. He could remember every item. But that box and its contents were nothing compared with what was still to come. They were all in for a big surprise.

Lucien swallowed his smile and finally closed his eyes.

One step at a time, Lucien. One step at a time.

29

The next slide showed the lid of the wooden box open, revealing a division down its center. As if on cue, everyone in the room, with the exception of Adrian Kennedy, leaned forward and squinted at the screen.

The compartment on the right was packed full of what at first seemed like just a bunch of colorful fabrics. The compartment on the left was filled with a variety of different jewelry items.

Silence.

More squinting.

A few chairs shuffled.

"Are those women's underwear?" Agent Taylor finally asked, indicating the compartment on the right.

"Let me clear that up for you," Kennedy said, clicking the remote-control button.

The image on the screen changed once more. It now showed all the contents from the box neatly arranged over a white surface. Taylor was right. They were all women's underwear, panties to be precise, in a multitude of colors, sizes, and styles, but now that they were all unbundled and displayed in rows, a previously unseen detail became clear. Many of the garments were covered with dried blood.

The jewelry items that had occupied the left compartment were also neatly arranged in rows, divided by type—rings, earrings, necklaces, bracelets, watches, chains, and even a couple of navel bars.

"Inside the right compartment we found fourteen pairs of women's underwear," Kennedy said, standing. "Out of those, and as you can see, eleven were covered in blood." He allowed the gravity of what he'd just said to sink in before continuing. "The garments vary in size, from extra small to extra large. They clearly belonged to different women. All the items have already been expedited to our forensics lab."

In general, token collectors take only one token from each victim, something to easily trigger strong memories of the victim and the murder act, as a reminder of their power. Often they target intimate items of clothing, fabric in close contact with the victim's skin. Some perpetrators, aroused sexually or otherwise by the power they command over their prey, believe they'll be able to smell the victim's fear on the item for months afterward, maybe years if properly stored. But taking two or more intimate items belonging to the same victim would not necessarily increase the satisfaction perpetrators get from reliving the murder act. One is usually more than enough.

Knowing this all too well, the agents in the room shifted uncomfortably in the suddenly stifling room.

"Jesus Christ," Jennifer Holden exclaimed. "So you're saying that we now might have another fourteen possible victims to add to the possible seven we've already got?"

"Twenty-six new possible victims," Hunter corrected her, pointing to the jewelry pieces on the screen.

Kennedy and Dr. Lambert were the only ones who showed no surprise.

"Right again," Dr. Lambert confirmed, nodding at the group. "Following the double-token theory, if Mr. Folter had already taken an underwear item from a victim, also taking a piece of jewelry from the same victim makes the second token pointless." He nodded at the screen. "We've got twelve pieces of jewelry. It would be safe to assume that the jewelry came from different victims. If we also assume that neither a piece of jewelry nor any of the underwear items came from one of the seven possible victims we already have, then we might be looking at twenty-six new victims, totaling thirty-three so far."

A few muttered curses were followed by deflated sighs and whispers.

"There's something else," Hunter said.

The room's attention returned to him.

"Two of those rings, all three watches, and one of those necklaces aren't feminine pieces of jewelry."

All eyes moved back to the screen.

"If these really belonged to his victims," Hunter moved on, "it doesn't look like Lucien killed only women."

30

At 7:30 a.m. sharp, the heavy metal door to the hall where Lucien was being held buzzed open. Hunter and Taylor started down the wide and well-lit corridor, which ran for about seventy-five yards. The cinder-block wall on the right was painted a dull shade of gray. The shining resin floor carried almost the same color, just a touch darker, with two guiding yellow lines running along the edge of it. A series of high-security cells ran along the left wall, ten in total. Each cell was separated by a wall as wide as the cell itself. In place of metal bars, the cells were all fronted by thick, shatterproof Plexiglas perforated by eight small conversation holes, each about half an inch in diameter. The cells were all empty, their lights turned off, with the exception of the one at the far end of the corridor. Despite being with the FBI for several years now, and having visited the BRIU building on many occasions, Taylor had never been down in sublevel five until now.

There was something quite ominous and sinister about that long stretch of corridor, as if they had just crossed the threshold between good and evil. The air inside it felt a touch too cold, a touch too dense, a touch less breathable.

Taylor did her best to fight the disconcerting shiver that sped up and down her spine as she took the first steps toward the last cell, but failed miserably. Something about that place reminded her of the Halloween haunted houses she used to be so scared of when she was a kid.

"I don't know about you," she said, steadying her body, "but I'd much rather do this up in the interrogation room."

"Unfortunately, we don't have a choice," Hunter replied as their shoes *click-clack*ed against the shiny floor with every step. He suddenly stopped and faced Taylor. "Courtney, let me tell you something about Lucien." His voice was barely louder than a whisper. He didn't want it to echo all the way to the last cell. "I'm sure he'll target you more than he will me. He'll try to get under your skin with comments, innuendos, direct digs, whatever, whatever he can think of. Some things will probably be very nasty. Just be prepared for it, okay? Don't let it affect you. If he manages to get into your mind, he'll rip you apart."

Taylor made a face. She already knew all this.

"I'm a big girl, Robert. I know how to take care of myself."

Hunter hoped she was right.

31

Two metal fold-up chairs had already been placed side by side at the end of the corridor, directly in front of the last cell.

Lucien Folter was lying on his bed, motionless, eyes open, staring at the ceiling. As the steps coming down the hallway toward him grew louder, he stood up, faced the Plexiglas, and waited. He looked completely relaxed, not an ounce of any sort of emotion showed on his face. A couple of seconds later Hunter and Taylor came into his line of sight, and the blank mask vanished, like an experienced actor who'd just been given his cue for the big scene.

He gave them a warm smile.

"Welcome to my new home," he said in a calm voice, looking around himself. "As temporary as it may be."

The cell was a rectangular box, eleven feet wide by thirteen feet deep. Other than the bed, which was mounted against the left wall, there was only a latrine and a sink against the far wall, and a small metal table with a metal bench, both bolted to the right wall and floor.

As if about to conduct a business meeting, Lucien pointed to the two chairs in the corridor.

"Please have a seat."

He waited for Hunter and Taylor to be seated before taking a seat himself at the edge of the bed.

"Seven thirty in the morning," Lucien said. "I love an early start. And as far as I can remember, so do you, Robert. Still can't sleep?"

Hunter said nothing. His insomnia wasn't a big secret, or something he kept hidden from anyone, anyway. He had started experiencing sleepless nights at the early age of seven.

With no family other than his father, coping with his mother's death proved a painful and lonely task. He would lie awake at night, too sad to fall asleep, too scared to close his eyes, too proud to cry.

It was just after his mother's funeral that he started fearing his dreams. Every time he closed his eyes he saw her face, crying, contorted with pain, begging for help, praying for death. He saw her once fit and healthy body so drained of life, so fragile and weak, she couldn't even sit up by herself. He saw a face that had once been beautiful, that had once carried the brightest smile and the kindest eyes he'd ever seen, transformed during those last few months into something unrecognizable. But it was still a face he'd never stopped loving.

Sleep and his dreams became the prison he'd do anything to escape. Insomnia was the logical answer his body and brain found to deal with his fear and the ghastly nightmares that came at night, a simple but effective defense mechanism.

Lucien studied Hunter's and Taylor's faces for several seconds. "You're still very good at not giving anything away, Robert," he said, shaking his finger in Hunter's direction. "Actually, I'd say you've gotten better at it, but you, Agent Taylor . . ." His finger moved to her. "Are close, but not quite there yet. I assume you've found the box.

"See, Agent Taylor." A new smile found its way onto Lucien's lips. "That quick glance you gave Robert just confirmed my suspicion. You still have a bit to learn."

Taylor looked unfazed.

Lucien's smile widened.

"You see Agent Taylor," he said, "keeping a steady poker face takes a lot of practice. Creating a deceptive facade takes a lot more energy though, isn't that right, Robert?" Lucien knew Hunter wouldn't reply, so he moved on. "Even you have to admit that I've now got mine down to perfection, haven't I? You thought you could always tell when I was lying, didn't you?" He breathed in. "And you could, all those years ago, but not anymore." Lucien paused and scratched his chin. "Let me see now. What was it again? Oh yes . . . this."

Lucien looked straight into Hunter's eyes, and suddenly his stare became a touch more focused, more determined. Then, for a fraction of a second, his lower-left eyelid tightened in an almost imperceptible movement. If you weren't looking for it, you wouldn't have seen it.

"Did you catch that, Agent Taylor?" Lucien followed his question with a smile. "Of course you didn't, but don't beat yourself up just yet. It's not your fault. You had no idea what you were looking for or where to look." His gaze moved to Hunter. "Robert noticed it because he knew he had to look at my eyes, especially my left one. I'll do it again, a little slower this time. Don't blink or you'll miss it, Agent Taylor."

He repeated his eye movement, this time with so much control it was almost frightening.

"You told me about it in college once, Robert, after a party, remember? We were both a little drunk, and you thought I'd taken no notice of it, didn't you?"

Hunter cast his mind back, and a hazy memory surfaced.

"But it *stayed* with me," Lucien continued. "You said that it was something very subtle, something not everyone would notice, but I knew that you could always pick it up. You always had a great eye for that kind of stuff, Robert. I didn't do it often. At least not if I was telling a simple white lie, but if it was anything more serious . . . BANG, my stare and my lower-left eyelid would give me away." Lucien used his thumb and forefinger to rub his eyes a couple of times. "So I practiced and practiced and practiced in front of a mirror until it was all gone. No more telltale signs. No more being betrayed by those tricky physiological motor reactions. I got so good at it that I could create new ones in a flash, anytime I liked, just to throw people off course. That is a terrifying thought, isn't it?"

Hunter and Taylor stayed quiet.

"I knew that you'd be looking for the telltale sign, Robert." A new smile. "I was fucking great, wasn't I? Oscar worthy." Without losing a beat, Lucien changed the subject and moved on. "I'd offer you a drink," he said, "but all I've got is tap water, and I only have one cup. Coffee would be nice." His stare lingered on Taylor.

She got the hint, looked up at the CCTV camera on the ceiling high above the cell, and gave it a single nod.

"Black with two sugars, if you please," Lucien said,

looking up at the same camera before addressing Hunter and Taylor again. "Okay, let me tell you how this is going to work. I'll allow you to ask me a few questions. I'll answer them truthfully, and I mean that. I won't lie. Then it's my turn to ask you a question. If you haven't answered me honestly, the interview is over for twenty-four hours, and we can start again the next day. And trust me, I'll be able to tell. I tell you the truth, you tell me the truth. Does that sound fair to you?"

Taylor frowned. "You want to ask us questions? About what?"

"Information is power, Agent Taylor. I like feeling powerful. Don't you?"

They all heard the door at the end of the corridor buzz open again. A marine carrying a cup of steaming coffee made his way toward them. Taylor took the cup, placed it in the Plexiglas tray, and slid it into the cell toward Lucien.

"Thank you, Agent Taylor," he said, retrieving the cup. He brought it to his nose and drew in a deep breath before sipping it. If the coffee was too hot, he showed no reaction. "Very nice." He nodded his approval. "Okay," he said, sitting back down. "Let's start the great reveal. What's your first question?"

32

Hunter had been silently studying his old friend since he and Taylor got to his cell. Lucien had an even more victorious, self-glorifying air about him that morning than he had the day before, but that wasn't all that surprising. Lucien knew he held the upper hand. He knew that at least for now, they all had to dance to his tune. Understandably, that seemed to please him immensely. But there was something else, something new about Lucien's attitude—conviction, confidence, deep pride.

Taylor glanced at Hunter, who made no move to ask the first question.

"So far we've found indications that you might've committed thirty-three murders," she began, her voice determinedly flat, calm, calculated, her eyes not shying away from Lucien's. "Is that correct, or are there more victims we don't yet know about?"

Lucien sipped his coffee again before shrugging matter-of-factly.

"That's a good first question, Agent Taylor, trying to figure out just how big a monster I am straightaway." He tilted his head back ever so slightly and started running his index finger from his Adam's apple to the tip of his chin, as if shaving. "But tell me this, if I'd murdered only one person, savagely or not, would that make me less of a monster than if I'd murdered thirty-three, or fifty-three, or one hundred and three?"

Taylor kept her cool. "Is that one of your questions for us?"

Lucien smiled, unconcerned. "No, it isn't. I was just curious, but never mind, 'cause like I said, Agent Taylor, it was a good first question. It just wasn't the right one. And that's very disappointing coming from a senior FBI agent like yourself. I was really expecting more from you." He looked at her in a derogatory way. "But I don't mind schooling you this once. After all, life is nothing but a big learning experience, isn't that right, Agent Taylor?"

"Indeed."

"Your first question should've had more purpose. It should've addressed the main topic of why you're here. The question should've prompted an answer that would've indicated if you're wasting time or not." Lucien sipped his coffee again before addressing Hunter. "But let's see if we can fix that for her, shall we? I still remember how good you used to be in college, Robert, always a step ahead of everyone else, including all the professors. Now, with so many years of experience as an LAPD detective, I'm guessing you've gotten better, sharper, even wittier. In this situation, what would your first question have been, Robert? And please don't disappoint Agent Taylor here. She wants to learn."

Hunter didn't have to look. He could feel Taylor's eyes on him.

Sitting back against the chair's backrest, Hunter's position was relaxed and calm. With his left leg crossed over his right, his hands resting on his thighs, there was no tension in his shoulders or neck.

"Don't keep us waiting, Robert," Lucien urged him. "Patience is a virtue, but a pain in the ass to master."

Hunter knew he had to play Lucien's game. There was nothing else he could do right now. "Location," he said at last. "Do you know the exact location of every body you disposed of?"

Lucien put his cup of coffee down on the floor, and began clapping slowly.

"He's good, isn't he?" Lucien asked Taylor in a sarcastic tone. "If I were you, I'd pay attention, Agent Taylor. You might learn a thing or two today."

Taylor did her best not to glare at him.

"You know why that's the right question, Agent Taylor?" he asked, his tone like that of a patient lecturer. "Because if I answer *no* to it, this whole thing is over. You can pack me up and send me off to the electric chair. I'm no use to you, or the FBI anymore." Without taking his eyes off Taylor, he picked up his coffee cup from the floor. "You're not here to get a confession from me, Agent Taylor. That part is done and dusted. *I am a killer.* I murdered *all* those people . . . brutally." There was a chilling pride in Lucien's last few words. "The only reason I'm still here is because you desperately need something from me." He glanced at Hunter. "The location of all the bodies. Not really because you need proof of what I've done, but because families need closure. They need to give their loved ones a proper burial, isn't that right, Agent Taylor?

"If I say I can't help you, there's no point in having any more interviews. There's no point in keeping me here, because I can't give you what you need." A ghost of a smile graced Lucien's lips. This was certainly amusing him. "Tell me, Agent Taylor, does it upset you that an outsider can do the job of an FBI agent better than you?"

Don't let it get to you, Hunter silently pleaded, as if his unvoiced thoughts could influence the agent's actions. *Don't get upset. Don't let him under your skin.* From the corner of his eye, he could see Taylor struggling with her anger, and if he could see it, so could Lucien.

But she remained silent.

Lucien chuckled and his attention returned to Hunter.

"The answer to your question, Robert, is—*yes*. I can tell you the location of all the bodies that *can* be found." He calmly sipped his coffee. "As you might understand, some can never be found. It's a physical impossibility. Oh," he said casually, "and I also know all of their identities by heart."

"You've got to give us something real, Lucien," Hunter said. He hadn't shifted from his relaxed position yet. "You've given us nothing but lies so far."

Lucien nodded and finished his coffee.

"I understand that, Robert." He closed his eyes and drew in a deep breath. His tranquility was eerie, as if he were merely sitting in a garden outside, appreciating the delicate perfume that scented the air, rather than locked in a cell inside one of the United States' most secretive prisons. "Megan Lowe," Lucien said without opening his eyes. "Twenty-eight years old. Born December sixteenth in Lewistown, Montana." He slowly ran the tip of his tongue across his upper lip. "Kate Barker, twenty-six years old. Born May eleventh in Seattle, Washington. Megan was abducted on July second, Kate on July fourth. Both were streetwalkers, working in Seattle, Washington. Megan was the brunette whose head was found inside the trunk of the car I was driving. Kate was the blond one."

Lucien finally opened his eyes and looked at Hunter.

"The remains of their bodies are still in Seattle. Would you like to write down the address?"

33

Director Adrian Kennedy, who was watching and listening to the interview from the holding cells' control room, immediately got the bureaucratic machine running to obtain a federal search warrant. Despite the early hour and the fact that Washington State was three hours behind Virginia, Kennedy managed to get a warrant signed by a Seattle federal judge in record time. Being an FBI director had its advantages.

Even though Lucien had told Hunter and Taylor that the key to the location where the two victims' remains were stored was on the same key chain they had used for the house in Murphy, Kennedy wasn't willing to wait. He wasn't about to send Hunter, Taylor, or any other agent all the way from Quantico to Seattle just to check if Lucien was lying again or not.

With a federal search warrant secured, Kennedy placed a call to the FBI field office on 1110 Third Avenue in Seattle, Washington. At 8:30 a.m. Pacific time, a team of two agents was dispatched to the address Lucien had provided.

"So where are we going, Ed?" Special Agent Sergio

Decker asked, as he took the driver's seat and switched on the engine of the midnight-black Ford SUV.

Special Agent in Charge Edgar Figueroa had just climbed into the passenger's seat. He was in his midthirties, tall and broad-shouldered, with a bodybuilder's physique. His dark hair was cropped to a third of an inch of his skull, and one just needed to look at his nose to know that it had been broken at least a couple of times.

"To check a self-storage unit on North Hundred and Thirtieth Street," he replied, buckling up.

Decker nodded, backed the car up, took a right on Third Avenue and headed northwest toward Seneca Street.

"What case is this?" he asked.

"Not ours," Figueroa replied. "I think a call came in from high up in Washington, DC, or Quantico. We're just going to verify the address."

"Narcs?" Decker questioned.

Figueroa shrugged and shook his head at the same time. "Not sure, but I don't think so. DEA isn't involved as far as I know. I wasn't told much, but I think this is supposed to be victims' remains."

Decker's eyebrows arched. "Stashed in a commercial storage unit?"

"That's the address we have," Figueroa confirmed.

Decker took another right and merged onto I-5 North, heading toward Vancouver. Traffic was slow.

"Do they have somebody in custody?" Decker asked.

"As far as I understand, yes. And again, I think they're holding him either in DC or Quantico." Another shrug from Figueroa. "Like I said, I wasn't told very much, but I did get the impression that this is something big."

"Do we have a warrant, or are we just going to talk our way through this, using our FBI charm?"

"We have a warrant," Figueroa said, consulting his watch. "A court marshal is meeting us at the address."

The trip from the office to the building took them twenty-six minutes. It looked like a regular warehouse, painted white, with the self-storage trade name in huge green letters across the front of the building. The large parking lot at the front of the building was practically empty. A young couple was unloading the contents of a rented white van onto an industrial-sized wheeled cart by loading dock number two.

Decker parked the SUV next to a small decorative garden directly in front of the main office. The ground was still wet from the rain that had stopped about an hour earlier, but judging by how dark the sky looked, there was more to come.

As both agents stepped out of the car, a woman, who looked to be in her early forties, exited a white Jeep Compass that was parked just a few yards away, four spaces to their right.

"I'm Federal Marshal Joanna Hughes," she said, offering her hand to each agent in turn.

"Shall we?" Hughes gestured toward reception.

An electronic *ding-ding* rang as Figueroa pushed the office door open and he, Decker, and Hughes stepped into the brightly lit rectangular room. Both FBI agents kept their dark shades on.

There was a small seating area to the left of the door. A light brown four-seater sofa and two matching armchairs had been positioned around a low circular chrome-and-glass table. A few magazines and several brochures advertising the business were neatly arranged on the tabletop. Sitting behind the wood and acrylic reception counter was a young man who looked no older than twenty-five. His eyes were glued to his smartphone and it took him at least five seconds to finally look up from the tiny screen.

"Can I help you?" he asked, putting the phone down next to the computer monitor in front of him as he stood up. He gave the visitors an overenthusiastic smile, as if to compensate for his inattention.

"Are you the person in charge here?" Marshal Hughes asked.

"That would be correct, ma'am." The kid nodded once. "How can I help you today?"

Hughes stepped closer and displayed her credentials. "I'm Federal Marshal Joanna Hughes," she said. "These two gentlemen are federal agents with the FBI."

Figueroa and Decker reached into their suit jacket pockets, producing their IDs.

The kid checked them before taking a step back. He looked a little confused, his smile fading. "Is there some sort of problem?"

Hughes handed him a piece of paper with the US government stamp on it.

"This is a federal search warrant giving us legal permission and right to search storage unit number three twenty-five in this establishment," she said calmly. "Would you be so kind as to open it for us?"

The kid looked at the warrant, read a few lines, made

a face as if it were written in Latin, and hesitated for a second. "I . . . I think I need to call my boss for this."

"What's your name, kid?" Decker asked.

"Billy."

Billy was about five foot eight with short blond hair, which was spiked in places with styling gel. He had three day's stubble and a couple of earrings in each ear.

"Okay, Billy, you can call whoever you like, but we don't really have time to wait." He nodded at the warrant. "As Federal Marshal Hughes explained, that piece of paper, which has been signed by a US federal judge, gives us the legal right to look inside unit three twenty-five, with or without your cooperation. Neither you, nor we, need your boss's permission to do so. That's all the permission we need right there. If you don't open the door for us, we're just going to have to bust it open, using any means necessary."

"And we won't be legally responsible for any damage caused," Figueroa added. "Do you understand what I'm saying?"

Billy had started to look very uncomfortable. His cell phone beeped on the counter, announcing a new text message, but he didn't even glance at it.

"That copy of the warrant stays with you," Decker said. "So you can show it to your boss, your lawyer, or whoever you please. That guarantees that you're not breaking the law, or company rules, or doing anything you shouldn't be doing." He paused and checked his watch. "We're on a pretty tight schedule here, Billy. So what is it going to be? Are you going to let us into the unit, or are we opening it ourselves?"

"You guys aren't punking me, are you?" Billy asked, his stare moving to the glass window behind both agents, as if he was trying to spot a hidden camera somewhere.

"This is official, Billy," Hughes replied, her tone telling Billy that this was no joke.

"You guys really FBI?" Billy now sounded a little thrilled.

"We really are," Decker replied.

"Look, I'd like to help," Billy said. "I can let you into the building. No problem. But I can't open the door to unit three twenty-five because it's padlocked. None of our doors has an actual locking mechanism, just a sliding bolt. Our customers can buy padlocks from us." He quickly indicated a display just behind him with several padlocks in all different sizes. "Or they can bring their own, but they're not required to supply us with extra keys. Once a unit is rented out, we don't have access to it anymore."

Figueroa nodded, and thought about it for a moment. "Okay. Can you give us the details of that account?"

"Sure." Billy started typing something into the computer behind the reception desk. "Here we go," he said after just a few seconds. "The unit is one of our medium, special ones—ten feet by ten feet."

"Special?" Decker asked.

"Yeah," Billy said. "It comes fitted with a power socket."

"Okay."

"It was rented out eight months ago, on January fourth, to a Mr. Liam Shaw," Billy continued, reading from his screen. "He paid for it a whole year in advance . . . cash."

"No surprise there," Decker said.

"The unit is down corridor F," Billy added. "I can take you there now if you like."

"Let's go," Figueroa and Decker said at the same time.

34

Until they had some sort of confirmation that Lucien was telling the truth about the self-storage unit in Seattle, no one saw any point in moving forward with the interviews. Director Kennedy told Hunter and Taylor that Washington FBI agents, armed with a federal search warrant, had already been sent to check the veracity of Lucien's statements, and they should have an answer in the next hour or less.

Taylor was sitting alone inside one of the conference rooms on sublevel three of the BRIU building, staring at the untouched cup of coffee on the table in front of her when Hunter opened the door and stepped inside.

"Are you okay?" he asked.

For a moment it seemed like Hunter's question hadn't reached her, but then she slowly turned and looked up at him.

"Yeah, I'm fine."

A few awkward, silent seconds followed.

"You did well down there," Hunter said, attempting to erase any trace of condescension from his tone.

"Oh yeah," Taylor replied sarcastically. "Except for starting out with the wrong first question, you mean."

"No," Hunter told her, taking a seat across the table from her. "That's where you're wrong, you see. No matter what first question you came up with, Courtney, Lucien would've thrown it back at you and tried to discredit you, tried to make you feel inferior, tried to shake your confidence and make you believe you're not good enough. He wants to get under your skin. And he knows he's good at it. In college he used to bully professors that way."

Taylor kept her eyes on Hunter.

"He wants to get under my skin too, but he knows me a little better than he does you, or at least he did, so right now he'll want to test the water with you to see how you respond, and he's going to keep on pushing harder and harder. You know that, don't you?"

"Let him push," Taylor replied firmly.

"Just remember that to Lucien this is like a game, Courtney . . . his game, because he knows he has the upper hand. Right now, there's only one thing we can do."

Taylor looked back at Hunter. "We play the game," she said.

Hunter shook his head. "Not the game, we play *his* game. We give him what he wants. Make him believe he's winning."

Adrian Kennedy pushed the conference-room door open and peeked inside. "Ah, here you are." He carried a blue folder with him.

"Anything from Seattle yet?" Hunter asked.

"Not yet," Kennedy responded. "We're still waiting, but it doesn't look like Lucien was lying about the identities of the women found in his trunk." He flipped open the folder. "Megan Lowe. She left Lewistown when she was sixteen, six months after her mother allowed her then boyfriend to move into their house. She first moved to Los Angeles, where she spent the next six years. Everything indicates that she was indeed a sex worker. After LA, Megan moved to Seattle. Line of work seemed to have stayed the same." He turned a page on the report he was reading. "Kate Barker. She left home when she was seventeen and moved in with a boyfriend, who at the time was an 'aspiring musician.' Not confirmed, but it seems like the boyfriend was the one who first got Kate to prostitute herself."

"Money for drugs?" Taylor asked.

Kennedy shrugged. "Probably. The abduction dates Lucien gave us, July second for Megan and July fourth for Kate, will be hard to confirm, since neither of them was ever reported missing."

That wasn't surprising. Prostitutes account for the third largest number of unsolved murders in the United States, just behind gang- and drug-related killings. Every day, thousands of sex workers are raped, assaulted, robbed, or abducted. They aren't targeted because of their attractiveness, or because they carry cash with them. They are targeted because they are easily accessible and extremely vulnerable, but most of all, because they are anonymous. The vast majority of street workers live alone, or share quarters with other prostitutes. When they have partners, the partner is usually their pimp. Many of them are runaways with little or no links to their families. Research shows that only two of every ten sex workers' disappearances are ever even reported.

Kennedy handed a copy of the report to Hunter and one to Taylor. The reports each carried mug shots of their subjects. Both women had been arrested a couple of times for prostitution. Despite the mug shots, it was impossible for anyone to match the photographs to the two heads found inside Lucien's trunk, such was the brutality of the wounds inflicted on them.

"If Lucien wasn't lying about their identities," Kennedy said, as he was leaving the room, "chances are, he isn't lying about Seattle either."

35

The inside of the storage facility was just as brightly lit as the reception office, with extra-wide corridors and rounded corners for ease of movement with wheeled carts and pallet trucks. The resin floor had been painted light green. It took Billy several minutes to guide them through all the turns and hallways until they reached corridor F. Unit three twenty-five was the third door on the left.

"Here we are," Billy said, indicating the unit.

Just as he'd explained earlier, centered on the right-hand edge of the white rolling door was a metal bolt, secured in place by a thick brass-colored padlock.

Figueroa and Decker moved forward to have a better look.

Unlike the military-grade padlock that Lucien had used to secure the door to the basement in the house in Murphy, this one was a shrouded Master ProSeries, not as impenetrable but still formidable.

"This is pretty heavy-duty," Figueroa said, looking at Decker and then at Billy. "Do you think you can breach it with that bolt cutter?"

Billy had brought a red and yellow forty-two-inch bolt cutter with him.

"No problem," Billy said, stepping forward. "We had to cut through a similar one a few weeks ago. I'm pretty sure this will be no different."

"So go ahead and do your thing, Billy," Figueroa said, stepping out of the way.

Billy opened the jaws of the cutter as wide as they would go and carefully positioned them around one of the shrouded ends of the padlock's shackle. He put most of his weight behind the cutter, and gave it a firm squeeze.

Clank.

The cutter slid off the padlock as if nothing had happened, but something bounced onto the floor and slid a couple of yards down the corridor. Billy had managed to cut off part of the protective covering circling the metal loop. Now the shackle was exposed on one side.

"I told you," Billy said, nodding at the cutter. "This bad boy is the shit. Now comes the easy part." He placed the cutter jaws around the exposed shackle and gave one more firm squeeze.

Click.

This time its jaws cut through the shackle as if slicing through wet clay.

Everyone looked impressed.

"I need to cut it again," Billy explained. "The shackle is too sturdy for us to be able to twist it out of place and free the lock. I need to cut a chunk off it."

"Knock yourself out, Billy," Decker said.

As the cutter sliced through the metal twice more, a small piece fell to the ground, leaving a sizable gap.

"And there you go," Billy announced triumphantly, removing the padlock from the door bolt.

"Great work, Billy," Figueroa said, amused by the kid's enthusiasm.

Billy stepped away and Figueroa slid the door bolt back and rolled the metal door up. All four of them stood still for a moment, staring into the almost empty, ten-feet-by-ten-feet storage unit. There was nothing there except for a large industrial chest freezer pushed up against the back wall.

Decker slipped on a pair of latex gloves. Figueroa did the same. "You can go back now, Billy. We'll call you if we need anything else."

Billy looked disappointed. "Can't I stay and have a look?"

"Not this time."

They all waited until he had rounded the corner before entering the storage unit. Hughes stayed a couple of paces behind both agents.

A low hum that came from the freezer's motor provided an unnerving background sound track. There was no lock on the freezer's lid.

Figueroa moved closer and studied it for several seconds, checking underneath and behind it as well.

"Looks okay," he said at last.

"So let's check inside," Decker replied.

Figueroa nodded and lifted the lid open.

The investigators frowned in almost perfect synchronization.

"What exactly are we looking for here, guys?" Hughes asked, bemused. "Supplies for an ice cream parlor?"

All they could see inside were stacks of gallon-sized plastic tubs of ice cream in a rainbow of flavors—

chocolate, vanilla, strawberry, pistachio, cookies and cream, apple cinnamon, and banana chocolate chip.

Decker was still frowning at all the tubs, but Figueroa had a much more concerned look on his face as he reached for one of them.

Holding the opaque white ice cream tub with his left hand, Figueroa slowly pulled the lid open.

Hughes's eyes went wide as she saw what was inside it. A second later, she vomited.

36

Hunter and Taylor were called into Director Adrian Kennedy's office fifty-five minutes after Kennedy had left them to be briefed on the fates of Megan Lowe and Kate Barker.

The office, which was located on the third floor of the BRIU building, was spacious and nicely decorated. There was an old-fashioned mahogany desk, two dark-brown Chesterfield leather armchairs, a furry rug that looked comfortable enough to sleep on, and a huge bookcase with at least one hundred leather-bound volumes. The walls were adorned mostly with framed diplomas, awards, and photographs of Kennedy posing next to political and government notables.

Kennedy was sitting behind his desk, his reading glasses high on his nose, staring at his oversized computer screen. "Come in," he called in response to the knock.

Taylor pushed the door open and stepped inside, Hunter following a couple of paces behind her.

"Don't sit down," Kennedy said, motioning them to come closer and nodding at his screen. "We got word from Seattle. Come have a look at this."

Hunter and Taylor moved past the armchairs and positioned themselves behind Kennedy's desk to his left and right, respectively. The screen showed only Kennedy's desktop. Hunter frowned, puzzled.

"About forty minutes ago," Kennedy began, "two of our agents and a US federal marshal breached the pad-lock on the storage unit's door in Seattle. This is what they found inside."

Kennedy clicked his mouse and brought back the application he had minimized seconds earlier. It was a regular image-viewing program.

"I received these photographs about five minutes ago," he explained.

The first picture on the screen was taken from just outside storage unit three twenty-five's open door. It was a standard, wide-angle crime-scene photograph, depicting the whole room, and giving a good idea of the size of the unit. Pushed up against the back wall was the chest freezer.

Kennedy clicked the mouse again for the next slide.

The second picture showed the freezer by itself, with its lid closed. Nothing suspicious there either.

Another click.

The third photograph was taken from a higher angle, directed downward, showing what the agents saw as they lifted the freezer's lid.

For a moment Taylor frowned at all the ice cream tubs.

"From now on it gets sick," Kennedy warned, then clicked his mouse again.

The image on the screen was substituted by a close-up snapshot of an agent holding one of the ice cream tubs in his left hand. Its lid had been pulled open.

Taylor hesitated for a moment while squinting, trying hard to understand what exactly she was looking at . . . and then she finally saw it.

"Oh, Christ," she whispered, bringing a hand to her mouth.

Hunter's stare remained on the screen.

Frozen inside the ice cream tub were two pairs of human eyeballs and a pair of human tongues.

It was easy to see why Taylor had struggled to understand the image at first. Due to dehydration and lack of blood flow, everything had shrunk in size. The eyeballs were to the left of the picture, stuck together like a bunch of grapes. The tongues sat to their right, also stuck together, one on top of the other, their oblong shapes creating an *X*.

Kennedy gave Hunter and Taylor a few more seconds to study the picture before clicking his mouse again. The next image showed a second ice cream tub. Inside it was a frozen human hand, severed at the wrist. No fingers. They had all been cut off.

Another click.

A second hand inside an ice cream tub.

One more click.

An ice cream tub full of fingers.

Kennedy stopped clicking.

"It goes on," he said. "There were sixty-eight ice cream tubs inside that freezer, every single one of them holding a frozen body part. Some of them held internal organs too, or parts of them . . . heart, liver, stomach . . . you get the picture, right?"

Hunter nodded.

"That section of the self-storage facility in Seattle has been locked down for the time being," Kennedy explained. "They guaranteed me two, three hours max, just so our forensics team can go over the entire unit and collect the freezer with all the ice cream tubs. The lab will do a DNA analysis and compare it with the one we've got from the severed heads in Lucien's trunk. Not that I have much doubt they'll match.

"The clerk working at the storage facility helped the agents breach the unit's door earlier, but he has no idea what was kept inside," Kennedy moved on. "We're keeping this as under wraps as we can. The press hasn't gotten word of it yet, and we'll try to keep it that way for as long as possible, but as we all know, Lucien Folter will have to be tried by a US court of law, so this story will eventually break. And when it does, it'll break big, because now I have no doubt that what we have locked up downstairs is a fucking monster."

37

Lucien had just finished the last set of his exercise routine when he heard the heavy metal door at the end of the corridor unlock, followed shortly by the sound of footsteps. He got up from the floor, used the sleeve of his orange jumpsuit to neatly wipe the sweat from his forehead, sat down at the edge of his bed, and waited calmly. When Hunter and Taylor appeared before him and took the seats in front of his cell, Lucien had a proud smirk on his lips.

"I'm guessing you had confirmation from Seattle," he said, his eyes slowly moving from Hunter's to Taylor's blank faces. "Too bad you didn't go there to see it for yourself. I think that I can safely say that my dismembering and chopping skills have become very polished over the years."

"Have you disposed of all the bodies in the exact same way?" Taylor asked. She didn't seem affected by Lucien's bragging. "By dismembering them?"

Lucien and Taylor held each other's stare for several seconds.

"No, not all of them," he replied matter-of-factly. "You see, Agent Taylor, at first, like all the scientists in your BRIU, I was curious. I really wanted to understand what drives a person to kill without emotion or remorse. The big question in my head was, are all psychopaths born that way, or can one be created out of sheer will? I read everything on the subject I could get my hands on, and nothing I found provided the answers I was looking for. There's nothing out there, Agent Taylor—no book, no thesis, no detailed work of any kind that will tell what really goes on in here." He tapped his index finger against his right temple. "Inside the mind of someone who becomes a senseless killer, someone who *teaches* himself to be a psychopath." Lucien smiled cryptically. "Maybe one day that will change. But allow me to give you a little preview."

Taylor calmly crossed her right leg over her left and waited.

"What so many seem to fail to understand, Agent Taylor, is that there's a huge learning curve when it comes to becoming a man like me. I've had to evolve, adapt, improvise, and grow more resourceful throughout the years." He gave them an unconcerned shrug. "But I always knew I would have to. Right from the start I wanted to try different methods . . . different approaches. Though death is universal, every victim has to be handled differently." Lucien made it sound as if killing was nothing more than a lab experiment. "But someone like me will always face one huge problem."

"And that is?" Taylor asked, her tone measured.

Lucien smiled at her humorlessly.

"Well, while you have countless resources and teams of agents and officers working around the clock to catch criminals, Agent Taylor, people like me are lone souls.

My means were very limited. Everything I had to rely on was in my head." He stared Taylor down coldly, still ignoring Hunter's gaze. "I'm sure you are aware that not so long ago, the FBI published a study showing that at any one time there are at least five hundred serial killers loose in the United States." He chuckled. "Astonishing, isn't it? People like me are a lot less rare than many might believe. I've encountered several other murderers throughout the years. People who *want* to torture and kill for no reason other than pure pleasure. People who hear voices, or think they do, telling them to go out and kill. People who believe they are doing some divine work on earth, ridding God's creation of sinners, or people who simply want to give their darkest desires wings. Some of them want to learn. They want to find someone who'd teach them. Someone like me."

Lucien gave Hunter and Taylor a few seconds to fully savor the implications of what he'd said.

"If I wanted to take on an apprentice, do you really think it would take me long to find one? All I would have to do is search the streets of any major city in this great country of ours." He spread his arms wide as if wanting to embrace the world. "The streets of America are overflowing with the next Ted Bundy, the next John Wayne Gacy, the next Lucien Folter."

As outrageous as the boastful claim sounded, Hunter knew Lucien was right.

"We could even have a talent show to search for America's next top serial killer." Lucien made a face as if he were seriously considering it. "I should actually suggest that to some cable TV channels. And it wouldn't surprise me if one did consider such a show, because one thing is for sure—they would have a bigger audience than for most of their other shit."

Memories of Hunter's latest investigation with the LAPD exploded in his mind like fireworks—a serial killer who had created his own reality murder show on the Internet. And just like Lucien had suggested, the audience had logged in to watch it in droves.

Lucien stood up, grabbed the plastic cup from the small metal table, walked over to the sink in the corner, and poured himself a drink before returning to the edge of the bed.

"But returning to your question, Agent Taylor," Lucien continued, "I didn't always dispose of my bodies in the same way." He had a sip of his water.

"Susan," Hunter said, breaking his silence. "You said she was your first victim."

Lucien's attention switched to Hunter.

"I knew you'd want to start with her, Robert. Not only because she was a friend, but also because you're right. I *did* tell you that she was my first one. And that really is the perfect place to start, isn't it?" He took a deep breath and the look in his eyes changed, as if he weren't bound by the walls around him anymore, as if his memories were so vivid he could touch them. "Let me tell you how it all began."

38

Palo Alto, California
Twenty-five years earlier

S o, are you really going to go traveling?" Lucien
asked, placing a new round of drinks on the table.

Susan Richards nodded. "I sure am."

Lucien and Susan had both graduated in psychology
from Stanford University just a week earlier, and were
still flying high on their achievement. They'd been celebrating every night since.

"Before I have to start job hunting," Susan said,
reaching for her drink—a double Jack Daniel's and
Coke—"I want to take a little time for myself, you
know? Visit some different places. Maybe even take a
trip to Europe. I've always wanted to go there."

Lucien laughed. "Job hunting? Have you gone mad?
We just graduated from *Stanford*, Susan, the top psychology program in the country. Jobs will be hunting
you."

"Maybe." Susan shrugged, seemingly unconcerned.
"What about you, Lucien, what will you do?"

"I'm not really sure, but I've been giving it a little thought lately, and I think that I might do the same as Robert."

"PhD?"

"I've been thinking about it, yeah. What do you think?"

"Yeah, if that's what you really want, go for it, Lucien."

Lucien tilted his head. "I just might."

"Speaking of Robert," Susan said, adjusting herself in her seat. "It's a pity that he had to go back to LA today."

Robert Hunter had been there for their graduation ceremony and for the first three nights of their week-long party spree, but he had taken the bus back to Los Angeles that morning to spend a week with his father before he had to return to Stanford to start his summer job as an assistant to two of his ex-professors during their summer courses.

"Yeah, I know," Lucien replied, sipping his new cocktail.

They were sitting at the Rocker Club in Crescent Park, on the north side of Palo Alto. It was their favorite lounge—the staff was friendly, the booze was cheap, the crowd was usually young and up for a good time, and the music was rocking and upbeat.

"He does miss his father quite a bit," Lucien added. "He's the only family he's got left."

"I know," Susan said.

Lucien nodded. "Don't you think it's a little funny how he never really talks about it? Even when he's drunk, Robert still manages to avoid the subject. I'm not sure, but I think that there's more to it than just standard trauma of losing a parent when young, don't you?"

Susan paused halfway through sipping her drink, smirking. "Oh, please don't."

"What?"

"Please tell me that you're not going to be one of those dopey psychology graduates who can barely have a conversation with someone without psychoanalyzing them, Lucien. Especially your friends."

"I . . ." Lucien shook his head with a half-embarrassed smile on his lips. "I wasn't psychoanalyzing Robert."

"Yes, you were."

"No, I wasn't. I was just saying that we've been roommates for four years. He's an odd person. Brightest guy I've ever met, but odd nonetheless, and I think that his mother's death might go a little deeper than he lets on."

"Oh really?" Susan said, putting her drink down on the table. "Like what, for example, Dr. Lucien? Let's hear your theory."

"I'm not a doctor, and I don't have a theory," Lucien replied. "I was just saying . . ." He waved his hand in a dismissive gesture. "Look, never mind. I'm not even sure why we're talking about this. We're here to party and celebrate." He reached for his drink. "So let's party and celebrate."

Susan raised her glass. "Yeah, I'll drink to that."

Guns N' Roses' "Sweet Child O' Mine" started playing through the speakers. Lucien finished his cocktail in two gulps.

"C'mon, let's go dance," he said, getting to his feet.

"But . . ." Susan pointed at her drink.

"Drink it down, girl . . . rock-and-roll style," Lucien urged.

Susan gulped her drink down, took Lucien's hand, and allowed him to drag her to the dance floor.

A couple of hours and several drinks later they were both ready to leave. Susan was well past drunkenness, though Lucien looked to be in much better shape.

"I think we should leave your car here and take a cab," Susan said, her words starting to skid into each other. "You can pick it up tomorrow sometime."

"Nah," Lucien came back. "I'm still good. I can drive."

"No you can't. You drank just as much as me, and I . . . am . . . wasted."

"Yeah, but I was drinking cocktails, not double shots of JD and Coke. You know the cocktails here are mainly juice with a splash of booze. I could drink them all night and still be okay to drive home."

Susan paused and regarded Lucien for a long instant. He did look pretty steady on his feet, and he was right—the cocktails at the Rocker Club weren't very strong.

"Are you sure you're okay to drive?"

"Positive."

Susan shrugged. "Okay then, but you're driving slowly, you hear? I'm going to keep my eye on you." She made a *V* with her index and middle fingers, pointed at her eyes, and then slowly moved her hand in the direction of Lucien's.

"Ten-four, ma'am," Lucien said, giving her a military salute.

Lucien had parked down the road, just around the corner. At that time of the morning, the street was deserted.

"Buckle up," he said, taking the driver's seat. "It's the law." He smiled.

"Says the man who had a truckload of cocktails before taking the wheel," Susan joked, struggling with the seat belt.

Lucien waited, giving her a look.

"I'm trying, all right?" she said, a little flustered. "I can't find the goddamn hole."

"Here, let me help you." Lucien leaned over, grabbed her seat belt buckle, and quickly slid it into its lock. Then, with no warning, he moved a little closer and kissed her full on the lips.

Susan pulled back, surprised, suddenly seeming much more sober. "Lucien, what are you doing?"

"What do you think I was doing?"

"Lucien . . . I'm . . . very sorry if I've given you the wrong impression tonight, or any other night. You're a fantastic person, a really good friend, and I get along with you great, but—"

"But you don't have those kinds of feelings for me," Lucien finished Susan's sentence for her. "Is that what you were about to say?"

Susan just stared at him.

"What if instead of me being the one sitting here, it were Robert?"

Susan was taken aback by the question.

"I bet you wouldn't pull back like you just did. I bet you'd be all over him like a two-dollar whore. Your clothes would probably be gone, and you'd be sitting on his lap, undoing his belt and begging for it."

"Lucien, what the hell is going on? It's like I don't even know you right now."

Lucien's eyes went stone cold, as if all the life and emotion had been sucked out of them.

"And what makes you think you ever knew me at all?"

The arctic tone of Lucien's words made Susan shiver. She was still struggling to understand what was happening when Lucien exploded into action, violently launching his body toward her, using his left hand to pin Susan's head against the passenger window.

Lucien hadn't fastened his seat belt, which gave him a lot more freedom of movement.

Susan tried to scream, but Lucien rapidly slid his hand over her mouth, muffling whatever sounds came out of it. With his right hand, he opened the small compartment that sat between the two front seats and reached inside.

Susan grabbed at Lucien's left hand and tried to push it away . . . tried to free her mouth . . . her head, but even if she'd been sober, he'd still be way too strong for her.

"It's okay, Susan," he whispered in her ear. "It'll all be over soon."

With incredible speed, Lucien's right hand shot toward Susan's face. She felt something prick the side of her neck, and in that instant, their eyes met.

Hers full of fear.

His full of evil.

39

FBI National Academy, Quantico, Virginia
The present

In a flat, unemotional voice, Lucien recounted the events that took place that night. All the while his eyes were locked on Hunter.

Hunter tried his best to remain impassive, but hearing Lucien's account of how he had subdued Susan had started to slowly tighten a knot in his throat. He shifted his weight in his chair, but hadn't yet broken eye contact with Lucien once.

Lucien paused, had another sip of his water, and waited.

"So you drugged her," Taylor finally said.

"I injected her with Propofol."

Taylor glanced at Hunter.

"It's a fast-acting general anesthetic," Lucien clarified. "It's incredible what you can get your hands on when you manage to get access to the medical-school building at Stanford."

"So what happened next?" Taylor asked. "Where did you take her? What did you do?"

"No, no, no," Lucien said with a slight shake of the head. "It's my turn to ask a question. That was the agreement, was it not? So far, this question game has been very one-sided."

"Fair enough," Taylor agreed. "Tell us what happened next and then ask your question."

"No deal. It's my turn now. Time to finally feed my curiosity." Lucien massaged the back of his neck for a moment before looking back at Hunter. "Tell me about when you were a kid, Robert. Tell me about your mother."

Hunter's jaw tightened.

Taylor looked a little confused.

"Quid pro quo," Lucien said. "You cops, or profilers, or federal agents, or whatever, are always looking to try to understand what makes people like me tick, isn't that right? You're always trying to figure out how the mind of a killer works. How can a human being have such disregard for another human life? How can someone become a monster like me?" Lucien delivered every word in a monotone. "Well, on the other hand, a monster like me would also like to know what makes people like you tick. The heroes of society . . . the best of the best . . . the ones who'd risk their lives for people they don't even know." He paused for effect. "You want to understand me. I want to understand you. It's as simple as that. And as Freud would tell you, Agent Taylor, if you want to delve deep into someone's psyche, if you want to understand the person they became, the best

place to start is with their childhood and their relation-
ship with their parents. Isn't that right, Robert?"

Hunter said nothing.

Lucien slowly cracked every knuckle on both of his
hands. The creepy, bone-creaking sound reverberated
against the cell walls.

"So, Robert, please indulge me in a twenty-five-year-
old curiosity of mine, will you?"

"I don't think so, Lucien," Hunter said, his voice as
serene as a priest's in a confessional.

"Oh, but I do, Robert," Lucien replied in the same
peaceful tone. "I really do. Because if you want to know
any more about what happened to Susan, *including
where you can find her remains*, you will indulge me."

The knot in Hunter's throat got a little tighter.

"Tell me what happened. How did your mother die?

"And please don't lie to me, Robert."

40

Hunter pictured Susan Richards's parents. He and Lucien had met them a couple of times when they'd made the trip from Nevada to Stanford to visit their daughter. They were a sweet couple. Hunter couldn't remember their names, but he remembered vividly how thrilled and proud they were of Susan for being accepted into such a prestigious university. She was the first person in either of their families to have ever gone to college.

Just like Hunter's parents, Susan's mother and father had come from poor backgrounds, and neither of them had been able to finish high school, having to drop out before the end of their freshmen years to find jobs of their own to help their families. When Susan was born, they'd promised themselves that they would do whatever it took to offer their daughter a better chance at life than the ones they had. Susan was only three months old when they started saving for her college fund.

According to the law, death in absentia, or presumption of death, occurs when a person has been missing for seven years or more, though the exact number varies slightly from state to state. Despite what the law might decree, in the absence of remains or any concrete proof, Hunter was sure that if Susan Richards's parents were still alive, they'd be holding on to a sliver of hope. The least he could do was give them some closure, and the chance to bury their daughter with dignity.

"My mother died of cancer when I was seven years old," Hunter said. He still looked pretty relaxed in his seat.

Lucien smiled triumphantly. "Yes, that much I already know, Robert. What type of cancer?"

"Glioblastoma multiforme."

"Oh! The most aggressive type of primary brain cancer. That must've been a tough blow," Lucien said, his voice emotionless. "How fast did it develop?"

"Fast enough," Hunter said. "Doctors found it too late. Within three months of the diagnosis she passed away."

It was Taylor's turn to shift her weight in her chair uncomfortably.

"Did she suffer?" Lucien asked.

Hunter's jaw tightened again.

Lucien leaned forward, placed his elbows on his knees, and slowly started rubbing his hands against each other.

"Tell me, Robert." The next four words were delivered slowly, with a pause between each of them. "Did your mother suffer? Did she scream in pain at night? Did she go from being a strong, smiling, vivacious person to an unrecognizable sack of skin and bones? Did she beg for death?"

Hunter could see that Lucien had switched his game, at least for the time being. He wasn't interested in getting under Taylor's skin anymore. Today, Hunter was his target. And Lucien was doing a damn good job.

"Yes," Hunter replied.

"Yes?" Lucien said. "Yes to what?"

"To everything."

"So say it."

Hunter breathed in.

Lucien waited.

"Yes, my mother suffered. Yes, she did scream in pain at night. Yes, she did go from being a strong, smiling, vivacious person to an unrecognizable sack of skin and bones, and yes, she did beg for death."

Taylor stole a peek at Hunter and felt goose bumps creep up all over her body.

"What was her name?" Lucien asked.

"Helen."

"Was she in a hospital or at home when she died?"

"At home," Hunter said. "She didn't want to be in a hospital."

"I see." Lucien nodded. "She wanted to be with her family . . . with her loved ones. Very noble, though strange and a little sadistic that she'd want her seven-year-old son to witness all of her suffering firsthand . . . all of her pain. I'm guessing it must've been something quite excruciating."

Through the avalanche of memories, keeping a steady face had become impossible. Hunter looked away and pressed his lips together, taking a moment to regain his composure. When he spoke again, his voice was as steady as he could muster, but there was no hiding the sadness in it.

"My mother worked as a cleaner for minimum wage.

My father worked nights as a security guard, and to complement the little money he earned, during the day he would take any odd job he could get. The end of every month was always a struggle in our house, even when they were both healthy. We had no savings because there was never anything left to save. My father's small health insurance wouldn't cover the costs. We couldn't afford the hospital bills. Home was the only place she could be."

A long silence dragged on.

"Wow, that's one *sad* story, Robert," Lucien finally said coldly. "I can practically hear the violins. Tell me, were you there when your mother died?"

Hunter shook his head. "No."

Lucien returned to a regular seating position and nodded calmly before standing up. "I told you that if you lied to me, Robert, I'd know. And that was a lie. This interview is over."

Taylor's surprised gaze darted between Hunter and Lucien.

"Fuck Susan's remains," Lucien said. "You will never find her. Good luck explaining that to her family."

41

Lucien turned and slowly walked over to the sink.

Taylor tensed in her seat, then Hunter lifted both of his hands in surrender. "Okay, Lucien, I'm sorry."

Lucien ran a hand through his hair, but kept his back to Hunter and Taylor. He took his time, as if he was considering Hunter's apology.

"Well, I guess I can't really blame you, can I, Robert?" he said at last. "You needed to give it a shot to see if I could really tell if you were lying or not. It's only logical. Why would you trust me now? I could never tell with you before, could I? You didn't really have any telltale signs. You were always the one who could keep a straight face through any situation." He finally turned to face his interrogators again. "Well, old friend, I guess you're either getting on in years, or I've gotten much, much better at reading people."

Hunter didn't doubt the latter for a second.

"So," Lucien continued, "for old times' sake I'm going to let this one slide, but don't lie to me anymore, Robert." He sat down again. "Maybe you would like to rephrase your answer?"

A short pause.

"Yes, I was home when my mother died," Hunter began again. "As I said, my father worked nights as a security guard, and my mother passed away during the night."

"So you were alone with your mother?"

Hunter nodded.

Lucien waited, but Hunter offered nothing more. "Don't stop now, Robert. Did her screams scare you at night?"

"Yes."

"But you didn't go hide in your room, did you?"

"No."

"And why not?"

"Because I was more scared of not being there for my mother if she needed me."

"And did she? On that last night? Did she need you?"

Hunter held his breath.

"Did she need you, Robert?"

Hunter saw something in Lucien's eyes that he hadn't noticed before—total certainty, as if he already knew all the answers. As if Lucien would know if Hunter deviated from the truth even a little bit.

"Yes," Hunter finally replied.

"How did she need you?" Lucien asked.

"Pills," Hunter said.

"What about them?"

"My mother used to take them. They made the pain go away, at least for a little while. But as the cancer grew stronger inside her, the effect of the pills grew weaker."

"So she needed more," Lucien said.

Hunter nodded.

A pensive look came over Lucien's face, but a moment later his lips stretched into a wicked smile.

"But they were prescription painkillers, right?" he said. "Probably very strong . . . probably schedule two . . . and probably opioids, right? Which means that exceeding the dosage was a big no-no. Those pills weren't by her bedside, were they, Robert? They couldn't have been. The risk of accidental overdose would've been too great. So where were they? In the bathroom? In the kitchen? Where? The pills, Robert, where were they kept?"

Hunter could hear the threat in his voice.

"My father kept them in the cupboard, in the kitchen."

"But your mother asked you for them that night."

"Yes."

Lucien scratched the scar on his left cheek.

"She couldn't handle the pain anymore, could she?" he pushed. "She'd rather be dead. In fact, she begged for death, and you played grim reaper, because you took them to her, didn't you? How many pills did you bring her, Robert?" Then it dawned on him and he lifted a hand as his eyes widened a touch. "You brought her the whole bottle, didn't you?"

Hunter said nothing, but his memory took him back to that night.

• • •

He sat alone in his room watching the heavy rain hammering against the window. He liked rain, especially heavy rain. Its thundering noise was almost enough to cover the crying, the moans of pain that came from the room next door . . . almost. He'd asked his father why the doctors didn't do something. Why they didn't take her to the hospital and make her better.

"There's nothing more that can be done," his father had said with tearful eyes as he placed two tablets next to a glass of water before hiding the medicine bottle deep inside the highest cupboard in their small kitchen.

"Can't we give her some more tablets, Dad? They help with her pain. She doesn't cry so much when she takes them."

"No, Robert," his father replied in an anxious voice. "Too many aren't good for her."

He had to take care of her when his father wasn't home, and back then his father worked nights.

Nights were always worse. Her screams sounded louder, her groans deeper and heavier with pain. They always made him shiver. Not like when he felt cold, but an intense shaking that came from deep within. Her illness had brought her so much pain, and he wished there was something he could do to help.

That night, seven-year-old Robert Hunter heard his mother call out and cautiously opened the door to her room. He felt like crying. Since she'd gotten ill, he felt like crying all the time, but his father had told him he mustn't.

Her illness made her look so different. She was so thin he could see her bones poking at her sagging skin. Her once striking long blond hair was now fine and frizzled. Her once sparkling eyes had lost all life and had sunk deep into their sockets.

Shaking, he paused by the door. His mother was curled up in a ball on the bed. Her knees pushed up against her chest, her arms wrapped tightly around her legs, her face contorted in pain. She screwed up her eyes and tried to focus on the tiny figure standing at the door.

"Please, baby," she whispered as she recognized her son. *"Can you help me? I can't take the pain anymore."*

It took all his strength to keep his tears locked in his throat. *"What can I do, Mom?"* His voice was as weak as hers. *"Do you want me to call Dad?"*

She managed only a delicate shake of the head. *"Dad can't help, honey, but you can. Could you come here . . . please? Can you help me?"*

"I can heat some milk up for you, Mom. You like hot milk."

He would do anything he could to see his mother smile again. As he stepped closer, she winced as a new surge of pain took over her body.

"Please, baby. Help me." Her breath was coming in short gasps.

Despite what his father had told him, he simply couldn't hold his tears anymore. They started rolling down his face.

His mother could now see he was scared and shaking. *"It's okay, honey. Everything will be fine,"* she said in a trembling voice.

He stepped closer still and placed his hand in hers.

"I love you, Mom."

His words brought tears to her eyes. *"I love you too, honey."* She gave his hand a frail squeeze. It was all she could muster. *"I need your help . . . please."*

"What can I do, Mom?"

"Can you get my pills for me? You know where they are, don't you?"

He ran the back of his right hand against his running nose. He looked scared. *"They're very high up,"* he said, hiding his eyes from her.

"Can't you reach them for me, baby? Please, you don't know how much it hurts."

His eyes were so full of tears that everything was blurred. His heart felt empty, and he felt as if all his strength had left him. Without saying a word, he turned around and opened the door.

His mother tried calling after him, but her voice was so weak it didn't travel.

He came back a few minutes later carrying a tray with a glass of water, two Oreos, and the bottle of medicine. She stared at it, hardly believing her eyes. She slowly pushed herself into a sitting position. He stepped closer, placed the tray on the bedside table, and handed her the glass of water.

She wanted to hug him so much, but she barely had the strength to move. Instead, she gave him the most honest smile he'd ever seen. She tried, but her fingers were too weak to twist open the bottle cap. She looked at him, and her eyes begged for help.

He took it from her trembling hands, pressed down on the cap, and twisted it counterclockwise before pouring two pills onto her hand. She placed them in her mouth and swallowed them without even sipping water. Her eyes pleaded for more.

"Dad told me that you shouldn't have more than eight of these a day, Mom. The two you just had make it ten today."

"You're so intelligent, my darling." She smiled again. "You're very special. I love you so much and I'm so sorry I won't see you grow up."

His eyes filled with tears once again as she wrapped her bony fingers around the medicine bottle.

He held on to it tightly.

"It's okay," she whispered. "It'll all be okay now."

Hesitantly, he let go. "Dad will be angry with me."

"No, he won't be, baby. I promise you." She placed two more pills in her mouth.

"I brought you these cookies." He pointed to the tray. "They're your favorite, Mom. Please have one. You didn't eat much today."

"I will, honey, in a while." She had a few more pills. "When Daddy comes home in the morning, tell him I love him, and that I always will. Can you do that for me?"

The boy nodded. His eyes locked on the now almost empty medicine bottle.

"Why don't you go read one of your books, darling? I know you love reading."

"I can read in here, Mom, so you're not alone. I can sit in the corner if you like. I won't make any noise, I promise."

She extended her hand and touched his hair. "I'll be okay now, honey. The pain's starting to go away." Her eyelids looked heavy.

"I'll guard the room then. I'll sit just outside the door."

She smiled wanly. "Guard the room?"

"You told me that sometimes God comes and takes sick people to heaven. I don't want him to take you, Mom. I'll sit by the door and if he comes I'll tell him to go away. I'll tell him that you're getting better and not to take you."

"You'll tell God to go away?"

He nodded vigorously.

She started crying again. "I'm going to miss you so much, Robert."

• • •

Taylor looked at Hunter and felt her heart shrivel inside her chest.

A cold smile cracked Lucien's lips, like ice over a dark, frozen lake. "So you left the room," he said.

Hunter nodded.

"And that was when the nightmares started," Lucien concluded, just like a psychologist who had finally broken through a patient's barrier.

With his gaze fixed on Lucien, Hunter finally shook the memory.

"Lucien," he said. The sadness had vanished from his voice, replaced with a steady intensity. "You have what you wanted. Now tell us what happened after you drugged Susan in the car."

42

La Honda, eighteen miles from Palo Alto, California
Twenty-five years earlier

Susan Richards was jolted awake by the loud sound of a heavy door slamming shut. Despite the sudden noise, she opened her eyes slowly, blinking constantly as if cornea-scratching grains of sand had been blown into them. Her eyelids felt heavy, and no matter how hard she tried, she couldn't get her eyes to focus. Her surroundings were nothing but a blur.

She felt dizzy, stuck in a hazy dream with no way of waking up. Her mouth was bone-dry and her tongue felt like sandpaper. Then she noticed the smell—damp, moldy, old, and sickening. She had no idea where she was, but it smelled as if the place had been neglected for years. In spite of the horrible smell, Susan's lungs demanded that she take in a full breath of air, and as she did, she could almost taste the rancid stench of the room. It only took one breath to make her gag.

All of a sudden, between desperate coughs, sharp and excruciating pain came to her. It took her exhausted body a few seconds to home in on its location. It was coming from her right arm.

Susan realized then that she was sitting on some sort of uncomfortable chair. Her wrists were tied together behind the chair's backrest, her ankles to the chair's legs. She was soaking wet, drenched with her own sweat. She tried lifting her head, which was slumped forward awkwardly, and the slight movement sent waves of nausea rippling through her stomach.

She couldn't identify the room's light source, maybe a corner lamp or an old lightbulb hanging overhead, but whatever it was, it bathed the room in a weak yellowish glow. Her eyes finally moved right and tried to focus on her aching arm. She still felt groggy, so it took a moment for her vision to steady itself and for the blurriness to dissipate. When it did, her heart filled with terror.

"Oh my God." The words dribbled out of her lips.

An enormous chunk of skin was missing from her arm—from her shoulder all the way down to her elbow. In its place she saw raw, blood-soaked flesh. For an instant, it looked as if the wound were alive. Blood had dripped down her arm, over her hands, through her fingers, and onto the concrete floor, forming a large crimson pool at the feet of the chair.

Susan jerked her head away and instantly vomited all over her lap. The effort made her feel even weaker, even dizzier.

"Sorry about that, Susan," she heard a familiar voice say. "You could never really stand the sight of blood, could you?"

Susan coughed a few more times and tried to spit

the awful taste of bile from her mouth. Her eyes moved forward, finally focusing on the figure standing in front of her.

"Lucien . . ." she said in a feeble whisper.

Images of last night at the Rocker Club flashed back at her. Then she remembered sitting in Lucien's car . . . the angry way he looked at her. And then nothing.

"What . . ." She was unable to finish the sentence, her throat far too frail to produce the sounds. Instinctively her eyes shot toward the raw flesh of her right arm once again and her whole body shivered.

"Oh," Lucien said unconcerned, reaching behind him. "Don't worry about that. I don't think you will miss this horrible thing, will you?"

He showed her a large glass jar filled with a pale-pink liquid. Something was floating in it, but Susan couldn't tell what it was.

"Oh, sorry," Lucien said, picking up on her confusion and reaching inside the jar with his gloved hand to collect the floating object. "Allow me to show you. The edges have curled in a bit now." He uncurled them and stretched the wet piece of skin he had carved off her arm less than an hour ago. "This is a hideous tattoo, Susan. I have no idea why you'd think that this was cool in any way."

Acidic bile flooded Susan's mouth, resulting in a new desperate frenzy of gags and coughs.

Amused, Lucien waited until it was over to resume his explanation.

"But I think that it will make a great souvenir," he said, nodding a couple of times. "And do you know what? I do think that I will give the token collector thing a shot. See how it makes me feel. Give the theory behind it a practical test. What do you think?"

Susan's head throbbed with the rhythm of her thudding heart. The rope that had been used to tie her wrists and ankles felt as if it had cut through to her bones. She tried to speak, but fear seemed to have erased every word from her terrified mind. Her eyes, on the other hand, reflected her fear and desperation.

Lucien returned the tattooed piece of skin to the jar.

"You know," he said. "I've had that syringe hidden in my car for almost a year now. I thought about using it many times. But never on you." Lucien moved on. "I thought about picking up a prostitute many times, though." He shrugged indifferently. "But unfortunately it didn't quite work out. I never really felt ready for it before, but tonight was different. I guess I can say that tonight I felt my first *real* killer's impulse."

Tears welled up in Susan's eyes. The air inside the room felt denser, even more polluted . . . almost unbreathable.

Lucien's eyes shone with a new purpose. Susan saw it, and that sent a new current of panic traveling through her body.

"I decided not to fight it," he proceeded, moving a step closer. "I decided to act on it. So I did. And here we are."

Susan tried to calm her breathing, tried to think. Everything still felt like a horrible dream, but if it were, why wasn't she waking up?

"Lucien . . ." she said, her voice rasping, catching in her swollen throat. "I don't know—"

"No, no, no," Lucien interrupted, shaking his left

index finger at her. "There's nothing you can say. Don't you see, Susan? There's no turning back now." He stretched his arms out to his sides, calling attention to the room. "We're here now. The process has started. The floodgates have opened . . . or any other clichéd metaphor you'd care to come up with. But no matter what, this is happening."

That was when Susan noticed the look in Lucien's eyes—distant and ice-cold . . . soulless. And it paralyzed her.

Her fear filled Lucien with excitement. He was expecting that excitement to conflict with something inside him—maybe morals, or sentimentality . . . he wasn't quite sure what, but *something*. That conflict never came. He felt nothing but exhilarated to be finally doing something he'd fantasized about for so long.

Susan wanted to speak, to scream, but her panic-frozen lips wouldn't move. Instead, her eyes begged him for mercy . . . mercy that never came.

Without warning, Lucien exploded forward, and in a flash, his hands were on Susan's neck.

Her eyes went wide with terror. Her neck tightened as her body tried to defend itself from the attack. Her jaw dropped open, gasping for air, but her brain knew that the battle was already lost. Lucien's thumbs were already compressing Susan's airway, while his large palms were applying enough pressure to her carotid arteries and jugular veins to cause significant occlusion, interfering with the flow of blood to her neck.

When Susan's body started kicking and wriggling on the chair, Lucien placed most of his body weight on her lap to keep her steady. That was when he felt something collapse under his thumbs. He knew then that he had crushed her larynx and trachea. Susan would be dead in seconds, but Lucien didn't stop squeezing until he had fractured the hyoid bone in her neck.

All the while, his mad, frantic eyes were locked onto Susan's dying ones.

43

Hunter sat in silence. Not once had he interrupted Lucien's unsentimental account of events.

"Before you ask," Lucien said, looking at Hunter, "there was no sexual gratification in what I did. I did not touch Susan in that way." He shrugged. "Truth be told, she was never supposed to be my first. She was never supposed to be a victim at all. She was never part of the thousands of fantasies I had before that day. It was just very unfortunate that it happened that way."

For some reason, Lucien felt that he should explain himself further.

"I know that you both know that people like me don't just suddenly decide to start killing and that's that. I know that you understand that we fantasize about hurting others for a long time. Some might start fantasizing when they're kids, some a lot later in life, but we all do, and we do it all the time. I guess I can say that my fascination with death started early. You see, my father was a great hunter. He used to take me hunting up in the mountains in Colorado, and there was something about the waiting, the stalking . . . and looking straight into the animal's eyes just before pulling the trigger. It captivated me."

Lucien scratched his chin while regarding Hunter and Taylor. Then he smiled.

"Look at the two of you. I can practically hear your brains working. The psychologist in you, Robert, and the law enforcer in you, Agent Taylor, already starting to make theoretic connections between my early hunting days and the killer I became." He laughed. "Before you ask, I didn't wet the bed when I was a kid, and I never liked setting fire to anything."

Lucien was referring to the Macdonald triad, a theory that concerns a set of three behavioral individualities—animal cruelty, obsession with fire setting, and persistent bed-wetting past the age of five. If all three are present together while a subject is young, they can be associated with violent tendencies later in life, particularly homicidal behavior. Though studies have shown that, statistically, no significant links between the triad and violent offenders have been found, the theory persists. Animal cruelty is by far the trait most often proven to manifest itself in the early lives of apprehended serial killers. Hunter and Taylor were both aware of that.

Lucien used his index finger to pick at something that was stuck between his two front teeth. "Well, knock yourselves out, guys. Analyze whatever you like, but I'm sure I will surprise you."

"You already have," Hunter said.

The edges of Lucien's lips curved up smugly.

"Despite my hunting days," he continued, "it was during my first year in high school that I started having dreams.

"In these dreams I wasn't hunting. I was hurting people. Sometimes people I knew, sometimes people I had never seen before. They were very violent. They should've been nightmares, but they filled me with excitement. So much that I didn't want to wake up. I didn't want them to stop . . . and that was when I started fantasizing during the day, while wide-awake. The starring role in these . . ." Lucien searched the air around him for the right words. "Let's say, *intense fantasies* of mine, usually belonged to people I disliked . . . teachers, school bullies, some family members . . . but not always. Anyway, Susan was never one of them. She was never part of any of my violent fantasies. She just happened to fit the *perfect* profile that night."

Lucien stood up, crossed over to the sink, and refilled his cup with water.

"That was the reason I wanted to study psychology and criminal behavior originally," he continued, returning to the edge of the bed. "To try to understand what was going on in my head. Why I had these violent thoughts swimming around in here." He tapped his right temple with the tip of his index finger. "Why I enjoyed them so much, and if there was anything I could do to get rid of them." He chuckled. "But wouldn't you know it? College had an adverse effect. The more theories I confronted about how psychologists believed the mind of a killer worked, the more intrigued I became." Lucien paused and had a sip of water. "I wanted to test them."

He leaned forward slightly. "I mean, weren't you intrigued too, Robert? As a student with such an eager mind, didn't you want to understand what *really* goes on inside a killer's head? What *really* makes them tick? Didn't you want to know if the theories we were taught were true, or just a pile of shit guesses put together by a bunch of nerdy psychologists?

"Well, I did," Lucien said when Hunter didn't speak. "The more psychologists I studied, the more I compared their analyses with how my fantasies made me feel. And then, one of those theories finally proved true for me."

Lucien looked at Taylor long and slow, his gaze resting on her chest, her legs.

"Care to take a guess at what theory that was, Agent Taylor?"

She wasn't in the mood for games, but she knew Lucien still held all the cards.

"Fantasies may one day not be enough," she said.

Lucien's smile widened. "Wow. You're getting better at this, Agent Taylor. That's absolutely right. I continued fantasizing until one day I realized that the fantasies just weren't enough. They weren't making me feel as good as they used to. To get the same high, I needed to go to the next level." His stare settled back on Hunter, changing slowly to what seemed to be a genuine expression of gratitude. "Then you changed everything, Robert."

44

Hunter stayed perfectly still, matching Lucien's gaze. It was Taylor who showed surprise.

"How do you mean?" she asked.

Lucien kept his eyes on Hunter a little longer, still looking for a reaction.

Nothing.

"It was only natural that Robert and I discuss our studies," Lucien began. "Two young and hungry minds trying to make sense of the crazy world we lived in, trying to be the best students we could be, and we were roommates too, of course. There was never a break from it. But it was during a debate in our second year at Stanford that Robert said something that really got my brain going."

Taylor peeked at Hunter's impassive face.

"I'll clarify it for you, Agent Taylor," Lucien offered with a smirk. "We were studying brain physiology. The debate was whether science would one day find a way to identify a sector of the brain, no matter how small, that controlled our urges to perform particular actions. Including becoming a killer.

"I hope you don't mind if I use the same example as

you did then, Robert," Lucien said. "I still remember it well." He didn't wait for a reply. "Two brothers," Lucien began, addressing Taylor. "Identical twins. Both were shown the same amount of love and affection by their parents. They went to the same schools, attended the same classes, and were taught the same moral values. In essence, there was absolutely no difference in their up-bringing. Now, let's say that these two brothers became avid music fans."

Taylor's frown was tiny, but Lucien still noticed it.

"Stay with me," he said condescendingly. "Things will get clearer." Lucien winked at Hunter. "And they both liked the same style of music and the same bands. They changed their looks and hairstyles to match the ones of their idols. They bought the albums." Lucien paused and smiled. "Well, that was back then; now they would just download the music, isn't that right? Anyway, they had the T-shirts, the baseball hats, the posters, the badges . . . everything. They went to every concert that came to their town. But there was one difference. Brother A was content with just being a music fan. He was happy to just go to the gigs, listen to the songs back in his room, and dress up like his idols. Brother B, on the other hand, wanted something more. Something inside him told him that he needed to be part of the music circus himself. He needed to experience the real deal. So brother B learned how to play an instrument, and he joined a band. And there we have it."

Lucien allowed his words to float in the air, giving Taylor a moment to digest them before moving on.

"It's that little difference that makes *all* the differ-ence, Agent Taylor. Why does brother B, after growing up in identical circumstances, want something that little bit more than brother A? Why is one content with just being a fan, and the other isn't?"

If Taylor was trying to formulate an answer, Lucien didn't wait to hear it.

"That same theory can easily be transposed with the desire to murder. Some people with violent tendencies may be content with just fantasizing, with watching violent films or reading violent books or looking at violent pictures on the Internet, or hitting a punching bag, or whatnot, but some . . ." He shook his head slowly. "Some will feel the need to go that little bit further. To become brother B. And it's this drive, the drive that makes us *want* something more than others, that Robert argued science will never be able to pinpoint physiologically, because that drive is what makes us *individuals*."

Hunter kept on observing Lucien. He was getting worked up by his own discourse, like a preacher delivering a fine and well-polished sermon in church, even more so because he could see that he'd made Taylor wonder. Still, the agent held firm.

"Are you saying that Robert's argument all those years ago is what tipped you into killing?" Taylor scoffed. "Are you looking for someone to blame for everything you've done? How typical."

Lucien threw his head back and laughed. "Not at all, Agent Taylor. I've done what I've done because I wanted to." He pointed a finger at Hunter. "But physiology aside, it got me thinking, old friend, because that was when I realized exactly what I needed to do. I needed to stop fantasizing. I needed to stop fighting the urge.

I needed to move it to the next level. I needed to become brother B. So I started planning. And believe me, I studied criminology in depth. I read and subscribed to specialized newspapers and magazines. I studied the writings of prominent forensic psychiatrists. I learned about sex murderers, serial murderers, military murderers, mass murderers, professional murderers. I studied massacres and murder conspiracies. I learned just about everything I could on the subject, but the one thing I paid particular attention to was perpetrators' mistakes. Especially the mistakes that led to their capture."

"Well, it looks like you didn't pay that much attention after all, given your current predicament," Taylor said. She allowed her eyes to circle around his cell.

Lucien wasn't bothered by Taylor's sharp comment.

"Oh, I paid more than enough attention, Agent Taylor. Unfortunately, no one can foresee accidents. The only reason I'm sitting here right now is not because I made a mistake, or because of any merit of your own or of the organization you work for, but because an unfortunate chain of chance events took place seven days ago. Events that were completely out of my control. Admit it, Agent Taylor, the FBI had no idea I existed. You weren't investigating me, any of my aliases, or any of the acts I committed."

"We would have eventually caught on to you," Taylor said.

"But of course you would have." Lucien grinned confidently. "Anyway, as I was saying, I started planning. And the first thing on my list was to find an isolated, anonymous place. Somewhere I wouldn't be disturbed. A place where I could take my time.

"I found it in La Honda, just an old, abandoned house in the middle of some woods. It was close enough to Stanford that it wouldn't take me long to get there. And the best thing about it was that I could use remote back roads to reach it. No one would spot me."

Lucien stood up and stretched his powerful frame.

"The place is still there," he said. "I visited it not that long ago. You know what? I've got a little bit of a headache and I'm getting hungry. So what do you say we all take a break?" He pulled his sleeve up and looked at his wrist as if he had a watch. "Let's start again in two hours, how does that sound?"

"Not good, Lucien," Hunter said, revealing the first signs of having lost patience with his former friend's ramblings and machinations. "Susan's remains—where are they?"

"Another two hours before you find out won't make a difference, Robert. It's not like you have to rush to save her, is it now?"

45

Outside the sun was shining brightly in yet another cloudless sky. It was the kind of warm and joyful weather that made most people smile for no apparent reason, but the magic of the day didn't seem to reach as far as the BRIU building.

Hunter had found an empty meeting room somewhere on the second floor. He was standing by the window, staring out at nothing at all when Taylor stepped inside and softly closed the door behind her.

"So there you are."

Without turning, Hunter checked his watch. It had only been ten minutes since they'd left Lucien in his cell.

"Are you all right?" Taylor asked, stepping closer.

"I'm fine," Hunter replied.

Taylor hesitated an instant. "Listen, I need to get out of here for a while."

Hunter turned and looked at her.

"I need to go outdoors for an hour or so, breathe some fresh air or something before I go back down into that basement."

Hunter could easily empathize with her caged feeling.

"I know a place not very far from here where they'll have tables outside on a day like this," Taylor added. "Their food is great, but if you're not hungry, their coffee is even better. What do you say we get the hell out of here for a bit?"

She didn't have to ask twice.

46

Despite having eaten their last meal over four and a half hours earlier, neither Hunter nor Taylor was hungry. Hunter ordered a simple black coffee, while Taylor went for a double espresso. They were sitting outside at one of the tables at a small Italian cantina–style restaurant on Garrisonville Road, less than a fifteen-minute drive from the FBI Academy.

Taylor stirred her coffee and watched the thin layer of dark-brown foam slowly disappear from its surface. She thought about telling Hunter how sorry she was for what had happened to his mother. She thought about telling him about her own mother, but then decided that the subject would benefit neither of them. She finished stirring her coffee and placed the spoon on the saucer, searching for something to say.

A tall young waitress, her long dark hair pulled back into a fishtail braid, stepped up to their table.

"Are you sure you wouldn't like to have a look at the menu?" she asked with a hint of an Italian accent. "I can recommend the gnocchi with the chef's special cheese, tomato, and basil sauce." She gave them a charming smile. "It's so good you'll want to lick the plate."

Gnocchi was Hunter's favorite Italian dish, but he still had no appetite.

"Wow, that does sound quite tempting," he said, matching her smile. "But I'm not very hungry today. Maybe another time." He nodded at Taylor.

"Yeah, I'm not hungry either. Just the coffee for me today, thanks."

"No problem," the waitress said. Paused. Looked back at them. "I hope you guys work things out," she added kindly. "You look good together." She gave them a quick smile before moving over to take the order of a small group sitting just a few tables away.

"Is that the vibe we're giving out?" Taylor laughed once the waitress was out of earshot.

Hunter shrugged, amused. "I guess."

For an instant Taylor looked almost embarrassed, but in a flash her game face was back on. "Do you really believe that Susan was never part of any of Lucien's violent fantasies?" she asked. "Do you believe she really was his first-ever victim? And that he didn't rape her?"

Hunter was waiting for his coffee to cool down a little. He leaned back in his chair. "Why do you think he would lie about any of that?"

"I'm not sure. I guess that what I'm trying to understand is—if Susan really was Lucien's first-ever victim, and he'd never had any *violent fantasies* about her, how come he went for her and not someone else . . . a stranger?"

Hunter frowned.

Taylor read his confusion. "No, I'm not talking about that particular night, or even that week, Robert. I know she had no job, that she planned to travel, and no one would miss her for a while. What I'm talking about is that despite the circumstances back then, she and Lucien were supposed to be friends. From what he said, he even had some romantic interest in her, which suggests some sort of emotional attachment."

Hunter's coffee had cooled down enough for him to have a healthy sip. "And you're thinking that it's got to be a lot harder for a perpetrator to kidnap, *partially skin*, and then kill someone he knew, someone who was supposedly a friend, someone he had a crush on."

"Exactly." Taylor nodded. "Especially if that person is his first-ever victim. If Lucien hadn't fantasized about killing Susan in particular, then why torture and kill a friend? He could've easily found an anonymous victim, a total stranger, someone he could've picked up in a bar or a club—a hooker, I don't know—but someone he had zero feelings for, someone he couldn't care less about."

"But to Lucien, that was exactly who Susan was."

Taylor looked confused for a second.

"You're trying to look at it with your own eyes, Courtney," Hunter said, putting his coffee cup back down on the table. "You're trying to understand it with your sane mind. And when you do that, emotions get in the way. You have to try to look at it through Lucien's eyes. His psychopathy isn't victim-centered."

Taylor held Hunter's gaze for a long while. Every agent with the FBI's Behavioral Research and Instruction Unit was aware that there are two major types of aggressive psychopaths. The first kind—victim-centered—are the ones for whom the victim is the most important part of the equation. The perpetrator fantasizes about a *specific* type of victim, so everyone he chooses has to match that type, fit the profile. And it usually boils down to physical type. With victim-centered psychopaths, the whole fantasy revolves around the way the victim looks. It's the victim's physical attributes that excite and turn them on. Most of the time their targets remind them of someone else. In those cases, there's always some sort of strong emotional connection, and nine out of ten times their fantasies will involve some sort of sexual act. The victim being sexually assaulted either before or after being murdered is almost a certainty.

The second major type of aggressive psychopaths— violence-centered—are the ones for whom the victim's profile is secondary. The most important part of the equation is the violence, not the victim. It's the killing act that pleasures them. They don't fantasize about a certain type of victim. They don't fantasize about having sex with the victim, because sex will bring them little or no pleasure at all. On the contrary, it's a distraction from the violence. What they fantasize about is torture, about how to inflict pain, about the godlike power that it gives them. To those psychopaths, anyone can become a victim, even friends and family. There is no distinction. Because of that, they achieve a much higher level of emotional detachment than their victim-centered counterparts. Emotions simply have no relevance.

"How do you know Lucien's psychopathy isn't victim-centered?" Taylor finally asked.

Hunter finished his coffee and used a paper napkin to dab his mouth.

"Because of the evidence we have so far."

Taylor leaned in slightly and cocked her head.

"The tokens that were found inside that box in Lucien's house, remember?" Hunter elaborated. "Not all of them came from women, and the ones that did drastically varied in size. That tells us that the victim's physical type and even gender aren't that important to him. But Lucien also told us so himself . . . twice."

Taylor paused, and Hunter could tell that she was searching her mental record of that morning's interview.

"He told us that when he was in high school he dreamed of hurting people," Hunter reminded her. "Sometimes people he knew, sometimes people he had never seen before . . . just random creations of his imagination—not a specific type.

"Then he told us that when he started fantasizing while wide-awake, the star roles in his violent fantasies usually belonged to people he disliked. Sometimes teachers, sometimes school bullies, sometimes family members . . . but not always. No physical attributes or gender came into play. In Lucien's dreams and fantasies, *who* he was hurting made no difference to him. What excited him was the act of murder itself."

Hunter consulted his watch. It was time to get going.

"Trust me, Courtney, whatever feelings Lucien felt for Susan wouldn't have stopped him. Not even love."

47

For lunch, Lucien had been given an aluminum tray containing one portion of bread, lumpy mashed potatoes, a few soggy coins of carrots, and two pieces of dry chicken, which were swimming in some sort of yellowish sauce. Everything lacked salt and tasted like cardboard. Despite the fact that the FBI had seemingly redefined tasteless food, Lucien didn't really mind. He wasn't eating for taste or pleasure. He ate to keep his body and mind fed, to give his muscles at least some of the nutrients they needed. He ate every last scrap.

Just ten minutes after he'd finished his lunch, Lucien heard the familiar buzzing and unlocking sound from the door at the end of the corridor.

"Two hours almost to the second," he said as Hunter and Taylor came into his line of sight. "I had a feeling you would be punctual." Lucien waited for them to take their seats. "Do you mind if I stand up and walk about a little while we talk? It helps me digest that crap you guys call food around here."

No one had any objections.

"So," Lucien said. "Where were we?"

Hunter and Taylor both knew that Lucien hadn't

forgotten where they'd left off. The question was just part of his game.

"Susan Richards," Taylor said, calmly crossing her legs, interlacing her fingers, and resting her right elbow on one of the chair's arms.

"Oh, yeah," Lucien replied as he slowly started pacing from left to right at the front of the cell. "What about her again?

"Oh, that's right. I was about to tell you about her remains, wasn't I?" There was a perverse quality to Lucien's suddenly bright smile. "Have you contacted her parents yet, Robert? Are they still alive?"

"What?"

"Susan's parents. We met them a couple of times, remember? Are they still alive?"

"Yes. They're still alive," Hunter confirmed.

Lucien nodded his understanding. "They seemed to be nice people. Will you be the one in charge of giving them the news?"

Hunter suspected he would be, but he was getting tired of Lucien's games. The way he saw it, right then, any answer was an answer, as long as it got Lucien talking.

"Yes."

"Will you be doing it over the phone, or do you intend to speak to them face-to-face?"

Any answer.

"Face-to-face."

Lucien chewed on that for a beat before returning to Hunter's original question. "You know, Robert, that night I experienced things . . . feelings, that until then I had only read about. That night, Robert, I could actually feel Susan's life fading away under my finger-tips." He glanced toward his hands before continuing. "I could feel her pulse under my palms, and the more I squeezed, the weaker it got." He turned and faced Hunter and Taylor one more time. "And that was when I was elevated. It was an out-of-body experience: I realized that the feeling so many had testified to was indeed true."

Taylor's eyes darted toward Hunter and then back to Lucien. "What feeling are you talking about?"

Lucien didn't answer, but his eyes passed the question over to Hunter.

"They call it a godlike feeling," Hunter said.

Lucien nodded once. "Right again, Robert. The godlike feeling. A feeling of such supreme power that it seemed beyond any human grasp. The power to extinguish life. And let me tell you, it's true what they say. That feeling changes your life forever. It's intoxicating, Robert, addictive, hypnotizing even. Especially if you're looking straight into the eyes of a person as you squeeze the life out of their bodies. That's the moment when you *become* God."

No, Hunter thought, *that's the moment when you delude yourself that you have.* He noticed Lucien's fingers slowly closing into fists before he turned and faced Taylor.

"Tell me, Agent Taylor, have you ever killed some-one?"

The question caught Taylor by surprise, and in a whirlwind of memory, her heartbeat took off like a fighter jet.

48

It had happened three years after Taylor graduated from the FBI Academy. She'd been assigned to the New York field office.

That night, Taylor had spent hours poring over NYPD's and New Jersey PD's combined investigation files on a serial killer they had named The Ad Killer, or TAK for short.

In the past ten months TAK had sodomized and killed six women—four in New York and two in New Jersey. All six of them had been private sex workers. All six of them fit a specific physical profile—dark shoulder-length hair, brown eyes, aged between nineteen and thirty-five, average weight, average height. The pseudonym The Ad Killer was used because the only solid fact the police had been able to gather over nine months of investigations was that all six women had placed private advertisements, offering their "tantric massage" services, in the back pages of free local newspapers.

After nine months and not much to show for the investigation, the mayor of New York had demanded that the chief of police request the assistance of the FBI.

Courtney Taylor was one of the two agents assigned to assist with the case.

It was past midnight when Taylor left the FBI office on the twenty-third floor of the Federal Plaza building that late October night. She drove through Manhattan slowly before taking the Queens-Midtown Tunnel toward her small one-bedroom apartment in Astoria. Suddenly she remembered that she had completely run out of several supplies back home.

"Oh, damn!" she breathed out, quickly swinging her car right and taking a parking spot just past a twenty-four-hour grocery store. As she turned off the engine, her stomach decided to remind her of its hunger by demonstrating its own version of a whale's mating call.

At that time of the morning the store wasn't busy at all—two, maybe three customers browsed the aisles. The young clerk at the counter nodded a robotic *good morning* at Taylor, before returning his attention to a dog-eared paperback.

Taylor grabbed a basket by the entrance and started throwing items into it. She'd just picked up a half gallon of milk from one of the fridges at the back of the store when she heard a commotion up front. She frowned and peeked around the corner, but saw nothing out of the ordinary. Still, her instincts told her that something wasn't right, and Taylor had learned a long time ago to always trust her instincts. She put the basket on the floor and walked around to the next aisle.

"Hurry the fuck up, man, or I'll blow your fucking brains all over this dirty floor. I ain't got all fucking night." The anxious, raised voice she heard sounded unstable.

Instantly, Taylor reached for her Glock 22, thumbed the safety off, and quietly chambered a round. Her stomach's rumble had gone quiet all of a sudden, giving way to a heavy-metal drum solo from her heart. This was no well-rehearsed, well-planned FBI operation. This was no drill. This was sheer bad luck. This was *real*, and this was happening right in front of her.

Crouching down to keep herself hidden from view, Taylor moved stealthily up the aisle toward the front counter. She paused before reaching the end of it, and through a gap between some shelves, angled herself to check the round surveillance mirror in one of the corners of the ceiling.

"Motherfucker, you think I'm playing wit' you?" she heard the anxious voice say. "You think this is a fucking game? You better speed the fuck up or I'll pop a cap in your ugly ass. You hear what I'm saying, homes?"

The drum solo in Taylor's heart gathered momentum. In the mirror she could see a single perpetrator. Tall and skinny, wearing blue jeans and a dark, baggy New York Yankees sweatshirt. With a red-and-black bandana covering most of his face, he was pointing a Beretta 92 semiautomatic pistol directly at the terrified store clerk's head.

Like a frantic chicken, the perpetrator quickly turned his head every few seconds to check the store's entrance and aisles, glancing fitfully from one to the other. Even from a distance Taylor could tell that he was completely wasted, wired up on some kind of drug. Taylor knew his volatile state could only make this night worse.

Despite his incessant checking, the kid with the Beretta was so out of it that he didn't even notice the police car that had just parked outside the shop.

Officer Turkowski wasn't responding to a distress call. That small grocery store, stashed away in a dark corner of Queens, had no silent alarm or panic button hidden behind the counter. No, Officer Turkowski simply got hungry and decided to grab a couple of doughnuts and maybe a few Twinkies to keep him going for the next hour or so. He could have grabbed a burrito from the Taco Bell on Jackson Avenue, but he was just around the corner from the twenty-four-hour grocery store, and decided that he wanted something sweet.

Turkowski was a young officer who had been with the NYPD for two and a half years. He'd only started doing biweekly solo patrols in the past two months.

He stepped out of his Crown Vic, and for once, closed the driver's door without slamming it.

Inside the shop, the terrified cashier had finished placing all the cash from the register into a paper bag, and was about to hand it over to his assailant when he saw the young police officer appear at the shop's door.

Turkowski saw the kid with the Beretta a second before the kid saw him. There was no time to call for backup. Hard-core police training kicked in, and in a flash he had unholstered his gun and had it aimed at the kid in a two-hand grip.

"Drop it," he called out, his voice steadier than he expected.

The kid had already forgotten everything about the money and the clerk. His only concern now was the cop with the gun. He swung his body around, and in a split second he had his Beretta aimed at Turkowski's chest.

"Fuck that, cop. You drop it," the kid said, holding his gun sideways in a one-hand grip—street-gangster style, obviously emulating what he'd seen of thugs on TV.

The kid was nervous, but he was no first timer. In an agile motion, as he pivoted his body to face the police officer, he had taken a step back and strategically positioned himself with his back to the front of the shop. He now had the store clerk slightly to his left, the police officer slightly to his right, and the shop aisles directly in front of him, giving him the best overall viewpoint of the entire scene.

Hiding in the aisle, Taylor had the kid's inverse viewpoint. The kid stood nearly directly in front of her.

"I said drop it," Turkowski repeated, easing himself one step to his right. "Put your weapon on the ground, take a step forward, and kneel down with your hands behind your head."

Still crouching, Taylor silently moved up the aisle toward the men. No one had noticed her yet. From her position, she got a better look at the entire scene, especially the perpetrator. The kid's eyes were wild with a mixture of adrenaline, anxiety, and drugs. His posture was rigid but fearless, as if he had everything under total control. Turkowski, on the other hand, seemed edgier.

"Fuck you, cop," the kid said, using his left hand to pull the red-and-black bandana down from his nose and mouth, allowing it to hang loosely around his neck, revealing his face.

Taylor knew that was a bad sign. By revealing his face, he showed he had nothing to lose. He planned on doing whatever it took to be the last one standing in their confrontation—no witnesses. Taylor had to act before the whole situation got out of control.

Too late.

As Taylor leaped to her feet, the entire scene seemed to play in slow motion, like a film on a big screen. The kid still hadn't noticed her, but he gave Officer Turkowski no chance . . . no warning. He squeezed the trigger on his Beretta 92 three times in quick succession.

The first bullet hit Turkowski in his right shoulder, rupturing tendons, shattering bone, and blowing a red mist of blood into the air. The second and third hit him square in the chest, directly over his heart, destroying the organ's left and right atria. Turkowski was dead before he hit the ground.

Despite the mess and the blood, the kid didn't panic. He swung quickly on the balls of his feet to face the store clerk, grabbed the bag with the cash, and raised his gun again. Since he'd already killed a cop, why leave a witness?

Taylor read that resolve in the kid's crazed eyes. She knew what was coming, and before he could turn the nightmare into a reality, she had stepped away from her cover and into clear view, her Glock 22 firmly aimed right at his back.

Through the corner of his eye, the kid caught a glimpse of movement coming from his right. He spun instinctively, his finger already starting to apply pressure to the trigger.

Taylor had no time to shout out a warning, but she also knew that it would make no difference. The kid wouldn't have responded. He would've shot her with the same determination with which he had shot the police officer.

Taylor squeezed her trigger only once.

The .40 Smith & Wesson bullet was intended to just wound, to incapacitate the kid by hitting him in the upper arm or shoulder. But the shot had been hurried and the target was in mid-movement. The bullet hit him higher than intended, a few inches to the right. The thief fell back, a chunk of his throat splattering onto the wall behind him.

It took him three and a half minutes to bleed out. It took the ambulance ten minutes to get to the store.

He was only eighteen years old.

49

Taylor wasn't prepared to go through any of what had happened that night all those years ago with Lucien, but she knew that if she answered truthfully he would pick at that wound until it bled. Expertly controlling any reactions that could give her away, she gave him her answer.

"No."

Lucien was observing Taylor closely, but this time her poker face seemed to work.

"Robert?" Lucien refocused his inquiry. "Don't lie to me now."

Once again, Hunter had the feeling that Lucien already knew the answer.

"Yes," he said. "Unfortunately, I've killed people in the line of duty."

"How many?"

Hunter didn't have to think about it. "I've shot and killed six people."

Lucien savored those words for an instant. "And you weren't overcome by a feeling of tremendous power? Not even once?"

"No, I wasn't." Hunter didn't hesitate. "If I could have avoided it, I would've."

For several seconds they exchanged a fierce stare, as if their eyes were fighting their own private tug-of-war.

"Susan's remains, Lucien," Hunter finally asked, once more. "Where are they?"

"Very well," Lucien agreed, breaking eye contact. He breathed in deeply. "As I said before, Robert, the place I used in La Honda is still there. Once the magic of the moment had worn off that night and I stopped shaking from the adrenaline rush, I knew I had to dispose of the body. That was just another reason why I chose that place—it was surrounded by woods." A careless shrug.

He started pacing again, his hands behind his back.

"So I dug for the rest of the night, all the way until morning. Ended up with a four, maybe five-foot-deep grave. I had already bought bags and bags of ground coffee to hide the scent and a few bottles of mountain lion urine, to scare off lesser predators.

"So I dumped her in and covered it all with some leaves and sticks. It's never been disturbed, by man or animal."

"Where is this house?" Hunter asked.

Lucien smiled and spent the next two minutes giving Hunter and Taylor specific instructions on how to get to it from Sears Ranch Road.

Standing directly in front of Hunter, Lucien paused. "Will you tell them everything? Will you tell them the truth about what I did?"

Hunter knew Lucien was talking about Susan's parents again.

"Yes."

"Hmmm . . . I wonder how they'll feel. What will their reaction be?"

"What do you care?" Taylor said evenly. "At least they'll now have closure. They'll be able to bury their daughter's remains with dignity, and rest assured that the monster who took her away from them will be locked up for the rest of his natural life."

"Oh no, I wasn't talking about that, Agent Taylor." Lucien licked his lips. "I meant . . . I wonder how they'll feel when they find out that they *ate* their own daughter."

50

Kennedy had decided to cancel all his appointments back in Washington and stay at Quantico, at least for another day or so. In all his years with the bureau, no suspect had intrigued him as much as Lucien Folter did.

He'd ordered a check on Susan Richards's parents late last night. Her father was now seventy-one and her mother sixty-nine, both retired. They were still living in the same old house in Boulder City, Nevada, and they were still calling the police departments in Palo Alto and Santa Clara County at least monthly asking for any news on their beloved daughter's case.

Kennedy and Dr. Lambert had been following all the interviews through the monitors in the holding cells' control room to near obsession. Every once in a while one of them would make a brief comment on something Lucien said, but mostly, they watched in rapt silence. As soon as Kennedy heard Lucien's directions to Susan's grave behind the house in La Honda, he reached for the phone on the desk in front of him.

Within seconds Kennedy was speaking to the special agent in charge of their field office in San Francisco.

Agent Bradley Simmons was a soft-spoken man who had been with the FBI for twenty years, nine of them with the San Francisco office. He still had a strong south Texas accent.

"Get in touch with the La Honda Police Department and County Sheriff's office *only* if you need to, you understand?" Kennedy said, once Agent Simmons had taken everything down. "This is *exclusively* an FBI operation. From what we understand, the location is isolated. It's by woods, no neighbors, no one around. Get onto it now, and get back to me the second you find anything."

Kennedy hung up and returned his attention to the monitors and the interview just in time to hear Lucien's last comment. His body tensed in apprehension.

"Did he just say that they *ate* their own daughter?"

Dr. Lambert sat before one of the monitors with a similarly shocked look on his face. He wanted to play back the recording in hopes he'd misheard, but he knew he didn't need to. Without diverting his attention from the screen, he nodded.

At that moment, there was a knock on the door to the control room. Chris Welch, a technician from Behavioral Analysis Unit 4, didn't wait for a reply, pushing the door open.

"Director Kennedy," the blond in his early forties greeted Kennedy as he stepped into the room. "Sorry to disturb you, sir. You asked me to notify you immediately if we came across anything that seemed relevant here." He nodded at the brown-and-black marbled notebook that had been retrieved from Lucien's house in Murphy for the BAU4 to scrutinize.

"I thought you'd like to have a look at this." Welch flipped open the notebook and handed it to Kennedy.

Kennedy's eyes scanned several pages before he let out a heavy breath.

"Jesus!"

51

Even with the ventilation system at full power, Hunter felt the beads of sweat that had formed on the nape of his neck slowly start to trickle down his back.

"*They what?*" he asked, his voice puncturing the shocked silence.

Lucien had turned to face the cell's back wall.

"Yes, you heard right, Robert," he said. "Susan's parents ate her . . ." He cocked his head to one side almost playfully. "I mean . . . not all of her, of course, just a few diced-up organs."

"How?" Hunter asked. "By then they'd already traveled back to Nevada after her graduation."

"Yes, I know," Lucien said. "I visited them."

"You did what?" Taylor this time.

Lucien faced them. "I visited them two days after that night. I was thoughtful enough to bring them a gift with . . . a casserole I baked myself."

Something pirouetted inside Taylor's stomach.

"A trip from Stanford to Boulder City in Nevada doesn't take that long," Lucien said to Taylor. "Susan had introduced us to them . . . Robert and I that is, a year or two before. We met them again after the graduation ceremony.

"They were a sweet couple," Lucien proceeded. "Susan was a sweet girl. I decided it was the right thing to do in the end."

"The right thing to do?" Taylor had been knocked off balance so hard that she couldn't contain herself. "How could that be the *right* thing to do?"

"You're the investigator in this case, Agent Taylor. You tell me," Lucien said. "Let me give you a pop quiz. Let's say this was a completely different investigation. Let's say that you didn't have me in custody. Let's say that you had a case where you found out that the Unknown Subject had fed some of his victim's organs to her family. What would your conclusion as to motive be, Agent Taylor? I'm interested to know."

Play his game. Let him believe he's winning. Hunter's words came back to Taylor. She knew that what Lucien wanted was to get under her skin, to shake her confidence. She now understood that every time she lost her temper, Lucien felt like he'd won another battle. *Give him what he wants.*

"Because you're a deranged psychopath?" she said with anger in her eyes, acting as convincingly as she could. "Because to you it sounded like something fun to do? Because it fed your God complex?"

Lucien crossed his arms over his chest and looked at Taylor, intrigued.

Sarcasm dripped from his words. "Spoken like a true professional. You know, I have always found that there's nothing as entertaining as seeing people feed off their emotions. The problem is, they cloud judgment and open the door to a world of mistakes. I learned that a long time ago. I'm surprised you haven't."

He bought it.

As if he didn't have a care in the world, Lucien pulled his sleeve up and again looked at his watchless wrist.

"Wow, time flies when you're having fun, doesn't it? And I guess you two have a lot of work to do now, don't you? You know . . . bones to dig up, explanations to make, stories to tell."

Leisurely, Lucien lay down on the bed and interlaced his fingers behind his head.

"Give Susan's parents my best for me, will you, Robert? Oh, and by the way, if you're wondering . . . yes, I did sit down and share dinner with them that night, followed by a lovely dessert."

52

Hunter's fist connected with the punching bag with so much force that it sent it swinging backward almost two feet. He'd been hitting one of the hundred-pound leather bags that hung from the ceiling in the BRIU building's boxing gym for just a little under an hour. His shirt and shorts were drenched in sweat, which poured down from his forehead. His whole body ached from the grueling workout. But he needed some time to think, to try to organize the thoughts inside his head, to disconnect, even if only for a few minutes, and for Hunter, heavy exercise did the trick more times than not.

Today was not one of those times. He felt mentally exhausted, and frustration ran through his body like bad blood. No matter how hard Hunter punched that bag or how much weight he lifted, he just couldn't seem to get rid of it.

"If I were thirty years younger, I'd spot you with that punching bag," Kennedy said, appearing at the door to the gym, deserted, except for Hunter. "But even so, the way you're hitting that thing, you'd probably put me through the wall. I'm surprised your hand isn't broken yet."

The long day and a full pack of cigarettes made Kennedy's hoarse voice sound even more so than usual.

Hunter delivered one final series of heavy punches to the bag—jab, jab, cross, left hook, cross. The bag swung erratically, as if it had had enough and finally been defeated, before Hunter embraced it into a stop. Panting, he rested his head against the bag for a moment, waiting for his breathing to slowly return to normal. Sweat dripped from his chin onto his shoes and the floor.

Kennedy stepped closer.

"Any news from La Honda?" Hunter asked at last, his head still down. He still hadn't released the bag.

Kennedy nodded with little enthusiasm, and then, realizing that Hunter couldn't see him, said simply, "Yes."

Hunter straightened.

Kennedy threw Hunter a towel. "The agents followed Lucien's instructions to the location and began digging. They dug for an hour." He handed Hunter a legal-size envelope. "And this is what they found."

Hunter quickly dried his face and hands before retrieving two printed photographs. As his eyes devoured the images, his heartbeat picked up speed once again.

The first photograph showed a full human skeleton, its bones old and discolored with time, lying inside a five-foot-deep grave.

The second was a close-up snapshot of the skull.

Hunter stared at the pictures in silence for several seconds, dwelling on the second one, as if he were attempting to mentally reconstruct Susan's face over her yellowed bones.

Kennedy took a step back, giving Hunter a moment

before he spoke again. "Since we already know that Lucien is a serial offender, protocol dictates that we now dig
up the entire site," Kennedy said. "Looking for possible
remains of other bodies will be a huge operation, and
there's no way of doing that without getting the local
authorities involved and bringing a Hollywood-sized
spotlight to this case."

"I'd wait a while, Adrian," Hunter said. He'd never
been a big fan of protocol, and especially not in this
case. "At least until we're finished interviewing him. So
far Lucien has been straight with us. If there are other
bodies buried around that same area, I have a feeling he
will tell us. Bringing media attention to this investigation right now won't benefit anyone."

Kennedy usually played by the book, but he was
inclined to agree with Hunter.

"It will take at least a couple of days for forensics to
confirm that what we've got really is Susan Richards's
skeleton," Kennedy said.

"It will be," Hunter replied, returning the printouts
to the envelope before he clarified further. "Lucien had
no reason to lie. We already know he killed Susan. He
told us that, and the framed tattooed skin in his basement confirmed it. If he had disposed of Susan's body in
a way that no remains could be found, he would've just
told us so." He jabbed a finger at the envelope. "If those
were the remains of someone else he killed, there would
be no point in telling us it was Susan's body either, because he knows we will be testing it anyway."

"I understand, but just to be on the safe side, I think
you'd better wait for official confirmation before contacting her parents."

Hunter nodded slowly before using the towel on his face and arms once more. Bringing the news to Susan's parents was one job he wasn't looking forward to. "I've got to take a shower."

"Come up to my office when you're done," Kennedy said. "There's something else I need to show you."

53

Twenty minutes later, his hair still wet from his shower, Hunter was back inside Director Kennedy's office. Special Agent Taylor was also there. Her blond hair was loose and wavy, falling naturally over her shoulders. She wore a dark pencil skirt with a blue blouse tucked in, black nylon stockings, and black strappy court shoes. Sitting in one of the armchairs in front of Kennedy's desk, she held the same photographs Hunter had looked at down in the gym, the ones of Susan Richards's remains.

Kennedy stood behind his desk.

"You still drink Scotch?" he asked Hunter.

Single-malt Scotch whiskey was Hunter's biggest passion. He knew how to appreciate its complexity. Though, sometimes just getting drunk worked fine.

Hunter nodded.

Kennedy walked over to the cabinet to his left, opened it, and retrieved three whiskey tumblers and a bottle of twenty-five-year-old Tomatin. He poured each of them a healthy dose, added a splash of water, and handed a glass to Hunter and one to Taylor.

"I need to ask you something, Robert," Kennedy said in a more serious tone.

Hunter sipped his Scotch and waited.

"Do you think Lucien was lying about the cannibalism?" Kennedy asked. "That's something that we have no way of proving."

"I can't see what he would achieve by lying about that," Hunter replied.

"Maybe he was going for the shock effect, Robert, and a little fame," Kennedy said.

Hunter shook his head. "Not Lucien. He doesn't want notoriety. At least not yet. As sickening as it sounds, I don't think he's lying . . . about eating some of Susan's flesh . . . or about feeding it to her parents."

Kennedy paused, doubt reflected in his eyes. "I've seen and heard a lot in my life, but what kind of evil mind drives anyone to do such a thing?"

Taylor looked at Hunter curiously.

He shrugged and looked away.

"I've read studies, interviews, books, papers, theses . . . you name it, about cannibal killers, serial or not," Kennedy added. "God knows we've had many of them down in those same cells over the years. And I understand that a good number of them believe that they do it because to them their victims are special, and the act of eating them solidifies their bond with their victims. That whole idea that if they eat even a small part of them, the victims will stay with them forever. I guess everyone deludes themselves in their own way. But feeding it to others . . . ?"

Hunter said nothing.

Kennedy pushed further.

"If you have anything that could throw any sort of light on the *why*s of this madness, Robert, please humor me, because I can't figure it out. Why did he feed her to her parents?"

Hunter sipped his drink again and leaned against the bookcase. "I think he did it because he felt guilty."

54

Kennedy's doubtful look bounced between Hunter and Taylor. Taylor didn't look at all surprised.

"Could you please elaborate, Robert," the director asked. "Because to me, feeding someone to her own parents doesn't quite sound like the actions of a person stricken by remorse."

"If Lucien is being truthful about Susan being his first victim," Hunter said, "and right now we have no reason to doubt that, then, as you know, guilt and remorse are the first two most common emotions that usually torment a first-time killer."

Kennedy and Taylor were both well aware of the studies Hunter alluded to. According to the FBI's Behavioral Research and Instruction Unit, *serial murder* is defined as a series of three or more killings, committed on three or more separate occasions, with a cooling-off period between murders. These murders must also have common characteristics such as to suggest the reasonable possibility that the crimes had been committed by the same person or persons.

That cooling-off period, especially between the initial killings of a series, was almost always due to the perpetrator or perpetrators experiencing intense, albeit temporary, feelings of regret.

Aggressors who eventually become serial murderers struggle with murderous urges, destructive impulses, and even rage attacks for a long time, sometimes years, finding them harder and harder to resist until the urges finally win the battle, just as in Lucien's case. The simple fact that they *struggle* clearly indicates that these subjects know that killing another human being is wrong. Guilty feelings are simply logical psychological responses to stepping outside the bounds of socially sanctioned behavior.

Most mentally healthy people can easily understand why. Most of us usually experience some level of guilt if we do something we know to be wrong—cheat on an exam, steal the paper from the neighbor's porch, tell a lie, or whatever. That sense of guilt is directly proportional to how wrong one believes one's actions are—the worse the actions, the bigger the guilt trips.

And for an ostensibly "sane" man like Lucien, bad actions don't come much worse than murder.

"Okay, I agree that Lucien must've struggled with different stages of guilt in the aftermath of murdering Susan," Kennedy admitted. "But I still can see no reason why, overwhelmed by guilt or not, he would've fed parts of her body to her own parents, Robert."

"I can see two *possible* reasons," Hunter said, with a hand gesture. "The first one you mentioned just a moment ago."

Kennedy's eyes squinted a fraction. "And what was that?"

"Believing that by consuming the flesh of their victims, the victims will then stay with them forever. They will become *part* of them," Taylor said in a half whisper. "Or whoever eats them." She allowed Kennedy a few seconds to reanalyze that statement.

Kennedy caught on quickly. "Jesus! Third-party transference." He looked at Hunter for confirmation, but proceeded anyway. "So Lucien believed that if *her parents* consumed some of her flesh, then Susan would stay with *them* forever?"

"As Lucien said," Taylor commented, "she was never supposed to be a victim, and he also thought that her parents were nice people. So Robert could be right. He might've done it because he felt guilty he'd taken their daughter away from them."

Kennedy considered that for a silent moment.

"And the second possibility?" he finally asked.

"The second reason links to the first," Hunter said. "Lucien told us that he used to hunt with his father, right?"

"Yes, I remember that," Kennedy said impatiently.

"He also said that his father was a great hunter."

"Yes, I remember that too."

"Okay; many hunters inherit a belief that's been passed down through generations and generations of Native Americans," Hunter explained.

Kennedy's eyebrows arched curiously.

"Native Americans never hunted for fun or sport. They hunted exclusively for food, and they believed that they must eat whatever they killed, always, because to eat their prey was to honor them. They believed that it kept their spirit alive in this world. It showed respect. To let their flesh go to waste, that would be a dishonor."

Kennedy didn't know that, but his memory flashed back to Susan Richards's file sitting on his desk. Her mother was second-generation Shoshone, a Native American tribe, mostly from the area that became the state of Nevada. Her family name was Tuari, which meant *young eagle*.

Taylor looked at Hunter, intrigued.

"I read a lot," Hunter offered before she was able to ask the question.

"So you think that, in his mind at least, Lucien was redeeming himself, even if only a little bit," Kennedy stated rather than asked. "He was being compassionate, even without their knowledge."

"Everyone deludes themselves in their own way," Hunter repeated Kennedy's words. "We can theorize as much as we like here, Adrian, but the only one who really knows what was going on inside his head is Lucien himself."

"So in that case, let me ask you this," Kennedy said. "Why do you think he took part? Lucien said that he sat down to have dinner with them that night."

"Because Lucien was experimenting."

Kennedy pinched the bridge of his nose as if he could feel an oncoming headache.

"In college Lucien didn't exactly doubt any of the theories behind these sadistic acts," he said. "He knew they were based on true accounts from apprehended offenders, but he was on the verge of becoming obsessed with the *feelings and emotions* described by such offenders."

Kennedy remembered something Lucien had said during one of the interviews. "He wanted to experience them for himself."

"Back then, he never said so in so many words," Hunter agreed. "But now we know that that was exactly what he wanted, to experiment. And that's what makes Lucien so different from most psychopaths I've ever come up against.

"We know that he killed Susan, his first victim, by strangulation," Hunter elaborated. "But if we compare her murder with his latest ones, the two victims in his trunk . . . the MO, the level of violence, everything has skyrocketed. I'm willing to bet that the violence in the murders he committed between the first and those last moved up a step at a time. But Lucien escalates not because he's being guided by uncontrollable urges inside him."

"He does it consciously," Taylor said, picking up Hunter's thread of thought. "He does it because he wants to know how it feels as he becomes more and more violent."

"That's a frightening thought," Kennedy said. "The level of determination and self-discipline one needs to keep escalating murder after murder for twenty-five years is mind-boggling. And you think he did it just so he could experience the feelings?"

Hunter had paused, his memory reaching for something long forgotten. "I'll be damned!" he finally exclaimed.

"What?" Kennedy asked.

"I can't believe he's really doing it," Hunter murmured.

"Doing what?"

"I think Lucien might've been writing an encyclopedia."

55

I remember a discussion we had once," Hunter said. "I think it was during our junior year. We were talking about emotional triggers and drives in extreme, violent murders—what psychological factors could cause an individual to brutally offend and reoffend."

"Okay," Kennedy said, intrigued.

"Bear in mind that notorious cannibal killers like Jeffrey Dahmer, Armin Meiwes, and Andrei Chikatilo hadn't been caught yet. Their interviews weren't on file."

Kennedy and Taylor both nodded together.

"As I've said," Hunter moved on, "Lucien didn't doubt the veracity of the accounts we had then, but he wasn't quite convinced by many of the theoretical rationales. He was obsessed with asking how they can know for sure."

"No one can," Taylor said. "Academic discourse operates on theoretical assumption, and without those testimonies—"

"Precisely," Hunter agreed. "And Lucien understood that."

"But he wasn't satisfied," Kennedy concluded.

"No, he wasn't. And that day he suggested something so far-fetched, I basically ignored it."

"And that was?"

Hunter took a deep breath while trying to remember the details.

"The crazy possibility of someone becoming a killer for an altruistic purpose," he finally said. "Lucien argued how groundbreaking it would be for criminal-behavior psychology if a fully mentally capable individual went on a killing rampage, escalating his or her way through different levels of violence, and experimenting with different methods and fantasies, while at the same time taking comprehensive notes of everything, including feelings and psychological states of mind at the time and in the aftermath of each murder. Some sort of in-depth psychological study of the mind of a killer, written by the killer himself . . . by choice.

"He believed that a notebook, or even a series of notebooks, filled with such true accounts would become an encyclopedia of knowledge, a bible of sorts to criminal-behavioral scientists."

As extreme as it sounds, Kennedy thought, *Lucien was right. Such a book would become one of the most-referred-to books by criminologists, psychologists, and law enforcement agents around the world.*

"I think that might be what he was doing," Hunter said, his thoughts beginning to turn his stomach. "Jumping from murder to murder, escalating the violence with each one, trying different things, different methods . . . and keeping a diary of how he felt, especially emotionally. In his mind, that would give him the excuse he wanted."

Kennedy's forehead creased as he looked at Hunter. "Excuse?"

"Lucien is a sociopath, no doubt about that—we know it and he knows it. The difference is: he's known it for a long time. He told us that, remember?"

Taylor nodded. "He started fantasizing while still in school."

"That's right, and I think that that knowledge hurt him. A regular kid shouldn't be fantasizing about killing people. Maybe it made him feel like something inside his brain was broken, that he didn't belong. He even told us that the reason why he decided to study criminal-behavior psychology was to understand himself."

"But that backfired," Kennedy said.

"No, it didn't," Hunter replied. "If anything, it pushed his imagination further. It made him come up with what to him sounded like a plausible motive."

"What better excuse to commit atrocious acts of violence than to fool yourself into believing that you're doing it for a noble cause," Taylor said, following Hunter's line of thought. "All in the name of research?"

"That false belief would've eased his internal pain," Hunter added. "Lucien could then start feeding his hunger because in his mind, he wasn't a sociopath anymore . . . He was a scientist, a researcher. Everyone deludes themselves in their own way, remember?"

Kennedy broke eye contact.

"Is there something else?" Hunter asked. "Something you're not telling us?"

Kennedy pursed his lips in reply. He walked to his desk, opened the top right-hand drawer, and pulled out a notebook. It was the same notebook Special Agent Chris Welch had handed him in the holding cells' control room earlier.

Hunter immediately recognized the notebook as one of the several he and Special Agent Taylor had seen in Lucien's basement.

"You might be all too right, Robert," Kennedy said. "Because we found this."

56

Hunter felt a wave of dread overtake him, one he'd unconsciously feared since the investigation's inception. He took the notebook from Kennedy's hands and flipped open its cover.

Taylor moved closer to see the document herself, but Kennedy handed her a folder containing photocopies of the first several pages of Lucien's notebook.

The first page pictured a crude black-and-white pencil sketch of a female face screaming, contorted in agony.

Hunter's eyes found Kennedy's, posing a silent question.

The BRIU director shook his head defeatedly, and gestured for Hunter to carry on.

Hunter turned the page, and immediately recognized Lucien's handwriting.

He began reading.

I guess my head is starting to change. At first, after every kill, I was overwhelmed by intense feelings of guilt, as I expected I would be. Some-

*times for months. I came close to turning myself
in many times. Many times I promised myself I'd
never do it again. But as time went by and the
guilty feelings began to lessen, slowly and steadily,
the desire to do it all again would come back. I
wanted it to come back. With every victim, my
guilt phase grew shorter and shorter, to the point
that they are now almost nonexistent—a couple
of days long, if that. There's no doubt that my
mind has adapted. Murder has become something that feels natural to me now. When I'm
out, I often look around and as my eyes settle on
someone in a bar, on a train, on the streets . . .
wherever I am, I find myself thinking of how
easily I could kill them. How much I could make
them scream. How much pain I could inflict before I actually give in. And those thoughts excite
me more than ever.*

*Getting rid of these thoughts has become harder
and harder, but the truth is, I don't want to get rid
of them. I now understand that killing can indeed
become a very powerful drug. More powerful than
any drug I've ever tried. And I am completely
hooked. But despite my addiction, one thing I've
learned is that I need some sort of trigger to finally
push me over the edge.*

*That trigger can be anything—a certain phys-
ical type that matches a specific look, the way
someone talks or looks at me, the way someone
dresses, the scent they're wearing, an action they
take, a mannerism they have . . . anything. It's*

not the same every time. I don't know it until I see it.

I saw it again last night.

It was late. I had just ordered my third double Scotch. I wasn't looking for anything or anyone. I just felt like getting drunk, that's all. Actually, I felt like getting obliterated. It was by chance that I found myself in Forest, Mississippi. I hadn't booked into a motel or anything. I figured I'd just get hammered, pass out in my car outside in the parking lot, wake up sometime the next day, and be on my way.

But things didn't happen that way.

I was sitting at the far end of the bar, keeping to myself. It was a slow night with not many customers. The bartender tried to be friendly and start a conversation, but I was curt enough that he quickly got the hint.

As the bartender poured me my next drink, a new face walked into the bar. He was big, a lot bigger than me—a mixture of muscle and greasy fat. He was taller too, by at least three to four inches. The bartender called him Jed.

Jed's hair was cut so short I wondered why he didn't just shave it all off. He had a jagged half-moon scar on the underside of his chin, clearly the result of someone taking the rear end of a broken bottle to his face. His nose had also been broken more than once, and his right ear looked a little out of shape, as if it'd been smashed against his skull. It didn't take someone with a lot of brain-

power to know that Jed liked to get himself into fights.

He took a seat at the bar, four stools to my left, and as he did, two other customers who were at the tables behind us got up and left.

Jed didn't seem very popular, and even from where I was sitting, he stank of cheap booze and stale sweat.

"Gimme a fucking beer, Tom," he called, his voice dragging a little. His pupils were the size of dinner plates, so he was definitely loaded on something heavier than just alcohol.

"C'mon, Jed," the bartender hesitated, keeping his voice even. "It's late, and you've certainly had enough for one night."

Jed's bulldog brow creased even further.

"Don't fucking tell me I've had enough, Tom."

His voice grew louder by a few decibels, and another customer sneaked out the door.

"I'll tell you when I've had enough. Now gimme a fucking beer before I shove one up your pussy little ass."

Tom grabbed a bottle of beer from the fridge, unscrewed its top, and placed it on the bar in front of Jed.

Jed took it and swallowed half of it down in three large gulps.

I didn't realize I was staring until Jed turned to me.

"What the fuck are you looking at?" he said, pushing his beer bottle to one side. "Are you some kind of fag?"

I didn't answer him, and still didn't look away.

"I asked you a question, fag."

Jed took another swig of his beer.

"You like what you see, fag?" He lifted his right arm and flexed his bicep like a bodybuilder before blowing me a kiss.

I was hypnotized by that sack of shit that called himself Jed.

"C'mon, Jed," the bartender tried to intervene, clearly foreseeing what was to come. "Let it go, man. The guy is just trying to have a quiet drink."

Tom looked at me with a face that said, Dude, please just go. You don't want this trouble, trust me.

I didn't move. I probably wasn't even blinking.

"Shut the fuck up, Tom," Jed said, pointing a finger at him, but looking at me. "I want to know why this fag likes looking at me so much. Do you want to fuck a real man tonight? Is that it, fag? Would you like a piece of this?" Jed used both hands to point to his massive gut.

My eyes slowly ran the length of his body, and that seemed to piss him off way past his limit. His jaw locked in anger. His face became even redder, and he stood up from his stool threateningly.

And that was it.

That was the trigger.

It wasn't his obnoxious way, or his smell, or the name-calling, or the fact that he was so damn ugly he probably had to sneak up on his mirror. It wasn't even that he didn't allow me to get drunk in peace.

It was the fact that he thought he could assert his superiority over me that did it. That pushed me over the edge.

Right there and then, I knew Jed would die that night.

57

Hunter stopped reading and looked at Kennedy.

Even though he was looking at the words upside down, Kennedy had been following Hunter's eyes and knew exactly where he'd paused.

"Read on," he said. "There's a twist."

I didn't face up to Jed. Not there. I wasn't about to get into a fistfight with him in a public place.

I placed thirty dollars on the bar to cover my drinks, got up, and took a couple of steps back.

"What's the problem, fag? Too scared?"

Tom quickly jumped in, putting himself between Jed and me.

"C'mon, Jed, there's no problem here. The guy didn't say anything, and he was just leaving, right?"

Tom twisted his neck to look at me, his eyes begging me not to engage.

I finally snapped out of my trance and began walking away.

"That's right, fag, get your pussy ass out of here before I fuck you up."

I opened the door and stepped outside into the warm and damp night.

I drove to the other side of the road and parked in a dark spot, next to a rusty Dumpster. From there I had a clear view of the bar's entrance.

I waited.

Jed walked out the door forty-six minutes later and staggered over to a battered Ford pickup truck. It took him almost a minute to manage to slot his key into the keyhole and open the door. He didn't drive off straightaway either. For a moment I thought that he would fall asleep in the truck, but he didn't. He lit up a spliff and smoked the whole damn thing before he turned on his engine.

I followed him, keeping my distance. But Jed's senses were so mushed, he wouldn't have noticed a pink elephant in a golden tutu following him.

Jed's driving was all over the place, and what scared me the most was the possibility of him being stopped by a cop. If that had happened, Jed would've spent the night in a cell for driving under the influence, and I would've had to walk away from my plans. Unfortunately, for Jed, Forest in Scott County, Mississippi, seemed deserted of cops that evening.

Jed lived just outside town, in a single-story, dirty, old, and faded-blue wooden house by the side of the road. There was no garage, and the driveway was nothing but dirt and gravel, flanked by shrubs and overgrown grass. He parked his truck by the rusty metal fence that circled the property, and smoked another spliff before finally wobbling his way into the house.

I parked down the block, waited twenty minutes, and very quietly crossed over to the house. The front door was locked, but it didn't take me long to find an open window. I knew there'd be one. With no air-conditioning in sight, the Mississippi night was too hot and stuffy for any alternative.

The inside of the house smelled of grease, fried onions, stale cigarettes, and dry rot. The place was filthy and an absolute mess, but after meeting Jed, I expected nothing less.

I tiptoed my way deeper through the dark. Finding the bedroom was easy. All I had to do was follow the snores, and Jed snored like a dinosaur in heat. But I didn't want to kill him in his bed. That would've been too easy.

I felt my blood bubbling inside my veins with excitement as my heart changed rhythm. My adrenal glands caught up to the new beat and began pumping at full throttle, while my mouth salivated like a hungry dog in a butcher shop. I wanted to prolong that feeling for as long as I could. Nothing is more exciting than hiding inside the victim's house and waiting for the right moment.

I chose a sharp knife from his kitchen. Thankfully there was a good selection to choose from. I knew that a fat greaseball like Jed would no doubt get up in the middle of the night and either hit the kitchen for some more food, or the bathroom to go piss a gallon. With that much booze inside him, the bathroom was a safer option. I hid behind the shower curtain where he wouldn't see me until it was too late.

I covered my shoes with plastic bags that I'd also found in the kitchen, carefully pulled the shower curtain back, climbed into his soiled bathtub, leaned back against the tiled wall, and waited. I can stay still for hours if I have to.

The waiting made my whole body tingle as if I were soaked in an Alka-Seltzer bath, high on my power.

Jed finally came into the bathroom ninety-four minutes later, dragging his feet.

I took a deep breath to keep myself from going for him too early. I had carved a small slit in the plastic curtain so I could see out. Looking lost, Jed paused once he entered the bathroom.

And then the right moment came.

58

Hunter and Taylor couldn't tear themselves away from the pages in Lucien's notebook.

Jed stretched his huge arms high above his head. He yawned, and even from behind the curtain I could smell his putrid breath. His eyes were bloodshot from a combination of the weed he'd smoked earlier, alcohol, and the heavy sleep he'd just woken up from. He was wearing nothing but a pair of filthy boxer shorts. He was so pathetic, it almost made me laugh.

For an instant it looked to me as if his eyes tried to focus on the shower curtain. Maybe he noticed the tear I'd created, I'll never know, but that was my cue.

I was so wired from adrenaline that I must've moved twice as fast as normal. He never saw me coming.

With my left hand, I pulled the shower curtain to one side, while throwing my body forward. My right hand and the knife created a high arc from right to left.

The blade hit Jed exactly where I wanted it to—across his neck and throat. The combination of the blade's sharpness and the strength of my movement would've proved lethal to anyone. The knife cut through skin and muscle as if they were made of rice paper. From the amount of arterial spray that hit my face and the curtain and wall behind me, I knew I had sliced through both of Jed's internal jugular veins, and ruptured his upper airway. His eyes settled on me for a brief moment, but I'm not sure he recognized me.

I didn't care if he knew or not because I was overcome with ecstasy. I grabbed the back of Jed's head with my left hand and pulled it back hard, exposing the fatal wound further. I enjoyed watching the blood squirt out of his neck, cascade down his body, and froth in his mouth. A muffled gurgling sound was all his vocal cords could produce. I held him in that position until his crazed eyes went still. Until the gurgling sound was gone. Until his body became nothing but deadweight.

After Jed fell to the ground, I stayed in the bathroom for another seven minutes, still high on all the adrenaline, endorphins, and serotonin that my brain had thrown at me. I felt no guilt. No remorse.

I washed my face and hands. I would burn my clothes as soon as I left the house.

It was time to move on.

But fate is a funny thing, and as I walked down the short corridor and past Jed's room, something caught my attention and I stopped. The door to the bedroom was wide open, and that was the first time I saw her.

It was hard to believe that a sack of shit like Jed could have a girlfriend. She wasn't his wife. Neither of them wore a wedding ring, but there she was, passed out on the bed. Surprisingly, she wasn't nearly as big or as ugly as Jed was—short dark hair, high cheekbones, delicate lips, and smooth honey-colored skin. She was attractive, very. How she ended up with Jed will always be a mystery to me.

I stood by the door, staring at her asleep in bed. I was still buzzing from cutting Jed's throat. How can an addict, high on his favorite drug, walk away when some more is so freely offered to him?

My body started to tingle again, and I felt the trigger go off inside my head for the second time in the same night. I decided that I wouldn't fight the urges anymore, so I carefully and quietly walked into the room and lay in bed beside her. I could still feel the warmth from where Jed had lain.

I didn't move for twenty-two minutes, watching Jed's girlfriend sleep, waiting, inhaling the scent from her hair, feeling the warmth of her body so close to mine.

Then she moved.

She rolled over and threw her arm over my chest in a sleepy hug, like couples do. Her eyes remained closed. Her hand fell on my shoulder, and I couldn't contain myself. As gently as I could, I took her hand, brought it over to my lips, and began kissing and licking her fingers. They smelled and tasted of hand cream.

I guess she enjoyed the kissing and nibbling, because she moaned quietly and slowly threw her leg over me. As it settled over me, she must've missed Jed's body volume. It took a few seconds for the signals to be decoded by her drowsy brain. Once they were, she frowned even before her eyes opened.

The light in the room wasn't great. All she had to go by was the full moon, now low in the sky outside the open window on the east wall. My face was half-obscured by shadows.

I guess I hadn't washed myself as well as I thought I did, because at that exact moment, a drop of Jed's blood dripped from my hair onto my forehead, ran down over my eyebrow, and onto the white pillowcase.

The woman blinked. A nervous blink, full of fear. She jerked her head back a couple of inches so her eyes could better focus, and as they did, fear froze them in place.

She saw a stranger with his clothes soaked in blood, lying where her boyfriend was supposed to be, staring into her eyes, with two of her fingers stuck in his mouth.

here are the others?" Hunter asked.

"That's the only one," Kennedy answered. "All the other notebooks found in the house in Murphy contained nothing but a few drawings and sketches. Nothing like this."

"But there must be others." Hunter was adamant. "Are you sure they checked through all the books and notebooks they found?"

"Yes. I'm sure," Kennedy confirmed. "Lucien must've kept them somewhere else, or scattered them around several different locations. That wouldn't surprise me, and that's something else you should find out during the course of your interviews."

Hunter's stare hardened, and Kennedy read its emotion clearly.

"Look, Robert, there's no way on earth I approve of what Lucien has done, but if you're right about him writing down everything he's done and experienced in notebooks, then it's already done, and it cannot be *undone*. If these notebooks do indeed exist, then we might as well have them. For one, they'll constitute evidence in a serial murder case that I have no doubt will go down as one of the most serious in history. Two, the psychological and behavioral knowledge . . . the understanding that we'll gain from those notes and texts may prove to be a game changer in our fight against extremely violent repeat offenders. As a law enforcement officer and as a psychologist you know that full well, Robert."

Hunter had no argument to rebut him.

"And there's nothing inside the storage facility in Seattle?" Taylor asked.

"Nothing but the freezer and the body parts," Kennedy confirmed.

"I checked with the Scott County Sheriff's Department in Mississippi," Kennedy moved on. "Jed Davis and his girlfriend, Melanie Rose, were butchered inside the house they shared just outside Forest twenty-one years ago. They were found by her mother, who dropped by with a homemade apple pie about two days after the incident. No one was ever arrested." He paused. "According to the medical examiner, Melanie Rose's head was hacked off with a kitchen knife. The head was left on the dining table in the living room. That was the first thing her mother saw when she looked in through the window." Kennedy looked at Hunter, the expression on his face sober. "He killed her just because she was home, Robert. He killed her for pure pleasure."

Hunter closed his eyes and pressed his lips against each other.

"You read the account," Kennedy added. "It was written the day after he butchered them. The narrative and the words are clear and concise; there's no sign of hysteria or even nervousness. We all know that that spells total emotional detachment. As you've said, his accounts are like a study into what goes on inside the mind of a vicious killer—how he thinks, how he feels, what drives him—prior, during, and after each attack. Call me selfish, Robert, but I want that knowledge. We *need* that knowledge. If those books exist, you need to get them for me."

Hunter walked over to the window and looked outside. Night and clouds had darkened the sky, but the view helped him see things clearer somehow, understand something that until now he hadn't. He cursed himself for not having seen it earlier.

"You will have them, Adrian," he said. "Because Lucien wants you to."

Taylor frowned.

"What do you mean?"

"This was all planned," Hunter said.

Taylor's and Kennedy's confusion intensified.

"What was all planned, Robert?" Taylor asked.

"Being caught." Hunter turned to face them. "Well, maybe the timing wasn't one hundred percent as planned. Maybe Lucien would've liked to carry on murdering for a while longer. He could never have predicted the accident in Wyoming that led us to him, but I think that he was always counting on being caught one day."

Kennedy took just a few seconds to board Hunter's thought ship. "Because what's the point in writing an encyclopedia on killing and behavioral motivation if no one will read it . . . or study it, right?"

Hunter agreed in silence.

Taylor wasn't as convinced. "Yeah, but then why would he want to be caught? He could've arranged for the books to be delivered to the FBI, or he could've sent them in anonymously."

"It wouldn't have had the same effect," Hunter disagreed.

"Robert is right," Kennedy backed him up. "The notebooks on their own wouldn't have had the same weight as catching the perpetrator. It would've taken us a lot longer to follow up on what they contained . . . if we ever did. There would always be doubts as to whether the books were a hoax or not. Having Lucien in custody . . . the interviews, him guiding us to the remains of his victims' bodies . . . it all adds to the whole credibility of the notebooks."

Kennedy paused as a new realization finally hit him. He looked at Hunter. "And that's why he asked for you."

Hunter breathed out and nodded.

"Because *you* add even more credibility to Lucien's character," Kennedy said. "You went to college together. You shared a dorm. You were the best of friends. You know how intelligent he is, and he knew that you could vouch for that." He walked over to the other side of his desk. "I bet he's counting on you to remember the conversation you had about the 'killing encyclopedia' idea. He knew you would remember Susan Richards. You were always a major part of his plan, Robert."

"So now that his credibility is more than established," Taylor cut in, "why not just ask him for the notebooks? If you're right, and the idea from the beginning was for the bureau to get those books, he should be forthcoming with the information."

"No, he won't be," Hunter said. "Not yet."

"And why is that?"

"Because he's not nearly finished with this game."

60

Hunter managed only three and a half erratic hours of sleep. He was up by 5:00 a.m. By 6:30 he'd been for a five-mile run, and at 7:30 he and Taylor were back down in sublevel five.

As he had been the previous day, Lucien was sitting at the edge of his bed, right leg crossed over his left, hands clasped together and resting on his lap, calmly waiting.

Hunter, Taylor, and Kennedy had decided the night before that pushing Lucien to talk about the notebooks now, if they indeed existed, wasn't the best strategy. His victims' remains were still the priority.

"I was wondering if you'd still be here or not, Robert," Lucien said as his interrogators took their seats. "I thought that maybe you'd want to see Susan's remains for yourself. You could've been halfway to Nevada to see her parents by now." He studied Hunter's expression, but got nothing. "You did find her, didn't you?" The question's tone completely lacking in concern.

"We found her," Taylor confirmed.

"Ah, but of course," Lucien said as though he'd just

remembered something. "Tests and more tests. You know that it's her, don't you, Robert?"

No reaction.

"But the FBI won't move a muscle until they have lab confirmation. It's protocol. Contacting her parents without being one hundred percent sure that you have Susan's remains would be careless, and potentially very damaging for both sides. That's understandable."

"Are there any other victims buried in the vicinity of the house in La Honda, Lucien?" Hunter asked.

Lucien smiled. "I did think about it. It's a great location. Hidden from everything. No one to sneak up on you." He shook his head. "But no. Susan was the only one in La Honda. This is a huge country, Robert. Similar places aren't that hard to find. Anyway, after Susan it took me a long time to get my shit together." He cracked the knuckles on his hands against each other. "Murder can be one hell of a dark time."

Hunter wasn't very interested in hearing Lucien's personal accounts of how he felt, and though he knew Lucien would want to stretch every interview as much as he could, he still pushed for the information he wanted.

"Just give us the name and the location of another victim, Lucien."

Lucien carried on as if he hadn't heard the question.

"On the days, weeks, months after Susan, as the adrenaline wore off, I was as sure as I could be that I'd never do it again. But as time went by, the desire to kill again started to creep up on me. And it came back stronger, more demanding. I missed the transcendent high. I missed the feeling of power I had that night with Susan. And I knew that my body as well as my brain was dying to experience it again."

"How long was it?" Taylor asked. "The cooling-off period? How long between Susan Richards and your second victim?"

"Seven hundred and nine days."

Lucien didn't even have to think about the answer. The number was etched in his brain. Every detail about *everything* he'd done was etched in his brain.

"I was already at Yale," he proceeded. "Her name was Karen Simpson."

Hunter frowned.

Lucien looked at him and nodded. "That's right, Robert, Karen was real, with all the tattoos, the lip and nose piercings, the left earlobe stretched to a half inch, the Bettie Page–style bangs . . . I met her at Yale, just like I told you, but I did lie about something. Karen was never a drug addict.

"As I told you before, she was a very sweet woman. She was also getting a PhD in psychology. We used to study together. In fact . . ." Lucien gave them a sly smile, one that said *I know something that you don't.* "Both of you have already made her acquaintance." He gave Hunter and Taylor a challenging look.

"The other framed tattoos down in that basement," Hunter said.

"That's right, Robert," Lucien agreed. "The cranes."

One of the pieces found in Lucien's basement had a colored tattoo of a pair of cranes. The design had been taken from a painting called *Two Cranes on a Snowy Pine*, by the artist Katsushika Hokusai.

"She had it tattooed on her upper right arm," Lucien said. "Now, despite Karen being only my second victim, I decided to get adventurous."

61

As I've said," Lucien continued, "the urges started coming back to me a few months after I left Stanford, but they didn't become unbearable until much later. At first I thought I could deal with them. I thought that they'd be easy to curb, but just like every repeat offender eventually finds out, I was wrong."

Lucien used both of his hands to rub the back of his neck while closing his eyes and tilting his head back. After several silent seconds he exhaled.

"There was a difference this time. As I said before, I had never looked at Susan as a potential victim until the night it all happened. This time, I knew Karen would be the one. I'd known it from the day I met her."

"What guided you toward that decision?" Taylor asked. "What made you choose Karen?"

Lucien made an impressed face. "Very good question, Agent Taylor. Looks like you're learning.

"I guess the first things that guided me toward Karen were her tattoos.

"You've got to remember that large colored tattoos weren't as popular twenty-three years ago as they are now," Lucien said. "Especially on women. They reminded me of Susan." His words were dry as a bone, sucking all the moisture out of the air. "I began having dreams about them. I began fantasizing about skinning those drawings off Karen's body just like I'd done to Susan. And that was when I realized that another theory was proving true.

"My brain kept going back to the same MO I had used with Susan, and we all know the reason why, don't we? Though it had been nowhere near perfect, I knew I'd feel more comfortable going back to an MO that had already worked. Familiarity, that's why repeat offenders rarely change their MO." He pointed to her notebook. "You can write that down if you want."

Lucien got up, poured himself a glass of water from the sink, and returned to the edge of his bed.

"But I decided that I wasn't looking for comfortable. I wasn't looking to do something I'd already done, to re-create the same high. That wasn't part of what I had planned. So I started to think about what I'd do differently. Even before I met Karen I knew I would do it again. There was no doubt in my mind anymore. The desire had become too great for me to resist it. So the search for a new hidden place began."

"Where is she?" Hunter asked.

"Oh, she's still in Connecticut," Lucien confirmed calmly. "Actually, not that far from New Haven and Yale University."

"Where exactly?" Hunter pushed.

More for effect than anything else, Lucien hesitated, moving his head from side to side as if half in doubt.

"I'll tell you, but let me ask you this first."

Taylor was observing Lucien attentively. She would never forget the evil smile he threw their way.

"Do you know what a LIN charge is?"

62

Yale University, New Haven, Connecticut
Twenty-three years earlier

Lucien met Karen Simpson at the beginning of his third semester at Yale. Karen had just transferred from a university in England, and was still settling in. Lucien had never forgotten the first time he saw . . . no, *heard* her. That was what caught his attention at first. Her voice . . . her British accent.

Karen raised her hand to ask a question right at the end of a rather boring lecture in Investigative Psychology and Offending Behavior. Lucien had already gathered his books and was preparing to leave when the sound of her voice made him stop. There was something in the calm and unconcerned way she pronounced every word, a charming cadence to her sentences that was almost hypnotizing. The icing on the cake was the way everything was dressed up in the most charismatic British accent.

Lucien's eyes found Karen sitting at the other end of the lecture hall, almost hidden away among the other students. His eyes followed her as class was dismissed. She couldn't have been any taller than five foot two, Lucien guessed. He took a step to the side to get a better look at her. Her makeup looked quite different—heavier, more gothic than most. She wore a dark T-shirt with *The Cure* written on it and a photograph of someone with messy dark hair, heavy black eye makeup, and badly applied red lipstick.

But what really grabbed his attention was the large tattoo on her upper right arm. As he caught sight of it, it stopped his breath for a moment or two. All of a sudden, his memory was bombarded with images of Susan and what had happened that night almost two years before. Images of him carefully slicing the skin off her arm. The thoughts brought with them a tremendous rush, something he hadn't felt since that night, and for an instant Lucien felt light-headed.

What is that? he thought as he composed himself, squinting at the tattoo. It looked like a couple of large birds, but from where he was standing he couldn't be sure. What he *was* sure of was that Karen Simpson would never graduate from Yale. Her fate would be much, much different.

It didn't take Lucien long at all to befriend Karen. In fact, it happened later that same day. He had followed her around campus from a distance, until a perfect opportunity presented itself midafternoon. Karen had just stepped out of the Psychiatric Hospital just south of the old campus, when she paused, seemingly looking for something inside her backpack. She rummaged through it for a few minutes before giving up. After letting go of a deep, exasperated breath, she allowed her eyes to circle around her, looking a little lost.

"Everything okay?" Lucien asked, recognizing his opportunity to tentatively approach. The expression on his face was pleasant, innocent.

Karen smiled shyly. "Yes, everything is fine. I just seem to have lost my campus map, which is not the best thing to do in your first week at a school this big."

"That's true," Lucien agreed with a sympathetic chuckle. "But you might be in luck. Give me a sec," he said, lifting a finger in a *wait* gesture before reaching into his own rucksack. "Here we go. I knew it would be here somewhere. Have this one." He handed Karen a new campus map.

"Oh!" Her eyes lit up with surprise. "Are you sure?"

"Yes, of course. I know my way around quite well. I just never really cleaned out my bag, so that map's been there for a while." He gave her a *What can you do?* kind of shrug. "Anyway, where do you need to go just now?"

"I'm trying to find Grove Street Cemetery."

Karen's British pronunciation of *cemetery* brought a new smile to Lucien's lips.

"Wow, that's quite a walk from here." He pointed south. "Why do you want to go to the cemetery, if you don't mind my asking?"

"Oh no, I don't really need the cemetery. That's just my point of reference. I need to go to Dunham Lab, but I remember that it's just across the road from there."

Lucien nodded. "Yes, that's right, but hey, I'm heading that way myself. I can walk you there if you like."

"Are you sure?"

"Yes, of course. I'm going to the Becton Center, which is right opposite."

"Oh, that's a piece of good fortune," Karen said, hooking her backpack over her right shoulder. "Well, if it really is no bother, that would be great. Thank you very much."

Then, with a thoughtful expression on his face, Lucien looked at Karen sideways. "Wait a second." He pointed a finger at her. "You were in the Investigative Psychology and Offending Behavior lecture this morning, weren't you?" His performance could've won him a place in drama school.

Surprise bloomed on Karen's face. "I was indeed. You were there?"

"Yeah, sitting right at the back. I'm getting a PhD in psychology."

Even more surprise now.

"So am I. I just transferred from University College London."

"Wow, London? I always wanted to go to London." Lucien offered his hand. "I'm Lucien, by the way."

And so it began.

Meeting Karen Simpson filled Lucien with an immense feeling of relief, as if he'd just found a long-lost piece of a puzzle that had been eating at his brain for months.

He didn't want to overdo it, though. He knew that people would see them together, so he didn't want to appear like he was Karen's best friend, or even a romantic interest. Those were the first people at whose doors the authorities would come knocking once she disappeared.

No, Lucien was careful to appear just like another student in Karen's circle of acquaintances.

His planning took another six months. Four of them were spent searching for a hidden place where he'd be able to imprison Karen and take his time with her, undisturbed. He finally found an abandoned shack hidden deep in the forestland by Lake Saltonstall, not that dissimilar to the one he'd found back in La Honda. One thing Lucien was very certain of was that he would skin Karen alive. The skinning process was what had given him the biggest high that night with Susan. And that meant that he would have to keep Karen in captivity for at least a few hours.

But Lucien also wanted to experiment. He didn't want to use his hands on Karen's neck like he'd done with Susan. He wanted something new, something different. The idea came to him one morning as a friend of his, who was studying molecular, cellular, and developmental biology at Yale, told him about an experiment gone badly wrong inside Pierce Laboratory. As his friend described what had happened, Lucien felt his blood prick inside his veins. He knew then how he wanted Karen to die.

63

Yale University closed for summer in mid-May. Lucien had been eagerly waiting and planning for it for some time, and he played his cards absolutely right.

Around April, Lucien had asked Karen if she intended to go back to England for summer vacation.

"Are you joking?" she had replied. "Summers in England are like a mild spring around here. I've been looking forward to my first summer in the United States for quite a while now."

"Are you staying on campus?"

"No, I don't think so. I'm thinking about taking a trip down to New York first. Maybe I'll get a new tattoo. There are some great studios down there. After that I was thinking I could perhaps travel to Florida and the coast. Spend a few days at the beach." Karen smiled.

"Are you planning on doing all that by yourself?" That was Lucien's key question.

Karen shrugged. "I guess." She looked at him inquisitively. "But I could do with a travel mate. What do you say, Lucien? It could be fun . . . New York, then the beach?"

Lucien saw the opportunity, but he screwed up his face and gave her a quick excuse, saying that he already had a few things organized—a few summer jobs. He knew that if he said yes, Karen would probably tell someone else that they'd be traveling together—a friend, a professor, her parents, whoever. Then, if she never came back from their summer trip, but he did, his name would be right at the top of the police's suspect list. On the other hand, if Karen disappeared when she was supposed to have taken a trip on her own, questions wouldn't start being asked until much later. Many would just assume that she had given up Yale after one semester and gone back to England. It probably wouldn't be until her parents started worrying about her lack of communication that alarm bells would start ringing.

They met again just before summer break, and Karen told Lucien that she was planning on leaving for her New York and Florida vacation in four days' time. That gave him three to get everything prepared. But he had been meticulously organizing for months. He had almost everything he needed in place. The only things missing were a few chemical canisters, and he knew exactly where to get them.

Lucien dropped by Karen's studio apartment the day before she was due to leave for New York. His plan was simple. He would invite her to take a drive with him to Lake Saltonstall that morning for a picnic, saying that they'd be back before nightfall. If Karen said that she couldn't for any reason, then Lucien would invite her for a quick *Have a good summer trip* drink later that evening, to which he was sure she would say yes. Anyway, the final purpose was the same—to be alone with Karen either at a remote picnic site, or inside his car before she was due to leave.

Karen said yes to the picnic.

Lucien picked her up at around 11:00 a.m. He drove at a steady pace, and the ride to the isolated location he'd chosen by the lake took just under twenty-five minutes. But this time Lucien didn't subdue his victim inside his car. There was no surprise attack. No needle to the neck. Lucien did actually prepare a picnic, with sandwiches, salads, fruit, doughnuts, chocolates, beer, and champagne. They ate, drank, and laughed like the best of friends. It was only when Lucien poured the last of the champagne into Karen's glass that he added enough sedative to throw her into a deep, dreamless sleep for at least an hour.

It took less than five minutes for the drug to work.

When Karen opened her eyes again there was no more picnic, no more outdoors. She came to very slowly, and the first thing she realized was that her head ached with such ferocity, it felt like an animal was inside her skull, clawing at her brain.

Through the pain, it took her eyes four whole minutes to finally regain focus in the poor light. As they did, she struggled to understand her surroundings. She was sitting inside a dark, stuffy, and soiled room. The walls were made of plain wood, like a large toolshed in someone's backyard. But something inside her told her that she wasn't near anyone's home . . . near anyone, at all. She was somewhere else. Somewhere no one would find her . . . a place where no one would hear her if she screamed. And as that realization dawned on her, that was exactly what she tried doing—screaming. But her lips weren't really moving. Her jaw wasn't moving either. Panic took hold of her body and she tried to look around. She was frozen.

Oh, Jesus!

She tried to move her fingers.

Nothing.

Her hands.

Nothing.

Her feet and toes.

Nothing.

Her legs and arms.

Nothing.

All she could move were her eyes.

She looked down and saw that she was sitting on some cheap metal chair, unrestrained. Her arms were loose and hanging by the sides of the chair.

For a second she thought she was dreaming, that she would very soon wake up back in her bed, that she would laugh and wonder why her brain had produced such tormenting images, but then there was movement to her right, and the fear she felt growing inside her told her that this was no dream.

Her eyes darted toward the shadows.

"Welcome back, sleepyhead," Lucien said, stepping out of the darkness.

It took Karen just a few seconds to notice that everything about him seemed different, starting with what he was wearing—a long, lab-like, plastic see-through coverall. His sneakers were covered with blue, plastic shoe covers.

Lucien smiled at her.

Karen tried to speak, but her tongue felt heavy and swollen. Only undecipherable noise came from her throat.

"Unfortunately you won't be able to say much," Lucien explained. "You see, Karen, I've injected you with a succinylcholine-based drug."

Fear exploded behind Karen's eyes.

As a psychology student, Karen knew the chemical's power. Succinylcholine is a neuromuscular-blocking agent. It blocks transmission at the neuromuscular joint, causing paralysis of whichever skeletal muscle is affected—in Karen's case, her entire body—though the nervous system stays intact.

She would still be able to feel everything.

Lucien checked his watch. "You'll be in this state for a while longer." He stepped closer. "You know, I'm not a big fan of tattoos. I'm not sure if I've told you that before, but I will admit that the design you have on your upper right arm is very nice. Japanese, isn't it?" As he said that, he moved his right hand from behind his back. The metallic blade he held glistened in the dim light.

There was no room for any more fear in Karen's eyes. They just glistened as unintelligible sounds escaped her throat.

Lucien stepped closer still.

"The main reason why I paralyzed you," he said, "was because I wouldn't want you to wiggle around and mess this up. This is very delicate work." He looked at the blade—a laser-sharp surgical scalpel. "This will hurt a little bit."

Tears rolled down Karen's cheeks.

"But the good news for you is that . . . I've done this before."

64

Karen implored her body to move. Despite her efforts, it simply wasn't enough. Her body just wouldn't respond, no matter how hard she willed it to.

Karen's head was slumped forward and leaned slightly to the right. Her chin almost touched her chest. Lucien had placed her in that position deliberately. He knew that once the drug had taken effect, Karen wouldn't be able to move her neck, only her eyes. He wanted her to be able to see.

And so she did.

As Lucien moved closer, her eyes shot right and she saw the scalpel pierce her skin and the blood come out of her arm, but she was so scared that it took several seconds for a sharp penetrating pain to finally hit her, releasing an animallike, guttural growl that came from deep inside her.

Slowly and skillfully, Lucien used the scalpel to rupture the skin at the top of Karen's shoulder blade. The first blob of blood seeped out, and he used a piece of gauze to clear it up. He proceeded to gradually slice and very carefully pull the skin off her arm.

The skinning, together with Karen's palpable fear,

filled Lucien with an exhilarating satisfaction he couldn't explain. It was better than any drug he could think of.

The entire process didn't take him very long, and at the end of it Lucien was floating on air, high on adrenaline and the huge amounts of endorphins his brain had released into his bloodstream. He would've completed the skinning in half the time, but Karen could only manage a few minutes before passing out. Lucien wanted her awake, he wanted her panic, and so he would interrupt the process to bring her back to consciousness by slapping her face before starting again. That took time.

When he was finally done, he waited for Karen to come to, then lifted the bloody tattoo to show her.

Her internal organs weren't paralyzed, and as her eyes caught sight of what used to be part of her upper right arm, her stomach shot half of its contents back up her esophagus.

"Don't worry, Karen," Lucien said as he began to clean the vomit from her lap.

Karen screamed inside her head at his touch.

"That's the only tattoo I want from you. I will not be taking any of your others."

Karen had five tattoos in total, but she wasn't in the least reassured.

"But I do have a surprise for you." Lucien got up and disappeared into the shadows.

Karen heard a muffled, scratching, metallic sound, as if Lucien had begun dragging a beer keg across the floor. When he reappeared, long minutes later, Lucien had with him a couple of metal tanks, very similar in appearance to the large oxygen tanks one would find in hospitals. But somehow Karen knew that what these tanks contained wouldn't be anything so harmless.

A hose was attached to the nozzle of each tank's top. Lucien placed the tanks about five feet in front of Karen's chair before returning to the shadows. Seconds later he returned once more, bringing with him an altered telescopic boom microphone stand, with two arms instead of one.

He placed the stand between Karen and the tanks before adjusting the two boom arms—one up at her chest, one down toward her waist.

Karen's eyes followed Lucien's every movement with an enormous sense of dread.

Lucien proceeded to hook a tank hose to each of the boom arms.

"I have a question for you, Karen. Have you ever heard of a LIN charge?"

He twisted both tanks so that their labels faced her helpless body. As she read them, understanding what their contents promised, her heart froze.

65

Taylor had frowned at the mention of LIN charges, but Hunter knew exactly what his former friend was talking about.

LN_2, LIN, and LN are all known abbreviations for liquid nitrogen. A LIN charge is a supercooled liquid nitrogen blast. It became known as a LIN charge because the military had created liquid nitrogen grenades and explosive charges that could be magnetically attached to structures like doors, walkways, bridges, and so on. Their main purpose was to hyperfreeze substances—alloys, metal, plastic, wood—making them extremely vulnerable and easy to breach. The real problem comes when a LIN charge hits human skin.

Liquid nitrogen grenades differ from all other known types of grenade in one simple way. Their charge doesn't need to break or penetrate the skin of their target in order to kill them.

The premise behind their effectiveness is based on

the special chemical properties of the most abundant mineral on earth—water.

Water is the only naturally occurring substance on the planet that expands when cooled. If a human body is struck by a blast of supercooled liquid nitrogen, it will become very cold, very fast. When that happens, blood cells will freeze instantly in what is known as a *shock freeze*. The real messy part comes because blood cells are made of approximately seventy percent water, and the water in the blood cells will begin to expand very rapidly. The result of all those water molecules in one's bloodstream expanding so quickly is total body hemorrhage.

Because of the supercooled charge, the molecules' expansion doesn't stop, and in consequence every single blood cell in the human body eventually explodes.

"I'll tell you this," Lucien said, after gleefully explaining the process to Hunter and Taylor. "What happened to her body once I blasted it with liquid nitrogen was hell-scary, even for me. It was like everything inside her exploded, and all that blood came pouring out through . . ." He sighed deeply and scratched his beard, sweeping his eyes over his barren cell. "Everywhere, really—her eyes, ears, nose, mouth . . . I spent four days just cleaning and disinfecting that shack so wild animals wouldn't take over once I was gone." Lucien paused, remembering. "My friend back at Yale told me what happened when they performed this experiment on a live frog in one of the labs. But even my fertile imagination didn't reach as far as reality."

Neither Hunter nor Taylor wanted to hear any more.

"The location, Lucien," Hunter asked. His voice was

steady and reasonable, despite his mounting horror. "Did you bury her around Lake Saltonstall?"

Lucien ran a finger around the grooves surrounding one of the cinder blocks on the wall to his left. "That I did. And I have a surprise for you. I revisited that place four more times after Karen, if you know what I mean." He pursed his lips, as if to ask *What could I do?* and followed it with a careless shrug. "It was a good site, well hidden."

"Are you saying we'll find five bodies there?" Taylor asked.

Lucien held them in suspense for a moment longer before nodding. "Uh-huh. Would you like their names?"

Taylor glared at him.

Lucien laughed. "But of course you would." He closed his eyes and breathed in as if his memory needed an extra burst of oxygen to function with its usual frightening clarity. When he reopened them again, they looked dead, emotionless. He began.

"Emily Evans, thirty-three years old from New York City. Owen Miller, twenty-six years old from Cleveland, Ohio. Rafaela Gomez, thirty-nine years old from Lancaster, Pennsylvania. And Leslie Jenkins, twenty-two years old from Toronto. She was an international student back at Yale."

Lucien paused and drew in another deep breath.

"Would you like me to tell you how they died as well?" His eyes didn't lose their flatness.

Hunter had no intention of sitting in that basement and listening to Lucien boast further.

"The location, Lucien, nothing more," Hunter said.

"Really?" Lucien made a disappointed face. "But it was just starting to get fun. Karen was only my second victim, after all. I got better with each one, believe me." He winked at Taylor suggestively. "Much better."

"The location, Lucien," she said. "Where in New Haven are these bodies?"

Lucien scratched his beard again.

"Of course I'll tell you. I promised I would, didn't I? But I've been telling *you* things for far too long now, and now it's my turn to ask a question again. That was the deal."

Hunter should've known that Lucien would attempt to turn the tables once more. "Tell us where the bodies are first, then, while the FBI verifies the site, you can ask your question."

Lucien inclined his head slightly in affirmation. "I can see your logic, but I'm sure that the FBI is already verifying the four names I've just given you." He looked up at the CCTV camera in the corner of the ceiling inside his cell and smiled at it. "Which means that I've given you something to keep you busy for the moment. So now it's my turn."

Lucien twisted his body slightly to properly face Hunter.

"Tell me about Jessica, Robert."

66

Back in the holding cells' control room, Director Kennedy was already on the phone to one of his research teams.

"I need proof that these people are real," he said to the lead agent. "Social Security numbers, driver's licenses, whatever." He dictated the first three names with the respective ages and hometowns, just as Lucien had mentioned. "The fourth person, Leslie Jenkins, is from Toronto, Canada. She was an international student at Yale in the early nineties. Check with Yale and, if need be, check with the Canadian embassy in Washington. I also need to know if these people were reported missing. Get back to me ASAP." He quickly put the phone down.

Kennedy massaged his temples, remembering once having a conversation with a military weapons expert who had joined the FBI. The weapons expert had showed him actual footage of what happens to a human body when it's exposed to a blast of supercooled liquid nitrogen. Kennedy had probably seen more dead bodies and attended more violent crime scenes than most people in the entire bureau, but he'd never seen anything quite like that footage.

Kennedy was ready to contact the FBI field office in New Haven, Connecticut, and ask them to dispatch a team to whatever location Lucien provided, when Lucien changed the game once more.

"Who's Jessica?" Dr. Lambert asked, looking at Kennedy.

Kennedy shook his head. "I have no idea."

67

"'m sorry?" Hunter said. No poker face could mask his surprise.

"Jessica Petersen," Lucien repeated, clearly enjoying Hunter's reaction. The name traveled through the air slowly, like smoke. "Tell me about Jessica Petersen, Robert. Who was she?"

Baffled, Hunter couldn't tear his eyes away from Lucien, his brain trying hard to understand what was happening.

Police or medical records, he thought, his mind racing. *That was the only possible way. Somehow Lucien had gained access to either police or medical records, or both.* Lucien already knew all the answers. Hunter's mind flashed back to his intuitive discomfort when Lucien asked about his mother. The medical examiner's report would've stated that Hunter's mother had died of an overdose, and put the time of death sometime in the middle of the night. Finding out that Hunter's father worked nights, and therefore wasn't at home, wouldn't have been very difficult. The only other person in that household at the time would have been a seven-year-old Robert Hunter. Lucien would've had no problem putting together most of what had really happened that night. He just needed Hunter to fill in the gaps.

"Who was she?" Lucien asked again, coolly.

Hunter blinked the confusion away. "Someone I knew years ago," he finally replied in the same tone.

"C'mon, Robert," Lucien shot back. "I know you can do better than that. And you know you can't lie to me."

Their stares battled for a moment.

"She's someone I used to date when I was young," Hunter said.

"How young?"

"Very. I met her just after I finished my PhD."

Lucien sat back on his bed and stretched his legs in front of him, getting as comfortable as he could in his tiny cell. "How long did you date her for?"

"Two years."

"Were you in love?" Lucien asked, tilting his head slightly to one side.

Hunter hesitated. "Lucien, what does this have to do with—"

"Just answer the question, Robert," Lucien cut him short. "I can ask whatever I like, relevant or not—that was the deal, and right now I would like you to tell me more about Jessica Petersen. Were you in love with her?"

Taylor shifted in her chair, uncomfortable at the tension growing between the two men.

Hunter's nod was subtle. "Yes, I was in love with Jessica."

"Did you make plans to marry her?"

Silence.

Lucien's eyebrows arched, indicating that he was waiting for an answer.

"Yes," Hunter said. "We were engaged."

For the briefest of moments Taylor heard Hunter's voice crack.

"Oh, that's interesting," Lucien commented. "So what went wrong? I know that you've never been married. So, what happened? How come you didn't marry the woman you were in love with? Did she leave you for someone else?"

Hunter gambled. "Yes, she found someone else. Someone better."

Lucien shook his head and noisily sucked his teeth, shaking his head at Hunter disdainfully. "Are you sure you want to test me again, Robert? Are you sure you want to lie to me? Because that's what you're doing right now." Lucien's gaze and voice both became hard as steel. "And I *really* don't like that."

Taylor kept a steady face, but her eyes reflected her confusion.

"You know what?" Hunter said, lifting his hands up. "I'm not talking about this."

"I think you'd better," Lucien countered.

"I don't think so," Hunter replied in the same gentle tone a psychologist would use to address a patient. "I came here because I thought I'd be helping an old friend. Someone I thought I knew. When they showed me your picture back in LA just a few days ago, I was sure that there had been some sort of bad mistake. I agreed to fly over here because I thought I could help the FBI clear all this up and prove you're not the man they think you are. I was wrong. I can't help because there's nothing to clear up. You are who you are, and you did what you did. But you said so yourself—there's no rush to any of this, because there's no one we can save. And when I leave, the FBI will carry on interrogating you about the locations of all your victims' remains."

Hunter peeked at Taylor. A frown had creased her forehead after she heard the word *leave*.

"They'll just use different methods," Hunter continued. "Less conventional ones. I'm sure you know what's coming. It might take a few days longer, but trust me, Lucien, in the end you will talk."

Hunter got up, ready to leave.

Lucien looked as calm as he ever had.

"I would really suggest that you sit back down, old friend, because you've misquoted me."

Hunter paused.

"I didn't say that there was no rush about any of this. I said that there was no rush in finding Susan's remains, because you couldn't save *her* anyway."

Something in Lucien's phrasing made Hunter's heartbeat stumble, pick itself up, and then stumble again.

"And I've never said that you couldn't save anyone. Because I think there's still time." A tense pause as Lucien looked at his wrist, consulting an invisible watch once again. "I haven't killed all the victims I've abducted, Robert." Lucien accompanied those words with a look so cold and devoid of feeling, it could've belonged to a cadaver. "One is still alive."

Part Three

A RACE AGAINST TIME

68

Hidden location
Three days earlier

She coughed and spluttered awake, or at least she thought she was awake. She couldn't really tell anymore. Her reality was more terrifying than her worst nightmares. Confusion surrounded her twenty-four hours a day, as her brain seemed to be in a constant state of haziness—half-numb, half-awake.

Due to the lack of sunlight, she had lost track of time a while ago. She knew she'd been locked in a stinking hellhole for a long time. To her it felt like years, but it could've been just months, or even weeks. Time just trickled by, and there was no way for her to keep count.

She could still remember the night she met him in that bar on the east side of town. He was older than she but charming, attractive, clearly well educated, funny, and really knew how to compliment a woman. He made her feel special. He made her feel like she could light up the sky. At the end of the night, he put her in a cab and didn't suggest joining her. He was polite and gentlemanly. He did ask her for her phone number, though.

She had to admit that she had been quite excited when he called just a few days later and asked if she would like to go out for dinner with him. With a huge smile on her face, she said yes.

He picked her up that evening, at around 7:00 p.m., but they never made it to a restaurant. As soon as she entered his car and buckled up, she felt something sting the side of her neck. He'd acted so fast she didn't even see his hand move. The next thing she could recall was waking up in this cold, damp room.

The room was exactly twelve paces by twelve paces. She'd counted and recounted it many times. The walls were crudely made of brick and mortar, the floor of rough cement. The door, which sat at the center of one of the walls, was made of metal with a rectangular, lockable viewing slot about five feet from the floor. Like a prison door. There was a thin and dirty mattress pushed against the back wall, and a blanket that smelled of wet dog; no pillow. In one corner there was a plastic bucket she was told to use as a toilet. There were no windows, and the weak yellowish bulb locked inside a metal mesh box at the center of the ceiling was on twenty-four/seven.

Since she'd been taken into captivity, she'd only seen her kidnapper a handful of times, when he would enter her cell to deliver food and water or a new roll of rough toilet paper, and to swap her toilet bucket for a clean one.

So far, he hadn't touched her. He never said much either. She would scream, beg, plead, try to talk, but he barely replied.

He scared her so much that on one occasion, she wet herself. One day, she gave in and asked him what he planned to do to her. He didn't reply with words. He simply looked at her, and in his eyes she saw something she'd never seen before—unadulterated evil.

Though she had completely lost track of time, she could still tell that some of the intervals between rations were stretching far too long.

Once, just after the third or fourth food delivery, she had waited for the door to open and tried surprise attacking him with all the strength she had in her, clawing at his face with her chipped nails. But it seemed like he'd been waiting for her to act all along, and before she was able to so much as scratch him, he punched her stomach so hard, she immediately doubled over and puked. She spent hours lying on the floor in a fetal position, contorted in pain, her abdomen sore and bruised.

Sometimes the rations were larger than others—more bottles of water, more packets of crackers and cookies, more candy bars, more loaves of bread, sometimes even fruit. Then he'd be gone for a long time. The larger the ration he brought her, the longer it would be before he came back, and the last batch of supplies she'd gotten was the largest of them all.

She didn't know exactly how long ago that was, but she knew it was longer than ever before. She had learned to stretch her supplies as much as possible. Usually by the time she was running out of food and water, he'd be back bringing her more, but not this time.

She had run out of food some time ago, maybe three or four days. To her it seemed longer. She ran out of water a day after that. She felt weak and dehydrated.

Her lips were dried and cracked. Because of how hungry she was, the cold and dampness of the room affected her more than ever. She spent most of her days curled up in a ball in a corner, wrapped up in that stinking blanket. But even so, she couldn't stop shivering.

Her throat had begun to feel like it was on fire since she ran out of water, but today more than ever. She desperately needed a drink. Her eyelids were heavy and it required an effort of will to force them open. Her head ached so that every movement she made felt as if it would be her last.

She brought a hand to her clammy forehead, and it felt as if she were touching hot metal. She was burning up.

With an amazing force of effort, she lifted her head and looked at the door. She thought she heard something. Steps, maybe. Someone coming.

As crazy as it seemed, a smile came to her lips. The human brain is a complex organ, and a fragile and shattered mind sometimes clutches at straws. Right there and then she didn't think of her captor as the man who could rape her repeatedly before killing her. She thought of him as the savior who was coming to bring her food and water.

She held on to the wall and slowly propped herself onto her feet. With the hesitant steps of a battle-weary soldier, she gradually made her way to the door and placed her ear against it.

"Hello . . ." she called in the weak voice of a scared child.

No reply.

"Hello . . . Are you out there? . . . Please? . . . Please can I have some water?" Her voice was now strangled with tears. She was shivering so badly her teeth were chattering.

"Please . . . ?" She began crying. "Please help me . . . ? Just a few drops of water, please."

She heard nothing but absolute silence.

She stayed on the floor by the door with her ear pressed hard against it for a long time—a couple of hours, probably. There was no noise. There never had been. Her tired brain was so desperate it was starting to trick her. Her fever was so high, she was starting to hallucinate.

It took some time for her sobs to subside. She wiped the tears from her eyes and her dirty cheeks, and with no strength left in her to get back up on her feet, she crawled back to her corner and her blanket on the other side of the room.

She was losing her mind. She could feel it.

As she curled herself back into a ball, she started whispering to herself. "Don't give up. Stay strong. You'll get through this. Stay strong . . ."

69

FBI National Academy, Quantico, Virginia
The present

M adeleine," Lucien said. He was still sitting on his
bed with his legs stretched in front of him, com-
fortably. "Her name is Madeleine Reed. But she likes to
be called Maddy.

"She's twenty-three years old. I picked her up on
April ninth, in Pittsburgh, but she was born in Blue
Springs City, Missouri." He jerked his head toward the
end of the corridor outside his cell. "You can go check it
out if you like. Her family must be going crazy by now."

Hunter and Taylor both knew that Adrian Kennedy
was listening in on the interview. He would have the
name and details confirmed in a matter of minutes.

"April ninth?" Taylor said, her eyes wide with surprise. "That was five months ago."

"It was indeed," Lucien agreed. "But don't worry,
Agent Taylor, I've got a little system that works. I've
honed it over the years." He smiled. "I leave her rations
of food and water before I leave, and Maddy is clever.

She figured out very quickly that she had to go easy on it, or else it would all run out before I got back with more. And I'll tell you, she became quite expert at it." He opened his hands and studied the veins crisscrossing the backs of them. "But I was supposed to be back four, maybe five days ago."

He allowed the seriousness of his words to punch everyone square in the face before he continued.

"If Maddy ran out of food and water a few days ago, she'd be very weak by now, no doubt about that, but she's probably still alive. Now, how long she'll stay that way? I can't tell you."

"Where is she?" Hunter asked.

"Tell me about Jessica Petersen," Lucien came back. "Tell me about the woman you loved."

Hunter sucked in a deep breath.

"Tell us where she is, Lucien, so we can save her, and I promise you that I'll tell you whatever you want to know."

Lucien rubbed the patch of skin between his eyebrows. "Umm." He pretended to think about it. "No. No deal. As I've said, now it's your turn to answer my questions. I've given you enough."

"I will answer them, Lucien," Hunter said. "I give you my word I will. But if she ran out of food and water four days ago, we need to get to her now."

Lucien remained unperturbed.

"What's the point in letting her die this way, Lucien?" Hunter pleaded. "You won't be there to watch her die. Whatever satisfaction you got from killing your victims, Madeleine's death will *not* give it to you."

"Probably not," Lucien agreed.

"So please, let her live."

Lucien was unfazed.

"It's over, Lucien. Look around you. You've been caught. By chance, but you've been caught. There's no point in taking anyone else's life." Hunter paused. "Please, there must still be something human inside you. Have mercy this once. Let us bring Madeleine in."

Lucien stood. "Nice speech, Robert," he said, pursing his lips. "Short, to the point, and with just the right amount of emotion. For a second there I thought your eyes would tear up." Sarcasm fit Lucien like a second skin. "But I *am* showing mercy. My kind of mercy. And this is how it works. First I want to hear about Jessica. Then, and only then, I'll tell you the location of Karen Simpson and the other four victims' remains in New Haven, and I'll tell you where Madeleine Reed is. After that, you and Agent Taylor can go be heroes."

Lucien saw Taylor check her watch nervously.

"Yes, you *are* losing time," he said, nodding. "Every second has suddenly become quite precious, hasn't it? You don't need me to tell you that dehydration can have irreversible neurological consequences. If you don't get a move on, she might be nothing more than a vegetable by the time you find her."

Lucien pointed to Hunter's chair.

"So sit your ass back down, Robert, and start talking."

70

Hunter exchanged a quick, worried look with Taylor, and returned to his seat.

"What do you want to know?" he asked, looking Lucien in the eye.

Lucien's smirk was triumphant. "I want to know what happened. How come you never married the woman you were engaged to? How come you and Jessica aren't together?"

"Because she passed away."

Taylor turned her head and caught great sadness in Hunter's gaze before he quickly looked down.

Lucien saw it too. "How?" he asked. "How did she die?"

Hunter knew he couldn't lie. "She was murdered," he replied.

Taylor couldn't check a gasp of surprise.

"Murdered?" Lucien said. "Okay, now this is getting interesting. Please do continue, Robert."

"There's nothing more to it. We were engaged and she was murdered before I had the chance to marry her. That's all there is."

"That's never *all there is*, Robert. Those are only the superficial facts, and they are not the purpose of this exercise of mine. Tell me how it happened. Were you there? Did you see it happen? Tell me how you felt. That's what I really want to know. The feelings deep inside you. The thoughts in your head."

Hunter hesitated for a split second.

"You can take as long as you want," Lucien challenged. "It doesn't bother me. But remember that the clock is ticking for poor Madeleine."

"No, I wasn't there," Hunter said. "If I were, it wouldn't have happened."

"That's a bold statement, Robert. So where were you?" Lucien sat back down at the edge of his bed. "Feel free to start at the beginning."

Hunter had never talked about Jessica to anyone. He found it better to keep some things locked inside, in a place he barely visited himself.

"I hadn't made detective for the LAPD yet," he began. "I was just a police officer with the central bureau. My partner and I were out doing rounds in the Rampart area that day."

"I'm listening," Lucien said when Hunter paused for a deep breath.

"Though Jess and I were engaged, we didn't live together," Hunter explained. "We were making arrangements to, once I became a detective, which was only a few weeks away, but at that time, we still lived in separate apartments. I was supposed to see her that night. We were having dinner together. She'd made reservations at a restaurant somewhere in West Hollywood. But toward the end of the afternoon, my partner and I were dispatched to check on a domestic-violence disturbance in Westlake.

"We got to the address in less than ten minutes, but it all sounded too quiet. That worried me. The husband must've seen our black-and-white unit approaching through the window. We got out, walked up to the door, and knocked. Actually, my partner, Kevin, knocked. I walked out to the side of the house to check the window."

"So what happened then?" Lucien urged Hunter.

"The husband shot Kevin with a sawed-off twelve-gauge shotgun through the mailbox flap on the door. He was hiding behind it, waiting for us." Hunter looked down at his hands. "The gun was loaded with heavy double-slug terminator ammo. From that distance, the round practically tore Kevin's body in half."

"Wait," Lucien said. "So just like that, this guy shot a cop through the door?"

Hunter nodded. "He was high on crack cocaine. Had been for several days. That was also the main reason for the domestic violence. His brain was soup. He'd locked his wife and his little daughter in the house and had been abusing and beating them. His little girl was six."

Even Lucien paused for thought. "So what did you do after he'd torn your partner in half with a shotgun?"

"I returned fire. I pulled Kevin away from the door and I returned fire."

"And . . . ?"

"I aimed low," Hunter said. "Lower half of the body. I wasn't looking for a kill shot, just to maim. Both of my shots got through, but with reduced velocity from breaching the door. The first hit the guy's right thigh, the second hit him in the groin."

Lucien coughed a laugh. "You shot his dick off?"

"It was unintentional."

This time it was a full, throaty laugh. "Well, if the scumbag was abusing his six-year-old little girl, then I guess he deserved it."

Taylor found it rich that someone like Lucien would call anyone a scumbag.

"He survived?" Lucien asked.

"Yes. I called for backup, but the amount of blood he was losing, together with being shot in the groin, scared him sober. Before backup and the ambulance arrived, he opened the door and gave himself up."

"But your partner didn't make it," Lucien concluded.

"No. He was dead before he hit the ground."

"Too bad," Lucien said with no emotion in his voice. "So, I guess that you never made it to dinner with Jess that night." He paused and studied Hunter. "Do you mind if I call her Jess?"

"Yes, I do."

Lucien nodded. "Okay, I apologize. I'll rephrase. So I guess that you never made it to dinner with *Jessica* that night."

"No, I didn't."

71

Los Angeles, California
Twenty years earlier

Hunter had helped place Kevin's body in the coroners' van before he was called upon to recount the details of what had happened to the detectives who'd been assigned to the case. After that, he drove to Harbor-UCLA Medical Center to check on the progress of the man he'd shot.

A doctor came out of the operating room to update him. The man, Marcus Colbert, would live, but he would walk with a limp for the rest of his life and he would never again have active sexual relations.

Hunter's head was an absolute mess, but he still had to go back to his precinct and fill in several reports before he could go home.

Protocol dictated that after a shoot-out with victim fatalities, the officers involved had to have several sessions with an LAPD shrink before they would be allowed to return to their full duties, pending a psychological evaluation. His captain told him that his first session with the appointed psychologist would be in two days' time.

Hunter sat in an empty room, staring at the pen in his hand and at the empty reports in front of him for a long moment. The events of that day kept playing and replaying in his mind like an old movie stuck on a loop. He couldn't believe Kevin was gone—shot dead by a paranoid crackhead on a binge. They'd been partners since Hunter had joined the LAPD a year and a half earlier. Kevin had been a good man.

By the time Hunter was done with the reports, it was nearing ten in the evening. Understandably, he'd forgotten all about his dinner plans with Jessica. He gave her a call to apologize and explain why he hadn't turned up or called earlier, but the phone just rang before going straight to the answering machine.

Jessica was a sweet woman, and she fully understood the complications that came with dating a law enforcement officer—the long hours, the last-minute cancellations, the worries for Hunter's well-being, everything. She also knew that once Hunter made detective, those complications would step up a level or two further, but she was in love, and to her, that was all that mattered.

Hunter left a short message apologizing, but he didn't go into any details. He would tell her everything when he saw her. For all her strength and resolve, Jessica was very sensitive, and though he'd tried to conceal it, he was sure that she would pick up the sadness in his voice, the seriousness of it all.

Hunter found it strange that Jessica hadn't answered the phone. He didn't believe she'd gone out, not at that time on a Tuesday evening. Maybe tonight she was just a little more upset than the previous times he had had to cancel on her right at the last minute. Despite his head being all over the place, he still managed to think clearly enough to stop by a twenty-four-hour grocery shop and pick her up some flowers as an apology.

He got to Jessica's place just before 11:00 p.m. As he parked on the street and looked up at her house, he was overwhelmed by a sensation of dread so intense it nauseated him. He'd never felt anything like it before. But then again, he'd never lost a partner before either.

Hunter stepped out of the car and approached the house, but with every step, the foreboding feeling multiplied exponentially.

Sixth sense, premonition, gut feeling, whatever name anyone would like to call it, Hunter's was screaming at him by the time he got to the door. Something wasn't right.

He had a copy of the keys, but he didn't need them. The front door was unlocked. Jessica never left the front door unlocked.

Hunter pushed the door open, stepped into Jessica's dark living room, and was immediately hit by a smell that practically paralyzed his heart and sent a wave of shivers up and down his spine.

Blood does not have any smell while flowing through one's body. It's only when it comes into contact with air that it acquires a distinctive, nonchemical, metallic scent, very similar to copper. Hunter had been surrounded by that same smell that afternoon.

"Oh, God, no," the terrified words dribbled from his lips.

The flowers hit the floor.

His trembling hand reached for the light switch.

As brightness bathed the room, Hunter's world was sent into darkness. A darkness so deep he wasn't sure he would ever find his way out of it again.

Jessica lay facedown in a pool of her own blood by the kitchen door. The living room around him was a mess—broken lamps, tossed furniture, open drawers—distinct signs of a struggle.

"Jess . . . Jess . . ." Hunter ran to her, calling out in a voice that didn't seem to belong to him.

He kneeled by her side, his trousers soaking in her blood.

"Oh, God . . ." His voice broke.

He reached for her and turned her over.

Jessica had been stabbed several times. There were lacerations on both of her arms, her hands, chest, abdomen, and neck.

Hunter looked at her beautiful face and his vision clouded with tears. Her lips had already faded to a pale color. The skin on her face and hands had acquired a peculiar shade of purple. Rigor mortis hadn't set in yet, but it was well on its way, which told Hunter that she'd been murdered less than four hours earlier—around the time he was supposed to have picked her up for dinner. That knowledge sent the darkness inside plunging to new depths. His soul seemed to leave him, leaving behind just an empty body, drowning in sorrow.

Gently, Hunter brushed her hair away from her face, kissed her forehead, brought her to his chest, and hugged her tight. He could still smell her delicate perfume. He could still feel the softness of her hair.

"I'm so sorry, Jess." A suffocating anguish drowned his words in emotion. "I'm so terribly sorry."

He held her in his arms until his tears stopped flowing.

If he could've exchanged places with her, if he could've breathed his life into her body, he would've done it. He would've given his life for hers without a second thought.

He finally let go of her, and as he turned his head he saw something he had completely missed in his horror and grief. Written in blood on one of the living-room walls were two words.

Cop whore.

72

FBI National Academy, Quantico, Virginia
The present

As Hunter told Lucien about that night, a dark, endless pit, like an old wound that had never fully healed, reopened in Hunter's stomach, dragging his heart down, and bringing back an emptiness inside him he'd fought twenty years to leave behind.

"So you lost both of your partners in the same night," Lucien said. If Hunter didn't know better, he would've sworn there was a pinch of sorrow in Lucien's voice.

Hunter blinked once, pushing the memory as far away from his mind as he could. "Madeleine, Lucien. Where is she?"

"Wait a second, old friend, not so fast."

"What do you mean not so fast," Hunter spat. "You've heard all there is to hear about what happened to Jessica. That was what you wanted, wasn't it?"

"No, that was just part of it. But since you told me what happened that night, I'll give you something in return. It's only fair. Are you listening?"

It took Lucien just two minutes to give them specific directions to the site by Lake Saltonstall in New Haven, where they'd find Karen Simpson's remains, together with those of the other four victims he'd mentioned.

"Now," Lucien said when he was done, "if you want me to give you Madeleine, let's go back to Jessica and what happened after she was murdered. Was the perpetrator ever caught?"

"Perpetrators," Hunter corrected him. "Forensics found two sets of prints in the house, neither of which matched anything in the police archives."

Lucien's expression showed surprise. "Was it a sexual attack?"

"No," Hunter replied. "She wasn't sexually assaulted. It was a robbery. They took the few items of jewelry she had, including the engagement ring on her finger, her purse, and all the cash she had in the house."

"A robbery?" Lucien seemed to find that strange.

So did Taylor, though she remained silent, digesting the gruesome story she'd just heard.

"So why kill her?" Lucien asked.

Hunter paused. Looked away. Looked back at Lucien. "Because of me."

Lucien waited, but Hunter didn't offer any more. "What do you mean, because of you? This was a revenge attack? Someone wanting to get back at you?"

"No," Hunter said. "Jessica had several photographs of the two of us together scattered around the house. In many of them I was in uniform. Those picture frames had all been smashed. Some had the word *pig* written in blood on them. Some had the words *Fuck the police*. That sort of thing."

As things became clearer, Lucien tilted sideways slowly. "So, once they found out that she was engaged to an LAPD officer, they decided to kill her, just for fun."

Hunter said nothing. He didn't even blink.

"Have you looked at gang members? Gangs have a hatred for the police practically hardwired into their brains, especially in a city like Los Angeles. The only other people who hate police officers as much are ex-cons, but if the fingerprints weren't on file, then those are clearly ruled out."

Hunter knew that full well, and he and the detectives assigned to the case had hammered every single gang contact they had for information. They got nothing, not even a whisper.

"We're wasting time here," Hunter said, irritation starting to come through in his voice. "There's nothing more to say about Jessica or that night. She was murdered. The people who did it have never been caught. Tell us where Madeleine is, Lucien. Let us bring her in."

Lucien still wasn't ready. "So you blamed yourself for her death." Lucien didn't ask. "Actually, you did it twice, didn't you? First for being a cop, because you knew that was the reason why they killed her. And second because you didn't make it to her house for dinnertime like you were supposed to."

Hunter stayed quiet.

"The human mind is a funny thing, isn't it?" Lucien spoke in a practiced therapist's voice—deep, calm, and reasonable. "Even though you know that neither of the two reasons you've been blaming yourself for years is actually your fault, even though you understand the psychology behind the *why* you've been blaming yourself, you still can't avert your guilt."

Lucien chuckled and got back on his feet. "Just because one understands psychology, Robert, doesn't mean one is immune to psychological traumas and pressures. Just because one is a doctor, doesn't mean one doesn't get sick."

Was that what Lucien was doing? Hunter asked himself. *He'd used Jessica's murder as an example to defend his own sordid actions. Just because Lucien knew that killing people was wrong, just because as a psychologist he probably understood his desires and where they came from didn't mean that he could control them.*

"And that's the reason why you've been a loner since then, isn't it, Robert?" Lucien said. "Because you blame yourself for what happened. She was killed because she was close to you. I bet you promised yourself you'd never let that happen again."

Hunter wasn't in the mood to be psychoanalyzed. He needed to end this. And he needed to do it now. Any answer would do. "Yes, that's the reason. Now tell us where Madeleine is."

"In a moment. You haven't satisfied the researcher in me yet, Robert. What I really want to know about is what happened inside your head after Jessica was murdered. The earthquake of feelings that I know you went through. You tell me that, and I'll give you Madeleine."

After twenty years, Hunter had learned how to live with those feelings. They were ingrained in everything he did, no matter how small.

"What is there to know?" he asked evenly.

"I want to know about the anger inside you, Robert.

The rage. I want to know if you were angry enough to kill. Did you dream of going after them?" Lucien asked. "The perpetrators? Jessica's killers?"

"An investigation was launched—" Hunter began.

"That's not what I asked," Lucien shot back with a shake of the head. "I want to know if *you* launched your own crusade to find her killers, Robert."

Hunter was about to reply when Lucien interrupted him.

"Don't lie to me now, Robert. Madeleine's life depends on it."

Hunter could feel Taylor's eyes on him, probing.

"Yes. I never stopped searching for them."

Hunter's answer seemed to excite Lucien.

"So here's the million-dollar question, Robert," he said. "If you found them, would you take them in? Or would you impose your own justice on them . . . your own revenge?"

Hunter scratched the back of his hand.

"You would kill them yourself, wouldn't you?" Lucien's smile was confident. "I can see it in your eyes, Robert. I saw it while you were reliving that night. I bet Agent Taylor saw it too. The anger. The rage. The hurt. Fuck being a detective. Fuck the law that you swore to uphold. *This* would take priority over everything. Over your own life. If you came face-to-face with the people who took Jessica from you, you'd murder them without an ounce of hesitation. I know you would. I know you've thought about it hundreds, maybe thousands of times."

Hunter breathed in through his nose, and out through his mouth, attempting to regain his calm.

"Hell, you might even torture them for a while just to enjoy seeing them suffer for what they did. That would be fun, wouldn't it?"

Lucien saw a muscle flex in Hunter's jaw, but still he continued.

"As I've said before," he continued, "under the right circumstances, anyone can become a killer. Even those who are supposed to protect and to serve." His dead stare could've frozen ice. "Remember, Robert, a murder is a murder. The reasons behind it have no relevance, whether it was justified revenge or a sadistic urge." He brought his face to less than an inch from the Plexiglas. "So one day, you still might become the same as me."

Lucien was indeed using Jessica's murder to, in a sick way, excuse the things he'd done, Hunter thought. *First appealing to psychological reason, now the emotional ones.* Hunter was sure that Lucien had read the police reports. Knowing Hunter as well as he had all those years ago, he would've figured out that Hunter had never stopped searching for Jessica's killers. He had pushed for Hunter to tell the story purposefully, so that he could degrade it and use it as a rationale for his own twisted acts.

Despite Hunter's anger, he still had only one priority. He figured that Lucien had achieved what he wanted. There was nothing else he could say. He tried once more, now nearly pleading.

"Tell us where Madeleine is, Lucien."

Lucien chuckled. "Okay. But I can't just tell you the location, Robert. I have to take you there."

73

Lucien's last words didn't surprise either Hunter or Taylor. In fact, they had both expected this. It was certainly logical. Because Madeleine's life depended on them getting to her quickly, it was too risky to rely on Lucien's verbal or written instructions. What if when they got to the vicinity of where their sole remaining living victim was held captive, the instructions suddenly became unclear because the surroundings had changed? What if they took a wrong turn? What if there was a mistake in the instructions, deliberate or not? They would lose valuable time trying to get Lucien to re-explain everything over a phone line or video link.

No, Lucien had to go with them. He had to personally guide them there.

Taylor's eyes sought Hunter's before giving Lucien a simple nod.

Lucien smiled. "There's one more thing," he said, winking at her. "There will be only the three of us on this trip. No other FBI agents. No one following us either, by land or air. You, Robert, and I—not a person more, not a person less. That's the deal. I won't tolerate negotiation of any kind. If you break the deal, or if I suspect that we're being followed, I guide you nowhere. Madeleine dies alone, forgotten and forsaken, and I'll make sure the press finds out why. I can live with that. Can you?"

Taylor knew she was in a no-win situation. Nothing had changed since they'd discovered that Lucien was the only one who could guide them to his victims' remains. He still held all the cards, even more so now that there was supposedly a live victim. He could call the shots any way he saw fit, and at the moment, there was nothing either Hunter or Taylor could do about it.

"As long as you understand that you'll be cuffed at the hands and ankles, and we'll be armed," Taylor said, echoing Lucien's tone. "You try anything, and I swear we'll gun you down. I can live with that. Can you?"

"I would've expected nothing less," Lucien replied.

"We'll be ready to leave in fifteen minutes." She stood up. "Where are we going?"

"I'll tell you when we're on our way," Lucien replied.

"I need to know if we need a plane or a car, at the very least."

Lucien nodded his agreement. "A plane first. Then a car."

"Give me more than that. I have to know how much fuel we'll need."

"Enough to get us to Illinois."

As Hunter and Taylor took their first steps toward the door at the end of the corridor, Lucien halted them.

"I guess that day is closer than you think, Robert," he said.

Hunter and Taylor paused and turned to face Lucien again.

"What day is that?" Hunter asked.

"The day that you might become the same as me." If Lucien's voice had sounded emotionless in their interviews, now it sounded like it could've come from some cold and ancient devil . . . completely heartless. "Because for the past two days, my friend, you've been sitting before the man you've been seeking for twenty years. I was the one who took Jessica from you."

74

Hunter didn't move, didn't breathe, didn't blink. It was like his whole body went into lockdown.

"What was that?" Taylor was the one who asked the quiet question.

Lucien's gaze was cemented on Hunter, but other than the initial frown of confusion at his statement, he got nothing else from the LAPD detective.

"You think I'm saying this just to get under your skin, don't you, Robert?"

"You obviously are," Taylor cut in. There was no disguising the irritation in her voice. "You ran out of tricks, and now you're just stalling to rile us up. You know what? I wouldn't be surprised if there is no Madeleine Reed held captive anywhere. I wouldn't be surprised if you just made her up because you ran out of acts for this little performance of yours. I think your chamber is empty. You're panicking, and firing blanks because you know the game is really up."

Lucien faced Taylor, his expression an unintelligible mask. "Is that really your argument, Agent Taylor? 'I'm firing blanks because I know the game is up'? Is that the best you can come up with?" He coughed a laugh before his stare turned to ice once more. "I could eat a bowl of alphabet soup and shit a better argument than that." Lucien jerked his chin at the CCTV camera just outside his cell. "Why don't you go ask your people who have been listening in on us? Go ask them if Madeleine Reed is real or not. I'm sure they've been busy running checks."

"Even if there is someone named Madeleine Reed from Pittsburgh, Pennsylvania," Taylor shot back, still keeping her composure, "who has been reported as missing sometime after April ninth, it doesn't mean you've got her, or that you even know where she is. You can obtain a list of names from every missing-persons bureau in the country over the Internet these days. You are well prepared for us. You've proved that over and over. I'm sure that even someone as arrogant as you must have entertained the possibility that one day you might be caught. It's reasonable to think that you'd have a few tricks already prepared for that eventuality. But even if you are the one who kidnapped Madeleine, you can give us no proof that she's still alive. You could've killed her months ago, and you know that there's no way we can know for sure. So now you just picked her name out of the many that you've tortured and murdered, and are using her to give you a last chance of getting out of here."

Taylor took a breath, waiting for either of the two men to speak.

Nothing.

"I wasn't joking when I said that we'll gun you down if you try anything," Taylor continued. "If you think this trip will give you a chance at escaping and we won't take decisive action because we think that you might have information that'll lead us to a live victim, then you're not as smart as you think you are."

"Now that's a much better argument than your firing-blanks metaphor, Agent Taylor," Lucien said, sardonically clapping his hands three times. "But as you've just pointed out, there's no way you can know for sure. So when you find out that there really is a Madeleine Reed, who was reported missing in Pittsburgh, Pennsylvania, after April ninth, can you really afford to call my bluff?" He gave her a couple of seconds to think about it before adding, "Because if you do and I'm not bluffing, the amount of shit that will rain on you and on the FBI will last a lifetime."

Hunter could barely listen. Lucien's words still echoed in his head. *Because for the past two days, my friend, you've been sitting before the man you've been seeking for twenty years. I was the one who took Jessica from you.*

Every atom in his body wanted to believe that Lucien was just bluffing, but Hunter had seen something in Lucien's eyes—a disquieting defiance that only came with certainty.

"I can see your thoughts racing behind your eyes, Robert," Lucien said, moving his attention away from Taylor. "You're trying to decide if I'm telling the truth or not. Maybe I can help you with that." He ran his tongue over his top lip. "Yellow-fronted house, number 5067 on the corner of Lemon Grove Avenue and North Oxford, in East Hollywood."

Hunter felt his throat constrict. Yet if Lucien had

read the police reports, that information would've been easy to obtain.

Once more Lucien seemed to read his mind.

"I know, I know," he conceded. "That proves nothing. An address is easy enough to acquire. But how about this. Out of the photographs you mentioned that Jessica had scattered around the house, the largest of them all was in a silver frame on a small table by the dark-brown leather sofa in the living room. The picture was of the two of you at some sort of LAPD dinner. You were in uniform and proudly displaying an award. She was wearing a purple dress with a matching purse. Her hair was loose, but thrown to one side, over her left shoulder."

Still with his gaze firmly set on Hunter, Lucien paused, before delivering a final blow.

"But you know the real difference between that and all the other photographs that had been vandalized in the house, don't you, Robert? That was the only one on which the word *pig* was written vertically, instead of horizontally."

75

Hunter's eyes were focused on Lucien, but not his mind. All of his thoughts had traveled back to the night that part of him had died along with Jessica. He didn't need to search far. Every detail of what he'd seen that night had been stored for eternity. Accessing those memories was painful, but simple. He could practically see the photograph Lucien was talking about, right in front of him—the smashed glass, the silver frame, and the word *pig* written in large blood letters—vertically. As Lucien had said, that had been the only photograph on which a word had been written that way.

Trying his best to think logically, Hunter somehow managed to restrain his anger before it overflowed his body.

If Lucien had somehow managed to get his hands on the crime-scene police reports from Jessica's murder, after all, then there was also a possibility that he'd managed to obtain copies of the crime-scene evidence report and inventory, which Hunter knew were very detailed.

Lucien picked up on his doubt.

"Still not convinced, huh? Aren't the brain's defense mechanisms intriguing, Robert? To try to avoid the intense psychological pain that it can feel coming, it will subconsciously try everything it can to find an alternative answer. It will even disregard facts and hang on to things it knows not to be true. I can't blame you, Robert. If I were in your shoes, I wouldn't want to believe it either. But the reality is—it's true."

"You're bluffing again." Taylor tried to diffuse the situation one more time, her voice angry and a few decibels louder than before. "Robert said that there were two perpetrators. Forensics found two sets of fingerprints at the scene. Are you going to tell us that you had a partner this once? *And,*" she stressed before Lucien could respond, "we now have your fingerprints on file. One of the first things the FBI's computer system does is to check the fingerprints of any apprehended individuals for matches against the records in our system, which are linked to any unsolved crimes. If your fingerprints had matched any of the ones found inside Jessica's home, or at the crime scene of any other unsolved crime, we would've had red alerts screaming at us from all four corners days ago."

Lucien waited patiently for Taylor to finish.

"I have brought it to your attention before, Agent Taylor, but you can be quite naive sometimes. Do you think that staging a crime scene is *hard*? Do you think that making a murder look like a by-product of a robbery is difficult? Do you think that acquiring and planting someone else's fingerprints inside Jessica's house would pose a problem for someone like me?" He laughed. "I can give you the names of the two men those fingerprints belonged to. Not that you'll be able to verify it anyway, but I can also give you the location where you'll find their remains. I wanted it to look like a robbery by gang members. I wanted the police to look for two suspects instead of one. Why do you think the FBI had no clue I existed, Agent Taylor? Why do you think that after so many murders, your Behavioral Research and Instruction Unit has never been able to link any of them? Why do you think you haven't been searching for a murderer who's been killing people for twenty-five years?"

Defeat and anger began to line Taylor's face, as Lucien's voice raised to a near howl of triumph before returning to its arctic calm.

"It's called *deception*, Agent Taylor. Making the police believe one thing, while the truth is something very different. It's an art, and I'm very good at it."

Lucien reverted his attention back to Hunter.

"Maybe this will clear the doubts from your mind once and for all, Robert. You said that all the jewelry Jessica had in the house had been stolen, but did you tell the detectives exactly what was taken?"

Hunter felt an uneasy sensation crawling like a rash across his skin.

"Of course not," Lucien said. "I doubt you knew every piece of jewelry she owned. But I can tell you exactly what was missing. She kept everything inside this cute little flowery box on the dresser in her room, next to another picture of you both. A picture that wasn't touched, wasn't vandalized. The two of you at the beach." He paused, and in Hunter's stricken face, saw the punch had hit its target. But he wasn't done yet. "I took the whole box. But from her body, other than the engagement ring you've already mentioned, I also took her two single-diamond earrings, and her dainty neck-lace. The pendant on it was a white gold hummingbird. Its eye was a tiny ruby."

No amount of self-discipline would've been able to keep Hunter's anger locked inside this time. He shot forward and slammed both of his fists against the Plexiglas.

Tears welled in Hunter's eyes. The deep pain in them was as clear as words on a page. Without even realizing he did so, he let a single word escape his lips through gritted teeth.

"Why?"

76

Hunter's outburst was so violent that it made Taylor jump on the spot. Lucien, on the other hand, barely blinked. He'd been expecting it for some time.

When Hunter's fists finally stopped their pounding, the skin on his hands had turned red raw and was already starting to bruise. His whole body was trembling with rage, heartbreak, and confusion. Lucien was simply enjoying the show, but he didn't fail to hear Hunter's question.

"You want to know why?" Lucien asked.

Hunter just glared at him. He couldn't stop shaking.

"The real reason is that I couldn't help it," Lucien explained. "I really missed you, Robert. I missed the only true friend I ever had. So eight months before the incident with Jessica, I decided to look you up in Los Angeles. I didn't get in contact with you first because I wanted to surprise you."

Hunter allowed his hands to drop to the sides of his body.

"I found out where you lived," Lucien continued. "That wasn't hard. So I just hung out around your apartment block one evening, waiting for you to come home. I thought that maybe after the huge surprise of seeing an old friend again we could go and grab a beer somewhere, talk about old times . . . catch up." Lucien shrugged. "Maybe deep inside I had a masochistic desire to see if you would pick anything up—any of my psychopathic traits, I mean. Maybe I wanted to check if you could see behind my everyday mask. Or maybe it wasn't that at all. Maybe I was so confident that I just wanted to put myself through a test, to prove to myself that I was really that good. And what better test than to spend a few days in the company of the best criminal-behavior psychologist I knew? Someone who was also a police officer, and about to become a detective. If you weren't able to read the signs, Robert, then who would?"

Hunter's stomach was in turmoil, and he had to concentrate hard not to be sick.

"But that night you didn't come home alone," Lucien proceeded. "I watched you park your car, get out, and like a gentleman, go around to the other side and open the passenger door for someone. Out stepped this beautiful woman. I have to hand it to you, Robert, she was stunning.

"I couldn't really tell you what it was exactly," Lucien said. "But I'd already learned that despite all the desires, despite all the violent thoughts and impulses one gets, despite the unstoppable drive to take someone's life, there still needs to be some sort of trigger to finally push one over the edge.

"With Jessica it was the way she looked at you when you took her hand to help her out of the car, Robert. The way she kissed you right there in the parking lot.

There was so much love between the two of you that I could feel it on my skin all the way from where I was standing."

Hunter's fingers closed into a fist once again.

"I tried, Robert. I tried to resist it. That's why I never approached you. I didn't *want* to do it. I didn't want to take Jessica from you. I left Los Angeles the next morning, and I did all I could to forget about her. If ever I tried to resist an urge, that was it. But what neither of you will ever understand is that once that trigger goes off inside your head, you're doomed. The obsession drives you crazy. You can delay it, but you can't contain it." Lucien tapped the tip of his index finger against his right temple several times. "It comes back night, after day, after night, hammering your brain, until you just can't take it anymore. Until the visions take over your life. And that point came eight months later."

Hunter took a step back from the Plexiglas. He now knew that Lucien's psychopathy had no limits. He also knew that he had been right in his earlier assumption. Years ago, during his Stanford years, Lucien had fooled himself into believing that he was embarking on noble, lifelong research, when in truth, all he was doing was coming up with a bullshit excuse to feed the blood-hungry sociopath inside him.

"So I planned everything to look like a robbery," Lucien said. "I killed two men just to get their fingerprints. I knew they would never be found, so no matter how hard and long the police searched for them, the prints would never be matched to anyone. I returned to Los Angeles. I saw the two of you together again, and then I followed her back to her place."

Even Taylor was now starting to feel numb.

"There was no torture," Lucien added, almost consolingly. "No sexual gratification. I did it as fast as I could, Robert."

"No torture?" Taylor interjected. "Robert said that there were stab wounds all over her body."

Lucien's eyes sought Hunter. "If the autopsy team was competent enough, they should've found out that her first wound, the one to her throat, was the fatal one. All the others were inflicted postmortem. That was part of my robbery deception."

That fact had always bothered Hunter once he'd read the autopsy report. He had put it down to a burst of anger from the perpetrators because Jessica was engaged to a police officer.

"I staged the scene with the broken picture frames, the vandalized photographs, the disturbed house, and the stolen jewelry and money. And that was it. That's how it happened. That's *why* it happened."

Hunter's eyes remained unblinking on Lucien's face as he stepped up against the Plexiglas once again, the fingers on both of his hands still clenched into fists.

"You were right before, Lucien." His voice was so calm, it scared Taylor. "Screw being a detective. Screw what I've sworn to uphold. You *are* a dead man."

77

Ninety seconds later, Hunter and Taylor were standing inside Director Adrian Kennedy's office. Dr. Lambert was also there.

"I understand that this whole scenario has changed for you, Robert," Kennedy said as Hunter stood looking out the window. "No one could've anticipated that sort of revelation, and I am deeply sorry. I'm not going to lie to you and say that I completely understand how you feel, because I don't. No one does." Kennedy's naturally hoarse voice was more fatigued than ever.

He walked over to his desk and picked up a printout before retrieving his reading glasses from his breast pocket.

"But there's one thing that hasn't changed," he said before reading from the document. "Madeleine Reed, twenty-three years old, born in Blue Springs City, Missouri, but at the time living in Pittsburgh, Pennsylvania. She was last seen by her housemate on April ninth, just before she left her apartment to go out for dinner with someone she'd met a few days earlier in a bar. Madeleine never came back that night, which her housemate found strange because Maddy—that's what everyone calls her—didn't make a habit of spending the night with anyone on a first date."

Hunter kept his focus on the world outside Kennedy's window.

"Two days later, she still hadn't turned up," Kennedy added. "That was when the housemate, Selena Nunez, went down to the police station and reported her missing. Despite all efforts from the investigators, they've gotten absolutely nowhere. No one knows what this mysterious man who took her out for dinner on the evening of April ninth looks like. The bartender at the place Madeleine was the night before remembers her. He also remembers seeing her talking with someone who looked a little older than her, but he didn't pay enough attention to the man's face to be able to give the police an accurate description." Kennedy adjusted his reading glasses on his nose. "Madeleine worked for CancerCare. Her specific job was to provide support and friendship to children with terminal cancer, Robert. It shouldn't matter to me, but she's a good person."

Kennedy offered the printout to Hunter.

Hunter didn't move.

"Look at her, Robert."

A few seconds went by before Hunter finally dragged his eyes away from the window and onto the sheet of paper Kennedy had in his hand. Attached to it was a second printout—a six-by-four portrait photograph of Madeleine Reed. She was an attractive girl, with light, smooth skin, green eyes, and hair that dropped in a vibrant black sheen past her shoulders. The smile she'd worn when the photograph was taken looked pure and innocent. She looked happy.

"The fact that Lucien might know where Madeleine Reed is being kept hasn't changed, Robert," Kennedy said again. "You can't walk away from this now. You can't turn your back on her."

Hunter studied the photograph for a while longer before returning the sheet to the director in silence.

Kennedy took the opportunity to press on. "I know you don't work for me, Robert, so I can't order you to do anything, but I do know you. I know what you stand for, and what you've dedicated your life to. And if you allow your emotions to dictate your actions now, no matter how hurt and angry you feel inside, you won't be able to live with yourself later. You know that full well."

A headache was pinching and pricking behind Hunter's eyes.

"I've been searching for Jessica's killers for twenty years, Adrian." Hunter's voice was low and full of hurt. "Not a day has gone by since her murder that I don't regret not being there for her that night. Not a day has gone by since that I haven't promised her that I would find them, and when I did, I would make them pay, no matter the consequences to myself."

"I understand that," Kennedy said.

"Do you?" Hunter questioned. "Do you, really?"

"Yes, I do."

"She was pregnant," Hunter said.

The air was knocked out of Kennedy's lungs. He looked back at Hunter with confusion evident on his face.

"Jessica was pregnant," Hunter repeated. "We had found out that morning, through one of those off-the-shelf pregnancy tests, but we could both feel it was accurate. That was the reason for her booking the restaurant that night. We were supposed to be celebrating. We were both . . ." Hunter paused to catch his breath. "So happy."

Taylor felt a paralyzing chill run through her. She wanted to say something, but she didn't know what, or how.

"Lucien didn't only take the woman that I was supposed to marry from me, Adrian," Hunter said. "He took away the family I was supposed to have."

Kennedy looked down at the floor in silence, his way of paying his respects and recognizing Hunter's pain.

Taylor looked at Hunter with sorrow in her eyes, but the expression on her face showed nothing but admiration. She couldn't even begin to envisage the sort of emotional pain he had had to get through, but she fully understood that such an event had the power to break people, physically and emotionally. It could destroy the strongest of spirits, making them give up on everything. Give up on life. But Hunter hadn't. He'd stayed with the LAPD. He'd stayed focused. He not only found the strength to get by day by day, but he also became the best at what he did.

"I'm sorry, old friend," Kennedy finally said. "I never knew that."

"No one did," Hunter replied. "Not even her family. We wanted to wait until Jess had seen the doctor so we had official confirmation." Hunter's gaze returned to the window. "I asked the coroner to omit it from the autopsy report. That was not the way I wanted her parents to find out, and I saw no point in adding to their pain."

"I can only imagine how devastating that must've been for you, Robert," Kennedy said after a long and dark silence. "And I am so sorry."

"And nevertheless, you want to put me inside an enclosed space with the person I've been searching for for twenty years and swore revenge on, without the security of a Plexiglas wall to hold me back."

"He's been caught, Robert," Kennedy replied in a measured voice. "Lucien is sitting in an underground, escape-proof prison cell five levels below the FBI's Behavioral Research and Instruction Unit. He *is* going to pay for everything he's done. He's going to pay for what he did to Jessica and to you." He pointed to the printout. "But this girl may die if you don't get on that plane with Lucien. I know you don't want to let that happen."

"You can send someone else."

"No we can't, Robert," said Taylor, who was standing by Kennedy's desk, turning to face him. "You heard what Lucien said downstairs. You, me, and him. Not a person less, not a person more. If Madeleine isn't already dead and we break that deal, she will die— alone—probably still holding on to some hope that someone will find her."

Hunter said nothing.

"Courtney is right," Kennedy said. "If Madeleine isn't already dead, we're losing precious time here. We've got to act now. Please don't let your anger and sorrow take away Madeleine's chances of being saved. Her *only* chance of being saved."

Hunter looked at Madeleine's photograph attached to the printout once again.

"She's not dead," he said, not an ounce of doubt in his voice.

"What?" Kennedy asked.

"You said *if Madeleine isn't already dead.*" Hunter shook his head. "Madeleine Reed definitely isn't dead. She's still alive."

78

The unwavering conviction in Hunter's voice was reassuring and confusing in equal measures.

Taylor's question came not in words, but from a slight shake of the head complemented by narrowing eyes.

"She's alive," Hunter reiterated.

"How can you be so sure?" Dr. Lambert asked. "Don't get me wrong, Detective Hunter. I do agree with Director Kennedy. I believe you must act now, but you must also be prepared for the fact that you could already be too late to save this poor girl's life, or even for the fact that Lucien could be sending you on a wild-goose chase. He's a deceiver by nature, with years of experience. As Agent Taylor said during your last interview, Lucien might be looking at this as his last chance to get outside, which increases the chances of him trying something."

"That could be," Hunter replied. "But Madeleine is still alive."

"So I'll repeat Dr. Lambert's question," Kennedy took over. "How can you be so sure, Robert?"

"Because Madeleine Reed is Lucien's trump card,"

Hunter said. "He's been holding on to it from day one. When did you first bring him here to the BRIU?"

"Seven days ago," Kennedy answered. "You know that."

"And yet, he hasn't mentioned her until now," Hunter reminded them. "As Dr. Lambert said, Lucien's got a lot of experience. He's been playing this game for a very long time. Even though he was caught by chance, every move he makes is calculated to the last detail. And any experienced player knows one major rule about his trumps."

"Never play them too soon," Taylor said. "You hold on to them until the best possible moment."

Hunter nodded. "Or until it's imperative that you do show them. You've all mentioned how impressive Lucien's internal clock and calculations are, right? He knows exactly how much food and water he's left Madeleine. He's already said that she's learned how to ration everything almost to perfection. He's calculated the threshold. He's known it from day one, and I'm sure he's got a very accurate idea of where her point of no return is. And yet he saw no reason to play his trump card until now. He wants to make this a race against time, because that puts us under pressure. A hell of a lot more pressure than just finding some victim's remains."

It took a second for Hunter's words to sink in.

"And that's also why he waited until now to reveal that he was your fiancée's killer," Dr. Lambert said, putting the pieces together. "Because it affects your state of mind. It destabilizes you. It makes you emotional, and therefore more vulnerable, more prone to mistakes. Lucien knew that full well."

Goose bumps ran up and down Taylor's skin.

"But that also makes Robert more volatile," she said. "If Lucien weren't behind that Plexiglas wall, he'd probably be dead now." Her gaze moved to Hunter, who returned her stare with one hundred percent conviction.

"And maybe that's exactly what he wants," Dr. Lambert said. "Not to try to escape while he's outside with you both, but suicide by cop."

"Why would he want that?" Taylor asked.

"Because whatever happens, Lucien wants to be remembered," Hunter said. "He wants the notoriety . . . the 'prestige' that comes with being a famous serial killer. He wants his legacy to be studied in psychology and criminology classrooms all over the world. That's one of the reasons he's been writing this encyclopedia of his, if that really is what he's been doing."

"I understand that," Taylor said. "But that will probably happen no matter what. He doesn't have to be killed to achieve it."

"True," Hunter agreed. "But he also understands that his reputation would get an exponential boost if he doesn't end his days behind bars, or get executed by the state. On the other hand, if he's shot dead by the FBI while they're trying to rescue his last victim . . ." Hunter shrugged.

"He becomes a legend," Dr. Lambert agreed.

"So if you think Madeleine Reed is still alive," Kennedy said, addressing Hunter, "and assuming that Lucien's got his calculations right, how long would you say we have, Robert?"

Hunter made a dubious face. "My best guess is that from the time he told us about Madeleine, we would've had around twenty hours to find her. After that, I wouldn't hold out too much hope."

Kennedy checked his watch. "So we've already lost an hour," he said. "We can't waste any more time here, Robert."

Madeleine's photograph was still on the desk. It looked like she was staring straight at them.

"Is the plane ready?" he said.

"It will be by the time you get to the runway," Kennedy replied. "But the two of you need to get ready first."

"Be prepared," Dr. Lambert said as everyone began moving. "Because I think you're right, Detective Hunter. Lucien will try to push both of you to the limit, and he knows that as things stand right now, he won't even need to push that hard. I think that once he gets out there again, he will do whatever it takes not to end up back in our grasp. Even if it costs him his life."

Hunter zipped up his jacket. "And I'm fine with that." He looked at Taylor. "As long as I'm the one who takes the shot."

79

Before heading down to the SUV that was already waiting for them by one of the security exits at the back of the building, Hunter and Taylor were both asked to hand in their shirts so that two state-of-the-art, wireless surveillance microphones and GPS devices could be fitted onto them. The microphones were disguised as regular buttons, but so that a single button didn't conspicuously differ from the others, every button on both shirts had to be replaced. The one just above their belly buttons held the microphone. It connected to a powerful but inconspicuous satellite transmitter that resembled a stick of gum via a small cable strapped to the small of their backs. Director Adrian Kennedy and his team would know their exact location at all times. But as soon as he got his shirt back, Hunter opposed the idea.

"The fake buttons aren't the same color as the original ones," he told Adrian Kennedy.

"They're close enough," Kennedy replied.

"Maybe for most people," Hunter said, "but not for Lucien."

"Are you telling me that you think he's noticed the color of the buttons on your and Agent Taylor's shirts?"

"Trust me. Lucien has noticed everything, Adrian. He's like a sponge."

"Well, this is the best we can do given our time frame," Kennedy said. "I need ears with you at all times, so we're going to have to roll with this."

This could be a costly mistake, Hunter thought.

Everything was already in place by the time Lucien was escorted out of the security exit by two marines ten minutes later. He was wearing the same orange prison jumpsuit he'd been wearing throughout the interviews. His hands and ankles were shackled by metal chains that looped around his waist, restricting his movements—his arms could not come up past his chest, and his step could never reach beyond one foot, making it impossible for him to run.

"Something is missing from this equation," Lucien said to Taylor, as she opened the back door of the SUV to allow him to climb in.

"Detective Hunter will meet us on the plane," Taylor said, knowing exactly what Lucien was referring to.

Lucien laughed. "But of course. He needs time to find himself and maybe check his emotions before this whole thing turns into a total fiasco, isn't that so, Agent Taylor?"

Taylor didn't reply. Instead, she simply held the door open while both marines helped him onto the backseat, locked his chains onto the metal loop on the car's floor, and handed the keys to Taylor.

"I love your sunglasses, Agent Taylor," Lucien said as

Taylor took the passenger seat. "They're very . . . FBI. Do you think I could get a pair, just for the sake of this trip?"

Taylor said nothing.

"I guess that would be a *no*, then."

Lucien looked at his cuffed hands for a short instant, and when he spoke again his voice was controlled and measured—no excitement, no anger, just a robotic, flat tone. "How do you think this is going to end, Agent Taylor?"

The driver, an African American marine who looked like he could probably bench-press the entire SUV, got the car in motion.

Taylor kept her eyes on the road.

"C'mon, Agent Taylor," Lucien insisted. "It's a fair question. I'm interested in knowing what your expectations are. You've done a great job so far. You've managed to obtain information that has led the FBI to retrieve the lost remains of three victims." He raised his eyebrows. "Assuming that your team is competent enough to follow instructions, you should also find the remains of the five victims I left in New Haven. And you have also managed to acquire information that might lead you to a live victim, and, if you succeed in saving her, that will make you a hero, Agent Taylor. That's not bad at all for just two days of interviews. So I think my question is quite fair. How do you think this whole thing is going to end up? Do you think you and Robert will become heroes, or will this turn into your worst nightmare?"

Taylor saw the driver's questioning eyes flick toward her for a fraction of a second.

"Do you think he will do it?" he insisted. "Do you think Robert will avenge Jessica's death? Do you think he'll forget everything he's stood for for most of his life and let his anger take over?"

No reply.

"Do you think he'll shoot me? Or will he use his hands—choke me until I stop breathing?"

Taylor didn't look, but she knew that Lucien's face would be wearing a sickening smile.

They left the FBI Academy compound, heading north toward Turner Field landing strip.

"How would you do it, Agent Taylor? If I had violently taken someone you were desperately in love with away from you, and left you with nothing but bloody doubts, how would you take your revenge on me?"

Taylor felt her blood warming inside her veins, but still, she swallowed every word that threatened to tumble out of her mouth.

"Let me tell you what I think, Agent Taylor. I think he will do it. I think Robert will break, and he will finally get his revenge. And I think that the only way you will be able to stop him is if you shoot him first. The big question is—will you?"

80

Hunter and two marines were waiting by the small, custom-made five-seat Learjet when the black SUV pulled up next to the plane.

Heavy clouds were starting to gather overhead, making it feel like the whole day was changing moods—bright being substituted by dark, blue by gray.

Taylor stepped out of the car and handed one of the marines the keys to Lucien's restraints. They took charge of unlocking him from the backseat and taking him onboard. As they walked past Hunter and took the few steps that led into the plane, Lucien turned and looked into Hunter's eyes. He saw nothing but hurt and anger, and had to fight an internal battle to avoid smiling.

Only when Lucien's chains had been securely locked onto the loops built into the floor of the plane beside one of its seats did Hunter and Taylor board the aircraft.

Lucien's seat was at the rear of the cabin, enclosed by a metal cage equipped with a military-grade, assault-proof electronic lock that could only be activated through a button by the pilot's cockpit.

Taylor placed her jacket on the seat just ahead and to

the right of Lucien's cage, but didn't sit down. Hunter took the seat across the aisle from her. The pilot was waiting patiently.

"So where are we going in Illinois?" Taylor asked Lucien.

"We're not," he replied matter-of-factly.

Taylor hesitated a beat. "What do you mean? You said we were going to Illinois."

"No, I didn't. I said we needed enough fuel to cover the distance from here to Illinois. If we do have enough fuel to get to Illinois, that means that we also have enough fuel to get to New Hampshire. That's where we're going."

Lucien's seat was stationary, but all the others in the cabin could twirl a full three hundred and sixty degrees. Hunter didn't swing his chair around to look at Lucien, but he wasn't surprised that Lucien was still playing games.

"New Hampshire," Taylor said.

"That's correct, Agent Taylor. 'Live free or die.'"

"Okay, so where in New Hampshire are we going?"

"You can tell the pilot to fly due north, toward the Canadian border. I'll give him more details when we enter New Hampshire's airspace."

Taylor passed the instructions to the pilot and returned to her seat. Like Hunter, she preferred not to face the prisoner.

A minute later the plane taxied to the end of the runway, and the pilot announced that they were clear for takeoff. The jet engines roared to life, and within twenty seconds they were airborne. As the plane veered right, the few rays of sunlight that managed to break through the dark clouds reflected sharply off the aircraft's fuselage.

Hunter fixed his eyes out the window as the ground below him slipped away. To him, the plane's bottled air felt denser than ever, as if it had been polluted by Lucien's presence.

Taylor sat still, eyes forward, trying to organize her thoughts. She had a bottle of still water with her, from which she took a tiny sip every minute or two. It wasn't because she was thirsty, it was just a nervous reflex, something her body practically forced her to do in order to try to calm herself down.

Hunter was also struggling to tamp down twenty years of anger and frustration that were dying to break free.

They'd been flying for over half an hour when Lucien spoke again.

"Do you believe that someone can be born evil, Agent Taylor?" he asked.

Taylor sipped her water again while her gaze moved across the aisle to Hunter. His full attention seemed to be on the world outside his window. It looked like he hadn't even heard the question.

In Taylor's silence, Lucien moved on.

"You do know that there are a great number of criminologists, criminal psychologists, and psychiatrists who believe that a person can be born evil, don't you? That some sort of evil gene exists."

Nothing from Taylor.

"Being evil, or overwhelmingly violent, could be a genetic condition. Do you think that's true, Agent Taylor? Do you think a newborn can actually *inherit* being evil, being a killer, just like one can inherit hemophilia, or red hair, or color blindness?"

Taylor took another silent sip of her water.

"C'mon, humor me, Agent Taylor," Lucien said. "In your opinion, can being a senseless killer like me be a product of genetic inheritance?"

Why hadn't they equipped this plane with a soundproof Plexiglas cage instead of a metal one?

"Twenty-seven," Lucien said, resting his head against the chair's backrest.

Reflexively, Taylor looked at Hunter again. He was still looking out the window, but she was sure he'd heard Lucien. Had he just completely changed subjects? Was he giving them coordinates? She spun her chair around.

"Twenty-seven?"

"Twenty-seven states," Lucien explained.

"I've visited sperm banks in twenty-seven different states. All under different names, and backed up by a résumé that would impress the queen of England. It's all part of another one of my ongoing experiments."

Taylor felt the acidic taste of bile rise up in her throat.

"So, if you believe that being a killer can be a product of genetic inheritance, Agent Taylor," Lucien said, "then in a few years' time, we might all have some surprises."

The cabin speakers crackled once before the pilot's voice came through.

"We're approaching the border between Massachusetts and New Hampshire. Do I have any new instructions?"

Lucien's face came alive.

"Let the adventure begin."

Hidden location
Two days earlier

Madeleine Reed blinked heavily several times before she was finally able to open her eyes. Focus did not come instantly. In fact, it took almost two minutes for shapes to start making sense.

She was still curled up against one of the corners in her cell, with the dirty, smelly blanket wrapped around her body like a cocoon. But no matter how tight she wrapped that disgusting rag around her, or how small she made herself, she couldn't keep the cold away—she couldn't stop shivering. The fever might've gone away, or gotten worse. She couldn't tell anymore. Every atom in her body ached with such intensity that she was constantly on the verge of passing out.

The only sound inside her cell was the buzzing of flies around the overflowing bucket of waste in the opposite corner.

Madeleine coughed a couple of times, and her dry throat felt as if it were on fire. The nauseating pain made her eyelids flutter like butterfly wings. She rested her head against the wall for a moment.

As she gathered herself together one more time, she looked at her unrecognizable, bony hands. Her nails were all broken, their beds crusted with dry blood. Her knuckles were red and swollen. She had never felt so weak, so hungry, so thirsty.

Madeleine realized that there were parts of her blanket that were still damp, probably from when her body was soaking wet due to her high fever. She was so desperate that in a moment of madness, she brought the blanket to her mouth and eagerly sucked on it, trying to get some of the moisture from the fabric onto her cracked lips and dry mouth. But what she got was a mouthful of dirt and such a revolting taste that it made her gag.

Empty plastic water bottles were scattered about the cell. Not even a drop was left in any of them, but that didn't stop Madeleine from reaching for one and trying again. She brought the bottle to her mouth and threw her head back, crunching and squeezing the bottle with both of her hands.

Nothing.

Exhausted by the effort, she let the bottle fall to the floor again.

Her eyelids fluttered one more time. Though desperately tired and overwhelmed by sadness, she still didn't want to fall back asleep. She knew that the extreme exhaustion she felt was her body shutting down. It just didn't have enough energy to stay awake. It didn't have enough energy to keep all of her organs working properly, like a corporation slowly closing its departments because it didn't have enough resources to keep them all operational.

Madeleine remembered watching a TV documentary about that once. A dehydrated and malnourished body will slowly eat itself away, first its fat stores, then the proteins and nutrients from its muscles, until they are all gone and their energy depleted. After that, the body will start shutting down. The liver and kidneys will stop functioning properly. The brain, made up as it is of seventy-five to eighty percent water, will really feel the damaging effects of dehydration. Its response will vary from person to person, and will be completely arbitrary, ranging from very vivid hallucinations to a total meltdown. At that point, the damage caused to the cerebral mass will be irreversible.

With no more nutrients, the body runs out of energy, becoming overexhausted. But nothing on earth is as complex and as intelligent as the human body. Even under such intense duress, its defense mechanism will work to the best of its ability. To try to save the little energy it has left, and to avoid the person dying in agonizing pain, the spent body will force itself to fall asleep, this time forever.

Madeleine knew she was dying. She knew that if she fell back asleep, she would probably never wake up again. But she also didn't know what else to do. She felt so tired that even moving a finger felt like running a marathon.

"I don't want to die," she whispered to herself. "I don't want to die like this. I don't want to die in this place. Somebody please help me."

Then a crazy idea came to her. She'd heard stories of

people who drank their own urine, and as disgusting as that might've sounded, her fatigued brain was fighting to keep her alive.

Without giving it another thought, Madeleine reached once more for one of the empty water bottles. With tremendous effort she got back on her feet, unbuttoned and unzipped her dirty and now ripped trousers, and pulled them down to her ankles. Her panties followed. Holding the bottle in the right position, she closed her eyes and concentrated as best as she could, squeezing her leg and stomach muscles tight.

Finally, after what seemed like an eternity, a few tiny drops splashed against the bottom of the bottle. Madeleine became so happy she started laughing hysterically. That was until she looked in the bottle.

The few drops of urine she had managed to squeeze out were a dark-amber color. She knew that was a very bad sign.

The darker the color of urine, the more dehydrated the body is.

The drops she had in that bottle were probably ninety-nine percent toxin. If she drank them, it would be like drinking poison. It wouldn't help her stay alive, it would merely speed her death.

She stared at the container in her hand for a long moment, the bottle shaking. She wanted to cry, but in her advanced stage of dehydration, her lacrimal glands could produce no tears.

Finally strength left her and she collapsed to the ground. The bottle rolled away across to the other side of her cell.

"I don't want to die." The words barely escaped her

trembling lips, but she couldn't battle anymore. Her vision blurred as her eyes closed. She had no more strength to keep herself awake.

She had no more hope.

She had no more faith.

She allowed herself to begin accepting the inevitable.

82

New Hampshire airspace
The present

Since Lucien's restraints didn't allow his hands to rise past his chest, he bent forward so he could scratch his nose.

Taylor had swiveled her chair around to face him, while Hunter still kept his facing forward.

"Okay," Taylor said. "So we've entered New Hampshire's airspace. Where do we go from here?"

Lucien took his time. "Damn, these are uncomfortable. You wouldn't be so kind as to scratch my nose for me, would you, Agent Taylor?"

She scowled at him in silence.

"Yeah, I didn't think so." Lucien finally sat back up. "Tell the pilot to keep on flying due north. Let me know when he is over White Mountain National Forest."

White Mountain National Forest is a federally managed forest that totals an area of 750,852 acres. About ninety-four percent of it is located in the state of New Hampshire. It's so vast, no aircraft could miss it.

Taylor passed the instructions to the pilot and returned to her seat.

They flew for another twenty-seven silent minutes before the pilot's voice came through the speakers again.

"We're just about to reach the southern border of White Mountain National Forest. Shall I keep on flying north, or is there a new piece of this puzzle he'd like to let me know of?"

Taylor faced Lucien one more time and waited.

Lucien was staring at the backs of his hands as if there were something mysterious on them only he could see.

"Now it gets good," he said without lifting his eyes. "Tell the pilot we're going to Berlin."

Taylor stared at him in disbelief. "Say that again."

"Relax, Agent Taylor," Lucien said. "I'm not referring to Berlin, Germany. That would've been too far-fetched, even for me. But if you check the map of New Hampshire, you'll find that just north of White Mountain National Forest, there's a small town called Berlin. Its municipal airport, interestingly enough, is located eight miles north, near another small town called Milan." He laughed. "Very European, isn't it?"

Taylor's expression relaxed a little.

"Tell the pilot we need to land at Berlin's municipal airport."

Taylor used the plane's intercom to pass on the new instructions to the pilot.

Hunter could hardly believe how well prepared Lucien was. *How long has he been planning this?* he asked himself.

The state of New Hampshire was one of the few that did not have a specific FBI field office. Its jurisdiction

fell under the Boston field office in Massachusetts—
way too far for Director Kennedy to dispatch a backup
team. Even though Lucien had given them detailed
instructions that no one was to follow them by land
or air, Hunter knew Adrian Kennedy wouldn't simply
comply with the requests of a serial murderer. But despite the director's desire for a plan B, with no FBI field
office in New Hampshire, if Adrian Kennedy wanted
a second, local team tagging Hunter and Taylor, he
would have to contact the county sheriff's department,
or the local police department. Neither was trained in
high-profile surveillance, and that was too high a risk.
Hunter had no doubt Lucien had factored all this into
his sick equation.

"I've just contacted the airport in Berlin." The pilot's
voice came through the cabin speakers one more time.
"We're clear for landing, and we'll be starting our de-
scent in five minutes."

One step at a time, Lucien thought to himself. *One
step at a time.*

83

After being airborne for exactly one hour and forty-eight minutes, the Learjet touched down at the small, rural landing strip, and quickly taxied to a spot at the end of the runway, away from the other small planes. The pilot had already alerted the airport's traffic-control center that the plane was an official FBI aircraft on federal business and not to be approached.

"So what now?" Hunter asked Lucien even before the plane came to a complete stop. This was the first time Hunter had addressed him since Quantico.

"Now we get a car," Lucien replied and made a dubious face. "But this isn't LAX, Robert. There are no car-rental companies in the airport's foyer. Actually, there isn't even a foyer." He jerked his head toward the window. "You'll see. You'll be lucky if you find a vending machine somewhere around here."

Taylor threw a questioning look at Hunter.

"You can call a rental company if you like," Lucien proceeded. "I'm sure you can get a number for one either in the town of Berlin or Milan, but it will take them about twenty-five minutes to get a car out here. If you don't want to wait, I suggest we improvise."

"Improvise?" Taylor said.

Lucien shrugged. "Commandeer a car or something. Like in the movies. You're the ones with FBI badges. I'm sure the folks around here would be very impressed by them."

Taylor considered what to do.

"Remember that every second counts for poor Madeleine," Lucien added. "So feel free to take as long as you like."

"You stay here with him," Hunter said, already moving toward the plane's door. "I'll go."

Taylor agreed with a nod. Right now she really didn't want to leave Hunter alone with their prisoner.

As soon as Hunter left the cabin, Lucien shut his eyes and seemed to fall back into one of his meditative states.

"Let's go," Hunter said as he stepped back onto the plane.

"We've got a car already?" Taylor asked, jumping to her feet. Hunter had been gone for less than three minutes.

He nodded. "I sort of borrowed it from the guy who runs air traffic control here."

"Fair enough," she said. She didn't need any more explanation. Taylor then unholstered her weapon and pointed it at Lucien. "Okay, we're going to do this step-by-step. When Robert presses the release button to the door of your cage, the floor chain loops will also disengage. You will then stand up—*slowly*—step out of the cell, and stop. Do you understand?"

Lucien nodded, unimpressed.

Taylor gave Hunter a nod. He hit the button by the

door to the cockpit before also unholstering his weapon and placing Lucien dead in his aim.

An electronic buzzing sound echoed loudly throughout the cabin. Lucien's cage door clicked open and retracted. The metal chains that kept his ankles and hands shackled together were also released from their floor and chair restraints.

"Up," Taylor said.

Lucien complied.

"Now step forward and outside the cage."

Lucien complied.

"Walk toward us and the exit, nice and slow."

Lucien complied.

Taylor moved over and positioned herself behind Lucien. Hunter stayed ahead of him. He went down the steps first. Lucien and Taylor followed shortly after.

A red Jeep Grand Cherokee was parked just a few feet from the plane. Hunter walked over and opened the back door.

"Nice car," Lucien commented.

"Get in," Hunter replied.

Lucien paused and looked around himself. There was no one around. Berlin's municipal airport was nothing more than a landing strip of asphalt built next to a forest. There was no waiting room, or lounge, or so much as a fast-food restaurant. Two midsized hangars, large enough to fit maybe a couple of private planes each, were located east of the runway. Just south of them were a few smaller administrative buildings. Nothing else.

Lucien looked up at the sky. Night was fast approaching, and with it a cold breeze was settling in. Lucien's hair flopped on his forehead and he flipped his head to flick it back in place. His eyes tracked the night for a long while, searching, listening.

"Get in," Hunter commanded again.

With shuffling steps, Lucien moved toward the car. Hunter held the door open. Like a starlet eager to preserve her modesty in a too-short dress, Lucien sat down first before bringing his legs in. With his hands and feet shackled to his waist, it was easier that way.

Hunter closed the door and signaled Taylor to go over to the other side. She did. Only once Taylor had taken her place in the backseat did Hunter get into the driver's seat.

Taylor's gun was still aimed at Lucien.

"I want your back against the seat," she said. "And your arm on the door's armrest at all times." She pulled down the backseat's center armrest, creating a flimsy division between Lucien and herself. "You make any sudden movements, and I swear I'll blow your kneecaps. Is that simple enough for you?"

"Perfectly simple," Lucien replied.

Hunter started the car.

"So where to from here?" he asked.

Lucien smiled.

"Absolutely nowhere."

84

FBI National Academy, Quantico, Virginia

Hunter had been right. Director Kennedy always had a plan B.

Exactly ten minutes after the Learjet transporting Hunter, Taylor, and Lucien took off, a second followed. This one was carrying five of Kennedy's top agents, all of them expert marksmen well trained in covert operations. With them, they had a satellite-tracking device specially tuned to track the GPS signals coming from Hunter's and Taylor's microphone buttons. They also had ears in the plane, as the surveillance microphones transmitted back not only to Director Kennedy at the FBI Academy, but also to the second jet and its agents.

Inside the FBI operations control room back at Quantico, Adrian Kennedy and Dr. Lambert were following both planes' progress on the radar screen. As soon as the first jet landed in Berlin's airport, Kennedy reached for the phone in his pocket.

"Director," Agent Nicholas Brody, the team leader

in the second jet, answered his cell phone before the second ring.

"Bird One just landed," Kennedy said.

"Yes, we saw," Brody replied.

"Tell your pilot to start flying in circles right now," Kennedy said. "Do not, and I repeat, do not fly through any airspace that is visible from the airport. I'll call you back when you're clear for landing."

"Roger that, sir."

Agent Brody disconnected from the call, passed the new instructions to the pilot, returned to his seat, and waited.

85

Hunter met Lucien's cold eyes in the rearview mirror. The smile on Lucien's lips was a mixture of arrogance and defiance.

"What was that?" Taylor asked, her patience more than wearing thin.

Lucien kept his gaze on the rearview mirror, his eyes battling with Hunter's.

"We're going absolutely nowhere," he said again, his tone controlled and even.

Hunter calmly turned the engine off.

"What do you mean, Lucien?"

"I mean exactly what I said back in my cell," Lucien said. "The deal was: just the three of us, no one following. You break the deal, I take you nowhere. I thought I'd made that perfectly clear."

Hunter took his hands off the steering wheel and turned his palms up in surrender.

"Do you see anyone other than the three of us? Anyone following us at all?"

"Not yet." Lucien replied confidently before his eyes moved up and to the right. "But they're up there, probably waiting, flying around in circles. You know it and I know it."

Taylor's inquisitive eyes also found Hunter's in the rearview mirror. He kept his gaze on Lucien.

"No, we don't know that," Hunter said. "And neither do you. You're making assumptions."

"My assumptions are always based on facts, Robert," Lucien said.

"Facts?" Taylor this time. "What facts?"

Lucien's stare finally left the rearview mirror and moved to Taylor. On its way Lucien noticed that her gun grip had slacked just a touch.

"Let's see, Agent Taylor, we can get a move on as soon as you and Robert take off your shirts and throw them out the window. How about that?"

"Excuse me?" Taylor said. The offended look she managed to make was expertly executed.

"Your shirts," Lucien repeated. "Take them off and throw them out the window."

Silence from Hunter and Taylor.

"You disappoint me, Robert," Lucien said. "Did you think I wouldn't notice the buttons on both of your shirts?"

A muscle flexed on Taylor's jaw.

Lucien addressed her. "It was a good try, but the colors don't quite match the ones you had earlier." He lifted his right index finger and pointed at Taylor's shirt. "Those are about two shades darker. I'm guessing that what we have here is a microphone, a GPS satellite transmitter, and perhaps a camera?

"Disappointing. I'd imagined that the FBI would be

more careful than that." Lucien shrugged. "But then again, I didn't give you guys that much notice, did I?"

Hunter thought back to his conversation with Director Kennedy in reference to the buttons—*This could be a costly mistake.*

"So," Lucien carried on, "we have a few options here. You can both take off your shirts and throw them out the window." He gave Taylor a provocative wink. "And that would no doubt add to my pleasure here in the backseat. Or you can rip the buttons off, one by one, and throw them out the window." Lucien was still staring at Taylor. "I bet you have a beautiful belly button, Agent Taylor."

"Fuck you." Taylor couldn't contain herself.

Lucien laughed. "Alternatively, you can keep your shirts on with the buttons intact and just rip off the satellite transmitters, which I'm sure are taped to your bodies somewhere.

"Please," Lucien added, "waste as much time as you like thinking about it." He placed his head against the leather headrest and closed his eyes. "Let me know when you've made up your minds."

Hunter unbuckled his seat belt, leaned forward a little, and ripped the satellite transmitter from his lower back.

With her weapon still aimed at Lucien, Taylor did the same.

• • •

Back in the control room in Quantico, Director Adrian Kennedy heard a scraping sound. A moment after that Hunter's microphone went completely silent. A couple of seconds later so did Taylor's. The dots that represented each of them on their radar screen faded to nothing.

The agent sitting at the radar station quickly typed several commands into his computer before finally looking up at Adrian Kennedy. "We've lost them, sir. I'm sorry. There's nothing we can do from here."

"Son of a bitch," Kennedy whispered between clenched teeth.

Inside Bird Two, circling the sky near Berlin's municipal airport, Agent Brody ran his hand through his close-cropped hair, and uttered the exact same thing.

86

That's much better," Lucien said once Hunter and Taylor had both dropped their satellite transmitters out their windows. "Now, let's be on the safe side, shall we? Take off your belts and drop them outside the window as well."

"Those were the only transmitters we had on," Taylor said.

"Noted," Lucien said with a polite nod. "But forgive me for not trusting you at this particular moment, Agent Taylor. Now, if you please, the belts."

Hunter and Taylor complied, dropping them outside the windows.

"Now empty your pockets. Change, credit cards, wallets, pens—all of it. And your watches too."

"How about this?" Taylor said, showing Lucien his key chain, the one they had used to gain access to the house in Murphy, North Carolina.

"Oh, you better hang on to that, Agent Taylor. We'll need it to get into this place."

Hunter and Taylor dropped their belongings out the windows.

"Don't worry," Lucien said. "I'm sure the pilot will

collect everything once we drive off. Nothing will be lost. Now, since we're on a roll here, let's do the same with your shoes too. Take them off and leave them outside."

"The shoes?" Taylor asked.

"I've seen transmitters hidden inside heels, Agent Taylor. And since you've already abused my trust once, I'm not leaving anything to chance. But if you care to waste more time, you'll get no opposition from me."

Seconds later, Hunter's boots and Taylor's shoes hit the asphalt by the side of the car.

Lucien leaned forward slowly and looked down at Taylor's bare feet.

"You have very pretty toes, Agent Taylor." He nodded his amusement. "Red, the color of passion. Interesting. Did you know that it's estimated that as many as thirty to forty percent of men have some sort of foot fetish? I'm sure that there are people out there who'd kill just to be able to touch those pretty toes."

Instinctively cringing at his words, Taylor moved her feet back under the seat.

Lucien laughed.

"And last but not least," he continued. "Let's get rid of the cell phones, shall we? We all know that they have trackable GPS systems."

As much as this upset them, Hunter and Taylor couldn't argue. Lucien still held all the cards in this game. They did as they were told, and the phones were discarded as well.

Satisfied, Lucien smiled at Hunter via the rearview mirror.

"I think we're good now," he said. "You can start the car again, Robert."

Hunter did, and the satellite navigation system came to life on the 8.4-inch touch screen on the dashboard.

"You won't need that," Lucien said. "There's no road name, or number or anything. Just a dirt path. I'll guide you. First thing we've got to do is get the hell out of this shithole of an airport."

87

FBI National Academy, Quantico, Virginia

D irector Kennedy stared at the radar screen inside the control room at the FBI Academy in Quantico for a long time, possibilities running wild inside his head.

"We can try to track the GPS signals in their cell phones," the agent at the radar station offered.

Kennedy shrugged. "We can give that a spin, but this guy is too smart. He figured out the buttons just because they were a couple of shades darker than the original ones, for Christ's sake. Who notices the color of buttons on someone else's shirt?"

"Someone who knows what to expect," Dr. Lambert said. "Lucien never expected the FBI to simply bend over and accept his demands. He knew we would try something, and he was ready for it."

"And that's exactly what I mean," Kennedy said. "If he was ready for the buttons, I don't think there's a chance he would allow Robert and Agent Taylor to proceed carrying their cell phones with them. Even a ten-year-old kid knows that a cell phone GPS system is trackable." He looked at the agent managing the controls. "But by all means, give it a spin."

The agent called up an internal FBI application on his computer. "What's the agent's name and title again?" he asked.

"Courtney Taylor," Kennedy replied. "She's with the Behavioral Research and Instruction Unit."

A few more keyboard clicks.

"Found her," the agent said.

The application he had called up on his screen listed the trackable GPS ID for every cell phone the bureau issued.

"Give me a few seconds." The agent began typing furiously. A moment later the word *locating* appeared on his screen, followed by three blinking dots. Just a few seconds after that the screen announced *GPS ID found*.

A new dot appeared on the radar system.

"The phone is live," the agent said. "The GPS is still transmitting, which means it hasn't been destroyed, and the battery is still in it. The location is exactly the same as we had before. They're still on the runway at Berlin's municipal airport."

"Either that," Kennedy said, "or they were told to leave their phones behind." He looked at Dr. Lambert, who nodded.

"That's what I would do."

The cell phone in Kennedy's pocket rang. It was Agent Brody from Bird Two.

"Director," Brody said once Kennedy answered the call, "our pilot has just been in contact with the pilot in Bird One. He said that the car with the target is gone, but they left behind a pile of stuff on the runway—cell phones, wallets, belts, even shoes. The target is taking no chances."

Kennedy had his answer.

"What do you suggest we do?" Brody asked. "With no ears on the ground, and no accurate target location, landing might be too risky, and even if we get away with it without the target noticing us, we don't have a signal to follow once we're on the ground."

"I understand," Kennedy said. "And the answer is: I'm not sure yet. Let me call you back once I figure something out." He disconnected. His tired brain was working hard to come up with an idea. And then a thought came to him. "The car," he said, looking at Dr. Lambert and then at the radar station agent. "Robert got the car from the guy who runs air traffic control at the airport. His name is Josh. We heard that whole conversation through Robert's button mic, remember? Josh said he just got the Jeep a couple of months ago."

"And a lot of new cars," the agent said, picking up on Kennedy's line of thought, "already come equipped with an antitheft satellite tracking system. It's definitely worth a try."

Kennedy nodded. "Let's get Josh on the phone right now."

88

As soon as he drove through the airport gates, Hunter found himself on East Side River Road.

"Make a left," Lucien said. "Then take your first right. We've got to cross the small bridge into the town of Milan. Unfortunately, it doesn't quite compare to the one in Italy. No duomo to see here. Actually, nothing to see here at all."

Hunter followed Lucien's instructions. They crossed the bridge and passed an elementary school on their right before coming to a T-junction at the top of the road.

"Hang a right, and just follow the road," Lucien commanded.

Hunter did, and within a few hundred yards he drove past a few houses—some small, some a little larger, but nothing extravagant.

"Welcome to the town of Milan, New Hampshire," Lucien said, jerking his chin toward the window. "There's nothing here but rednecks, fields, and solitude. It's a great place to disappear, go under the radar. No one will disturb you here. No one cares. And that's one of the greatest things about America—it's riddled with towns like these. In every state you visit, you'll find tons of Milans and Berlins and Murphys and Shitkickers-villes. Just godforsaken places where many of the streets don't even have names, where people don't notice if you keep to yourself."

Taylor felt the weight of Lucien's key chain in her pocket and thought back to the seventeen keys it held. Each one of them could belong to a different anonymous hovel.

Lucien read her like a book.

"You're wondering how I come upon these places, aren't you, Agent Taylor?"

"No, I'm not," Taylor replied, just to contradict Lucien. "I don't really care."

Hunter checked her in his rearview mirror.

Taylor's reply didn't deter Lucien from his lesson.

"They are actually quite easy to come by," he explained. "You can buy neglected, abandoned, half-destroyed places that no one wants or cares about anymore for next to nothing. If there is an owner, he or she usually just wants to get rid of the burden, so they'll consider almost any offer. No refurbishment needed either. On the contrary, the more fucked-up, dirty, rotten, and putrid the place is, the better. And you know why that is, don't you, Robert?"

Hunter kept his eyes on the road, but he knew exactly why. *The fear factor.* You throw an abducted victim into a rancid, dark place, infested with rats or cockroaches, and the location alone will scare the life out of them.

Lucien didn't wait for an answer this time; he knew that Hunter knew. He moved his head from side to side, and then forward and backward to try to release some of the tension in his neck.

"This particular house," he continued, "was sheer luck, but a great find. It belonged to someone I met while at Yale. His great-grandfather built it one hundred years ago. The house was passed down from generation to generation, being refurbished twice before it finally ended up as my friend's property, but he hated everything about this place—the location, the looks, the layout and, according to him, its legacy and its history. In his mind, the house was cursed, a jinx. His mother died in an accident in the backyard. A few years later, his father hanged himself in the kitchen. His grandfather also died there. He said that he never wanted to see this place again. If he did, he'd burn it to the ground. I offered to buy it from him, but he wouldn't have it. He just gave me the keys, signed away the deed, and said *Take it. It's yours.*"

Once they passed the initial cluster of houses, the scenery began to change. To their right, following the banks of the river, were nicely cropped fields that stretched as far as the eye could see. To their left was nothing but densely populated forests.

After about two miles, Hunter started noticing several unmarked dirt paths that sprang out from the main road, leading deeper into the forest fields on their left. From his vantage, he couldn't see how deep they went, or where they led.

Lucien was still watching Hunter in the rearview mirror.

"You're wondering which one of these will take you to where Madeleine is, aren't you, Robert?"

Hunter locked eyes with him for a quick moment.

Lucien gave Hunter a tight smile. "Well, we'll be there soon enough. And for your sake, I really hope we're not too late."

89

The road swerved slightly to the left, then to the right, then to the left again. There were no crossroads or tight bends, just more dirt paths that appeared every so often, branching away from the main road and into the unknown. The forestland to their left seemed to become thicker the farther they went. Hunter switched the Jeep's inside lights on as the darkness deepened. There was no way he would allow Lucien to hide his movements.

"How much farther?" Taylor asked.

Lucien turned and looked out his window before carrying his gaze across to the one on the other side.

"Not long."

The road curved left again in a half-moon shape, following the contour of the river on their right. The orderly fields were all but gone, replaced by dense trees.

"Keep your eyes peeled for a sharp left turn that's coming up, Robert," Lucien said. "Not a dirt path."

Hunter slowed down and drove for another one hundred and fifty yards.

"Yep," Lucien nodded. "That's the one. Right ahead."

Hunter bent left.

The road seemed to stretch forever into undiluted blackness. Since they'd left the airport, not a single vehicle had crossed their path. No one had appeared in their rearview mirror either. The farther they went, the more it felt like they were driving away from civilization and into some sort of twilight world.

They drove for another mile before the road became a bumpy dirt path. Hunter shifted down and wondered if he should engage the four-wheel drive just in case.

"We're lucky," Lucien said. "It looks like there's been no rain lately. These roads can easily turn into a nightmare of pools and mud when rain comes."

Hunter slowed down a little more, moving from one side of the road to the other to avoid potholes, doing his best so the car wouldn't jerk any more than necessary.

"There's a right turn coming up," Lucien announced, tilting his head to one side to get a better look at the windshield. "We need to take it, Robert."

"This one?" Hunter asked, slowing and pointing to a turn about twenty-five yards ahead of them.

"That's it."

The road got bumpier still. The next mile seemed to take them an eternity.

"One more left turn," Lucien said, "coming up, and we'll be almost there, but keep your eyes open, Robert—it's a tiny path, and it's quite hidden away."

Hunter veered left. The trail was barely wide enough for the Jeep to fit through, and shrubs and bushes scraped the side of the vehicle.

"Oops," Lucien commented. "I don't think the air traffic controller back at the airport will be happy about this, but then again, since his car was commandeered by the FBI, I'm sure it will be federally insured."

This time Hunter had nowhere to go to swerve away from the bigger bumps and potholes. Lucky for them that they were in a brand-new car, Hunter thought, and the suspension was strong and steady.

After another half a mile, the road came to an abrupt end. Hunter put the car in neutral and looked around. Taylor did the same. There was nothing but forest surrounding them.

"Did we take a wrong turn somewhere?" Taylor asked.

"No," Lucien replied. "This is it."

Taylor looked out the window again. All she saw were the Jeep's headlights' reflections on the shrubs and trees.

"This is it?" she repeated incredulously. "Where?"

Lucien nodded toward the forest in front of them. "We have to walk the rest of the way. You can't get there by car."

90

Hunter was the first to leave the Jeep. Once he was out, he unholstered his weapon and opened the back door for Lucien. Taylor followed shortly after.

"Now what?" she asked, looking around.

"Through there," Lucien said, indicating a few loose tree branches that'd been piled up against each other just ahead and to the right of where the Jeep was parked.

"We're walking with no light and no shoes?" Taylor asked Hunter, indicating their bare feet.

"Not much I can do about the shoes," he replied before reaching back inside the car for the glove compartment. He came back with a Maglite Pro LED flashlight. "But we do have light."

"That's handy," Taylor said.

"I knew night was approaching," Hunter said. "And I wasn't counting on Lucien's hiding place being straightforward. So I also asked the air traffic controller for a flashlight."

"Robert Hunter," Lucien said, nodding and pursing his lips appraisingly. "Always thinking a step ahead. Too bad you didn't foresee the shoe problem, but don't worry Agent Taylor, we don't have to walk far. Hey, if I can make it all shackled up like this, you should have no problem with those pretty feet of yours."

"Let's go," Hunter commanded, eager to cut his time with Lucien as short as possible.

They assumed the same formation as when they had deplaned. Hunter took point, Lucien came second, and Taylor stayed four to five steps behind Lucien, her weapon always trained just a couple of inches below his neckline.

Hunter quickly removed the branches Lucien had indicated, revealing a well-worn trail.

"Just follow it," Lucien said. "The place isn't very far from here."

Despite already being in a hurry, Hunter was filled with an extra sense of urgency, as if something he couldn't quite pinpoint was off. But he couldn't dwell on it. Madeleine Reed was waiting.

"Let's move," he said.

The flashlight had a wide, ultrabright beam, which made things a little easier.

They took to the trail, and surprisingly, Lucien didn't try to slow them down with the excuse of his shackled legs. He didn't have to. Pebbles and sharp-edged sticks forced Hunter and Taylor to move more tentatively than they would've liked.

They had covered only about thirty yards when the track swerved hard right, then left, and then it really felt as if they had crossed through some sort of twilight gate. All of a sudden, the bushes, trees, and scrubs gave way to a plain field—a clearing in the middle of nowhere.

"And here we are," Lucien said with a proud smile.

Hunter and Taylor paused, their eyes scanning around in disbelief.

"What the hell is this?"

91

Hunter shined his flashlight on the structure before them.

It was a squared, ivy-covered brick house in the style of one hundred years ago, with white Romanesque columns outside the front entryway, which had surely once been imposing. Now, only two of the original four were still standing, and those had cracks running from top to bottom.

Whatever remained of its first incarnation as some-one's grand hillside home was now merely memory. Add to that the disfiguration caused by the elements and a total disregard and lack of care for the property, and the result was the carcass of the house they had in front of them—a battered shell of a home.

Three of the four outside walls still remained, but they all had holes and major fissures in them, as if the house belonged in a Middle Eastern war zone. The south wall, on the right side of the house, had almost entirely crumbled into a pile of rubble. Most of the internal walls had also collapsed, filling what remained of the place with debris. The roof had caved in almost everywhere, with the exception of the old living room at the front of the house, the corridor beyond it, and the kitchen on the left, where it was still partially in place. Wild vegetation had grown through the floorboards and among the rubble. The windows were all broken, and some of the window frames had been ripped from the walls as if by an internal explosion.

"Welcome to one of my favorite hiding places," Lucien said.

"This is bullshit." Taylor couldn't hide the anger in her voice. "You're telling us that you left Madeleine somewhere in this ghost shell of a house—no windows, no doors, no walls, and she never walked out?"

Lucien's gaze flashed to Taylor, his eyes dark vials filled with venom.

"Not somewhere inside it, Agent Taylor." He paused and ran his tongue over his bottom lip like a lizard. "Buried underneath it."

92

Lucien's words sent a rash of fear crawling across Taylor's skin. Her confused gaze immediately returned to what was left of the house, before moving to the soil surrounding it.

"Well, not exactly buried," Lucien clarified. "Let me show you." He lifted both cuffed hands and pointed toward the north side of the disfigured structure. "Through there."

In a hurry, Hunter and the flashlight took point again. Lucien and Taylor followed.

"My friend's grandfather," Lucien said as they started walking, "and by *friend* I mean the person I got this place from, was a hard-core, old-school patriot. I was told that he had his best years in this house during the United States versus the Soviet Union era. You know, 'death to all communists' kind of thing. And he really subscribed to that ideology. Nuclear power was still in its infancy. But there was plenty of talk about a possible atomic war between the two countries."

As soon as they reached the side of the house, Hunter and Taylor understood what Lucien was talking about.

Halfway along the north wall stood a large, thick

metal basement-entry double door. The doors were locked together by a Sargent and Greenleaf military-grade padlock, very similar to the one they'd found in the house in Murphy.

"My friend's grandfather," Lucien continued, "in his paranoia and deep belief that an atomic war was inevitable and imminent, refurbished the whole place, extending and adding a substantial bomb shelter to the original basement." He nodded at the padlocked doors. "The house might look like an earthquake site, but the shelter has more than lived up to its expectations." He indicated the padlock. "The key for that is on the key chain."

Taylor reached for it immediately.

"Which one?" she asked urgently, holding up the bunch of keys with one hand, her gun still trained on Lucien.

Lucien leaned forward and squinted at them for a second. "The sixth one starting from your left."

Taylor holstered her gun and selected the key, knowing that Hunter had his weapon aimed at Lucien, and reached for the padlock.

Hunter and Lucien waited, and as they did, Hunter's uneasy sensation that something wasn't quite right came back to him. He looked around for an instant.

"What's at the back of the house?" he asked.

Lucien studied him for a moment, and then let his gaze move toward the far end of the house.

"A very badly treated backyard," he replied. "There's a large pond as well, which now looks more like a deep pool of mud. Would you like me to give you a tour? I have all the time in the world."

Click. The padlock came undone. Taylor unhooked it from the doors and threw it away before grabbing one of the handles and pulling it toward her. The door barely moved.

"Heavy, aren't they?" Lucien commented. "As I've said, this isn't a regular cellar, Agent Taylor. It's a fallout shelter."

"I'll do it," Hunter said.

Taylor unholstered her gun once more, and stepped back while Hunter first pulled the right door open, then the left.

They were immediately hit by a breath of warm, stale air. The doors revealed a concrete staircase that took them down deeper than they would've imagined. There were at least thirty steps.

Hunter led the way, hurrying.

At the bottom, they were greeted by another heavy metal door with a sturdy lock.

"The seventh key," Lucien announced. "The one to the right of the one you used on the padlock."

Taylor moved forward and unlocked the door before pushing it open.

The air inside the dark room beyond it was leaden with dust, and felt even staler, but there was something else in the air, something that both Hunter and Taylor easily recognized. They'd been around it too many times.

It was the smell of death.

93

Sometimes sour, sometimes putrid, sometimes sickly sweet, sometimes bitter, sometimes nauseating, and most of the time a combination of everything bad.

Most would say that there's no specific smell to death, but it chokes your heart and saddens your soul in a way that nothing else does.

Hunter and Taylor were filled with a disquieting fear. *We've wasted too much time. We're too late.*

Hunter shined the beam of his flashlight into the room and moved it around almost frantically.

It was empty.

Lucien took a deep, healthy breath, like a hungry man taking in the aroma of freshly cooked food.

"Wow, I missed this smell."

"Madeleine?" Taylor called into the room, her gaze chasing after the beam of the flashlight. "Madeleine?"

"It would've been very stupid of me if I had left Madeleine locked inside the very first room one comes to in the shelter, wouldn't it?"

"Where is she?" Taylor asked.

"There's a light switch on the wall to the right of the door," Lucien told them.

Hunter reached for it.

A feeble, yellowish bulb at the center of the ceiling flicked a couple of times, as if in doubt whether it would come on or not. It finally did, and it brought with it an electronic hiss that echoed annoyingly around the room.

Hunter's eyes searched the place.

It was a semibare space twenty feet square. Two of the thick, solid concrete walls were adorned by a few handmade bookshelves, all of them loaded with dusty books. The wall to the left of where they stood had a single steel door in its center, with a dappled gunmetal look to its surface, as though it were supposed to draw the eye. Against the wall directly in front of them was a console desk that must've been at least sixty years old, where a multitude of buttons, switches, levers, and old-fashioned dial gauges could be found. A blank computer monitor hung on the wall just above the console desk. This was definitely the shelter's main control room.

The floor was simple polished concrete. A plethora of metal and PVC pipes of different diameters crisscrossed the ceiling in all directions, disappearing through the walls. A couple of medium-sized square cardboard and wooden boxes were piled on top of each other in one corner of the room. They looked to be full of supplies.

How many victims has Lucien tortured and killed after locking them away in this hellhole? Hunter thought.

"Madeleine is through that door," Lucien said. "I suggest you hurry."

"Which key?" Taylor asked, holding the key chain up to Lucien once again.

"Second to last key on your right."

Taylor holstered her weapon and moved purposefully toward the gunmetal door. Lucien and Hunter followed and the formation inverted: now Hunter took the rear, three steps behind Lucien.

Taylor slotted the key into the lock and twisted it left. With two loud clicks, the lock chamber rotated three hundred and sixty degrees once, then twice.

Taylor's heart picked up speed as she turned the handle and began pushing the door open.

Police instincts, hypersensitivity, training, experience, psychic ability, whatever it is that one draws on in these situations, Hunter and Taylor both sensed it at the same moment—a new life, a new presence, as if unlocking the door had given the cue for their cop's intuition to kick in.

Once again an identical thought crossed both of their minds. *Maybe we're not too late. There's still hope.*

But that hope vanished fast, because that new life, that presence they'd sensed, wasn't past the door ahead of them. It was behind them.

94

*C*lick.

Before Hunter or Taylor had a chance to turn around, they heard the sound of a bullet being chambered into a 9mm semiautomatic handgun.

"If either of you two fuckheads move, I'll blow your fucking head off. Is that clear?" The voice that came from the opposite end of the room was sharp, firm, and young. "Now get your goddamn hands above your heads."

Hunter tried to identify the specific direction from which the voice was coming. It seemed to have emanated from the general direction of the piled boxes, but there was hardly enough space behind them for a full-grown man or woman to hide. His next sentence, though, came from a different direction altogether, which meant he was moving. The reverberation inside the room, coupled with the incessant lightbulb hiss, made pinpointing the newcomer's exact location an almost impossible task.

Hunter was pretty sure that he could spin around and squeeze out a shot before whoever it was realized what was happening, but guessing wouldn't cut it, because if he missed, he'd be a dead man. He couldn't risk it.

"Did you all fucking hear me or what?" the young voice said again, but this time with a disturbed edge to it. "Hands above your heads."

Hunter and Taylor finally lifted their hands.

Lucien turned and smiled triumphantly at Hunter as he moved past him.

"I did good, didn't I?" the young voice asked. "I followed the instructions just like you taught me."

"You did great." Hunter and Taylor heard Lucien reassure whoever else had joined them. "Okay," Lucien said, now addressing them. "This is when I have to ask you both to put your guns on the floor, and without turning around, kick them back toward me, one at a time. Robert, you go first. Nice and easy. Let me add that my friend here has a very itchy trigger finger. And he never misses."

A few seconds ticked by.

"The fuck you waiting for, big guy?" the young voice said. "Let's go. Put your gun on the floor and kick it back before I put a hole in the back of your head."

Hunter cursed himself. His instincts had been telling him that things didn't feel quite right since they'd gotten to the derelict house. But in his hurry to try to save Madeleine, he had disregarded them, and proceeded inside the fallout shelter without properly checking the control room.

"Do it, Robert," Lucien said. "He really will blow your brains all over these walls."

"Fucking right I will. You think this is a game, big guy?"

The voice had moved closer. Hunter was almost certain that he was just a little to his right, but Hunter was now holding his weapon high above his head, while the kid behind him had his directly aimed at Hunter's skull. The advantage had swung the other way. There was no way out.

"Okay," he said.

"Nice and slowly," Lucien commanded. "Squat down, place your gun on the floor, then get back to a standing position before kicking it back toward me."

Hunter did as he was told.

"Your turn, Agent Taylor," Lucien said.

Taylor didn't move.

"Bitch, did you hear what he said?" the young voice asked with overwhelming anger.

Lucien lifted his hands, signaling for his accomplice to give him a minute.

"I'm well aware of many of the FBI's protocol field rules, Agent Taylor," he said, keeping his voice steady and unthreatening. "I'm also aware that some of those rules are not supposed to have any exceptions whatso-ever. High on that list is the rule that mandates that an FBI agent 'shall never surrender his or her weapon to a suspect or perpetrator during a hostage situation,'" Lucien quoted.

"Make no mistake here, Agent Taylor, this isn't your typical hostage situation. This is a life-and-death situa-tion . . . for you and Robert, that is. If you don't slide your weapon over to me, you *will* die. It's not a threat. It's a certainty. You need to make a judgment call, and you need to do it quickly."

"Fuck this explaining bullshit, Lucien," the young

voice blurted out. "Let's just kill these two fucks and get it over with."

The new ring to the kid's voice told Hunter that he was right on the edge, and it wouldn't take much to tip him over.

"Your call, Agent Taylor," Lucien said. "You've got five seconds; four . . ."

Hunter's gaze was fixed on Taylor's tense body. "Don't be a fool, Courtney," he said under his breath.

"Three, two . . ."

Hunter got ready to move.

"Okay," Taylor said.

Hunter breathed out.

Taylor proceeded to slowly place her weapon on the ground before using her foot to slide it across the floor toward Lucien.

Hunter and Taylor heard the sound of metal chains scraping the floor for an instant.

Lucien had picked up Taylor's gun.

"Nah-ah," the young voice said as Taylor began to turn. "No one told you to turn around, bitch. Keep your eyes on the goddamn door in front of you, or I'll blow your fucking head off."

Taylor paused.

"He really means it, Agent Taylor," Lucien said.

"Does this bitch think I'm kidding?"

Even without looking, Hunter and Taylor could sense that the newcomer's aim had moved to the back of her head. All he needed was a reason.

Taylor didn't give him one. She finally complied, and her eyes returned to the door.

"Now I'm going to have to ask you both to kneel

down, and put your hands behind your heads," Lucien said, while at the same time, unseen to Hunter and Taylor, signaling his accomplice. "Do it now."

Once more, Hunter and Taylor had no way out. They had to do as they were told.

"So what now?" Taylor asked. "You're just going to shoot us in the back?"

"Not my style, Agent Taylor," Lucien replied.

Clunk.

They heard the sharp sound of metal cutting through metal. A few seconds later they heard it again, this time followed by that of a chain running through a loop before falling to the ground.

"I was just being cautious while I got rid of these chains. Oh, now this is much better."

The next sound Hunter and Taylor heard was a loud thud, as a heavy metal object was thrown across the room to the other side and collided with the wall.

"Now please, stand up and turn around," Lucien commanded.

They did.

Standing next to Lucien, holding a Heckler & Koch USP9 semiautomatic handgun, was a wiry man, a little like a professional horse-racing jockey in build. He was only about twenty-five years old. He wore a crooked smile that seemed to bend in the same direction that he hunched his shoulder, giving him a skewed and somewhat menacing look. His head was completely shaven, and his blue eyes glowed with an unsettling intensity. He had a large, badly healed scar that ran from the left side of his chin all the way to the back of his right ear, crossing his right cheek. Even from a distance, Hunter could tell that the scar had been made either by a blunt knife, or a thick piece of glass. Across the room he also saw the heavy-duty forty-eight-inch bolt cutter that Lucien had used to free himself.

"Remember when I told you that I could easily find an apprentice if I wanted to?" Lucien said with a lopsided grin. "Well, I *did* want to, and just as I'd said, it wasn't hard at all. So let me introduce you to Ghost." He gestured toward the kid to his right. "I call him that because he moves like one, so light and silent you won't ever hear him coming. And due to his size and amazing flexibility, he's able to hide in places you can't even imagine." Lucien allowed his gaze to drift to the cardboard boxes. "I know it's hard to believe, but he was actually inside one of those."

One of Ghost's front teeth was chipped. Every few seconds he nervously ran his tongue across its jagged edge, giving him an edgy look, as if he could lose control at any second.

"I like her," Ghost said, his gaze falling over Taylor as if she were naked. "And she's got nice toes. I *reeeeally* like that. Let's just kill the big guy and take her with us. We can have some fun with her."

Taylor didn't shy away from Ghost's eyes, the anger in her stare colliding with the desire in his.

"Did you arrange everything the way we planned?" Lucien asked Ghost as he rubbed his chafed wrists.

Ghost nodded, his attention still on Taylor.

"I don't want you to think that I've been lying to you all this time," Lucien said. "Because I haven't. Why don't you open that door, Agent Taylor?" He indicated the gunmetal door. "And see what lies behind it."

Taylor held Lucien's stare for a while longer before turning around and pushing the door open. On the ceiling of the corridor beyond it, two weak fluorescent tubes flicked and buzzed as if they were about to blow. Their light seemed to travel down the hallway in slow motion, and as it reached the passage's end, Taylor's heart almost stopped beating.

95

The corridor was long and narrow, the walls made of solid concrete, just like the shelter's control room. Several doors lined both sides of the hallway and seemed to lead the eye to one directly at the hallway's end, which was propped open.

The light coming from the fluorescent tubes wasn't strong enough to reach the last room, so all they got was a sort of hazy silhouette, but even so, Hunter and Taylor had no problem identifying the shape of a naked woman's body. She sat on a chair, her head slumped forward awkwardly. Her hands seemed to be tied behind her back, and she certainly wasn't moving.

Taylor felt a nauseating shiver in the pit of her stomach.

"Ghost," Lucien said. "The lights." He nodded at the control desk.

With his attention still locked on Hunter and Taylor, Ghost took a couple of steps to his right and flicked a switch on the old-fashioned console.

Another weak lightbulb struggled to come to life for

a few seconds before finally engaging. As it illuminated the girl's pale form, every muscle in Hunter's body tensed.

Madeleine Reed wasn't dead. But compared with the picture they'd seen of her inside Director Kennedy's office just hours before, she wasn't even a shadow of the woman she used to be. Her weight had drastically plummeted. Her smooth skin looked like it had aged forty years in just a few months, and it now clung to her bones. The dark circles under her eyes were so intense, they gave her a cadaver's appearance. Her lips were dry and chapped.

As the light inside the room came on, Madeleine blinked desperately several times. Her sad and confused eyes struggled with the brightness after who knows how many hours of darkness. Focus took a while, but when it finally came, her drained brain had to battle to understand the images in front of her. She slowly lifted her head, and the look on her face went from puzzled to hopeful and then to pleading before at last settling on desperation. Her lips moved, but if any words did come out, their sound wasn't strong enough to reach anyone at the other end of the hallway.

With the room now under its own light, Hunter and Taylor could finally see the entire picture.

Madeleine's hands were tied to each other behind the chair's backrest. Her feet were tied to the chair's legs.

As her eyes at last registered people at the other end of the corridor, she started shaking. Her breath came in little gasps, as if there weren't enough oxygen in the room.

"Madeleine," Hunter said, reading the first signs of acute panic on her face. He knew she'd been conditioned. She'd been tortured and scared for so long that her immediate psychological response to seeing anyone down in that hellhole was to flood her body with terror. Right now, to her, everyone was a threat, because everyone she'd met down there had tortured her.

"Listen to me, honey." Hunter's voice was as calm and as warm as he could make it sound. "My name is Robert Hunter, and I'm with the FBI. We're here to help you. Stay calm and we'll get you out of here, okay?"

Hunter felt so useless saying those words. He wanted to go to Madeleine, free her hands and feet, get her out of that fallout shelter, and reassure her that she was safe, that the nightmare was over, that no one would hurt her anymore. But he couldn't do any of that. All he could do was throw empty words down that corridor's length, and hope that it was enough to keep Madeleine from losing control.

Madeleine's lips moved again, and again. The sound of her words wasn't strong enough to reach his ears in the control room. But Hunter had no problem reading her lips.

"Please help me . . ."

Hunter quickly peeked at Ghost. He was standing by the control console, his weapon firmly in his grip, his stare burning a hole in the back of Taylor's head. Lucien was standing just a step to his left, but his attention seemed to be everywhere. Nothing would escape him. If Hunter tried anything, he'd be dead.

Lucien nodded at Ghost, who flicked a different switch on the control console. The door to the room Madeleine was in slammed shut, no doubt sending even more fear rushing to every molecule in her body.

Reflexively, Taylor immediately turned to face Lucien and Ghost. "No. Please, no."

The suddenness of her movement caught Ghost by surprise, almost tipping him over the edge, his arm tensing even further and his finger half squeezing the trigger on his gun.

"You better stay where you are, bitch."

"Please," Taylor said, her hands up in surrender. "Shutting the door on her will make her panic even more."

Lucien nodded. "Yes, I know."

Anger radiated from Taylor. "You son of a bitch."

"Let her go, Lucien," Hunter said. "Let Madeleine go. You don't need her anymore. You don't need to take her life. She means nothing to you. Take me and let her go. Let Courtney take Madeleine out of here, and take me."

"You dumb fuck," Ghost said. His gun was still aimed at Taylor. "Reality check, big guy—we already have you, and the whore inside the room, and the pretty FBI bitch with the nice toes here." He blew Taylor a kiss. "Soon you'll be all mine, bitch. And I'll make you scream. You can bet on that."

"Fuck you, you tiny, pencil-dicked, ugly fuck," she said, her self-control completely escaping her.

Maybe it was Taylor's words, or maybe Ghost had just had enough of this game, but the overload switch in his head flicked.

"No," he nearly drooled the word. "Fuck you, you stupid whore." He squeezed the trigger.

96

FBI National Academy, Quantico, Virginia
Forty-five minutes earlier

It didn't take the FBI long to get in contact with Joshua
Foster, the air traffic controller at Berlin's municipal
airport. The call was immediately transferred to Director Kennedy in the control room.

"Mr. Foster," Kennedy said, switching the call to
speakerphone. "My name is Adrian Kennedy. I'm the
director of the National Center for the Analysis of Violent Crime and of Behavioral Analysis Unit 4 of the
FBI. I believe that you were in contact with one of our
agents just moments ago. His name is Robert Hunter.
You handed him the keys to your Jeep."

"Ummm, that's correct." Understandably, there was
a nervous edge to Joshua Foster's voice.

"Okay, Mr. Foster, please listen carefully," Kennedy
said. "This is very important. I understand your car is
brand-new."

"Yeah, well, I got it about two months ago."

"That's great. Now did the car come equipped

with a location transponder, a GPS locator, in case of theft?"

"Actually, yes, it did."

Kennedy's face lit up.

"But I don't have the transponder tracking code with me," Foster said, anticipating Kennedy's next question. "It's back at my house."

"We don't need it," the agent at the radar station took over. "All we need is the car's license-plate number, and I can find the transponder tracking code from here."

"Oh, okay." Foster gave them his Jeep's license-plate number.

"Thank you very much, Mr. Foster," Kennedy said. "You've been a great help."

"Could I ask—" Foster tried saying, but Kennedy had already disconnected the call.

"How long will it take you to find this tracking code?" Kennedy asked the agent at the radar station.

"Not long at all," the agent replied, already typing something into his computer.

As Kennedy waited, his cell phone rang again. It was Special Agent Moyer, the agent in charge of the expedition sent to Lake Saltonstall in New Haven. They were looking for Karen Simpson's remains, together with those of Lucien's four other victims.

"Director," Moyer said, his voice firm but a little subdued, as if to show respect. "Sir, the information is one hundred percent legit. So far we've dug out the remains of exactly five bodies." There was an awkward pause. "Would you like us to continue digging? The area here is pretty vast, and if this was the perpetrator's preferred burial ground, who knows how many more we might find."

"No, that won't be necessary," Kennedy replied. "You won't find any more bodies." He had no doubt Lucien had told the truth. "Just prep the ones you found for transport. We'll need them here in Quantico ASAP."

"Understood, sir."

"Good work, Agent Moyer," Kennedy said before hanging up.

"Got the transponder tracking code," the agent at the radar station announced, as he entered a few more commands into his computer.

Everyone's eyes were glued to his screen.

"Tracking now."

The seconds felt like minutes. Finally, the map on the agent's screen repositioned itself to show the location of a bright, pulsating dot.

"We've got the Jeep's location," the agent said excitedly. A short pause. "And it doesn't look like they're moving anymore."

"Yes, I see that," Kennedy said, frowning at the screen. "But where the hell are they exactly?"

"Right in the middle of absolutely nowhere, by the looks of it," Dr. Lambert commented.

According to the map, the Jeep was parked at the end of a nameless dirt path deep inside a dense forestland several miles from Berlin's municipal airport.

"We need a satellite image of the area instead of a map," Kennedy said.

"Give me a second," the agent replied and immediately started typing again.

Two seconds later the map on his screen was swapped for a satellite image of the area.

Everyone frowned at the screen for a moment.

"What is this?" Kennedy asked, pointing at what looked like a construction site not that far from where the Jeep was parked.

The agent zoomed in on it and readjusted the resolution. "It looks like an old abandoned house or building of some sort," he answered. "Or at least what's left of it."

"That's it," Kennedy said. "That's where they are. That's where Lucien is keeping his victim." He reached for his cell phone and called Agent Brody inside Bird Two. They needed to land and get to that house—*now.*

97

White Mountain National Forest
The present

Hunter saw it before it actually happened.

He saw something explode behind Ghost's cold eyes, as if he'd been injected with pure anger and evil, and pushed past the point of no return. But this time Hunter wasn't able to move fast enough. Ghost's trigger reaction took only a split second, and as the hammer hit the firing pin in the gun, it seemed to Hunter that he'd activated a real-life slow-motion switch. He practically saw the bullet leave the gun barrel, travel through the air, and whizz past the right side of his face, missing it by just a fraction. He began turning toward Taylor reflexively, but he didn't have to see her to know the result. From that distance, even a novice wouldn't have missed, and he could see that Ghost was no first timer. A millisecond after the shot, he felt the warmth of splattered blood and brain matter hit the back of his neck and the side of his face, as Taylor's head exploded with the impact of the fragmenting bullet.

The air filled with the smell of cordite.

Hunter still managed to turn fast enough to see Taylor's body be propelled backward and slam against the dappled gunmetal door before falling to the ground. The wall behind her was colored crimson with speckles of flesh, gray matter, and blond hair. The bullet had hit her almost perfectly right between the eyes. Due to Ghost's diminutive height and his position in relation to Taylor, the bullet had traveled at a slight upward and left-to-right angle. The damage was mind-boggling. Most of the upper-right part of her head and cranium was missing, blown off by the Civil Defense bullet—a special type of round designed to mushroom and fragment on impact, sending tiny pieces in all directions.

Taylor never had a chance.

Hunter quickly turned back to face Ghost, whose aim had now moved to Hunter's face.

"Make a move, tough guy. C'mon, make a move, and I'll blow your brains all over her rotting corpse."

Hunter felt every fiber in his body go rigid with anger, and he had to use all his willpower not to lunge at Ghost. Instead he just stood there, his breathing labored, his hands shaking, but not from fear.

"Yeah, that's what I thought," Ghost said. "Not so tough after all, are you?"

"WHAT THE FUCK WAS THAT?" Lucien shouted. He looked even more surprised than Hunter was.

Ghost kept his weapon trained on Hunter. "The bitch was getting on my nerves," he replied in a serious but unconcerned voice. "No one talks to me that way."

Lucien took a step back, running a hand across his forehead.

"The bitch got what she deserved." Ghost shrugged. "What does it matter anyway? You and I know that they would never have walked out of here alive. And all this chitchat bullshit was pissing me off, so I just sped things up for her." He nodded at Hunter. "And you know what? I'm gonna do the same for him."

The young man's face burned with sadistic desire, and Hunter saw the same determination of moments ago flood Ghost's eyes.

There was no time for a reaction.

Another squeeze of the trigger.

Just like before, the bullet found its target with amazing accuracy.

98

Sky above the town of Milan, New Hampshire
Forty minutes earlier

Inside Bird Two, Agent Brody and his team were starting to lose hope.

Their plane had been circling the outer perimeter of Berlin's airport for several minutes. The pilot and Brody both knew that they'd need a plan of action soon. The plane had enough fuel for another half hour of flying, but if they weren't landing in Berlin, they would need to land somewhere else and refuel before flying back to Quantico.

The nearest airport to Berlin was in Gorham—ten minutes due south, depending on the wind. As a precautionary measure, the pilot always allowed an extra ten minutes of flight time in case of unforeseen circumstances. That left them with a maximum of another ten, maybe fifteen minutes to circle.

Brody had his cell phone on the table in front of him, staring at its dark screen as if hypnotized. When he finally checked his watch, another seven minutes had passed. Three more minutes and this operation was over. He had to call Kennedy.

As he reached for his phone, it rang.

99

White Mountain National Forest
The present

This wasn't the first time Hunter had stared down the barrel of a gun. It wasn't the first time he'd been in a life-and-death situation either, but Ghost was both too far away for Hunter to get to him in time and too close for Hunter to be able to dive away from the bullet.

This time, there was no way out.

In that split second before Ghost squeezed the trigger, all Hunter could think of was how sorry he was for not being able to protect Taylor, and for not fulfilling the promise he'd made to Jessica all those years ago as he held her mutilated body in his arms.

Hunter didn't close his eyes. He would not give Ghost the satisfaction. He didn't even blink. And that was how he was able to see his head explode.

It was a perfect shot. The bullet hit Ghost in his left temple. Its hollow-point cavity was immediately filled with fluids and tissue, forcing it to mushroom as it began traveling past the cranium wall and across Ghost's brain, savagely ripping apart everything in its path.

The mushroom effect of a hollow point reduces the bullet's velocity considerably, and in most cases there will be no exit wound. The bullet will generally lodge itself within its target. But again, at such close range, the power of a .45-caliber round was more than enough to propel the bullet all the way through Ghost's shaved head.

When it occurs, the exit wound of a mushroomed .45 Civil Defense bullet is impressive. In Ghost's case, it was the size of a grapefruit. Half of the right side of his face, from his ear to the top of his head, cracked open as if an alien being had hatched from it.

The terribly loud sound of the fired shot made Hunter jerk, but he still kept his eyes open. He saw the anger, the determination, and the evil dissipate from Ghost's eyes as his whole body was nearly lifted from the ground by the force of the bullet's impact. It slammed against the control console and flopped to the ground like an empty flour sack, a pool of blood quickly forming around his head.

His gun hit the console, sliding away to the other side of the room, disappearing somewhere behind the cardboard boxes.

Hunter's heart raced. Adrenaline flooded his every vein until he shook from it. His gaze finally moved to Lucien. He could still see a thin plume of smoke in the air from Lucien's shot. Before he could react further, Lucien aimed Taylor's gun at Hunter.

"Stay right where you are, Robert. I really don't want

to, but if need be, I'll put a bullet right through your heart. And you know I mean it."

Hunter stared at him, unable to hide his surprise at what Lucien had just done.

"I never liked him anyway," Lucien explained in his usual matter-of-fact manner. "He was just a dumb, sadistic kid with no purpose, who was traumatized when he was young and loved torturing and killing people just for the fun of it."

Coming from Lucien, that last comment seemed to Hunter to be pretty rich.

"And he just outlived his usefulness," Lucien moved on, not even a pinch of remorse or pity in his tone. "Like all the ones before him. They all do eventually, so I have to find myself a new little helper."

Hunter's focus was on Lucien's gun.

"Believe me if you like, but I had no intention of killing Agent Taylor, unless I absolutely had to, but unfortunately she touched on a delicate subject when it came to Ghost. His family was dysfunctional, to say the least. Both of his parents abused him physically and psychologically in ways that are hard for even me to imagine. They forced him to walk around naked all the time and made fun of him constantly, especially of his manhood, calling him a series of derogatory names. Would you like to guess one of them?"

Hunter breathed in. "Pencil dick."

Lucien nodded once. "That's the one. Unfortunately, Agent Taylor had no way of knowing that."

For a deeply traumatized and disturbed person, a single word, a sound, a color, an image, a smell . . . even simple things can easily reopen terribly painful wounds. Usually the person's reaction is unpredictable, but in the case of a violent person, the stimulus can trigger extreme outbursts. For a psychopath like Ghost, that violent reaction is usually fatal.

"When Ghost was seventeen years old," Lucien added, "he had finally had enough. He tied his father to a bed, castrated him, and left him to bleed to death. After that, he used a baseball bat to beat his mother's head into a paste. He was too damaged. I knew I'd be getting rid of him soon anyway."

Despite the bloody chaos of the control room, Hunter forced himself to think as clearly as he possibly could. His main concern was still Madeleine, and he turned his head to look down the corridor behind him. His eyes caught a glimpse of Taylor's body on the floor, and his heart sank yet again. He looked back at Lucien.

"Let Madeleine go, Lucien," he said one more time. "Please. If you really want another victim, take me instead. She means nothing to you."

"True, and that's exactly why I *should* kill her, Robert," Lucien said. "Because she means nothing to me. Now, you were my best friend. We have history. Why would I want to kill you instead of her?"

"Because you already took half my life when you took Jessica from me," Hunter replied. "And I know you don't like to leave things half-done."

As much as Hunter tried to hide it, Lucien recognized real emotion in his voice.

"So this is your chance, Lucien," Hunter continued. "Let her go and finish what you started with me, because if you don't, I *will* kill you."

Despite the seriousness of his words, Hunter's voice was library soft and steady.

"Okay," Lucien said, taking a step closer to the blood-covered control console, his weapon still targeting Hunter's heart. "Let's see if you are a man of your word, Robert." He flicked a switch, and the door at the end of the corridor swung open again.

Hunter turned and faced the hallway.

Madeleine immediately looked up. She looked even more petrified than before.

Hunter knew that she'd heard both shots.

Lucien jerked his gun toward the hallway. "Let's go join her, shall we? I have one last surprise for you."

100

Hunter had to step over Taylor's body to reach the hallway. Lucien followed, but at a safe distance. There was no way Hunter could mount an attack before Lucien fired at least two shots at him.

As Hunter started down the corridor, Madeleine's eyes met his and he could see only one thing in them—pure terror.

"Please help me."

This time Hunter could finally hear her. Her weak and quivering voice was drowning in tears.

"Madeleine, please just stay calm," Hunter said in his most confident voice. "Everything will be just fine."

Madeleine's gaze moved past Hunter and found Lucien, and it was as if the monster that had haunted her worst nightmares since she was a little girl had just materialized in front of her. Fear grew inside her to hurricane strength as she began screaming and twisting her body in the chair.

"Madeleine," Hunter said again. "Look at me."

She didn't.

"Look at me, Madeleine," he repeated, firmer this time.

Her stare moved to Hunter.

"That's right. Good girl. Keep your eyes on me and try to stay calm. I'll get you out of here." He hated himself for lying to the desperate girl, but there wasn't much else he could do.

Madeleine still looked terribly scared, but something in Hunter's tone seemed to work. She looked directly at him and stopped screaming abruptly.

"Get in, turn left, walk five paces, and kneel down, Robert," Lucien said as they got to the door.

Hunter did as he was told.

The room was completely bare, except for the chair where Madeleine sat and a small cabinet with two drawers at the opposite end. There was a faint scent of urine and vomit, fighting the harsher odor of disinfectant that he'd noticed, as if someone had been violently ill, and the cleanup had been sloppy.

Lucien entered the room after him, turned right, and approached the cabinet. He opened the top drawer and reached for something inside.

Madeleine's eyes turned toward him.

"Look at me, Madeleine," Hunter called again. "Don't worry about him. Keep your eyes on me. C'mon, this way."

"You are very good with hostages, Robert," Lucien said, moving to the left side of Madeleine's chair.

Hunter finally saw what Lucien had retrieved from the drawer—a stainless-steel blade, about five inches long.

"You know," Lucien said, "I really hate guns." With a quick hand movement he released the ammo clip from Taylor's .45 Springfield Professional. It fell to the floor, and he kicked it behind him, across the room from where Hunter was. He quickly pulled back the slide, ejecting the bullet in the chamber.

Hunter finally began to see his chance.

Lucien then depressed the recoil spring plug. In no time at all, he had completely stripped the gun, dropping its separate parts to the ground.

Hunter exhaled, his muscles tense and ready as he wondered if he could get to Lucien fast enough.

"Don't even think about it, Robert," Lucien said, taking a step forward and positioning himself partially behind Madeleine's chair. The blade, now in his left hand, moved to her neck, while his right hand pulled her head back by the hair. He could see that Hunter was dying to lunge at him. "You move a muscle, and I'll slice her neck open."

Hunter held steady.

"I know you despise me, old buddy," Lucien said, smiling slightly, almost apologetically. "And I don't blame you. Without knowing the real purpose behind everything I've done, anyone would. To everyone else I'm a sadistic psychopath who's been torturing and killing people for twenty-five years, right? But to you I'm much more than that. I'm the person you've been hunting for decades. The person who so savagely mutilated the only woman you've ever loved. The woman you were going to marry. The woman who would give you a family again."

Hunter felt his rage gather strength.

"But I'm much more than that," Lucien said. "In time you'll understand. I'm leaving you and the FBI a gift." He jerked his head in the corridor's direction. "You'll have no problems finding it. But that will come later, because right now I'm going to give you a chance to fulfill the promise you made to yourself and to Jessica all those years ago, Robert. And this is going to be the only chance you'll ever get, because if you don't kill me now, you'll *never* see me again. Not in this lifetime."

Hunter's heart shifted gears.

"The only problem is," Lucien continued, "the moral dilemma that is about to throw your conscience into a torment, old buddy." Lucien's gaze flicked to Madeleine for a moment before returning to Hunter. "Let me clarify what I mean by asking you one single question." He paused, his stare piercing. "And that question is—if you come after me now, how are you going to get her to a hospital before she bleeds to death?"

In a superfast movement, Lucien moved the knife down Madeleine's body, and stabbed her just under her rib cage. The blade penetrated all the way to its handle.

Hunter's eyes widened in shock.

"No," he shouted, springing forward, but Lucien was ready for him. Before Hunter could get to his feet, Lucien used the sole of his boot to kick him square in the chest. The powerful blow sent a winded Hunter tumbling backward. Lucien extracted the knife from

Madeleine's gasping body, opening the wound, and causing it to start bleeding profusely.

"Keep your promise to Jessica, or save Madeleine, Robert," Lucien called as he sprinted toward the door. "You can't do both. Make your choice, old friend."

101

It took Hunter a moment to catch his breath, and when he did, his lungs and his chest burned as if he'd inhaled hot coal. Reflexively, his hand moved to his chest, and his eyes to the door. His socks scrambled across the floor, trying to regain some sort of grip.

Once they finally did, his instincts kicked in. He dashed toward the door. There was no way that he was letting Lucien get away from him. He knew Lucien meant what he'd said—if Hunter didn't kill him now, he'd likely never get another chance. Lucien had surely planned his escape to the last detail. It had taken the FBI twenty-five years to apprehend him the first time— who knew if they ever would again?

Hunter had taken only three steps in the direction of the corridor when he caught a glimpse of Madeleine, blood pouring from her open wound. Her head had slumped forward again. Her eyelids were half-shut. Life was fast draining out of her.

Hunter had a pretty good understanding of anatomy. The wound was to Madeleine's left side of the abdomen, just under her rib cage. The blade Lucien had used was about five inches long, and he had driven the entire thing into her flesh. Judging by the amount of blood she was losing, Lucien had punctured a vascular organ.

Upper-left side, Hunter thought. *The blade punctured her spleen.*

He also noticed that Lucien had twisted the blade as he removed it from her body, enlarging the rupture to the organ and the entire wound channel. If Hunter didn't contain her bleeding now, in three to five minutes Madeleine would be dead from loss of blood. Even if he managed to contain the external bleeding, there was nothing he could do about the internal hemorrhaging. He still had to get her to a hospital and an operating room fast.

Hunter blinked in frustration. His priorities were colliding, just as Lucien had predicted.

Lucien was getting away.

You'll never see me again. Not in this lifetime.

Keep your promise to Jessica, or save Madeleine, Robert. You can't do both. Make your choice, old friend.

Hunter blinked once more, and then rushed toward Madeleine.

He kneeled down next to her, ripped his shirt from his body, jumbled it into a ball, and using his left hand, placed it over the wound, applying just enough pressure. The shirt was immediately soaked in her blood.

"Look at me, Madeleine," he said, while he stretched his right arm out, reaching for the blade that Lucien had dropped. "Look at me," he said again.

She didn't.

Streeeetch. Got it.

"Madeleine, look at me."

She tried, but her eyelids began to flutter.

"No, no, no. Stay with me, honey. Don't close your eyes. I know you're tired and hurt, but I need you to stay with me, okay? I'm going to get you out of here."

Hunter took a quick look behind the chair. Madeleine's hands were tied together with a plastic cable tie, as were her feet to the chair's legs. Still applying pressure to the wound with his left hand, he tilted his body to the right and used the blade to slice through the cable behind the chair.

Madeleine's hands fell loosely to her sides, as if she were a rag doll.

Hunter quickly sliced through the two cable ties at her feet.

"Madeleine . . ." He dropped the blade and reached for her face. Touching her chin, he gently shook her head from side to side. "Stay with me, honey. Stay with me."

Madeleine's drowsy eyes found his face.

"That's it. Keep your eyes on mine." He reached for her left hand and placed it on the shirt over her wound. "I need you to hold on to this and press it against your body as hard as you can. Do you understand, honey?"

He reached for her right hand and placed it over her left, helping her hold the shirt with both hands.

Madeleine didn't respond.

"Hold on to it and press it against you as hard as you can, okay?"

She tried, but she was far too weak to apply enough pressure to properly contain the bleeding. Hunter would have to do it himself, but he also needed to carry her out of the fallout shelter, into the Jeep outside, to which he still had the keys in his pocket, and then get her to a hospital. Unless he became an octopus in the next second or so, pulling that off would be near impossible.

Think, Robert, think, he told himself, looking around the room for something to help.

He thought about running back to the shelter's control room and searching the place for some sort of tape or rope, anything he could tie around her body to hold his shirt in place, but time was something he didn't have.

Think, Robert, think.

That was when his thought process went from A to Z in a split second—Ghost. Ghost had a small frame, with a very narrow waist, but Madeleine had lost so much weight that he was sure that Ghost's belt could loop around her torso.

"Maddy, hold on to this shirt as tight as you can. I'll be right back."

Madeleine looked at him with sleepy eyes.

"Hold on to it tight, honey," he repeated. "I'll be right back."

Hunter let go of her hands. Immediately more blood flowed out of her wound. Hunter had to move fast.

He got to his feet and sprinted down the corridor. He reached the control room and Ghost's body in three seconds.

Ghost was wearing a cheap black leather belt with a conventional square-frame-and-prong buckle. Hunter undid it and pulled it off his waist with a single strong pull. In no time at all he was flying back down the corridor. By the time he reached Madeleine again, he'd lost only nine seconds.

Madeleine had almost dropped the shirt.

"I'm here, Maddy, I'm here," he said.

Using his right hand, Hunter lifted Madeleine's back from the chair's backrest and wrapped Ghost's belt around her torso and over his blood-soaked shirt.

"This is going to feel a little tight, okay?" he said, and gave the belt a strong tug.

Madeleine coughed several times. No blood in her mouth. That was a good sign.

It was a perfect fit. The buckle slotted into the first hole.

"Okay, honey, I'm going to pick you up, and we're getting the hell out of this place, okay? I'm going to get you to a hospital. Stay with me. I know you're tired, but don't fall asleep, okay? Keep your eyes open. Ready? Here we go."

Hunter picked her up from the chair with both arms and got to his feet. The improvised belt tourniquet stayed in place. Madeleine coughed again. Still no blood.

"Madeleine, put your hands around my neck."

With great effort, she did. Then she looked straight into Hunter's eyes and, in a weak voice, she said five words.

"I don't want to die."

Hunter dashed out of the room and down the corridor as fast as he could.

102

Outside, the darkness was almost absolute, but after the basement, fresh night air was a godsend.

Hunter still had the Maglite in his pocket, so he adjusted his position on the steps—left leg two steps higher than the right—and awkwardly reached for the flashlight with his left hand. Grabbed it. Switched it on.

Madeleine was struggling to keep her eyes open.

"You're doing fine, honey. Stay awake. It feels good to be outside, doesn't it?"

"Yes," she whispered, almost managing a smile.

Hunter's sense of direction was as sharp as they came. They had approached the basement entrance from his left, so he turned and started moving that way, fast.

Debris, rocks, and sticks began digging at the soles of his feet, but he gritted his teeth and blocked out the pain as best as he could.

"You're doing great, Madeleine. We'll be in the car in just a moment, okay?"

Madeleine didn't reply. Her head dropped to Hunter's shoulder.

"No, no, no . . . Hey, no dozing off now. Tell me your name, honey. What's your full name?"

"Huh?"

"Your name. Tell me your full name, honey?"

Hunter also wanted to test her level of consciousness.

"Maddy," she replied.

Her whisper was getting weaker. Despite the tourniquet, her blood was now covering Hunter's arms and the whole lower half of his torso, and beginning to soak the top of his trousers. Some had spurted upward as he ran, spraying his chest and face with warmth.

"That's great. That's really great. Is Maddy short for something?"

"Madeleine."

"Wow, that's a beautiful name. But what's your last name?"

No reply.

"Maddy, wake up. Stay with me, honey. What's your last name? Tell me your last name."

Nothing. Hunter was losing her.

He took his eyes off his path to look at her face, and that was when he felt something cut the sole of his left foot. The pain shot up his leg like a rocket, causing him to stumble awkwardly, lose his balance, and almost fall to the ground. The shake and stumble jerked Madeleine awake. Her eyes butterflied open and she looked at him at last.

Despite the pain, Hunter smiled. "We're almost there. Keep your eyes open, okay?"

Hunter's running had turned into a desperate limp, as his left foot screamed in agony every time it touched the ground.

They finally reached the front of the house.

"FBI. Stop right where you are or we'll put you

down." The shout came from Hunter's left. He turned his head in that direction, but a light immediately shone on his face, preventing him from seeing who had called the order.

Hunter came to an abrupt halt.

In the next second, four other lights appeared out of the darkness—one more to Hunter's left, two to his right, and one directly in front of him. All the lights together provided enough brightness for Hunter to better see what he was faced with. He was surrounded by FBI agents. All of them had their weapons trained directly on him. No doubt this was Kennedy's backup team.

"Place the girl on the ground and take three steps back," the same person who had instructed him a moment ago yelled out.

"I'm *with* the FBI," Hunter shouted back, a touch of anger overshadowing any relief in his voice. "My name is Robert Hunter. I had to dispose of my credentials back on the runway of Berlin's municipal airport. You can check with Director Adrian Kennedy if you like, but do it on your own time, because this girl needs *immediate* medical assistance."

Agent Brody took a step closer and squinted at Hunter's face. It took his memory an extra couple of seconds to match Hunter's blood-streaked face to the photograph Director Kennedy had emailed him.

"Stand down. He's with us," Brody instructed his team, urgently moving toward Hunter. "We expected two of you," he said as he got to Hunter. "Agent Taylor?"

Hunter shook his head, telling Brody everything he needed to know.

Two other agents joined them. The remaining two kept their distances, checking the perimeter.

"And the prisoner?" Brody asked, as they started moving toward where the Jeep was parked.

"On the run," Hunter answered. "Where's your car?"

"Parked behind the Jeep you took from the air traffic controller."

"When did you get here?" Hunter asked.

"About a minute ago. We were just moving toward the house when we saw you come out."

"And you didn't cross paths with Lucien?"

They reached the cars, Brody's team's GMC SUV parked next to the commandeered Jeep.

"No."

One of the agents opened the back door. The other helped Hunter place Madeleine on the backseat. He gently brushed the hair from her forehead.

Hunter looked at the agent holding the car keys.

"You need to get her to a hospital. Now."

The agent was already buckling himself into the driver's seat.

"I'll get her there."

Hunter turned to the second agent. "Get in the back with her. *Do not* let her fall asleep. Tell the medical team that she received a stab wound to the upper-left side of her abdomen, approximately five inches deep. The blade reached the spleen, and was twisted counterclockwise on its way out."

He nodded and jumped into the car.

Madeleine's lips moved.

"What was that, sweetheart?" Hunter asked, leaning down. His right ear came within an inch of her lips.

"Please don't leave me." Her voice was barely audible now. Shock was setting in.

"I won't. I promise. These men are going to take you to a hospital now so they can treat you, okay? I'll be right behind them. I won't leave you. First, I'm going to get the bastard who did this to you."

Hunter closed the door and nodded at the driver. "Go."

103

A s the car pulled away, Hunter faced Agent Brody.

"You came in this way and you didn't cross paths with Lucien?" he asked again.

"No," Brody confirmed.

Hunter's gaze moved to the forest surrounding them.

"But there's another way to get to this house," Brody said.

Hunter looked at him.

"You can see it if you look at a satellite picture of this area, or even a map," Brody explained. "There's a road that goes around the long way. It takes you up to the back of the house."

"Let's go," Hunter said.

They quickly moved back toward the crumbling building. The remaining two agents promptly joined them. They ran past the stairs that led down to hell and continued toward the rear of the property.

Lucien had told the truth. The house's backyard was as dilapidated as the building itself. There were the remains of what once had been a small pond. A wide concrete pathway was cracked and full of holes. Parked to the right of the dirt path that led away from the house was a beat-up fifteen-year-old Ford Bronco. They all drew their weapons and approached the car slowly and carefully. It was empty. No doubt, that was the vehicle Ghost had used to access the property.

This time it was Brody's turn to study the forest surrounding the house.

"Do you think he's on foot?" he asked. "Tracking away through the forest?"

Hunter walked over to the dirt path, kneeled down, and used his flashlight to check the ground.

"No," he replied after a few seconds. "He's got a motorbike." He pointed to the tire tracks he'd found.

"What kind of head start has he got on us?" Brody asked.

"Five to six minutes."

Brody reached for his cell phone. "He can't be that far, then. I'll call Director Kennedy. He'll be able to organize roadblocks all around the perimeter."

Hunter closed his eyes and cursed himself again for not seeing this coming. He said nothing to Agent Brody, but he knew roadblocks wouldn't work. Not in this forsaken place, and not with the minimal amount of time they had.

Hunter was sure the towns of Berlin and Milan didn't have the manpower or vehicles for an airtight roadblock. He'd be surprised if both of their police departments together amounted to more than eight men and four cars. Kennedy would have to request the help of the police departments in adjacent cities, and the closest FBI field office was a whole state away. By the time Kennedy managed to get what he needed to try to contain the area, Lucien would certainly have already crossed state lines.

His old friend had left absolutely nothing to chance.

104

Four hours later

The entire fallout shelter was now swarming with FBI personnel. As with Ghost's, Courtney Taylor's body had been placed in a zip-up body bag and taken to the airport, where it was to be flown back to the chief medical examiner in Quantico.

Brody's team made it to the Androscoggin Valley Hospital in Berlin in record time. Madeleine Reed was still being operated on, but the doctors had told both agents that due to the precarious condition her body was in—very malnourished and partially dehydrated—her chances of survival weren't good. But as long as there was a chance, there was hope.

Hunter and Director Kennedy were in the shelter's control room. Hunter had run Kennedy through everything that had happened since they'd lost their satellite communication back at the airport.

Kennedy listened to the report with a somber expression. When Hunter told him how Agent Taylor was executed at point-blank range, and the reason for her execution, Kennedy squeezed his eyes tight and dropped his chin to his chest.

"How did this happen, Robert?" Kennedy finally asked when Hunter was done. "How come this Ghost character was here waiting for you? He couldn't just have been here the whole time, could he?"

"Probably not," Hunter replied.

"How could he know exactly when you were coming?"

"He didn't."

Kennedy was visibly annoyed. "What do you mean, Robert?"

Hunter had been thinking about this for some time.

"The FBI has certain secret procedures that will only come into action if a code word is spoken, or a code number is keyed in, or something along those lines, right?"

Kennedy nodded and paused for a second. "You're saying that Lucien had a dormant procedure in place? A preplanned strategy in case he was captured?"

"I'm sure he did. There's a reason why Lucien has managed to torture and kill so many people for so many years without anyone suspecting a damn thing, Adrian, even people close to him. He's too well prepared. What happened here was planned a long time ago."

While he pondered Hunter's words, Kennedy let his eyes circle the room once again. They paused on the pool of blood by the door that led into the corridor— Agent Taylor's blood. Sadness and anger collided inside his eyes.

"I'm sure that Lucien told the truth about having left Madeleine with enough food and water to last her just a few days," Hunter carried on. "But a simple code word or signal would've gotten this whole plan in motion. If he hadn't already been here, Ghost would've made the trip from wherever he was to keep her from dying. He obviously got here with plenty of time because he managed to feed and rehydrate her. He knew that within days of the signal, Lucien would've made whomever had him in custody bring him here."

Kennedy stayed quiet, his mind sifting through the information.

"Ghost wasn't his first-ever 'apprentice,'" Hunter added. "Lucien said so."

Kennedy looked at Hunter, intrigued.

"Lucien said that Ghost had outlived his usefulness, *like all the ones before him*. He said that they all do eventually, so he just finds himself a new little helper. I'm sure that the only reason Lucien found apprentices was so that a plan like this could work if he ever needed it. He probably found them, taught them the procedures, kept them for a while, then got rid of them."

"Because in the long run they'd become liabilities," Kennedy said. "A risk he didn't need."

Hunter nodded.

Kennedy still looked uncertain. "But to get the procedure in motion, Lucien would've had to have gotten the signal out to this Ghost character. So how did he do that?"

"A phone call."

Kennedy shook his head. "He wasn't granted any phone calls."

"Since he was taken in by the FBI, you mean," Hunter replied. "But he was arrested by the sheriff's department in Wheatland, Wyoming. Any calls then?"

A pause, then Kennedy shut his eyes for a second as if in pain.

"Son of a bitch," he whispered. He now remembered reading in the arrest report that the arrested subject was granted a single phone call. The call went unanswered. A code telephone number—a dead line that was never supposed to ring, unless . . . That was the signal.

"Then how did this Ghost guy get in here?" Kennedy asked. "You said that the door to this hellhole was padlocked from the outside."

"Last room on the right down the corridor," Hunter answered. "There's a door inside that leads to another passageway, which leads to an exit at the back of the house. Ghost got in through there. The first room on the left," Hunter said, pointing to the corridor, "is an observation room with two computer monitors. Lucien had CCTV cameras equipped with motion sensors hidden outside. As soon as anything moved within range of the cameras, a red light alarm would go off inside the whole shelter." Hunter indicated a red bulb on the wall behind Kennedy. "One of the cameras is set on a tree at the end of the dirt path that leads to the front of the house."

"Where you parked the Jeep," Kennedy said.

"That's right. That would've given Ghost more than enough time to pull Madeleine out of her cell—the last room on the left—tie her to the chair, and hide inside that box."

Kennedy turned and looked at the cardboard boxes pushed up against a dark corner.

"He hid in there?"

Hunter nodded.

"A very well-prepared trap," Kennedy said. "Lucien put you and Agent Taylor under incredible pressure to save a hostage's life. He put you under even more mental pressure by revealing he was your fiancée's murderer just minutes before forcing you to bring him here. The door was padlocked from the outside, and we all believed that Lucien always worked alone. There was no reason for you or Agent Taylor to suspect that there'd be someone waiting for you."

"I still should've checked the room properly," Hunter said. "I'm so terribly sorry for what happened to Courtney."

Neither man said anything for about a minute.

"He's not going to stop killing," Kennedy finally said. "We both know that. And when he kills again, we'll pick up the trail and we'll hunt him down."

"No, we won't," Hunter said.

Kennedy glared at him.

"He killed for twenty-five years without anyone ever knowing, Adrian. There were no links. Lucien doesn't follow a pattern. He doesn't repeat the same MO. He experiments. He kills indiscriminately—old, young, male, female, blond, brunette, American, foreigner. Nothing matters to him, except the experience of the crime. He could kill someone later today . . . He could have done it already, for all we know. We could find the body, search the scene, and we still wouldn't be able to say with any certainty if the murderer had been Lucien or not."

"So you believe what he told you?" Kennedy asked. "That we'll never see him again?"

Hunter nodded. "Unless we manage to outsmart him."

"And how do you propose we do that?"

"Maybe we can find something in those books."

Kennedy's gaze moved to the dust-covered books on the shelves.

"Those are the notebooks you were looking for," Hunter explained. "Lucien told me that he was leaving us a gift. Well, that's it. There are fifty-three books in total. All of them are somewhere between two hundred and fifty and three hundred pages long."

Kennedy approached one of the shelves, picked up one of the notebooks at random, and flipped it open. There was no date stamp, no mention of time whatsoever on the handwritten pages. Groups of full pages were separated by a single blank one, as if to isolate them into numberless and nameless chapters.

"I don't know exactly what we'll find until we go through all of them thoroughly," Hunter said. "But I did have an idea."

"I'm listening."

"I skimmed through a couple before you got here. Judging by what I saw, these books contain not only Lucien's emotions, frame of mind, how he felt during the buildup to and aftermath of a murder, his different MOs, and so on, but also everything he did, everyone he met, and *everywhere* he's been since he started this murderous encyclopedia, including hideout places like this one. Places no one else knows about."

Kennedy caught on fast. "And right now Lucien needs a place to go. The house in Murphy and this fallout shelter are not the only two properties he has under his wing."

"Precisely."

"Our problem is that if you're right, Lucien might be halfway there already, and I'm sure he won't hide in the same place for long. He'll get organized quickly, and then he'll probably vanish."

Kennedy looked back at the shelves. Fifty-three books, each about three hundred pages long. Hunter could see the doubt in his eyes.

"How quickly can you organize a team of the best speed-readers you can find, Adrian?" he asked. "People who can skim through pages fast, looking for something specific. In this case, locations."

Kennedy checked his watch. "If I can get on it now, by the time I get these books back to Quantico, in just under two hours' time, I'll have a team there waiting for me."

"So if we're fast enough, we'll have our list by the morning . . ." Hunter said.

"Then we'll hit every place on that list at the same time," Kennedy finished the thought.

"I know it's a long shot," Hunter said, "but with Lucien we need to take every shot we have, because we won't get many." He walked over to the bookshelves and collected eight random books.

"What are you doing?" Kennedy asked.

"I'm the fastest speed-reader you'll find. I'll go through these, and you can get your people to go through the rest. You'll have my list in a few hours." Hunter started moving toward the exit.

"Where are you going?"

"To the hospital. I promised Madeleine that I would be there."

Kennedy knew that the prospect of being helpful by

compiling a list of places wasn't the only reason Hunter wanted to go through those notebooks. If he could, he would've taken them all.

"Robert," Kennedy called.

Hunter paused.

"Finding Jessica's passage will not soothe your pain entirely. You know that. On the contrary, it will feed the anger and the hurt."

Hunter studied Kennedy for a brief moment. "As I said, Adrian, you'll have my list in a few hours."

105

The doctors had just finished operating on Madeleine Reed when Hunter got to the hospital. She had lost a lot of blood. A minute or two longer getting her to the operating room, and there would have been nothing they could've done for her. But the belt tourniquet had done a good-enough job. If not for that, she would've died from loss of blood five minutes *before* the agents got her to the emergency unit.

The doctors also told Hunter that the operation had gone as well as they could expect. They had managed to contain the internal bleeding and suture the spleen wound before the organ failed, but Madeleine's strength had already been at its minimum before they operated. Now, all they could do was wait and hope that Madeleine's body and her will to stay alive would be strong enough. The next few hours were absolutely critical. At the moment, machines were keeping her alive.

Hunter sat in an armchair in the corner, just a few feet away from Madeleine's hospital bed. She lay flat and still under a thin coverlet. Variously sized tubes extended from her mouth, nose, and arms, and connected

to two machines on each side of the bed. Even with
the coverlet, Hunter could tell that her abdomen was
heavily bandaged. The heart monitor on the right side
of the bed beeped steadily, drawing a hypnotic peak line
on its dark monitor screen.

Before taking a seat, Hunter had stared at Madeleine's face for a long time. She looked peaceful, and for
the first time in God knows how long, not scared.

Her parents had been notified just about half an
hour earlier, and they were on their way from Missouri.

"I know you're strong enough, Maddy," Hunter had
whispered to her. "And I know that you can beat this.
This time Lucien won't win. Don't let him win. I know
you'll walk out of here."

Hunter had been flying through Lucien's notebooks all night. It was 4:18 a.m. and he'd already
skimmed through six of the eight he had with him.
So far his list contained three different locations Lucien had used as torture chambers, each in a different
state.

He hadn't come across any mention of Jessica and
what had happened that fateful night twenty years ago
in Los Angeles. Truthfully, he didn't really know if he
was relieved or angered. He wasn't sure how he would
feel if he did come across the pages that described that
night's events.

Hunter sped through the pages for another twenty
minutes when something made him stop. It wasn't
something on the page he was on, but something his
eyes had skipped over a couple of pages back. His tired
brain had taken a few extra seconds to process it. He

quickly flipped back to the page and read the passage again.

Where had he heard that before?

Hunter racked his brain.

And then, finally, it came to him.

106

Hunter quickly found a bathroom down an empty hospital hallway. Once inside, he reached for his cell phone and dialed Kennedy's number. He knew Kennedy would still be awake.

Kennedy answered his phone on the second ring. "You've read through all eight notebooks already?"

"Almost there," Hunter replied. "One more to go. How's your team doing?"

"They've each been through four of the notebooks, but I've got nine of them going, five notebooks each. At this rate, we should have a list by dawn."

"That would be great," Hunter said. "But you'll have to ask them all to go back to the beginning and start again. They need to look for something other than the locations. Create another list."

"What? What do you mean, Robert? What else? What other list?"

Hunter quickly told him.

"Why?"

Hunter explained the reason why. He could almost hear Kennedy thinking.

"I'll be damned," Kennedy said, breathing out heavily. "Do you think . . . ?"

"It's another shot," Hunter replied. "And we agreed to take every shot we could."

"Absolutely." Another thoughtful pause. "If you're right, Robert, we *might* get a result. The problem is that the result could come tomorrow, next week, next month, or anytime in the next twenty or thirty years. There's no way of knowing."

"To get my hands on Lucien, I'm prepared to wait."

"Okay," Kennedy agreed. "But the team is just about to finish with the locations list, and you know that we can't lose time on that, so let's get that finished first and then I'll tell them to start again."

"Okay. You'll have my list of potential locations within the next hour." Hunter disconnected and went back to Madeleine's room.

He finished skimming through the last notebook he had with him in thirty-one minutes—no new locations. He texted Kennedy his findings, went back to the first notebook, and started the process all over again.

Kennedy called Hunter at 11:22 a.m.

"I thought you'd like to know," he said, "we have fifteen locations in total, spread across fifteen states. FBI and SWAT teams are getting ready as we speak. We should be ready to coordinate a mass crackdown in about an hour to an hour and a half."

"Sounds good," Hunter said.

"How are you doing with the second list?"

"Almost there. Give me another half hour. How's your team doing?"

"Living on strong black coffee."

"Yeah, I guess I can relate."

"They should also be finished soon. How's Madeleine doing?"

"Still unresponsive."

"I'm sorry to hear."

"Once you get the new list, you know what to do, right Adrian?"

"Yes, of course."

They disconnected.

Back inside Madeleine's hospital room, it took Hunter just another twenty-four minutes to complete his new list. This time he had four entries. He texted the new list to Kennedy and received a reply in five seconds: "Will initiate procedures as soon as I have all the entries. Locations crackdown will be in T-53 minutes. Will keep you posted."

107

Hunter received the next text message from Kennedy exactly fifty-three minutes later.

"Locations crackdown is a go. Will keep you posted. Second list now completed—every procedure initiated."

There was nothing Hunter could do now but sit and wait. He massaged the back of his neck. Exhaustion had slowly worn its way into his brain, joints, and muscles. Every time he moved, he could feel the tendons pulling tight across his whole body, as if they were about to snap. He closed his eyes only for a moment, and the next thing he felt was his cell phone vibrate in his chest pocket.

Hunter had dozed off for an hour and fourteen minutes. To him, it felt like two seconds. He quickly left the room and answered Kennedy's call.

"We've drawn a blank, Robert," Kennedy said. "Lucien was at none of the sites." Kennedy's voice was defeated, hopeless. "And it doesn't seem like he's been in any of them for weeks. Judging by the photographs I've received from the crackdown teams, some of these places were practically slaughterhouses. You wouldn't believe the torture paraphernalia found in them."

Sadly, Hunter was sure he would.

"It will take our forensics teams weeks, maybe months to sift through everything in those fifteen places, and it still might give us no clue as to Lucien's whereabouts. I'd say that those notebooks are our best bet for finding anything on his current whereabouts . . . if there is anything to be found. But now they have to be read thoroughly and scrutinized to the minutest detail, and that will also take a long time." Without realizing it, Kennedy let out a beaten sigh. He had no doubt that by the time they finished analyzing everything Lucien had left behind, he would be long gone, vanished forever. As Lucien himself had said, they'd never see him again.

Hunter felt so tired he couldn't think straight. He was fresh out of ideas.

108

Hunter came to a sudden stop as he returned to Madeleine's hospital room. All the hairs on the back of his neck stood on end. Madeleine was still lying flat and still, but her eyelids were struggling with their own weight, flickering desperately.

Hunter rushed to her bedside.

"Madeleine?"

Hunter gently touched her hand. "Madeleine, remember me?"

She blinked again and her eyes finally found his face. She didn't say a word, but her lips stretched into a thin smile.

Hunter smiled back. "I knew you'd beat this," he whispered. "I'm going to go get a doctor. I'll be right back."

She gave his hand the faintest of squeezes.

Hunter rushed out of the room and in less than a minute was back with a short, plump doctor who walked as if carrying his body weight was an everyday penitence. As the doctor approached Madeleine's bed, Hunter felt his cell phone vibrate in his chest pocket again. He excused himself and quickly left the room.

"Robert," Kennedy said as Hunter answered it. "The second list, the idea you came up with."

"Yes, what about it?"

"You're not going to believe this."

109

John F. Kennedy International Airport, New York
Seven hours later

Would you like a drink while we wait for the rest of the passengers to board, Mr. Tailor-Cotton?" the young first-class stewardess asked with a bright smile. Her blond hair was pulled back and styled into a perfect bun, and her carefully applied makeup accentuated her facial features perfectly. "Perhaps champagne, or maybe a cocktail?" she offered.

The passenger's eyes broke away from the window and found her pretty face. The name tag on her blouse read *Kate.* He smiled back.

"Champagne would be perfect." His voice was soft, with a gentle Canadian accent. His dark-green eyes had an intense, intelligent glint.

The smile never left the stewardess's lips. She found Mr. Tailor-Cotton mysteriously charming.

"Great choice," she said in reply. "I'll be right back with a glass."

"Excuse me, Kate?" he called as she was turning away. "How long before we take off?"

"We have a full flight tonight," she replied. "And we just started boarding all the other seating sections. If no one is late, we should start taxiing toward the runway in no more than thirty minutes."

"Oh, that's great. Thank you."

"But if there's anything I can do to make this short wait more comfortable for you, just let me know." Her smile gained a flirtatious sparkle.

Mr. Tailor-Cotton nodded, with a flirtatious smile of his own. "I'll keep that in mind."

His gaze followed her as she started down the aisle. When she disappeared past the dividing curtain, his attention returned to the window.

"I've heard that the beaches in Brazil are simply breathtaking," the passenger sitting directly behind Mr. Tailor-Cotton said, leaning forward. "I've never been there before, but they sound like paradise on earth."

For a split second, Mr. Tailor-Cotton's heart froze. Then he smiled at his own reflection staring back at him from the airplane window. He would recognize that voice anywhere.

The passenger behind him stood up, moved forward, and casually leaned against the armrest of the single seat across the aisle.

"Hello, Robert," Mr. Tailor-Cotton said, turning his head to look at Hunter.

"Hello, Lucien," Hunter replied calmly.

"You look awful," Lucien commented.

"I know," Hunter admitted. "You, on the other

hand, look amazing. Different hair color, contact lenses, the beard is gone, even your scar. All that in the space of just a few hours."

Lucien accepted the compliment graciously.

"You can do wonders with a little makeup and prosthetics, if you know what you're doing."

"And you have mastered that Canadian accent to perfection," Hunter admitted. "Nova Scotia, right?"

Lucien smiled. "You still have a great ear, Robert. That's right. Halifax. But I do have a collection of accents I've mastered. Would you like to hear some of them?"

That last sentence was delivered with a perfect Midwestern accent—Minnesota to be precise.

"Not right now," Hunter replied.

Lucien looked at his nails, unconcerned. "How's Madeleine?"

"She's alive. She'll make a full recovery."

Lucien looked back at Hunter. "You mean physically, right? Because mentally she's probably fucked-up for life."

Hunter's stare hardened. He knew Lucien was right. The trauma Madeleine had experienced would stay with her for the rest of her life.

"How did you find me?" Lucien finally asked.

"Your notebooks," Hunter explained. "Your encyclopedia. Your 'gift' to us, as you put it. I still remember the day you mentioned the idea to me back at Stanford."

Lucien smiled. "You thought it was crazy."

Hunter nodded. "I still do."

"Well, the crazy idea became a reality, Robert. And the information inside those books will forever change the way the FBI, the NCAVC, the BRIU, and every other law enforcement agency in this country, maybe in the world, look at people like me. It will make you understand things that up to now no one ever has, and otherwise never would. Intimate thoughts that have never been explained. Things that will exponentially better your chances of capturing those offenders. That's my gift to you, and to this fucked-up world. My work and those books will be studied and referenced for generations to come." He shrugged. "So what if I took a few lives in the name of research? Knowledge comes at a price, Robert. Some much higher than others."

Hunter nodded as his eyebrows arched. "All that knowledge about psychology and criminal behavior, and you failed to see your own psychosis. You're not a researcher, Lucien, much less a scientist. You're just another run-of-the-mill killer, and to justify your actions and feed the sociopath inside you, you deluded yourself into believing that what you were doing was for a noble cause. It's pathetic, really, because it's not even original. It's been done so many times before."

"Nothing I've done has been done before, Robert," Lucien shot back.

Hunter shrugged carelessly. "I'm not your therapist, Lucien. I'm not here to help you and this isn't a session, so you can keep deluding yourself as much as you like. No one cares, but the good thing is that in your books, you were kind enough to note absolutely everything concerning your experiments—locations, methods used, victims' names, and much more. I spent the night going through them."

"You read through fifty-three books in one night?"

"No, but I managed to skim through a few. And that's where I got lucky, and you didn't."

Lucien's expression showed interest.

"While reading one of them, I came across the name of one of your victims that sounded familiar—Liam Shaw."

Lucien's eyes went cold.

"It took me a little while to place it," Hunter said. "But I did eventually remember. That was the name you were using when you were first arrested in Wyoming."

Lucien stayed quiet.

"You were also kind enough to very thoroughly describe all your victims," Hunter continued. "And that was when I realized that Liam Shaw shared several physical characteristics with you—height, body type, complexion, facial shape, even the shapes of his eyes, nose, and mouth. You were of similar age too.

"Then I remembered something else you'd said in one of our interviews. You told Courtney that the reason you were caught wasn't thanks to the FBI. They weren't investigating any of your murders, or any of the *aliases* you used."

Lucien shifted in his seat.

"Well, that got me thinking, so I went back and checked for all the other *male* victims you described in the books. There weren't that many, but all of them shared those same physical characteristics with you."

Lucien scratched his chin.

Hunter tucked his hands inside his trouser pockets. "And that was why you picked them. Not because you particularly wanted them to be part of your en-cyclopedia of torture and death, but because you were creating a list of identities you could steal at the drop of a dime."

Lucien's gaze moved back to the window and the darkness outside.

"Some of your male victims were prostitutes," Hunter moved on. "Some were people who were down on their luck, but all of them had one major thing in common—they were all loners. People who were misunderstood and probably cast aside by their family and friends somewhere else. People who had left their lives behind to start something new in a new city. People with no attachments to anyone. The ones who'd never get reported as missing. The forgettables. The ones no one would miss."

"They've always made the best victims," Lucien said.

"Because of their natural physical resemblance to you, taking their place was never a hard thing to do—a little makeup, some hair dye, maybe some contact lenses, a new accent, and good-bye Lucien Folter, hello new identity. In this case, Anthony Tailor-Cotton, from Halifax, Canada."

"So you and the FBI spent the night flying through those books, looking for every male victim's name you could find."

Hunter nodded. "We put out a nationwide APB on all of them. But I'll admit that our hopes were very, very low. The best we were hoping for was that maybe, if we were very lucky, a few years from now one of those names would show up in a credit-card transaction somewhere. Just a sniff of a clue to where you could be. Now, you can imagine our surprise when within a couple of hours we got word that Anthony Tailor-Cotton, holder of a Canadian passport, just like one of the victims described in one of your notebooks, had purchased a ticket for a flight to Brazil tonight."

"I guess I should've taken an earlier flight," Lucien commented.

Hunter knew that initially Lucien would've had two options. One was to stay in the United States and lie low for a while . . . a long while. While doing so he would probably have to live under the shroud of a disguise. His name would've made the list of the top ten most wanted by the FBI, and his picture would've been circulated to every police department and sheriff's office in the country in hours. Lucien Folter wasn't the unknown ghost of a killer he used to be.

Option number two was to disappear quickly, preferably somewhere outside the United States. Hunter knew that Lucien didn't underestimate the FBI. He knew that his encyclopedia would be scrutinized to the utmost detail, because that was exactly what he wanted. He was counting on the bureau linking the name of one of his victims to the same name he was using when he was arrested, and then making the physical connection between all of his male victims and himself. So if Lucien disappeared quickly and to somewhere outside the United States, then when all those connections were made it wouldn't matter, because the FBI wouldn't have the jurisdiction to get their hands on him anyway. He just never imagined that the bureau would manage to connect everything in a matter of hours.

"Maybe you should've," Hunter said. "Like I said, this time I got lucky and you didn't, because the name

Liam Shaw just so happened to be in one of the eight books I had with me. If I hadn't come across that name, it would've probably taken the FBI a few months to connect the dots, by which time you would've been long gone."

All of a sudden, the dividing curtains at the front of the aircraft were pulled aside and Director Adrian Kennedy, together with four other FBI agents, began making their way toward Hunter. At the opposite end of the aisle, four armed NYPD SWAT officers appeared and were also making their way toward them.

For the first time Lucien showed real surprise.

"You're going to hand me over to the FBI?"

Hunter said nothing.

"That's disappointing, Robert. I thought you were a man of your word. I thought that you had promised not only yourself, but also the memory of your *murdered* fiancée, that you'd find the person who had so violently taken Jessica from your life, and kill him. That's what you've been searching for for twenty years, isn't it? To avenge Jessica's death. Well, here I am, old friend. All you have to do is put a bullet through my head and your twenty-year-long search is over. You can be proud of yourself." Lucien quickly checked the aisles. "So c'mon, Robert. Here I am, a sitting duck. I promise you I won't react. It'll be an easy shot."

Hunter shifted on his feet.

Kennedy and his agents drew closer.

"I thought you said that more than anything else, Jessica deserved justice. Are you telling me that you're going to betray that promise, Robert? You're going to betray the memory of the only person you ever loved?

The woman who you wanted for your wife? The woman who was carrying your baby?"

Hunter froze.

Lucien saw the hurt in his face. He pushed.

"Yes, I knew she was pregnant. She told me when she begged me not to kill her, but I did it anyway. And did you know that yours was the last name that came out of her lips before I cut her throat open? Before I murdered her and your child?"

Hunter saw red as Lucien taunted him. The thoughts inside his head made no sense anymore. His actions were no longer guided by sense and logic, but by pure rage. His hand shook with devastating anger when he reached for his gun holster.

Kennedy saw the look in Hunter's eyes, but he was still several steps away from him.

"ROBERT, DON'T DO IT," he shouted down the aisle.

Too late.

110

Hunter had acted so fast Lucien barely had time to flinch. Hunter saw his body go rigid, but not from fear or expectation, but from satisfaction in his accomplishment of making Hunter finally lose control. That satisfaction was short-lived.

Hunter dropped a pair of handcuffs on Lucien's lap.

Lucien looked up at him, confused. Hunter held no gun.

"You're right," Hunter said. "Jessica deserves justice. Her parents deserve justice. My unborn child deserves justice. And I deserve justice for what you've done. Nothing would please me more than to put a bullet in your head right here, right now. But we're not the only ones who deserve justice for what you've done, Lucien. The parents, the families, and the friends of every single victim you tortured and killed over so many years deserve justice too. They deserve to know what really happened to the people most of them still believe are just missing. They deserve to know where the remains of their loved ones are. They deserve to be able to give them a proper burial according to their beliefs. And most of all, they deserve to know that the monster who'd killed those loved ones will never kill again."

Hunter looked at Kennedy, who was now just a couple of feet away, and then back at Lucien.

"For that reason, yes, I'll betray my promise to myself and to Jessica. And this time there will be no more interviews, no more talks, Lucien. You have no more bargaining power, because we have your books, and everything we need to know is on those pages, including the location of the remains of every one of your victims. This really is where it ends for you."

Hunter nodded at the SWAT agents to his left. "You can take him now."

111

The next day

Despite his insomnia and the carnival of thoughts dancing in his head, Hunter was so exhausted that he finally managed to sleep for a few hours.

After Lucien's arrest, he had flown back to Quantico. As Kennedy had put it earlier, he was still officially *on loan* to the FBI, and as such, he needed to file his last report. That was completed late the previous night.

Hunter woke just before dawn. Kennedy arranged for an FBI jet to fly him back to Los Angeles early in the morning, and Hunter couldn't wait to get out of that place. Everything still felt too surreal. Only a few days ago, he was supposed to be boarding a plane to Hawaii: his first vacation in so long that he couldn't remember the last time he had taken a few days off. Instead, he was whisked away to the FBI Behavioral Research and Instruction Unit in Quantico, and into something that could only be described as a hellish nightmare. So much was revealed in so little time, his head seemed like it would never stop spinning.

Hunter was all ready to go. His few belongings were already packed into his backpack, and he had nothing else to do but wait for the driver to come pick him up. He walked over to the window on the east wall and placed his cup of coffee on the ledge. Outside, still under cover of night, several FBI recruits had already started their grueling exercise and running routines.

Hunter looked up at the star-filled sky as he reached for his wallet. From it he retrieved a twenty-year-old photograph. The colors had partially faded, but other than that, the picture was still in pretty good condition.

Hunter had taken that photo himself, a day after he and Jessica got engaged. She was standing on Santa Monica pier, smiling at the camera, her eyes glistening with an overwhelming happiness. As he stared at the photograph, Hunter's heart filled with a barrage of old and brand-new emotions. He felt a knot coming to his throat, but then he remembered the words Director Kennedy had told him in the early hours of the morning.

"Before you go, Robert, I want to make sure you understand something. I'm not going to pretend I know, because I can't even begin to imagine what's going on inside your mind right now. But I can tell you this: no matter what, you *must* stand proud, because thanks to you, we estimate that we'll be able to bring closure and final peace of mind to at least eighty families around the United States. Lucien's twenty-five-year murder spree is finally over. You ended it. Don't ever forget that."

Hunter knew he never would.

Turn the page for a preview of

I AM
DEATH

by Chris Carter

Coming soon from Emily Bestler Books

"Oh, thank you so much for coming on such short notice, Nicole," Audrey Bennett said, opening the front door to her white-fronted, two-story house in upper Laurel Canyon, a very affluent neighborhood in the Hollywood Hills.

Nicole gave Audrey a bright smile.

"It's no problem at all, Ms. Bennett."

Born and raised in Evansville, Indiana, Nicole Wilson spoke with a distinctive Midwestern accent. She wasn't very tall—about five foot three—and her looks weren't exactly what fashion magazines would call striking, but she was charming and had a disarming smile.

"Come in, come in," Audrey said, ushering Nicole inside with a hurried hand gesture.

"Sorry I'm a little late," Nicole said, stepping inside as she consulted her watch. It was just past 8:30 in the evening.

Audrey chuckled. "You've got to be the only person in the whole of Los Angeles who considers anything under ten minutes as being late, Nicole. Everyone else I know calls it 'fashionably on time.'"

Nicole smiled, but despite the comment, she still looked a little embarrassed. She prided herself on being a very punctual person.

"That's a beautiful dress, Ms. Bennett. Are you going anywhere special tonight?"

Audrey pursed her lips and twisted them to one side. "Dinner party at a judge's house." She leaned toward Nicole and her next words came out as a whisper. "They are sooooo boring."

Nicole giggled.

"Oh, hello, Nicole," James, Audrey's husband, said, coming down the arched staircase from the house's second floor. He wore an elegant dark-blue suit with a silk striped tie and a matching silk handkerchief just peeking out of his jacket pocket. His butterscotch-blond hair was combed back, and as always, not a strand seemed to be out of place.

"Are you ready, honey?" he asked his wife before quickly checking his Patek Philippe watch. "We've got to go."

"Yes, I know, I'll be right there, James," Audrey replied before turning to face Nicole again. "Josh's already asleep," she explained. "He's been playing and running around all day, which was great, because by eight o'clock he was so exhausted he was dozing off in front of the TV. We took him to bed and he crashed before his head hit the pillow."

"Oh, bless him," Nicole commented.

"From the amount of running the little devil did

today," James said as he approached Audrey and Nicole, "he should sleep right through to the morning. You should have an easy night." He grabbed Audrey's coat from the leather armchair and helped his wife into it. "We've really got to go, honey," he whispered into her ear before kissing her neck.

"I know, I know." Audrey motioned toward the door just past the river-rock fireplace on the east wall of their large living room. "Help yourself to anything you like from the kitchen. You know where everything is, right?"

Nicole nodded once.

"If Josh wakes up and asks for any more chocolate cake, *do not give it to him*. The last thing he needs is another sugar rush in the middle of the night."

"Okay," Nicole replied, renewing her smile.

"We might be quite late tonight," Audrey continued. "But I'll call you later just to check everything is all right."

"Enjoy your night," Nicole said, accompanying them to the door.

As Audrey took the few steps down from her front porch, she looked back at Nicole and mouthed the word "boring."

After closing the door, Nicole went upstairs and tiptoed to Josh's room. The three-year-old boy was sleeping like an angel, his arms wrapped around a stuffed toy creature with huge eyes and ears. From the bedroom door, Nicole stared at him for a long while. He looked so adorable with his blond flock of curly hair and rosy cheeks that she felt like cuddling up to him, but she didn't dare wake him. Instead, she blew him a kiss from the door and returned downstairs.

In the TV room, Nicole watched about an hour of some old comedy before her stomach started making noises. Only then she remembered that Audrey Bennett had said something about a chocolate cake. She looked at her watch. It was definitely time for a snack, and a slice of cake sounded just perfect. She left the room and went back upstairs to check on Josh again. He was in such a deep sleep, he hadn't even moved positions. Returning downstairs, Nicole crossed to the other side of the living room and opened the kitchen door, stepping inside.

"Whoa!" she yelled in fright, jumping back.

"Whoa!" the man sitting at the breakfast table, having a sandwich, yelled a millisecond after Nicole. Instinctively, and also in fright, he dropped the sandwich and kicked back from the table, immediately standing up and knocking over his glass of milk. His chair tipped over behind him.

"Who the hell are you?" Nicole asked in an anxious voice, taking a defensive step back.

The man gazed at her for a couple of seconds, confused, as if trying to figure out what was happening. "I'm Mark," he finally responded, using both hands to point at himself.

They stared at each other for a moment longer, and Mark quickly realized that his name meant absolutely nothing to the woman.

"Mark?" he repeated, turning every sentence into

a question, as if Nicole should've known all this. "Audrey's cousin from Texas? I'm here for a couple of days for a job interview? I'm staying in the apartment above the garage in the back?" He used his thumb to point over his right shoulder.

Nicole's questioning stare intensified.

"Audrey and James told you about me, didn't they?"

"No." She shook her head.

"Oh!" Mark looked even more confused now. "Umm, as I've said, I'm Mark, Audrey's cousin. You must be Nicole, the babysitter, right? They said you'd be coming. And I'm sorry, I really didn't mean to scare you, though I guess you've already paid me back in kind." He placed his right hand over his chest, tapping his fingers over his heart a few times. "I almost had a heart attack just now."

Nicole's stare relaxed a fraction.

"I flew in this morning for a big job interview downtown this afternoon," Mark explained.

He was dressed in what looked to be a brand-new suit, very elegant. He also looked quite attractive.

"I just got back from it about ten minutes ago," he continued. "And suddenly my stomach reminded me that I hadn't had any food all day." He tilted his head to one side. "I can't eat when I'm nervous. So I just came in for a quick sandwich and a glass of milk." His eyes moved to where he had been sitting and he chuckled. "Which is now all over the table and starting to drip onto the floor."

He picked up his chair and looked around for something to clean up the mess. He found a roll of paper towels next to a large fruit bowl on the kitchen counter.

"I'm a little surprised that Audrey forgot to tell you I was staying over," Mark said as he began mopping up the milk from the floor.

"Well, they were in a bit of a hurry," Nicole conceded, her posture not as tense as moments ago. "Ms. Bennett asked me if I could get here by eight o'clock, but the earliest I could make it was eight thirty."

"Oh, okay. Is Josh still awake? I'd like to say goodnight if I could."

Nicole shook her head. "No. He's out like a light."

"He's a great kid," Mark said as he bundled up all the soaked paper towels and dumped them in the trash can.

Nicole kept her full attention on him. "You know, you look a little familiar. Have I met you before?"

"No," Mark replied. "This is actually my first ever visit to LA. But it's probably from the photographs in the TV room and in James's study. I'm in two of them. Plus, Audrey and I have the same eyes."

"Oh . . . the photographs. That must be it," Nicole said, a hazy memory playing at the edge of her mind but not quite materializing.

A distant cell phone ring broke the awkward silence that had followed.

"Is that your phone?" Mark asked.

Nicole nodded.

"That's probably Audrey calling to say that she forgot to tell you about me." He shrugged and smiled. "Too late."

Nicole smiled back. "Let me go get that." She left the kitchen and returned to the living room, where she retrieved her cell phone from her bag. The call was indeed from Audrey Bennett.

"Hi, Ms. Bennett, how's the dinner party?"

"Even more boring than I expected, Nicole. This is going to be a long night. Anyway, I'm just calling to check that everything is all right."

"Yes, everything's fine," Nicole replied.

"Has Josh woken up at all?"

"No, no. I just checked on him again a moment ago. He looks like he's out for the count."

"Oh, that's great."

"By the way, I just met Mark in the kitchen."

There was some loud background noise coming from Audrey's side.

"Sorry, Nicole, what did you say?"

"That I just met Mark, your cousin from Texas who's staying in the garage apartment. I walked in on him having a sandwich in the kitchen. We scared the hell out of each other!" She giggled.

There was a couple of seconds' delay before Audrey replied.

"Nicole, where is he? Has he gone up to Josh's room?"

"No, he's still in the kitchen."

"Okay, listen to me." Audrey's voice was serious and shaky. "As quickly and as quietly as you can, go get Josh and get out of the house. I'm calling the police right now."

"What?"

"Nicole, I don't have a cousin named Mark from Texas. We don't have anyone staying in the garage apartment. Get out of the house . . . *now*. Do you underst—"

CLUNK.

"Nicole? *Nicole?*"

The line went dead.

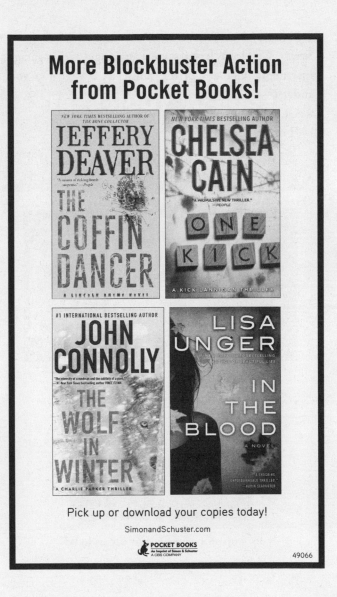